PRAISE FOR ANDY REMIC

"If you thought Theon Greyjoy's castration scene in *Game of Thrones* was a little restrained, then *The Iron Wolves* could be the epic fantasy potboiler for you... Combining George RR Martin-inspired visceral violence with a touch of *Slaine*-style bombastic barbarism and a plot straight out of *The Lord of the Rings*..."
SFX

"Add to the mix a good dollop of battlefield humour, a good handful of Howard's style backed up with a stark descriptiveness and it's a tale that gives Remic a firm footing within the genre."
Falcata Times

"*Soul Stealers* is fast, brutal and above all unmissable, there is quite simply nothing out there that can currently compare to Andy Remic's unrelenting, unforgiving and unflinching style. The new King of Heroic Fantasy has arrived. 5 *****"
SFBook.com

"*Kell's Legend* is a roller coaster ride of a book that grabbed me right from the first page and tore off at a rate of knots like I hadn't seen in a long time."
Graeme's Fantasy Book Review

"The Iron Wolves is a perfect introduction to a new hardcore fantasy series. Based on the evidence displayed, you can count me in. Bring it on!"
The Eloquent Page

ALSO BY ANDY REMIC

FANTASY
THE RAGE OF KINGS
The Iron Wolves

THE CLOCKWORK VAMPIRE CHRONICLES
Kell's Legend
Soul Stealers
Vampire Warlords
The Clockwork Vampire Chronicles [omnibus]

THRILLERS
Spiral
Quake
Warhead
Serial Killers Incorporated

SCIENCE FICTION
War Machine
Biohell
Hardcore
Cloneworld
Theme Planet
Toxicity
SIM

FOR CHILDREN
Rocket Cat

SCREENPLAYS
Impurity
After the War

ANDY REMIC

The White Towers

A BLOOD, WAR & REQUIEM NOVEL

ANGRY
ROBOT

ANGRY ROBOT
A member of the Osprey Group

Lace Market House,
54-56 High Pavement,
Nottingham,
NG1 1HW,
UK

Angry Robot/Osprey Publishing,
PO Box 3985,
New York,
NY 10185-3985,
USA

www.angryrobotbooks.com
Elf rats have left the building!

An Angry Robot paperback original 2014

Cover art by Lee Gibbons
Set in Meridien by Argh! Oxford.

Distributed in the United States by Random House, Inc., New York.

ISBN 978 0 85766 357 3
Ebook ISBN 978 0 85766 359 7

Printed in the United States of America

9 8 7 6 5 4 3 2 1

This book is dedicated to Dorothy Lumley, with much love.

Dot, as the proprietor of the Dorian Literary Agency, *endured* many of my very first attempts at writing – giving a young, insecure, desperate author positive encouragement and advice whilst many shitty editors/agents replied with – quite frankly – embarrassingly bad photocopied "get stuffed" sheets of toilet paper (I still have the evidence, in a big stack under the bed).

Dot was different. Dot cared. Dot nurtured. Dot *loved* The Business. It was in her blood, and in the glitter of her mischievous eyes. She wasn't in it for the money. She was in it for the *love*. In 1996 I wrote to Dot with *Theme Planet* (version 1.0), saying "I think you're the right babe for the gig". She replied, saying she'd enjoyed the book very much and would "love to represent me". A few years later, we had a deal with Orbit and I was a published author. Wow! *Bam!* Dream achieved.

When I found out Dot didn't have long left to live, I offered her the only thing I could think of that would really mean something: a dedication in my next novel. This one. This seemed to please her. And so, with great love, I raise a glass to Dorothy Lumley – and dedicate *The White Towers* to "the right babe for the gig". Rest in peace, Dot.

DEATHSHADOW

Iron dark clouds filled the sky. Thunder rumbled. Lightning cut the horizon into a jagged jigsaw, and hail smashed down on the broken up, earthquake-ravaged plain rippling before the walls of Desekra Fortress.

On the battlements, a makeshift gallows had been erected. The platform stepped out beyond the primary Desekra wall, Sanderlek, giving those to be hung a generous and violently picturesque view. There were five of them. Five prisoners, each with a thick rope noose around their necks, each with a black silk hood hiding cold iron eyes and mouths set in grim lines of betrayal. Their hands had been bound behind their backs, and boots kicked against trapdoors connected to pulleys and a single brass lever.

"The Iron Wolves have been found guilty on twelve counts of treason against His Majesty, King Yoon of Vagandrak," read a small, pompous fat man from a vellum scroll. "These counts amount to theft, extortion, the murder of General Dalgoran, the kidnapping and imprisonment of various members of the royal family…"

"I'll fucking show him imprisonment," murmured Narnok the Axeman, bristling.

"If you hadn't had your pants round your ankles, we wouldn't be in this mess," snapped Dek.

"Thus proclaims Mr Two Kegs," growled Narnok. "Maybe if *you* could hold your ale a little better, you might have heard the stampede to your door!"

"Silence amongst the prisoners!" squawked the bureaucrat.

"Or what?" bellowed Narnok. "You'll fucking hang us?" His laughter roared across the walls of Desekra Fortress.

The list of misdemeanours continued, and King Yoon of Vagandrak observed these, his prisoners, the Iron Wolves of legend and a multitude of children's stories; the Iron Wolves who – twenty years previous – had driven back thousands of invading mud-orcs and killed the sorcerer, Morkagoth; and in these past few days, reunited in anger, hate and loathing, older, wiser, more bitter and twisted and cynical, had repeated the act of defence and attack as Orlana the Changer, the Horse Lady; had brought yet more death and destruction to the borders of Vagandrak. Only this time, the carnage had been far more terrible, incredibly more destructive; for Kiki, the Captain of the Iron Wolves, had found inside herself the buried magick of the *Shamathe*, the magick of the Equiem, and had unleashed her fury across the Plains of Zakora. Desekra Fortress, the Pass of Splintered Bones, the Mountains of Skarandos, and the whole world, it seemed, had trembled as the mammoth earthquake smashed through the earth, sucking down tens of thousands of mud-orcs, back into the bowels of the world that had conjured them – and dragging down the kicking, screaming figure of Orlana with a million tonnes of collapsing granite.

Now, for risking their lives, for smashing the enemies of Vagandrak, King Yoon had chosen a simple reward.

Death by hanging.

"I have one thing to say," came the demure, measured voice of Kiki. Yoon made a throat-cutting gesture, but it was too late. Kiki continued, "Orlana the Changer, the Horse Lady, is far from dead. She will be back, Yoon. Back real soon. And who will protect you from her Equiem magick then?"

"Now," said King Yoon, dark eyes flashing dangerously at the hangman. "Do it now. *Do it now*!"

The hangman reached out and, with trembling, gloved fingers, took hold of a brass lever that operated the simple pulleys that, in turn, dropped the trapdoors beneath the hooded victims.

There came a *crack* as Narnok's ropes snapped under the huge axeman's writhing muscles, and he ripped off his hood, unhooked his noose, and, reaching forward, grabbed the pompous little bureaucrat, dragging him into a crushing bear-hug. "Help!" squeaked the little man, Narnok's crisscross scarred face up close and personal as Narnok pulled an ornate dagger from a sheath at the bureaucrat's hip. His arm came back and snapped forward. The dagger appeared, stubby and black, in the hangman's eye, and he gurgled as blood spattered the gallows. He slid from the trapdoor handle, sinking quietly into an embryonic heap.

"Bastards," growled Narnok, bad breath filling the bureaucrat's face, and, with grunt and a tug, he broke the man's spine with an audible crack and back-handed him from the gallows where the body toppled, a broken doll, into the rocks and deep chasms yawning below the fortress wall...

Yoon, blinking, suddenly screamed, "Kill him!" and ten of his elite guards rushed forward, led by Captain Dokta. Narnok ducked a sword-sweep, front-kicked Dokta from the battlements, and grabbed a sword by the blade with a slap. He stared into the surprised soldier's face, kicked him in the balls, slammed the sword left, where the hilt cut a groove across a soldier's eyes making him drop his blade and scrabble at the blood and flaps of opened flesh. Narnok took the sword's handle, weighed it thoughtfully, then launched a blistering attack: beheading one soldier; disembowelling a second so he fell to his knees clutching an armful of his own bloody bowels, cradled like some perverse abdominal abortion; then put the point of the blade through a third soldier's throat, skewering his bobbing apple and severing his spine so he collapsed like a sack of horse shit.

Narnok leapt to his colleagues' rescue, sword slashing down to cut the bonds of Dek, then Kiki, then Zastarte, and finally Trista. They removed silk hoods and loosened nooses, lifting them over their heads. Grim eyes met the soldiers of Vagandrak on the killing ground below.

Leaping down from the gallows, they grabbed weapons from the soldiers Narnok had slain. Bright steel gleamed under the storm clouds. The Iron Wolves formed a line on the battlements, weighing the odds, then suddenly charged at Yoon, at his remaining guards. Yoon screamed, high pitched and feral, and turned, slipping, then scrambling along on his hands and feet in what would have been a comical manner fit for the stage, if it hadn't been for five very real deadly killers in pursuit.

Kiki blocked an overhead sword strike, sparks showered, she punched the man in the throat, back-handed her blade across a second soldier's thigh, cutting the leg clean off and forcing him to collapse. Then the point of the blade skewered the eye of the man before her and she was over him even as he dropped, leaping, both boots landing atop Yoon and flattening him to the ground. When the King opened his eyes, Kiki was crouched beside him, a slender dagger to his throat. She jabbed it, just a little, and blood trickled free.

"Weapons down!" she bellowed, and gradually the fighting around stopped.

Kiki stood, dragging Yoon up with her.

"I'll have you... you... you *hung for this!*" frothed the king, apoplectic with rage.

"Yeah? You already tried that," said Kiki, smoothly, and tossed her sword to Dek who caught the weapon neatly from the air and rounded on the disabled soldiers. He grinned at them.

"Looks like you're shit out of luck, boys," he growled.

Kiki got a good handful of King Yoon's shaggy black hair and, with the dagger still spiking his throat, drew him close to her lithe, powerful body. She said, quietly, in his ear, "This is the way it's going to play out, *Your Highness*. We're going to retreat. Slowly. You're going to come with us. You've made it clear you want us dead, and us saving your damned country is not something which seems to bother you. A great shame. We'd give our lives for this realm, and you'd happily take them for no reason. The point is – our backs are against the wall. So don't think I won't slit your fucking throat. After all that's happened, it'd be a damn pleasure. Understand?" She shook him. "You *understand*?"

"Yes, yes... it hurts, please, stop pressing the knife in..."

"*You lot!*" bellowed Narnok, and the soldiers gathered

below stared up at him. Some looked at their boots in shame. "We fucking fought alongside you, like brothers, we held back the bloody mud-orcs together, shoulder to shoulder, our blood mixed on the battlements. And you stand there and watch your mad bastard of a king try to break our necks!"

Sergeant Dunda stepped forward, still clutching his axe, his bearded face lifted towards the Iron Wolves on the battlements. "Narnok, son, you can't do it this way. You may think him mad – *we* may think him mad – but he's *the King*, by all the gods! His word is Law!"

"Sometimes, you have to take a stand," rumbled Narnok, his one good eye sweeping across the gathered men.

"Yoon will have the whole of Vagandrak hunt you down," said Dunda, his voice level, neutral.

"Then so be it," said Narnok.

"We need to move," growled Kiki, pulling Yoon ever tighter.

"Follow me," said Dek, and started edging down the stone stairwell, both swords before him, his dark eyes full of murder. "Lads, you there, we're of the same land, and I don't want to cut off your heads; but if you force me to it, I will."

"Back off!" screeched Yoon. "Give them space, for the love of your king and country!"

The Iron Wolves reached the bottom of the steps at the same time the storm unleashed a fury of icy hail over Desekra Fortress. Ice rattled across the battlements, a great sweep slamming down and playing music on armour and helmets and shields. Thunder boomed in the mountains like the clash of titans; like the end of the world.

Kiki led the way now, with Zastarte and Trista, Dek and Narnok walking backwards, weapons bristling.

"We can take them," hissed Captain Dokta, dragging himself alongside Sergeant Dunda. He'd only just recovered from being front-kicked from the battlements; a fall of some twenty feet. He was lucky not to have broken his spine. "Call for the crossbows!"

"No," rumbled Dunda, his eyes fixed on the Iron Wolves. "Let them go. For now. Their blood rage is high. Last thing we want is a dead king's blood and body on *our* hands."

The Iron Wolves made their way to the tunnel beneath the second Desekra Wall, where Narnok pulled across a heavy iron gate and barred it, cutting off the majority of the remaining soldiers. From there, they moved to the nearest prison block, ducking inside, Kiki coming last with King Yoon as her living, breathing, royal-endorsed shield.

"Where now?" panted Dek, as gloom closed in. Outside, ice rattled on the cobbles and battlements, filling the world with a hushed white noise.

"Back underground," said Kiki, crouching to touch the soil. Her eyes were gleaming. "We head down. Into the tunnels. And get as far away from this place as is humanly possible."

"Human?" said Dek, raising an eyebrow.

Kiki chuckled, but there was no humour there. "You know what I mean."

They moved to the back of the empty prison block, filled with an old lingering stench of urine and vomit, towards a narrow door with a winding set of stone steps that led down to the dungeons proper; far beneath the main Keep. Yoon fought for a moment at the narrow doorway, his eyes filled with dread, fingers scratching at the portal edges.

"No. No!"

"I can strangle you unconscious and carry you down, if you like?" said Narnok amiably, looming close, his terribly scarred face and destroyed eye like the mask of some cut-up hell demon.

Yoon stared at him. "I'll walk," he said, mouth dry. "But my men – my army! – know this. They will hunt you down! They will slaughter you, like young squealing pigs in a tin shed filled with their own blood and shit!"

Narnok slapped the king across the back of the head, nearly pitching the man down the narrow spiral steps. "If you say so, lad. If you say so," muttered the huge axeman.

The Iron Wolves descended… down, into the darkness. Into a subterranean world of shadows.

FROM THE FIRE

For a long time, he truly believed he was condemned to Hell. Fire roared like a furnace. Flames burned high, scorching, searing, and all he could hear was a high-pitched female voice screaming; a tortured banshee; an eldritch sound. All he could see were glowing coals, as if they'd filled up the world before his eyes – had *become* his eyes. And then he slowly realised that the female screaming was his own, and the knowledge filled him with a chilled terror which dropped down through his bones to his very core. Feebly, he started to crawl, over fire and glowing stone, and sensed a massive movement around him. It was the huge, burning building shifting, groaning, growling, cracking, as if this structure and the fire were titanic monsters in some incredible, slow-paced battle. But he knew the fire would triumph. It always did.

Eventually the screaming stopped. *His* screaming stopped. Everything was dry, and hot, and blurred with hot mercury tears. Then the world fell away and tumbled down and darkness became his mistress.

He awoke to the sound of running water. It was beautiful. Perhaps the most beautiful thing he'd ever heard. Music.

Pure music. A symphony of Nature. And then the pain hit him, like a sledgehammer in the back of the head, and he gasped as needles flooded every vein, every organ, every atom of his body and he opened his mouth to scream, and his skin made crackling noises, and only a croak vomited out. The pain pounded him in great pulsing waves and with a sigh, he lowered his face to the frozen soil and registered a little puddle of ice, before he passed into darkness again.

Water. The water was cool. He pushed his hands under his body, feebly lifting himself up and then forward to slump onto his chest. White. Everywhere was white. He could smell smoke. He could smell burned pork. He could taste ash. He lifted himself again, and jerked himself forward. There were bushes. They briefly registered as a flash of tangled green. He lifted himself, slumped forward. Lifted himself. Slumped forward. Every movement screamed through his muscles. Every breath tore through his lungs like hot knives. He panted, and tried to cry, but there were no tears. His tongue, a dry stalk, licked lips like ruptured bark.

Danger. There was great danger! Men with swords.

Fire.

Forward. He pushed himself forward. It took a million years.

Stars were born. Flared. And died.

And still he pushed towards the flowing, musical stream, inching closer, and closer, and closer, and finally he reached a slope, and rolled down with a gasp through powdered snow to lie at the edge. The edges of the water were frozen, glittering like fine crystal. He could see his own breath smoking, now, and he brought his hand up to his gaze and almost wretched at the blackened, hooked claw, great cracks in the hard-cooked flesh weeping trickles of blood and pus...

It cannot be.

That cannot be my hand.

How could this awful thing happen to me?

He removed the claw from before his eyes and struggled forward, every inch of flesh pulsing him with waves of pain as if in some sick competition to make him puke. He slid over ice, then splashed into the flowing water and it was like instant orgasm. He gasped, the freezing water shocking him, and felt himself carried away, drifting away from the life-threatening danger. The men. With swords.

The men. And a name.

Dek.

He choked and spluttered a few times, flapping like a stranded fish in an ironic reversal, and gasped as he went down a low waterfall head-first, splashing into the pool, bobbing like an embalmed cadaver, limbs useless and trailing as the current picked him up once more and spun him around, drifting him downstream. It seemed to go on for some time, although he sensed he was drifting in and out of consciousness.

What happened? questioned his confused mind, over and over again.

How did I get here? But the answers would not come, and all he could remember were men, and swords, and talk of money, then burning wood, the roar of a terrible angry leviathan, bright flames all around and screaming, screaming as his clothes burned, his beard and hair caught fire, and he ran, then crawled on his knees, then squirmed like a snake on its belly to be free of the searing heat…

There came a gentle crunch as he came to rest on a crescent of pebbles. The stream bent here, and he had come to rest in a side-pool. He moved his arms slowly and tried to push himself up, but slumped back into the water, face first, spitting bubbles.

Maybe he was drowning? He did not care. At least the water was ice cold. Chilling him to the bone.

Anything but fire. Anything but the heat.

He shuddered.

Dek. Dek, the bastard. It had been a trap. Lantern oil. Mother's house. Trapped, with other members of the Red Thumb Gangs…

He fell swiftly down. Into darkness.

He knew he would die.

There came… a shaking.

"Agathe! Agathe! Come quickly!" Hands on him, instant agony, and a muttering, a woman's voice but gravelled and croaking. "Oh, by the Sweet Mother, oh my word, oh my God! What have we here? What's happened to you, poor boy? Oh my word! AGATHE!"

"What is it, what is it?" The grumbling of an old crone.

"Come quickly, there's a poor young man here!"

"Oh my, what happened?"

"I don't know, here, help me lift him. Oh my poor back, I can't do this, go and get the cart and be swift about it!"

Words whispered into his ear. "You hold on, you poor, poor man. Don't you dare let go. We'll look after you now. I'm Grace, that was my sister Agathe, she'll bring the pony and cart. Don't you worry about a thing."

The clop of hooves. Every jolt made him scream and the pain returned in great pulsing waves as his hands clawed, nails scratching at the wooden boards. He felt an incisor snap as his teeth ground together. He tried to weep, but nothing came, and he panted in frustration, and wished with all his heart that he were dead.

A smell. Sweetness. Honey. And something else. Almost like… cream. And blackberries. Slowly, gradually, finally, coolness crept over him. He was aware of no movement, no sound, no vision, just that beautiful sweet smell, and that gradual enveloping coolness. Eventually, hearing seemed to return, with various cracks and pops, and a feeling of pressure released inside his head. He worked his jaw from side to side and his whole face felt odd, solid almost, like he wore a mask that had been glued to him. He lifted his hand to explore, but heard a tut, a "Hush, what're you doing?", and his hand was guided away.

His eyes flickered open.

Two old women stood, gazing down at him. One was holding a large tub in frail, wrinkled hands; the other a wooden spatula.

"Ahh, he's awake. What're you called, boy?"

"I…" But he could not speak.

"Ahh, lost for words. But don't worry. We'll look after you. We'll take care of you. Been in a fire, you have. Oh, but I'm losing my manners, my name is Grace, and this is my sister, Agathe. But then, I think I already told you that. It's been all hands on deck since we found you. Burned, you were. Lying in the stream. Brought you back here on our cart, we did. Boy, you're a heavy young man! You were wearing chainmail that had almost become a part of you, thanks to the fire. We had to sedate you and use a blunt knife to prize each ring from your flesh."

"Grace! He won't be wanting to know that, now."

"Yes, yes, sorry. How do you feel? You must feel terrible. We've made an unguent from various ingredients, it will cool your skin, and draw any bad pus from the open flesh. Oh look, Agathe, he's trying to speak again."

"He'll need water, Grace. Give the poor boy some water."

Grace took a small cup and held it to his lips. He drank. It was, in all truth, the most incredible thing he had ever tasted. No wine, or ale, or sweet fruit juice could ever compare to that first conscious drink of pure, cool, soothing water.

He spluttered, and Grace removed the cup.

"Thank you," he croaked.

"What's your name, boy?"

"I…" and he realised he could not remember. So he licked his cracked open lips, and instead, said, "Thank you. Agathe. Grace. For rescuing. Me."

"Do you remember what happened?"

"There was a fire."

"You don't say, young man!" smiled Grace.

Agathe kicked her, and Grace scowled, bending to rub her ankle.

He drank more water, but still his tongue was made of old oak, still his mouth rinsed with ash. As he licked his lips, he wondered if the taste of fire would ever go away.

"Do you remember anything else?"

He remembered men with swords, firelight glimmering on polished blades. He remembered Dek, the large pit-fighter with iron-dark eyes, and talk of the money he owed to the Red Thumb Gang. But he said nothing. If these old ladies heard talk of warriors and gangs, they might not be so keen to nurse him back to health. If indeed, he *could* be nursed back to health.

"No," he finally managed. "Need. To sleep."

"Of course, dear. Of course."

Again, his face felt tight, odd, and he tried to lift his hand. Grace stopped him, gently, and returned his clawed, blackened appendage to the white cotton sheets. "No, no, young man. We have placed linen gauze over most of your face. It keeps the cream in place, keeps your skin moist. We're going to wrap you up pretty well. We've dealt with burns before. We know what we're doing."

"How?"

"Agathe here used to be a nurse in the city hospital. In Vagan."

"Oh. That's… good. Sleep… now."

Grace patted his hand. "Yes, you poor, poor man. You get some much needed rest."

Salvond sat high in the tree. It was a fabulous tree, an ancient oak, gnarled and twisted and… Salvond closed his eyes for a few moments. *Nigh on four hundred years old*. A section was blackened from a previous lightning strike, maybe a hundred years previous, and once more, closing his eyes Salvond felt himself sink into the bark, through the cambium, through sapwood and finally into the heartwood. He felt the slow beat of the tree's heart, its soul. And he relived the lightning strike, a series of feelings that linked to form a memory. And Salvond soothed the ancient oak. Sent his own pulses through heartwood, through sapwood, and he felt the oak respond to him, acknowledging him, accepting him.

Slowly, he opened his eyes. The two old women were pulling the blackened, tortured man from the pool and man-handling him, with curses and creaks, into a low wooden cart. Salvond remained perfectly still, his own skin – like bark – blending perfectly into the oak which had accepted him, made him its own. Slowly, Salvond's outer cells shifted, *mutated*, more and more until he was perfectly invisible against the oak. Only his black eyes could be seen. And the red of his mouth when he licked bark-rough lips.

The two women pulled the cart to their cottage nearby. Salvond listened and, through the sap, through the run of water through the soil, through tiny vibrations bounced from singing birds and clicking insects, he heard their dialogue.

Finally, night fell: a gradual, settling cloak.

There came a crunch as Salvond leapt from the oak and landed in the snow, awkwardly, his twisted back, his different-length legs, one rigid and straight, one with two supple knee joints, all combining to make him crooked and disjointed. Salvond hobbled through the snow towards the cottage, slowly, his bark-like skin masking him in the darkness, his thick, wiry, grey-green hair like so much gorse and bramble.

He slowed by the window. Inside, the glow of an oil lantern illuminated the blackened man in a bed of white cotton sheets, his visible arms and face covered in cream and gauzes, the two old women chatting to him amiably.

Salvond sent out quests. They emerged from his toes, growing through the soil, easing through tiny cracks in the brickwork and the old, porous foundations of the cottage. It took *hours*. Like roots, questing for water. Only these roots required a different currency; they sought knowledge. They quested into joists, then through the wood of the wide, warped, woodworm-infested floorboards. Finally, they oozed into the very wooden legs of the bed, pushing upwards into the down mattress and finally, into the–

Man.

Crowe tossed and turned beneath the sheets.

Images flickered in Salvond's mind as he moved backwards through this man's life, witnessing the fights and the stabbings, the money extortion for the Red Thumb Gangs in Zanne; the beatings and murders and the rapes. Salvond came to Crowe's initiation into the Red Thumbs, and experienced how the hard, mercenary, ambitious young man had turned on his best friend, stabbing him with a black-bladed dagger, quite literally, in the back. Blood on his hands. Again, back through time. *Back*. An alcoholic father. A weary, worn, beaten down mother who also, finally, turned to the cheap and nasty gin. Running free as a wild child. Wild, and wicked, and unchecked.

Perfect, thought Salvond.

And gradually, over the next three hours, his quests withdrew, back into himself, carrying information and understanding. Salvond knew this man. He had experienced this man's *life*. He knew what made him *tick*. Just like the clockwork of the Engineers.

As dawn was breaking, Salvond turned and hobbled into the bushes. He moved back to the ancient oak and, awkwardly, with great pain, managed to climb up into its branches and regain his former position.

Give it time, thought Salvond, and emitted a sigh like a heavy, creaking branch shifted by the wind.

He needs to suffer. More. A lot more.
Only then, will he appreciate my gift.

Minutes flowed into hours flowed into days flowed into weeks. Slowly, with the passing of time, Crowe started to heal. He wasn't aware of it at first, for his whole life had boiled down to a simple cycle of hot flesh, followed by applied cream and a soothing coolness. Within this cycle were also the herbs which Agathe and Grace crushed with pestle and mortar, and sprinkled into clear spring water. This, Crowe drank with increasing greed, as he realised the herbs' painkilling qualities; and with the drug came a blissful floating on a river of warm honey... for a while. Then the pain would creep in at the edges again, and Crowe would find himself growing increasingly agitated as he waited for the old women to appear at his door, bearing soothing cream and that glass of water in trembling frail old hands. Every footstep became a torture, and he wanted to scream, "Give me the herbs, give me the fucking glass!", but he did not, he lay there, suffering, grinding his teeth as bits of pain flared up and down his body and arms and legs and face and he felt like weeping, begging, dying.

Sometimes, the nights were the worst. He'd awake from some dream, in which he was still trapped in the burning house, with Dek and Ragorek outside, pointing at him, laughing as his hair caught fire and the flesh melted from his face. And once he had woken from such a torment, he'd lie in the cool stillness of the old cottage, listening to it, to the creak of its timbers, the occasional scamper of a mouse beneath floorboards, sometimes one of the old women would rise in the night and sit on their

shared commode, and he'd listen to the tinkle of their
piss in the wide stained ceramic pot.

Sometimes, he would strain against the bed as if
straining against chains, for he was trapped by his injuries,
shackled by his burns, and the pain would return and he
knew he was hours from the magical, pain relieving herbs;
and he knew it was going to be a long, torturous night.

Sometimes, he wished, truly wished, he had died in
that fire.

Because at least, then, it would have been an instant
release from this agony.

Crowe appreciated the simple pleasures in life. A *lack* of
the intense and all-consuming pain. A cool glass of water.
A bite of warm, soft, home-baked bread. Cold cream on his
burns. A chilled flannel on his brow. Distant bird song in
the hedgerows. A breeze from the open window. The taste
of fresh milk. A soft egg melting on his tortured tongue.
Soothing words from Agathe and Grace. Their confidence
in his recovery.

Four weeks after Agathe and Grace had found him in the
pool near their cottage, they helped him for the first time
to the front door. His hands were wrapped in bandages
and he held a hand-carved walking stick in each hand,
sturdy ash, to help support his weakened legs. He hobbled
forward, disjointed, hissing in pain, but then the daylight
hit him, and the smells from the open woodland to the
right, the river to the left. The ground was crisp with night
frost, and a cool breeze wafted towards him.

Crowe stepped out, then almost fell, and Agathe caught
his elbow. That contact made him gasp, but he ground

his teeth and tottered out, like a babe taking steps for the first time. There was a rough sawn bench, about ten steps away, and Agathe helped him towards it. He slumped down, with a soaring sense of elation, of achievement, despite the ridiculousness of such a simple feat. Once, Crowe could run ten miles and fight a bare-knuckle boxing match at the end. Now, he was either a babe or an old man, depending on how you viewed his jerky, puppet movements.

"Well done," said Agathe, sitting next to him.

"Thank you." He looked at her then, looked at her for the first time since the two old women had struggled with his burned carcass from the pond. He looked into her grey eyes, which twinkled in their pouch of wrinkled skin. Her face was slightly jaundiced, wrinkled heavy across the forehead, flesh saggy under her chin. Her hair was white and gently curled, falling to her shoulders. Crowe placed her age at around late sixties. He smiled. The sunlight glittered from her white hair, turning it silver. She was beautiful.

"Thank you," he said, simply. Then looked away, reddening. Or fancying he would redden, if his face hadn't been burned pork and scorched kindling.

"My pleasure," said Agathe, laying a hand on his shoulder. "We couldn't let you die, young man. What kind of people would we be, then? What kind of evil would live in our hearts, to let a young innocent perish whilst we stood by and did naught?"

Crowe thought of the women he'd raped. He thought of the men he'd beaten, clubbing them to the ground with bloody fists. He thought of the men and women he'd held on the end of his dagger, hearing the delicate crunch as steel chewed through flesh, and tears filled eyes, and he felt the elation, the joy of killing somebody, of robbing their life. Shame filled him. Filled him deep.

"You are good women," he said, eventually.

"Oh, nonsense. We just try to do what is right. Look!"

Crowe glanced up. A robin, soft, brown, with bright red breast, had landed on a branch. Its little head turned, watching them. Crowe realised it was the first time he had ever observed such a thing. Birds were not something that entered his lexicon, nor his consciousness. Whores, fighting, liquor. Yes. Red-breasted robins? Not a priority of observation. And yet here he sat, with an old woman resting her hand on his shoulder, filled with wonder at cool water and cooler air, watching the intelligent actions of a twitchy little robin.

You've gone fucking soft, he told himself.

And he grinned then, despite the way the motion cracked the blackened skin of his face. Suddenly, life felt good. Not *amazing*. But... do-able. He'd moved away from thoughts of suicide. A new hope filled him. It felt incredible.

"Come on, I'll help you inside. I'll make some tea, and Grace has baked soft scones. We have fresh blackberry jam. You'll enjoy it. You'll see."

"Thank you," he said again, and meant it from the bottom of his blackened, terrible heart.

Daylight was fading early, and sky-stacked clouds threatened snow. The back door to the cottage was half open, and a young deer had wandered in from the forest. It trusted Agathe and Grace, for they often left food out for the creature. A bowl was there, filled with fruit, wild flowers and nuts. The fawn's nostrils twitched and it moved forward, checking around with care, before lowering its muzzle into the bowl and savouring the offering. No sound intruded on the scene, except the nearby stream running through its frozen channel. But the deer lifted its head and, suddenly, for no apparent reason, its ears pinned back against its skull and it bolted, zig-zagging as it disappeared through the trees.

Inside the kitchen, Agathe was standing, staring out of the window as tea brewed in a pot. She'd seen the deer arrive, but had not heard it depart. So when the cracking of a twig brought her from her day-dreaming, her reverie, she thought it was still the deer and a smile broadened her wrinkled face…

But the shadow that fell across the threshold to the kitchen was not the deer. It was a small, hunkered, twisted creature with skin like bark and dark eyes that glittered. It hobbled into the kitchen and stood, staring at Agathe. She gasped, hand coming to her mouth.

"You," she hissed, in awe and terror.

"You know me, then?" said Salvond, voice a curious mixture of low and musical, and yet also cracked, degraded.

"I know what you are," said Agathe, voice low and level, eyes fixed on the elf rat. "I know you are a scourge. Cast out. Filled with poison, with plague. Go on! Get out!"

"You are mistaken," said Salvond, moving closer.

Agathe grabbed a bread knife from the table beside her, and slashed it in front of her. "I said stay back! You are diseased! Get out of my house! Grace! Grace!"

"I wouldn't do that," said Salvond, face cracking into a broken smile.

Agathe launched herself at the creature, knife plunging down. Despite his deformities, the elf rat side-stepped the attack, his own corrugated, twisted fingers lashing out and closing like powerful tree roots around Agathe's throat. He squeezed. She gasped, and the knife clattered to the kitchen flags.

Salvond glanced left, down the corridor towards the front room where Crowe was sleeping. He squeezed harder, and Agathe's legs went weak, collapsing at the knees – but still she remained in position as Salvond exerted pressure, held her there…

"Leave her be!" screamed Grace, hitting Salvond over the back of the head with a hefty log. But rather than collapse, or even shift, Salvond remained solid in place and turned slowly on Grace, who lifted the chunk of oak again, her intention to crack the elf rat's skull clean open. His hand came up, and tendrils like tree roots flowed from a circular wound in his palm. They wrapped around Grace's elderly face and she screamed, a scream which became quickly muffled. There were tiny crackling sounds as more strands snapped out, engulfing Grace's whole head. They wrapped around her, quivering, questing, entombing her completely and then pushing into her mouth, into her ears, up her nose, pushing into her eye sockets past her writhing, rolling eyeballs; then with the slow, gentle, unbending pressure that can send tree roots through lime mortar, these invading strands eased forward into Grace's skull. Her legs gave way suddenly, she sagged, held there, and then Salvond eased her to the floor and turned back to Agathe. She was purple, her own eyes rolling in disbelief and horror.

"I'm sorry, Old One," soothed Salvond, almost in sorrow. "But it has to be this way." Within the next minute Agathe, also, was dead.

Salvond straightened a little, his spine making crackling noises and the roots came back to him, wavering, quivering, and he closed his eyes for a moment as they were accepted back into his own body. Then he turned, and stared down the short corridor towards Crowe.

The elf rat limped across threadbare carpet. At the sound of his approach, Crowe's eyes fluttered and opened, and his blackened, crisped, well-cooked face turned from frown to grimace…

"Who are you?" he said.

"My name is Salvond."

"Where's Agathe? And Grace?"

"They are… sleeping a while."

Crowe started to struggle up, his movements weak and obviously causing him great pain. Reality came flooding over the dam of his security, and he realised, in a split second, how vulnerable he was. And as he looked into Salvond's ancient dark eyes, a kind of understanding came to him. He stopped struggling and lay there, teeth bared, growling softly, burned fingers clenching and unclenching the blankets.

"You killed them?"

"Yes." Salvond shuffled a little closer. He was within striking distance now. Crowe summoned up every ounce of strength and energy he had. This disgusting, terrible creature had murdered the two reasons Crowe was still alive; it had crushed their old beauty to shards. Something broke inside Crowe, and part of his old self came back. Part of his old bad self: distorted, crooked, cynical, hateful, merciless… something dead.

"You've come to kill me?" he snarled, finally, froth on his flecked lips, preparing to launch himself at the curiously disjointed monster.

"No, my dear boy," said Salvond, bending over him, his hand reaching out. Tendrils started to squirm and spiral from the palm of his hand which caught Crowe's attention and held him fascinated, hypnotised, in terror. "I've come to save you. And to learn from you. And to use you. You will become one of us. You will show me... *how* you humans work."

THE ANCIENT

The knocking came hard and fast, shaking the heavy door in its smooth teak frame. Grumbling, her wrinkled face squinting as she lit a lantern, Haleesa pulled a heavy robe around her ancient, stooped shoulders and padded barefoot across the hard soil floor.

The knocking came again, and mumbling, "Ha, it's enough to wake the dead," Haleesa threw open the portal to reveal the fury of the raging elements outside her thick-walled cabin. Rain slammed in diagonal sheets, and thunder rumbled distantly as the howl of the wind swept into the cabin, bringing the scent of the nearby forest.

"Is there no peace in the Palkran Settlement tonight?" scowled Haleesa.

"Come, come quickly." A round white face peered up from the darkness, flickering and strangely demonic in the wildly whipping flame of the fish-oil lantern. Miraculously, the flame did not extinguish, and the rain-soaked woman was beckoned across the cabin's threshold and into the dry warmth by Haleesa's wrinkled claw.

"Some problem?"

"Sweyn sent me to fetch the *Shamathe*. Gwynneth is having difficulty with her child. She is ready to deliver the babe… but cannot. You understand?"

Nodding, Haleesa pulled another, heavier, hooded shawl about her delicate shoulders, and gestured for the girl to lead the way through the storm.

The long hall was well lit and filled with warmth from a large fire-pit after the wildness of the storm-raped forest, and the young girl led a dripping Haleesa past roaring flames which the old woman fixed with a look of lingering despondency. And then they were through, into a room with a low cot and a scene dragged screaming from nightmare…

A man, Sweyn, stood to one side, his face drawn tight with weariness, his fingers rubbing the palms of his sweating hands in an unconscious display of fear. Two women were kneeling beside the low cot upon which writhed a beautiful woman with long dark hair. She was naked, her hair a waterfall of velvet across her milk-gorged breasts. Her legs were open, labia and inner thighs smeared with blood and amniotic fluid which had soaked the rough wool blankets beneath her.

Haleesa dropped her shawl. "Your first child, Gwynneth?"

The woman met the *Shamathe*'s gaze and held it, face contorted in pain. She nodded, her darting tongue licking at sweat-smeared lips.

A brave woman, thought Haleesa. She must be in great pain.

Her hands slid over Gwynneth's distended belly, squeezing gently, feeling the curves and bulges within; then she dropped to her knees and her fingers probed inside Gwynneth's vagina with the expert touch of a practised midwife.

"You have a restrictive pelvis," observed Haleesa. She met Gwynneth's gaze once more, and smiled warmly, her wrinkled, dark-skinned face beaming from under thick grey curls. "Don't worry, lass, it will be all right. I will look after you."

Two hours had passed, and Sweyn had left the room and was slumped by the fire, a bottle of pear brandy in his hands, his mouth a line holding the cage of his dry fear in place.

"The babe is coming," whispered Haleesa.

Gwynneth screamed, back arching as she pushed with all her might. Violent contractions forced her to squirm and buck, to twist and writhe, like a cat-torn rabbit with a broken spine. From between Gwynneth's thighs Haleesa witnessed a sudden sprout of bristly dark hair, and *instantly* she knew something was wrong. *Badly wrong*. A chill whisper scythed through her soul like a razor slicing icy flesh. The feeling came not due to her skills as a midwife, but more her experience – her *senses* and her *understanding* – as a *Shamathe*. A woman in tune with the earth and rocks and trees and mountains; a child of Nature.

Her hands dropped swiftly as the crown of the babe's head forced free and she applied pressure to stop Gwynneth ejecting the babe too quickly and thereby ripping herself apart – and damaging the child in the process. Gwynneth's quim stretched wide as the head appeared in full, and instantly Haleesa muttered the bitter tasting sour hissing words of *form illusion*…

The delivery was over in minutes, but instead of giving the babe to its mother, Haleesa cut the cord and wrapped the tiny pink wailing toddler in her shawl, close to her own breast. The old woman's eyes narrowed, her breathing coming in ragged pants, and she muttered a variety of minor charms. Only then did she look up, to meet the questioning gaze from the woman lying prostrate and exhausted. Gwynneth was wrapped in a blanket, her face ashen with weariness, her friend clasping her hand tightly so that pink skin turned white under clenching knuckles.

"Can…" a confused pause. "Can I hold her?"

Haleesa considered refusing, but gathering her remaining strength she muttered a strengthening of *form illusion* and handed over the babe. The little girl gurgled happily and Gwynneth smiled down at her child, her eyes bright with the joy of a new life, the happiness of birth, the awe of creation. She fumbled with her breast as if to suckle the child, but Haleesa stepped forward and lifted the babe from Gwynneth's startled arms.

"But… what?"

"This child is seriously ill. The laboured birth damaged her internally. I must take her for healing."

Gwynneth's face fell, and Haleesa forced the words from her unwilling mouth. "I will not play games with you, Gwynneth; the babe might die during the night. You must trust me, and let me do my work. I swear to you, I will give my life to save her."

"Can… can I come with you?"

"Best I work alone."

"But–"

Sweyn, who had stepped back into the room to witness the birth, whispered, "Shusht," and, kneeling, took his wife in his arms. "It is the right of *Shamathe*. She will not harm the child…" But it was there, in Gwynneth's eyes – the mistrust, the suspicion, and her gaze followed

Haleesa's retreating shawl as the old woman left the room and the hall, with the heavily swaddled babe; and disappeared into the storm.

"If she harms my baby, I will kill her," spat Gwynneth, and tears rolled down her chalk ashen cheeks.

As Haleesa bent her head against the hammering rain, she allowed the illusion to fall and felt the reality of the babe beneath her shawl. Swallowing back revulsion, she cut left down a narrow track and under the broad-shouldered shelter of vast, towering, swaying pine trees. The Lords of the Forest. The rain was less offensive here, less aggressive; Haleesa halted by a wide trunk which had fallen years earlier and had been stripped of bark. Rummaging in her robes she produced the babe and laid it against the roughness of the trunk. It did not cry – in fact it made no sound. Its birth cries and subsequent gurgles had been a simple *word illusion* cast by Haleesa.

She met this newborn babe's gaze and was shocked to see cognition there in the dark, iron-coloured eyes. She swallowed and allowed her own gaze to travel the ruined shell of the girl – although the child resembled no girl Haleesa had ever seen. Her head was topped with a ragged sprouting of wiry black hair. Her skin was mottled yellow, appearing almost scaled, and slick with a thick, oily substance. The nose was twisted and the teeth – for this newborn already had teeth – were tiny and pointed and glinted nastily from within ill-fitting lips. Like a fish, thought Haleesa as her eyes moved down, examining the spindly body and the arms and legs. There were no hands or feet, instead the arms and legs tapered to splintered points where jagged protrusions of bone shone with blood and were barely coated by the greasy, yellow skin. The babe's orifices shone under the delicate forest light below a bulging obscene belly, and were bright with pus weeping from urethra and anus. A tongue darted out, licking at white, brittle lips. The babe waved the jagged stumps of her arms in the air and Haleesa took another step back.

Leave her, screamed the words in her mind.

Leave her to...

(ah)... *die*.

But she could feel it – could feel the calling, feel the energies, feel the *mana* within the child. This little girl, this tiny, disfigured, horribly malformed child had been born *Shamathe*.

Like me, realised Haleesa, with a gradual rising horror.

Before she changed her mind, and forcing down rising nausea, Haleesa gathered the stinking babe in her arms. She could feel pus leaking through her shawl, burning against her skin, and she swallowed back her revulsion with a prayer of calm. She hurried through the night, oblivious to the threat of wolves or bears, until she reached the opening and her beckoning cabin at the foot of the cliff which reared up into sheer, black mountains above; ominous and foreboding; threatening, and yet strangely protective.

The rain was relenting as Haleesa slammed shut the door and threw three bolts across the slightly warped timbers. She laid the child on a thick wolfskin rug on the floor, and fetched a jug of goat's milk. She held the babe's head – the skin felt strange, like burned and greasy parchment – and allowed the babe to gulp greedily at the milk.

The girl was eager, and milk spilled down her yellowed skin: glistening jewels against a portrait of obscenity.

I should have told Gwynneth, thought Haleesa, suddenly. Should have told her the babe was dead...

And as she lay down on her bed, burrowing under the heavy furs and blankets, she heard the babe make a single sound, the first sound the child had uttered since its painful, horrible birth.

The child sighed in utter contentment.

The following morning, soon after sunrise, as Haleesa was preparing a breakfast of porridge and honeyed bread, there came a knocking at her door. This, at least, she had been expecting.

She shuffled forward, opening the portal and staring stoically at the young face of Gwynneth. Haleesa did not smile – she forced her face into a look of neutrality. She took the girl by the hand and brought her inside, leaving a nervous Sweyn standing beside the two ponies.

"Is she all right? Tell me!"

"I have bad news," said Haleesa, casting the word illusion. The babe cried out in the corner, in a small cot, as if in great pain.

"Tell me! Please!" A look of horror. Hands held to mouth.

"Prepare yourself, Gwynneth. Your child is seriously ill. She has a damaged heart, and I will have to keep her here for a while, to administer herbal remedies and keep a watchful eye in case she should suddenly stop breathing..."

"Oh no!"

"Be brave, child," said Haleesa, her voice softening. "You are of the *Palkran*. Be strong."

With these words, Gwynneth dried her eyes and stared at the babe. "Can I... can I hold her for a while?"

"Of course. Be gentle. Any sudden movement could kill her."

Gwynneth nodded, and picked up the babe, cradling the smooth skin to her shawl and looking down into deep brown eyes. They blinked, staring back as if with sentience: a connection.

"Have you thought of a name?"

"Yes. I shall call her Lorna."

"It is a pretty name. Now, come, put her to sleep, she needs much rest in this state."

Laying the babe gently, Gwynneth stared hard at Haleesa. "How long will she have to stay here?"

Haleesa shrugged. "A few months, maybe as many as six. It depends on her condition. It is very serious, I promise you." She placed a wrinkled claw on the girl's shoulder. "She may die, Gwynneth. You must understand this. You must prepare for this eventuality."

Nodding, tears wet on her cheeks, the girl left the warmth of the cabin and shivered in the strong fresh breeze. Haleesa followed her outside, breathing deep the scents of the forest. "If there's anything we can do to help you..." said Sweyn.

Haleesa nodded. "Another time." She watched the couple lead their ponies into the forest, picking a route between the towering trees. There were no paths leading to Haleesa's cabin – and that was the way she wanted it to stay.

Returning, the old woman picked up the child and pulled a small basket onto her arm. One part of her deception had been truth, at least – that of medicine. Not for the child, but for herself. Constantly casting illusions was draining her of power… and as the wind bit into her skin she felt the weight of many, many years pressing down upon her, felt her aged body betraying her.

To be young again, she thought wearily.

To be radiant in the prime of youth!

She stepped under the shadow of the trees and everything fell away into silence. No birds chattered in these parts. No wind moved the massive, perfumed evergreens. This part of the Palkran lands was silent, untouched by any life.

Haleesa picked her way carefully between the trees. Rarely did she look down, but every time she did she saw the babe staring up at her with that disconcerting intelligent gaze. Not once did the child – Lorna – cry out. Not once did she whimper for her mother. Not once did she gurgle, or chuckle, or make any sound associated with a babe. She was as silent as–

Silent as a corpse, thought Haleesa.

The journey took an hour, much of it uphill across the lower flanks of the mountains, which were layered with not just pine and elm, but ash and oak, ancient and twisted. Eventually, she came to a narrow valley devoid of trees, and picked her way with care between the boulders which littered the rocky floor.

The wind howled, eerie, like hunting ghosts through the cleft in the mountain bulk. As usual, in this place, Haleesa felt as if she were being watched.

"Rock and earth, fire and ash," she muttered, and placed Lorna down on a wide, flat stone veined with quartz. The babe followed Haleesa with her eyes as the old woman hobbled away, stooping to pick herbs, which she placed in the basket on her arm. Haleesa could feel the child's gaze boring into her back and she rallied against the impulse to turn.

And all the while her thoughts returned to her own father, and her own blood, all those many years ago…

the wind, screaming across a hilltop

towering storm-clouds, a mammoth black wall of billowing oppression, piling up and upon itself as it gathered and bulged with iron and copper streaks to finally pound the pitiful mortals below, crushing them with its magnitude

"*You have the gift,*" *said her father, looking down into the eyes of a seven year-old Haleesa.* "*You are* Shamathe; *you carry the blood of the Shaman. Your* mana *runs powerful through your blood and you are connected to the land, to the soil, the rock, the water, the mountains, the trees, to all life…*"

"*How do you know this?*" *asked Haleesa, her voice high-pitched, girlish, a child's utterance as her eyes shifted uneasily to the violent storm overhead.*

Her father smiled. "*I, too, possess the wealth of the elementals; the legacy of the Equiem. But I am a man, and in my blood the* mana *runs weak. Only a female can truly connect and use the power which the earth, the water, the air and the fire can offer. Use your gifts wisely, little Haleesa. Use them for the power of Good.*"

Haleesa's grip had tightened, as she clung to her father's huge, spade-like hand. "*You sound like you are going away, father.*"

He glanced at the clouds.

"*Aye, Little One.*"

"*Don't leave me!*"

"*Not yet, child.*" *He ruffled her hair.*

Thunder rumbled in the distance, and they looked together over the vast expanse of trees, a sweeping carpet beneath them. In the gloom, distant fires glittered, eyes in the belly of the forest beast.

"There will come a time," he whispered, his words almost lost in the roar of the heightening wind, "when another, like you, will come. But she will be a god, or a demon; a saviour, or a destroyer. Her power will be like nothing this world has ever seen..." He shivered. Then smiled at Haleesa. "I think you will meet her... and when that time comes, you must be ready, Haleesa."

"Ready for what?"

"Ready for whatever must be done. The vision is unclear. It is like a coin: double-sided and always spinning."

Lightning forked, smashing into the forest below. Haleesa felt her hair crackle and her muscles became taut. She glanced up at her father. His face was grim – his eyes fixed on the fast-approaching storm which rushed across the world.

Sheets of rain came slamming at them like knives; instantly they were soaked. Haleesa could not understand why her father did not take her under cover, away from the rain and the wind and the threat of

lightning.

The spear lanced from the turmoil, a jagged bolt screaming towards the earth. Haleesa felt nothing, only heard a high-pitched cry and felt immense heat – heat searing her hand and the right side of her face...

When she awoke, her father was gone, a blackened smear staining the earth where he'd been smashed into oblivion. She looked down at her fingers, and could feel the tingle of his energies... and realised in that instant, in that moment of death and connection, he had given her his power; passed on to her his knowledge, his skills, his wisdom as he passed from life to death... a parting gift.

Haleesa blinked. She found she was staring at her fingers, remembering that final touch. She felt tears trickling against her wrinkled, ancient skin. So long ago. But you never forget. You *never* forget.

Dabbing away the tears with the hem of her shawl, she placed a few more herbs in the basket; Dubweed, Redsaal, and Grey Glove. Then she turned – and froze.

Three huge, grey wolves sat in silence around the stone tablet on which rested the deformed, yellow-skinned babe, Lorna.

Haleesa blinked, and slowly released a breath. *Impossible*, screamed her mind. She would have heard them approach; she would have *felt* the presence of such beasts, for she was connected to the forest and the earth and the animals that inhabited this realm.

Haleesa stared hard at the animals. Each was four feet tall at the shoulders and heavily muscled. Their fur was a deep, thick grey: winter coats. One of the wolves had a black streak across its muzzle, and it stared at her, eyes cool and appraising.

Words of power leapt into Haleesa's mind and she felt the bite of energy welling from the earth beneath her feet, into her. But she stayed the words. Her lips were dry and she felt her legs trembling.

She took a step forward.

One of the wolves growled, and she saw a string of saliva pool to the ground.

Hungry, came the unbidden word in her mind. They were hungry. And yet they did not attack.

She took another step. She was five paces from the babe, which was watching her in that eerie silence.

"Good wolves," muttered Haleesa.

She took another step closer. Again, the words of power came blazing red and hot into her mind, and high on adrenaline Haleesa felt her youth again, felt the surge of *Shamathe* power. She was three paces from the nearest –

and largest – wolf, now. His baleful yellow eyes were fixed on her, and his lips peeled back revealing huge, jagged yellow fangs. The growl came from his belly and was a bass rumble, terrifying Haleesa to her core.

She forced another step, and another; then slowly, gently, bent and picked up the child. Lorna snuggled against Haleesa's breast and was immediately asleep.

The wolves turned and loped off into the forest.

Haleesa sank to the rock, her chest heaving, red pin-pricks of light flashing in her mind as she cradled the babe.

What magic is this, she mused, staring hard at the sleeping child.

Had they been summoned? And if so, for what purpose? And by a one day-old child?

She laughed, her laugh the insane cackle of an old crone, but strangely without humour.

Whatever. It is still good to be alive, she thought, and gathering herself together she stepped warily through the trees, eyes alert for movement, the ugly bundle in her arms asleep and breathing steadily.

Haleesa looked down, and the babe sighed.

Lorna was content.

During the weeks following the birth of Lorna, Sweyn and Gwynneth visited their horribly disfigured babe daily – blissfully unaware of her deformities. However, Haleesa soon became weary of the deception, her powers constantly drained. Her emulation began to change, and she made the child less communicative. She forced the babe's illusion to appear pallid, waxen and unmoving. A fish-wax doll with shallow breathing and a burning fever.

And then, one day, Sweyn and Gwynneth did not come.

They came the following morning, with presents of bread, honey and sausage for Haleesa. Sweyn cut some wood with an old axe kept in a shed beside the cabin, and then they left. It was three days before they returned, and Haleesa continued with her form illusion of the child in poor health, lying still and waxen, chilled and silent.

The weeks flowed by.

When Lorna was six months old, her parents visited just once a week – sometimes every two. Many times Sweyn did not attend, for he was out cutting wood with other men of the tribe, or was away buying or selling pigs at the market fifteen miles to the north.

By the time Lorna was a year old, her parents had practically given up their visits. During the last nine months, Gwynneth had been blessed with another child, a little girl, and the child had emerged – under the fearful gaze of a trembling and wary Haleesa – with a healthy pink complexion, a mop of golden curls and the lusty cries of the newborn.

Gwynneth called this fresh new whole perfect little girl "Suza", and she was blessed by the local priest and the parents had their new toy. Gwynneth would still visit Lorna every few months, out of guilt, if nothing else, but was now occupied with the upbringing of the new baby girl – and Haleesa was glad to see the pain slowly drift and dissipate like woodsmoke from the young, once-tortured woman.

The enviable strength of the human spirit to adapt and progress, she thought, with just a hint of bitterness.

Lorna was walking before she was two, and balanced on the spiked stumps of her deformed legs she was able to step carefully around Haleesa's cabin. Her eyes were always – *always* fixed on Haleesa and the old woman found this gaze, peering up from a mottled yellow face, utterly unnerving.

Lorna's hair had grown: a long, ragged trail of wiry black strands. She had grown in stature, filling out, her face becoming more round, her tiny pointed teeth nestling in the cavern of her fish mouth.

Her first word, on the day of her second birthday, had been: "*Mudder.*"

Haleesa had smiled, and shook her head. "No, I am not mudder. Gwynneth – the lady with long brown hair who visits – she is your mudder."

The girl shook her head, and pointed with the spike of one serrated arm. "You mudder," she whispered, then smiled, showing her tiny pointed teeth. Haleesa felt a ripple of goose bumps traverse her back and flanks, and she shivered, forcing a smile she did not feel.

Stepping outside to fetch some wood, Haleesa almost jumped out of her skin to see the three huge wolves sitting at the edge of the forest. Their pale yellow eyes were fixed on her and they made no sound.

Forcing herself forward, the old woman shuffled around the side of the cabin and hoisted a small log in her arms. Turning, she saw that the wolves had gone and, muttering to herself in annoyance and confusion, she returned to the cabin.

As the months passed, Lorna grew and learned with stunning speed. By the age of three she could speak quite clearly, holding reasonably complex discussions with Haleesa and asking about her missing hands.

"The Gods decided not to give you hands and feet," said Haleesa carefully, adding more wood to the flickering fire. Outside, snow was falling and the forest was a scene of beauty, one best experienced from the warmth of a friendly hearth. Through the cold panes of glass Haleesa watched the spinning flakes for some minutes as Lorna digested this piece of information.

The girl finally smiled. "There are no Gods," she said softly, her tongue darting to lick her yellowed lips. Her small round face looked up earnestly at her teacher and adoptive parent.

"And why not?"

"I can feel it."

"What can you feel?" Haleesa was intrigued as to how the girl would answer. She tilted her head, her wrinkled fingers rubbing at her chin as she waited for a reply.

Lorna closed her eyes. Her nostrils flared.

"I can feel your sadness. You are sorry for me. Deep within you carry the shame of your deceit – you lied to keep me here, to protect me. They would have left me in the forest to die, to be eaten by the wolves."

Haleesa took a deep breath.

"Then you understand. About the fear your appearance will provoke." Lorna nodded, her deep brown eyes fixed on Haleesa. "One day you may have the power to change this, to physically alter yourself. But for now, you must rely on *illusion*."

"What is that?" A child once more.

"Close your eyes."

"Yes."

"Listen to the fire. Feel the heat."

"Yes."

"The heat is energy. Everything is energy. What other people call magic, spells, the *Shamathe* feel as energy and they have the ability to move this energy around. You understand?"

"Yes. Energy. Spells. Move around."

"Good. Now take five deep breaths, and face the fire."

Lorna did so.

"Tell me what you see?"

Haleesa tried not to show her shock at the young girl's response. She had expected "Nothing – my eyes are closed!" but instead, Lorna whispered, "I can see an orange shape, flickering around and above where the flames are."

"You must pull that energy towards yourself. I cannot teach you how."

For long minutes they sat there, the young deformed child perfectly still, her closed eyes facing the flames, the old woman sitting back with a large pot of sweet tea in her liver-spotted hands.

Lorna's eyes came open. "I cannot," she said, simply.

"It will come," said Haleesa kindly.

"I know," said Lorna with a twisted smile.

That night, Lorna wailed in her sleep, thrashing her stumps madly as she twisted and turned, sweat gleaming on her naked yellow skin. Haleesa was there, cradling her head as deep brown eyes flared open.

"Quiet, little one. It is a dream."

"No. He is born."

Haleesa frowned and saw Lorna lick her lips with her quick, darting tongue.

"Who is born?"

"The King," whispered Lorna, "The Soul Taker," and

then refused to say more. She closed her eyes, cuddled under her blankets, and was asleep once more before Haleesa had even crossed the room back to her own cot.

Haleesa lay for a long time in the darkness, listening to the wind sighing outside, and wondering what Lorna *had* seen in her dreams. In her nightmares?

Haleesa shivered, and closed her eyes, praying for the morning.

They sat on the hilltop, overlooking the Palkran Settlement. Their seat was an old, lightning blasted log, and despite the snow the sun had come out and there was no wind. Haleesa felt the weather was very pleasant and she allowed the warm rays to lick across her aged, wrinkled face.

"Where is my mother's house?"

Haleesa pointed, to a conical adobe with a straw roof. As they watched, Gwynneth, once more pregnant, emerged holding the hand of a laughing, golden-haired girl. Haleesa shifted her gaze to watch Lorna, but the deformed girl's eyes and face were impassive, unreadable.

Gwynneth and the child disappeared between other houses and were lost in the bustle of people. It was market day, and the Palkran Settlement was a hive of activity despite the snow.

"I will try to pull the fire energy once more," said Lorna suddenly.

"What fire?" asked Haleesa.

"The sun," said Lorna, and before Haleesa could stop her the child had transferred her gaze on the glowing copper orb squatting low in the heavens. Haleesa surged to her feet, panic giving her movements urgency and she reached out towards Lorna–

"No."

The word was a command and Haleesa rocked to a halt. She knew that to focus on the sun would tear a human, even a *Shamathe*, physically apart. And yet... yet...

Haleesa felt the *flow*. It surrounded Lorna with a warmth which radiated and Haleesa sank to the ground, ignoring the cold of the snow in her bones as her eyes widened and she stared at the young child before her... a child performing the impossible... the channelling of the sun's direct energies...

Lorna laughed, a truly joyous sound from such an ugly shell.

"It feels wonderful," she breathed. "It tickles!"

"You must stop."

Lorna's gaze suddenly snapped to Haleesa, and the old woman saw the child's eyes had turned from deep iron to a soft copper.

"You must stop," cried Haleesa.

"I will never stop," whispered Lorna, and her eyes glowed, then faded, and the ugly little child smiled. She stepped towards Haleesa, but the old woman scrambled away across the snow.

"What you did, child... it was impossible."

"Nothing is impossible," said Lorna. The child turned her gaze back down on the village. Gwynneth was there once more, returning to her hut with her golden-haired young girl, and waddling with the awkwardness of her internal passenger. Haleesa wondered what was going through the mind of her protégée.

"Let us go home," said Lorna. "I am very hungry."

CATACOMBS

Kiki, captain of the Iron Wolves, led the way into the subterranean gloom under Desekra Fortress. Her face was grim, hand on the hilt of one short sword, her bobbed brown hair tied back into a tight pony-tail, her iron eyes grim, hard set, and scowling. Her instinct was to turn around, face King Yoon – her King, *the* King of Vagandrak, Chief Warden of the North, Defender of the Skarandos... and hack her sword into his fucking head.

Dek padded up close behind, and she half-turned, seeing his grinning face in the flickering light from the brand she carried. "What are you smiling at?"

"It turned out okay in the end," rumbled the broad-chested, badly tattooed pit-fighter. "Didn't it, Keeks?"

"Hmm. That's one way of looking at it, Dek. If it hadn't been for Narnok snapping those ropes, we'd be dangling corpses over the mud-orc killing ground right about now. And all thanks to that insane, maggot-infested bastard, Yoon."

"Well. I'm sure he had his reasons."

"Had his *what?* Have you gone fucking insane?"

"Kiki, calm down. I said he had his reasons, not that I

agreed with them. I like my neck unbroken, thanks very much, although I've got to admit, I'm a hard man to kill. It'd have to be a very strong rope." He thought about it. "And a very long drop."

Kiki stared, and coughed. "Well it was both of those; I think the fall from the walls of Desekra is big enough to crack even your unfaltering warrior's ego. The problem here is what kind of liability Yoon is going to prove. He's been nothing but a scourge against the people of Vagandrak."

"You should talk to him. When we stop," said Dek. He smiled amiably. "If you'll let us stop. He may yet be a man who surprises you."

Kiki nodded, but found a rage boiling inside herself, bubbling dangerously. She did not dare speak to Yoon. Yet. She knew she would lose her temper – and the last time that happened, she awoke a demon in her soul; she awoke the *Shamathe* and collapsed the battleground before the Desekra Fortress into a thousand caverns and ancient mines deep below the ground, sucking down thousands of warring, battling mud-orcs; sucking down Orlana, the Changer – otherwise known as the Horse Lady – down to her Eternal Doom.

Kiki took a deep breath and tried not to think about what nestled inside her. Tried not to think of her past. Her childhood. Of the Seed. And her sister, oh, her terrible, brooding, dark sister.

Well, I won't allow it, came the slithering voice of Suza, her tomb-demon, her eternal tormentor, sliding sideways into the charnel house of Kiki's skull and bringing flashing images of maggot-infested corpses, of dead babies in coffins, of priests staked out to die, of death and putrefaction and a certainty of every single mortal man's own imminent useless stinking death.

You cannot stop me, thought Kiki, gritting her teeth so hard there came a crack.

You did well, back there. Very clever. Very noble. Honourable Kiki! Saving the people of Vagandrak from the slavering, terrible, unholy mud-orcs; God bless her little golden glowing soul. You fucking idiot. Where did it get you? Yoon turned on you. Stabbed you in the back. Ripped your heart from your chest and your womb from your abdomen. You think that maniac wanted his people saving? He was giving them over to Orlana; sacrificing you all to the Horse Lady.

But… why? Why would a king do that to his people?

Why not? cackled Suza. *Like you really care, bitch. Like you really give a bejewelled fuck.*

"Kiki!" rumbled Narnok, from the back, where he'd looped some rope around Yoon's neck and was dragging the bound king along like a dog. The King's eyes were wide and mad, his mouth muttering curses in a language Kiki had never before heard as spit drooled down the rich embroidery of his silk and cotton robe. "If my memory serves, there's an old storeroom up ahead. One of Dalgoran's little stashes for the Old Raids."

Kiki nodded, and she noted the sudden gleam in Narnok's single eye amidst the writhing mess of his razor-scarred face. "Go on. Ask the question."

Narnok's voice dropped to a hiss, like the fevered insistence of an insane zealot. *"The curse, Kiki! You promised us; said Dalgoran told us how to lift the curse!"*

"And I shall," she said, uneasily, remembering Dalgoran's words – shortly before the old, noble general died by his own hand. *Deep below Desekra Fortress, beneath*

Zula, the keep, there is a chamber. Inside it there is a chest. Everything you need to lift the curse is inside that chest... This key unlocks both the chamber and the chest. You will understand, when you see it. He'd given her a bronze key which she wore on a loop of leather against her breast even as they spoke. Involuntarily, her hand came up, feeling the solidity of the bronze key through the soft cotton of her shirt. Nobody knew she had the key. *Nobody.* And if they did? She glanced around at her companions; at her *Iron Wolves.* Would they still be standing, talking?

First came Narnok, the huge axeman: bitter, twisted, hating humanity because of what his wife, Katuna, had done to him – over, ultimately, money. He also hated Dek, for Dek had been drawn into the spider's web of seduction and deceit, and had betrayed one of his most trusted friends by taking Katuna to bed; Katuna, with her long dark curls, flashing eyes, and perfect olive skin. The fact she had then employed Xander the torturer to cut up Narnok's face and put-out one of his eyes with acid had done nothing to temper the huge axeman's view of the world and the insects that scurried about on its surface. Damaged wasn't the half of it; but then, deep inside, weren't they all?

Dek. Handsome Dek! A tall, athletic pit-fighter, with a broken nose and a hatred of his brother after what went on with their dying mum. But now Ragorek was dead, and Dek seemed to have mellowed, remembering a time long ago when he and Kiki had been young recruits, and more: lovers. But when Dek slept with Katuna, betraying Narnok, he had also betrayed Kiki. She still remembered the pain in his eyes when she'd screamed at him, screamed that she'd slit his throat, cut off his balls, eat out his heart. She hadn't meant it, but it had had to be said. And now, years on, *decades* on, after so much sleep and wine and the addictive curse of the honey-leaf... well. That world seemed another lifetime, filled with different people, different lovers; lovers who'd helped dilute the pain.

The next Iron Wolf was Zastarte: handsome, dashing, *stunning*, with his slim rapier and witty banter, his expertise at giving women pleasure and his love of burning people alive. Amoral, twisted, decadent, he had changed since the old battles with mud-orcs and the sorcerer Morkagoth; or had he? Kiki remembered Zastarte from the Before Times – he'd always had a merciless streak. Had always been... mean? Ruled by money, sex, and later fame after the Iron Wolves became heroes; his merciless, amoral streak had grown dominant, yes; but, more importantly, it had always been there: more powerful than the curse that ran through all their blood, all their flesh. You could trust Zastarte, as long as there was good solid gold at the end of the mission. And maybe a few buxom wenches to lighten the darkness in his soul.

Trista was the very essence of beauty and the beast, yet another twisted individual. A great swordswoman, her husband had betrayed her and she'd spent many an evening hunting down newlyweds and murdering them in their conjugal bed – so, as it appeared in her twisted reality, they could be together... forever. No betrayal for those visited by Trista. No cheating lies and backstabbing treachery. She also had an unusual, predatory streak; Narnok had once compared her to the female spider that mated, then ate its mate. He said she was a predatory cannibal; and to sleep with her, was to die. Although Trista had been offended at the time, Narnok had been pretty astute with his observations.

And finally. Finally? Kiki turned her critical eye on herself. Kiki, Captain of the Iron Wolves, a dazzlingly accomplished warrior. But after the fame of turning back the mud-orcs at the Pass of Splintered Bones, of heading out into No Man's Land and confronting Morkagoth the Sorcerer, and beating him using the curse of the Iron Wolves... Kiki had discovered she had a tumour close to her heart. The King, Yoon's father, had showered them with money, jewels, lands, and Kiki had used a small fortune seeking the best medical advice in Vagandrak and beyond. When one brave surgeon finally cut her open, he had immediately sewn her back up again. To operate, he advised her, to *remove* the tumour would be to kill her stone dead. And so Kiki had fallen into bad ways, losing herself in the world of the honey-leaf, self-pity, drugs and liquor and meaningless sex – constantly mocked by the voice of her dead sister, Suza, taunting her inside her own tortured skull. Until the aged General Dalgoran had come looking for her, with a new mission.

And now. *Now* she held the key to releasing the Iron Wolves from the curse they suffered. Just like she had promised, if they accompanied her back to Desekra to face the new threat of massing mud-orcs and the Horse Lady, Orlana. And they had. They had all stuck to their side of the bargain. And, she realised, she could – she *could* release them from the curse, if she so chose. They could search for Dalgoran's secret chamber and drink the potion or wear the magick fucking ring – whatever secret was hidden in the box which would unbind the magick locking the Iron Wolves together. But...

But.

With a primeval instinct, Kiki knew this thing wasn't over. Knew the horrors visiting Vagandrak, although it seemed they had been turned aside once more... well, something inside her screamed more loudly than her dead bitch sister. And to release the Iron Wolves from their united curse would be to... *weaken* a massive force for good in the land. Kiki knew she owed it to Dalgoran, to King Tarek, to General Jagged and all the tens of thousands of soldiers who had given their lives protecting the good land of Vagandrak.

This thing wasn't over. Kiki knew it in her soul.

She gave a cough, and took a deep breath, straightening herself and staring into Narnok's single intense eye.

"I will do as was promised," said Kiki, slowly. "But we must head deeper. Deep down under Desekra and towards the north, under the Mountains of Skarandos. Because this thing, this unleashed evil – it isn't over. To give away that which binds us together, it would be to weaken us out of all context. You understand?"

Narnok gave a grim smile, and a single nod. Kiki felt her heart melt, for she understood his sacrifice. When Dalgoran had brought them all together, they'd been a disparate bunch, filled with hate. Now – they were more a unit. The Iron Wolves were truly back.

"We are with you, Kiki," said Dek, giving her a smile.

"Good," she said.

They continued down the steeply sloping tunnel, and after a half hour they emerged into a large, round, stone chamber, with ancient curved oak benches set about the dry walls. They were deep beneath Desekra Fortress now. But the portals which led off from this hub, all heading steeply downwards, blew with stale cold air like the last rattling breath from the sour mouth of a mud-orc corpse.

Prince Zastarte – dandy, womaniser – placed a silk sleeve over his mouth. "This place is unholy. It was not made by men and is not fit for men." He caught Trista's scowl and flashed her a smile. "Or women, dear heart," he amended. "You know I meant no offence."

"Good," said the beautiful, golden curled Trista, stepping past him, "or I'd have to slit open your belly like I was gutting a rotten fish." Only then did Zastarte catch a glimpse of the short-handled, jewelled dagger nearly completely hidden in her hand. Trista. Beauty and the beast. The sexual cannibal.

"Charmed, I'm sure, my dear."

"Enough shit," rumbled Narnok, tugging Yoon into the chamber behind him on his length of rope. "Kiki has the keys here. We stock up on weapons, provisions, anything we think might be useful. It's going to be a long journey down under the Skarandos Mountains, away from our enemies, and none of it's going to be pleasant, that's for sure."

Yoon stared at the five Iron Wolves, his eyes bulging. "What? You madmen think you can travel these tunnels all the way under the mountains? Are you serious? And you're taking *me* with you?"

"Well, what did you expect, Yoon? Turn around and head back out so your elite soldiers can hack us down one by one? No, son, you're coming with us. We go deep. We go far. And we kill anything that stands in our fucking way."

Yoon visibly trembled, paled. His long black curls were lank and plastered to his face and neck with damp cold sweat. He looked not an inch the battle king portrayed on the tapestries at the Royal Apartments in Vagan, the War Capital of Vagandrak, despite his athletic build and the fact he'd been trained by the best warriors in the realm.

Yoon licked fish-pale lips. "Him, him, that one, he has the right idea." He gestured wildly at Zastarte. "This place is unholy. Not fit for men. There are things down there!" Yoon's eyes flitted from one Iron Wolf to the next, to the next. His hands, tied tightly behind his back, were clammy with the same sweat that shone across his brow.

Narnok stepped closer, and Yoon blanched, his head moving back from the terrifying, scarred gaze and single working eye of the huge axeman. "You talk like you've been down here recent-like," breathed Narnok, dangerously quiet.

"No, no!"

"Oh, I think you have, little worm." Narnok hefted his axe and held a blade under Yoon's chin. "Speak more, little king."

"No, well, I might have explored a little; it is my fucking fortress after all!" he snapped, anger and madness flashing for a minute across his face, through his eyes. He struggled at the ropes, hoping to snap them in the same fashion Narnok had snapped his own bonds back on the gallows at Desekra, but without luck. Or the required strength. Narnok was something special.

"Good," said Narnok, straightening. "That means you can show us the way."

"What?" shrieked Yoon. "Are you insane? I'm not showing you, you, you fucking *traitors and infidels*... not showing you anything!"

"Well, lad, looks like I'll be removing that kingly head from those kingly shoulders," grinned Narnok, and loomed yet closer.

"Leave him!" snapped Kiki. "We haven't got time for this. As far as we know, that bastard could be feeding us lies and horse shit. We'll move on down through the tunnels, heading north and west. Dalgoran, God rest his soul, told me about the deeper tunnels, which form a network right under the mountains." She glanced at Yoon and gave a nasty smile. "The King's Guard will have to be extremely dedicated indeed to follow us that far into the unexplored wilderness beneath the mountains."

Yoon scowled, but remained silent.

The Iron Wolves filled packs with supplies; dried and salted beef and fish; daggers; canteens of water; fish oil for the brands Kiki and Dek carried; and emergency candles for lanterns, which they found hanging in a bundle against one wall. They noted how well stocked this supply chamber was; it was obviously used with a regularity that surprised them all. Kiki asked Yoon, but he was no longer talking.

They moved on, Kiki leading the way, Narnok dragging Yoon like a dog. Zastarte and Trista were curiously silent, each withdrawn and growing more so the deeper the Iron Wolves descended into the subterranean darkness. Dek was the only one who seemed even remotely happy. Happy to escape the noose. Happy to escape battling mud-orcs and insane witch-queens. In a world of sudden violence and the necessity of the blade, to Dek, wandering through a few gloomy tunnels was a veritable party.

The tunnel they followed was wide, with a sandy floor. It sloped gradually down, and they trekked in silence. In the sand, there were boot prints, but there was no way of telling how old they were. Kiki kept her hand on the hilt of her short sword, just in case.

They journeyed for several hours, in silence, with Yoon making the occasional grunting sound or muttered curse as Narnok kept the king close to hand. As the ceiling grew lower, so Narnok muttered his own curses for it forced him to walk with a stoop, bent over, and he began to rub at his neck and spine as shooting pains bothered him.

Eventually, the tunnel split, then split again, and Kiki stopped, gathering her bearings. She glanced at Yoon, but the king looked away, pale face worm-like in the gloom, dark curls gleaming like insect carapace.

Kiki led them down a narrow tunnel, so narrow they could only move in single file. Occasionally they had to turn sideways themselves, to squeeze through narrow apertures, and once they came to what looked like an old rock fall that had been cleared above. They scrambled over a pile of large rocks, glancing up nervously at where it appeared huge, blocky boulders hung in a precarious balance, ready to tumble.

"Is that safe?" grumbled Narnok, grazing his knees as he climbed. He took it out on Yoon, tugging hard on the rope. Yoon made a strangled grunting sound.

"Is anything, in life?" replied Kiki from up ahead, her voice almost metallic as it reverberated.

"Suppose not," muttered Narnok.

The scramble led to a large, hollowed-out chamber. Their firelight illuminated the rocks in streaks of silver and red. Kiki stared at the scene, confused for a moment until she realised there was a huge pool of water, an underground lake, which reflected the rocky angularities and protuberances of the ceiling. There were ledges to either side of the lake, and Kiki picked the left hand one that rose to a level just a few inches above the still, mirrored platter.

"Not sure about this," said Narnok, uneasily, following the others onto the narrow ledge. "I don't like water at the best of times; it's only good for eels and fishes."

"The interesting thing is," said Yoon, stumbling along the ledge after him, "this lake formed because of the flash floods."

Narnok stopped, and turned, and stared at Yoon. "You what?"

"Flash floods." Yoon grinned almost maniacally, and seemed to gain some major satisfaction at the discomfort on the big axeman's face.

"What does that bloody mean?"

"Storms, above, high up in the Skarandos Mountains. There are several fissures above here, high above, I believe. Sometimes, if the weather is bad – like now, during winter, for example – the mountains can dump millions of gallons of water, which come running down gaps in the rocks, finding their way and flooding chambers like this in seconds. I've had a lot of my men drown down here during exploration."

Narnok stared at him, then glanced along the ledge to where Kiki had stopped and was frowning at him with a *what the Hell is wrong now?* face. Narnok growled, "This maggot says this chamber can flood!" He tried to keep the panicky whine from his voice, and was mostly unsuccessful.

"All the more reason to hurry along, then," said Kiki through gritted teeth.

"But... I don't want to drown," said Narnok.

"Look at it this way," said Dek. "If you drown, so does Yoon."

They moved down the ledge, firelight dancing from walls and glowing against the lake's surface like a sun's dying rays over a distant world. The whole scene was intensely beautiful, filled with fire and subtle pastels. But Kiki was staring off ahead, mind working hard as she tried to remember, *tried to remember*, Dalgoran's quiet words...

And that's where it falls down, bitch, said Suza, voice crowing like a diseased cockerel in Kiki's mind.

Kiki paused. Her head titled sideways a little. *I thought you'd given up haunting me. I thought you'd crawled off somewhere to die; some poisonous little hole, some abandoned tomb, some place of death and desecration.*

Sweet words, sister of mine. Maybe I'm already there, trapped in some poisonous little hole. Inside your head, bitch. A place of anger and hate, a place of self-pity and internal betrayals. I can see your every thought, and trust me when I say your mind is not a pleasant place to be.

Kiki heard her own laughter inside her skull. She blinked. The world seemed to have gone into slow motion. The flames in the brand flickered, casting light across the underground lake, and yet she felt suddenly like the still water had become a huge mouth, opening like a vertical tunnel leading down to the bowels of the earth where she'd be swallowed whole and chewed into a bloody mass of mashed up bones and pulped flesh by teeth made of rock – deep down in the World Engine...

She took a deep breath, hand reaching out to steady herself against the wall. It seemed to take an age.

I want you gone, Suza. I want you out of my head.

You cannot banish me, and Kiki could not miss the smugness in Suza's tone. *With all your power, with the curse of the Iron Wolves, with the* mana *of the* Shamathe *running through your blood and bones and brains, you fucking cannot even get rid of me. Because you killed me, bitch, and I, also, carried the seed of the* Shamathe. *And I fled my dying shell. And I fled into you. I am part of you, now, dear sister. Until the day you, and I, both die.*

Kiki blinked, snapping out of it, and dropped to one knee, suddenly panting. It was like waking from a dream. A really bad dream.

"Kiki!" And Dek was there, tight beside her, his powerful body supporting her.

"I'm fine, Dek, I'm fine." She stood, leaning against the wall for a moment.

"What happened?"

Kiki gave a narrow smile. "Bad ghosts. Come on, before one of Yoon's flash floods comes thundering down and sends us swimming with the fishes."

"You don't believe that, do you?" said Dek, and she saw in his eyes the gleam of emotion. He cared for her. He cared for her, dearly.

She smiled, and patted his hand in thanks.

"After everything that's happened in the last few weeks, I don't know what to believe any more," she said.

The underground lake was an hour behind them. The tunnel had levelled out, was reasonably wide and had a breeze blowing through to cool the Iron Wolves and their unwelcome captive.

Kiki halted, and waited for the others to catch up.

They all stopped, and stared, and then looked to Kiki.

"What, by all the demons in the Furnace, and by the Tails of the Seven Sisters, is that?" said Zastarte, smoothing back his curls.

"It's slime," said Dek, and knelt beside the glowing yellow substance. He reached out as if to touch it, then thought better and withdrew his hand. "Looks a little like when a slug has passed on by."

"Well, it goes all the way down there, dear boy," said Zastarte, pointing with his fine-bladed rapier. "That would take a lot of slugs."

They all peered at the pale, sickly substance. It mainly coated the floor of the tunnel, but up ahead they could see it on the walls as well.

"Is it dangerous, d'you think?" rumbled Narnok.

"Ask your little dog, there," said Dek.

Narnok turned on Yoon. "Is it dangerous, lad? Eh?"

Yoon gave a shrug. "It's the worms. We came across them several months ago. They are dangerous, but primitive. Nothing an axe through the head can't solve, axeman. And I'm pretty sure you'll be the right thuggish brute for the job." Yoon sneered up at Narnok.

"You never answered the question," rumbled Narnok, and before the king could retort, he dragged him to the edge of the faintly glowing slime and threw him down. Yoon cried out, and span around on the ground. The slime coated his hands and legs and finely embroidered coat. His head snapped up and he glared at Narnok with murder in his eyes.

"You fucking psychopath!" Yoon shrieked. He scrambled to his feet, slipping several times in the slime which now seemed to coat everything. "It could have been poisonous! It could have burned my flesh from my bones!"

"Well? Is it?"

Yoon stared at Narnok, mouth flapping. "Is it what?"

"Is it poisonous? Or burning you like a particularly bad case of syphilis?"

"What? No!"

"Well, stop moaning, lad. And remember," he loomed close, baring his teeth in what might have been a smile, but was more reminiscent of something big and dark living in the caves below a deep river, "when I ask you a question, I expect a fucking answer. You hear me?" He reached out, grabbed Yoon by the throat, and shook him.

"I hear you," gurgled the king.

"Come on," said Kiki. "At least you proved one thing. It seems to be... safe. If that's the right word."

"Unless it has some terrible chemical side effect," flourished Zastarte, and he smiled, his beautiful face cracking into a glow of handsome ruggedness. "Something that, I don't know, damages us over a period of time, maybe socially as well as psychologically?"

"Prince Zastarte, we're all psychologically damaged. Or had you forgotten our curse?"

"It may be a curse to you, dear Kiki, but if I'm brutally honest, the ladies enjoy a little bit of the animal in their adventures. Aren't I right, Trista, my beautiful little scorpion?"

"You certainly stink like an animal," said Trista, and smiled sweetly.

"I rest my case," said Zastarte, and patted his mouth and nose with the lace ruffs of his silk shirt.

Kiki led the way through the tunnel, boots squelching through the sticky mess. The further they moved, the thicker the slime appeared, and the faint, almost fluorescent glow made it almost unnecessary for the fire torches they carried.

"You could put them out," said Dek, catching Kiki up.

She glanced at him. She looked ashen. Weary, drawn, gaunt. She forced a smile. "I thought we might have a sudden need for fire," she said, and Dek gave a thoughtful nod.

"You look tired, Keeks. Is it time for a stop?"

"When we get past this... area," she said. "I couldn't sleep here if I was dead on my feet. Which I practically am." She gave a weak smile, and Dek reached out, touching her shoulder.

"Hang in there, Captain," he said, his eyes shining, mouth forming a smile.

"I'll do my best, Dek. Just hope my best is good enough."

As they travelled, so a bad smell started to seep into the tunnels. It was rancid, like rotting fish and bad eggs, woven intricately into an aroma that made a human want to puke. Zastarte was the most offended. He pulled out a tiny little green bottle, and as Narnok and Dek watched with absolute disbelief, he squirted a little perfume onto a silk embroidered handkerchief and held it over his mouth and nose. He saw their stares.

"What?"

"You really are a fucking girl," rumbled Narnok, scratching at his scarred chin.

"Hey," said Zastarte, words muffled from behind the silk, "is it my fault I'm such a sensitive, delicate soul? I confess, despite being an expert in the lore of exploring a woman, and indeed on the intricacies of experimenting with a torture victim, one thing that really invades me worse than any anal rape is a truly offensive aroma." He frowned from behind his perfumed barrier. "I cannot help it that the rest of you are stinking heathens who do not wash their armpits and are happy to carry rancid lice in their lank and un-honeyed hair. Why, you all bring shame to the concept of warriors with honour and nobility, when a damsel is being rescued from certain death, the last thing she needs is some hairy brutal oaf with all the toiletry finesse of a rutting hog."

Dek stepped closer. "You really think you contain honour and nobility? Kiki told me what she saw. Down in that cellar." Dek's mouth had formed a casual snarl.

Zastarte either missed the implied threat or was completely insensitive to it. He waved his hand, a casual swatting away of Dek's words. "Yes, yes, I concede, maybe I haven't got *that much* honour and nobility. But I certainly *carry myself* that way, and it's only this damn curse, I believe, which has twisted me into something... amoral." He smiled. "But enough about me. Onwards, through the stench! I am now armoured against its putrefaction!"

As they moved forward, so the stench increased in its potency until Kiki and Trista, especially, could hardly bear it any longer. They, also, were covering their mouths and only Narnok seemed completely unaffected by the poison.

They reached the chamber after an hour of trekking through the bad smell and the glowing trails of slime; it was large, opening out into a cavern of some considerable size. Here, the walls were pebble-smooth and gleamed in the ethereal light. But it was the contents scattered across the floor in neat rows that made the Iron Wolves and their prisoner halt, boots clacking, staring with open mouths.

"What, in the name of the Chaos Halls, are *those*?" hissed Dek, eyes narrowed, drawing his sword unconsciously with a slither of oiled steel on leather.

"I don't know," said Kiki, and her head snapped around, focusing on King Yoon. "But *he* does. Explain, bastard, or I'll have Narnok here cut out your liver."

Yoon seemed unruffled by the threat, and he looked at the Iron Wolves, one by one by one, his eyes passing over and through them. Then he smiled, and it was the evil crescent of a curved razor blade. "You really don't understand what you're getting yourselves into, do you, little people? I warned you not to come down here. I warned you this place was... *dangerous*." He savoured the word, and his eyes moved past the Iron Wolves to the pods which lay clustered across the floor of the huge chamber. Each pod was about the size of a horse, its surface corrugated and white like the ribs on a dead animal. Each pod was divided into six or seven discrete bubbled segments, like cocoons joined at a central hub. They glowed, softly, pulsing white.

"They look like eggs, insect larvae, something like that," rumbled Narnok, choosing his words with delicate care.

Yoon glanced at him. "Yes, axeman. You are correct. These are the *leski worms*. Not good, my friends. Not good at all. My men only come through here at certain times; we have logged their hatching cycles. It took a long time. And cost a lot of lives. But then," and his eyes assessed them all with cool calculation, "you common people are so fucking expendable."

"Let me kill him, Kiki. Please let me kill him," growled Narnok.

"No." She shook her head. But now she was smiling. "Well, Yoon, we're going this way. And you're going to lead. So let's hope you've remembered the way, and remembered the fucking hatching times because you're going to be first in line if some terrible creature comes looking for blood."

"As you wish," said King Yoon, stiffly, and was pushed ahead by Narnok.

They moved slowly, silently, through the vast chamber. The rocky ground was thick with sticky secretions, and the stench was truly unbearable. Now, all the Iron Wolves had drawn their weapons and had subtly shifted from travellers making progress through tunnels to... something else. They moved with a natural, predatory wariness; heads and eyes were constantly moving, scanning, calculating, waiting for any sign of enemy or attack. None spoke, and they unconsciously fanned out, taking up a certain formation which they had used time and time again in battle, where each was able to protect the flank of another dependant on left or right handedness and proficiency with weapons. Kiki, for example, fought with two short swords; to her right was Narnok, right handed and holding his mighty twin-bladed axe; to her left was Dek, his main long sword in his left hand; and behind came Zastarte and Trista, completing their unit. All they lacked was Mola, but nobody had heard or seen anything of the older, secretive, man for decades.

Time seemed to slow as they passed through the chamber, picking each footstep with care, taking their time in this realm of the unknown. As they reached the centre, so strange, distant acoustics picked up the roar of an underground river which seemed to grow louder the closer to the centre they approached. Narnok felt the hairs

prickling on the back of his neck in fear as he remembered
Yoon's words, and the big man seemed unusually anxious.

"I don't like this," he muttered, after a while, and wiped
a sheen of sweat from his brow.

"Just focus," came Kiki's calming words, her soothing
tones, "and we'll get out of here alive."

Through treacle minutes they moved, until finally
a distant maw, a cave at the other side of the chamber
beckoned. This widened as they approached, until it was a
giant mouth leading to a black-ribbed throat from which
a cool, soothing breeze emerged fresh with the scent of
running water. The sounds of the underground river
had grown louder, until, as the Iron Wolves entered the
tunnel, it boomed and thrashed *above* them.

They moved on into darkness. Slowly, the slime trails
dissipated and they allowed at least one worry to drift away
like dragon smoke, to be replaced with a different kind
of fear. Somewhere above, a river ran through channels
of rock. No terrible thing. Except the further they now
progressed down this new, wide, high-ceilinged tunnel of
black rock and stalactites, the more they noticed trickles
of water running down the walls, and occasional drips
coming from what appeared, on inspection with Narnok's
torch, to be *cracks*.

"Not good," muttered Dek, as the river boomed above.

"That's a bloody understatement," croaked Narnok.

"Keep moving," said Kiki, and they pushed on,
travelling with great weariness, like walking cadavers; like
echoes of the undead.

Finally, leaving the river behind and taking more
branching tunnels, they found a cave with a sandy floor

where they could camp, and eat, and sleep. They unrolled thin blankets, for now the rocky tunnels were damp and cool, and after tying Yoon so tight he could barely move a finger, they slept, Zastarte taking first watch as he usually did. The Prince was almost reptilian in his lack of a need for sleep. He claimed it was what helped make him such a magnificent lover.

Kiki slept, and did not dream. It was a sleep of exhaustion. And utter, total recharge. For a while.

Sometimes, her dreams were happy. Sometimes, they were sad. Sometimes, they were downright fucking evil. There was one recurring dream that haunted her. The settings changed. Sometimes forest. Sometimes an undulating, snowy plain bordered by dark, towering pines where the yellow eyes of wolves watched from the shadows above slick, bloodstained muzzles. Occasionally, the dream contained a sterile white room, with a large white cup central to the chamber. That was the only furniture. In the white cup sat a perfectly fitting black ball which pulsed gently. In all the variations of the dreams there was one constant. Five figures, wreathed in shadow. Tall, lithe, featureless. They were there to kill her. And they always did.

When Kiki awoke, groggy, half within her sleep world, half within the real, her thoughts drifted long and low like winter mist, and she thought back to Dalgoran, and to the honey-leaf she had so recently craved. She thought about Dalgoran's suicide, and how the noble old general had been willing to take his own life, to step through the portal to the final destination so that he could, hopefully, spend an eternity with his loving wife Farsala. Kiki liked to think he'd killed himself because of the strange, dark magick of the forest through which they'd travelled – Sayansora alv Drakka, the Forest of Suicide, the Forest of Angry Spirits, the Sea of Trees – but somewhere, deep inside her own soul, she knew it had been the general's own choice. His own decision. He was a man of ramrod iron. He'd made his own choices in life. Why not in death?

Will anybody ever love me like that? she thought.

Enough to kill for? Enough to die for?

Three times, in her life, she had been in love. Or so she thought. And, she admitted, the last time had been at the height of her honey-leaf addiction and she *probably* hadn't been the most attentive girlfriend. That made her smile. *Girlfriend.* Wasn't she beyond thinking of herself as a girl?

Dek crouched beside her, and touched her shoulder.

"Mmm?"

"Time to move, Kiki." She stared up at him, and the broad-shouldered pit-fighter caught the strangeness in her look. "What?" he said. "What is it?"

"I was just thinking about you."

"You were? Nice thoughts, I hope. I saw what you did to Orlana the Changer and her army of mud-orcs. *Whoosh!* Instant earthquake. When we have a moment, I'd like to talk to you about that."

She smiled. "Yes. They were. Nice thoughts, I mean. About you."

"Good." Dek straightened himself. "It's time to move. Our mentally deviated torturer prince has scouted ahead – said he's found something big. Something amazing."

"Down here? Like what?"

Dek shrugged. "I don't know. He was pretty impressed by something, though. And it takes a lot to impress the dandy bastard."

"I'm not sure I like the sound of that. I don't like surprises. Not when I'm a hunted woman."

"Believe me," said Dek, thinking back to his debts with the Red Thumb Gangs, "you get used to it."

"Down here," said Zastarte. There was almost music in his voice, and he sounded a little like an excited child unwrapping presents on his birthday. "Trust me, guys, you will be amazed! I was amazed, and it takes a fucking lot of shit to amaze me, so trust me, you will be completely amazed!"

Dek leaned in to Kiki. "Do you think it might be amazing?" he whispered, and Kiki snorted a giggle.

The tunnel ended abruptly on a ledge, which split, winding around alternate sides of the massive cavern. But it was the contents of the vast cavern which had so inspired Zastarte's uncharacteristic outburst.

A huge part of the central cavern contained a building. Nothing natural, not rock or stone; this was iron, grey, and foreboding, with sheer walls forty or fifty feet high, smooth and impenetrable. The roof, from what the Iron Wolves could see from their vantage point, was also smooth iron so that the huge edifice formed an almost perfect cube.

"Good, eh?" enthused Zastarte.

"What is it?" said Dek, slowly, eyes narrowed.

Narnok prodded Yoon. "Go on, lad, spill the beans, before I spill your guts."

"I cannot say," spoke Yoon, softly.

"Cannot, or will not?"

"I told you people not to come down here."

"It's a prison, isn't it?" said Kiki, head tilting to one side, bobbed brown hair falling to her left shoulder. "You can see a door, way down there. A studded portal. The whole thing, it's a prison, or a holding cell. I'm right, aren't I, you obstinate and secretive little bastard?"

Yoon looked at her, and pursed his lips, and said nothing.

"We should go and explore," said Zastarte, who seemed to have come alive after his apparent depression at heading deeper underground, dropping beneath the earth as if walking towards his own tomb and burial. "There could be... treasure!"

"There could be big hard fuckers with swords," snapped Dek. "I strongly suggest we circumnavigate. We have no need to go into this place. It would be tactical foolishness; an unnecessary risk."

Kiki was still staring at Yoon. "What's in there?" she said.

"You'll never get in."

Kiki lifted her bunch of keys; General Dalgoran's keys, from when he had been in charge of Desekra Fortress years – *decades* – earlier. "You think so, do you, King Yoon?"

Yoon visibly paled, despite the gloom of the tunnel and the reflection of strange, ethereal light. It was as if the metal gleamed, supplying its own visibility from some intrinsic light source.

"This is a bad place," said Trista, pushing back her golden curls, her eyes seeming to glow in this underworld.

"Dek's right. We need to leave here. Many, many bad things have happened – are still happening. This is a haunted realm, Kiki."

"Ach, horse piss and nonsense!" declared Zastarte. "Nothing the Iron Wolves, in all their heroics and combined battle expertise, couldn't handle! I suggest a fluid, swift and decisive entry, which is what I suggest to all the ladies." He winked in the gloom. "Unless you've all suddenly turned into a bunch of spineless lick pussies. No offence meant."

"Listen to Dek and Trista," whispered Yoon, with passion, and Kiki felt herself flinch. In all the time she had known King Yoon, this was the first time he had ever referred to them by name. Now, it seemed, "peasant" or "you" just wasn't good enough. He turned and stared at Kiki, his eyes curiously fixed, his breathing coming in short, sharp pants. "There are some things in this life you do not want to discover. There are some things stranger, some things more decadent than even you would wish to explore. And that's coming from *me*, the King of Vagandrak, after witnessing *you*, a cursed and deviated woman, a *Shamathe*, summon a fucking *earthquake* to take out the witch queen Orlana and her filthy, mud-orc scum. Do you hear what I am saying, sweet Kiki, my mass-murdering little witch?"

Kiki considered this, face hard, eyes shadowed. Then she turned, and her eyes tracked the long sweeping ledges that followed the walls of the vast cavern, and eventually dropped to ground level where undulating rock formed a plateau leading to the massive iron prison.

"Get your shit together, Wolves. We're going in."

Dek gave her a questioning stare. "Why?" he said, finally.

Kiki glanced at King Yoon. "Because anything this bastard is trying to protect so bad – well, that's something we need to investigate. Don't you agree, *King Yoon of Vagandrak*? Of course you don't. Well, prepare to offer up your deepest, darkest secrets. We're the Iron Wolves, fucker, and we're not in this for the fame, the glory, the power or the fucking money."

INFILTRATION

They moved through the sewers and the underground tunnels. They slithered and crept and crawled through the deep, dark, slimy places within the web of pipe outlets, within underground walkways, beneath the city's dark secret caverns and cellars and tannery sluices and slaughterhouse gutters leading to rivers and surrounding marshes with the pulp of mashed and rotting offal.

Each one came, a crooked, bent, disjointed figure, arthritic and broken, with bent backs and odd shaped legs, with twisted arms and gnarled fingers. Their skin was like bark, some brown and soft, some grey and gnarled, some black and cracked. Their hair appeared as moss, and nodules rippled across corrugated skin like knots in wood. Many had long, curved claws of black; like mottled razors. Many carried ancient swords, chipped and battered, blackened and worn.

Despite their many deformities, the elf rats moved with care, gradually, choosing footsteps, splashing through shit and piss and offal and fish heads, the detritus, the cast-offs, the waste of the humans *above* who had taken their villages, taken their towns, usurped their cities, stolen their Realm.

The main sewer outlet from Vagan, the War Capital of Vagandrak, was long and high and wide. It served a population of near a hundred thousand, so had to have ample capacity. The elf rats surged through this, clumping together in tens, in hundreds... in thousands. They bobbed, sleek and wet and stained with shit, until they reached their first major obstacle. Centuries earlier, fearing some armed force might use the sewers to mount an invasion, huge iron bars had been fitted to the major inlets and sewage outlets serving the city of Vagan. And, here, the elf rats faltered, for each bar was like a tree trunk – only a tree trunk fashioned from pitted iron and sunk into deep stone anchor-blocks with precision masonry and ancient lime mortar.

"Wait!" came the hiss, and through the throng of distorted creatures hobbled one who was old, older than centuries. He wore a cloak of brown, interwoven with branches from his Heart Tree, and he hobbled forward as if in great pain. He reached the waist-thick bars and surveyed them for long moments. Then, slowly, he reached out and his hand connected with the metal. Quests grew from his fingers, thin black roots that emerged and began to twist and twine around the iron, burrowing into the solid surface like pikes gnawing through fish flesh and bone.

Slowly, the elf rat's eyes closed, and his black bark lips began to mutter, to murmur, to summon and send, for this was Bazaroth aea Quazaquiel, Sorcerer to the Elf Rat King Daranganoth, and the most feared, merciless, powerful magick enchanter ever to walk the Elf Rat lands of Zalazar.

Zalazar. The Banished Place.

The quests had spread and were whipping, snapping, writhing. They burrowed through the first pillar with sparks and a mass of writhing, glowing black, then on, to the next pillar, and the next, eating through the heavy iron like some incredibly potent acid. The rest of the elf rats shifted backwards in respect and fear. One did not cross Bazaroth, for the sorcerer was ill tempered and capricious.

There came several great *cracks*, and with a sigh like the dying of worlds the arched, ancient brick ceiling sagged. There were crashes as ten, then twenty of the pillars came thundering down into the torrent of sewage, and the elf rats waited a respectful few moments as the thousands of whipping, whirling quests, like a feeding frenzy of thin black eels, snapped and withdrew into Bazaroth's bleeding, gnarled hands. Then the sorcerer turned. And the sorcerer smiled with crooked teeth; fangs like splintered dead wood.

"Advance!" he croaked, and pointed, and the elf rats surged forward through the collected shit of the War Capital.

Grenan and Johan were grumbling again as they played blood-knuckle dice in the guard house on the southeast corner watch, down near the tanneries. They were grumbling because, despite the recent snow, the river still stank like a dead dog after three days rotting in the sun.

"I bet Frenal and Cashmik having got bloody tannery duty again," complained Grenan, throwing down his runecards as he realised the radiant, open glow on Johan's face was indicative of an impending win. "Go on. Take your bastard money. Buy a whore. I hope you get syphilis."

"Now now, Grenan, nobody likes a sore loser," grinned Johan, leaning forward and scooping the large pile of coin towards himself with both bear paws.

"Wait!" snapped Grenan, holding up a hand. Johan froze, grin locked to his face like the snarl on a cadaver.

"What, Gren? You can see I winned."

"No, hold on, let's see your runecards."

"Aww, Gren, you bloody know I winned!"

"Show!"

Slowly, the bear that was Johan turned over his runecards and Grenan's face was a beautiful portrait as he realised Johan held, perhaps, the worst hand dealt since the beginning of Time; certainly, since the beginnings of Fish Wife Rune Poker.

"Why, you bluffing, bluffing bastard, you cheating son of a cheating son's bitch! I just cannot believe you did that to me! You cheating, lying, dirty bastard horse shagger! You would have sat there like a bear with its cock in its hand and let me give you my winnings. I don't believe it! Is there no honesty left in the world? Is there no honour amongst thieves, I ask ye? Oh, you dirty, drooling scumbag."

"But Gren, you did it to me last Tuesday!" There was genuine agony in Johan's voice. "*And* the week before that, when we was playing down at Stanmore's Fish Market. *You* said that all's fair in love, war and Fish Wife Rune Poker. That's what *you* said. Now you're getting all aggravated when I did to you what you did to me. Now that's a double standard, that is."

"Listen, my friend. It's not a double standard because *I* taught you the bloody game in the first place! Taught you everything I knows! So, if I hadn't of taught ye, then you wouldn't be able to win in the first place, would ye? So, if anything, I should be entitled to more winnings and you shouldn't be allowed to cheat like ye did!"

Johan's broad, simple face wrinkled into a frown as he tried to follow Grenan's logic – or lack of it. And Grenan cackled as he pulled *his* new winnings towards himself and thought about the exotic whores down Mary Street at Old Cassandra's. Some new ones had come in on a ship via the Crystal Sea, said to be from deep south in Zakora, foreign with all sorts of neat and dirty tricks. One man, Big Nank, had told him lots of stories. Dumb Big Nank, they should call him. Spent a whole month's salary in less than a week, and left his wife with no money for rent or food for the five children who nagged him relentlessly.

Grenan chuckled to himself, and knew he had to be more wary...

He realised Johan was speaking to him.

"Eh, lad?"

"I said, 'What's that noise?' Didn't you hear it? Or were you thinking of those new uns down at Old Cassandra's?"

Grenan stared at Johan with his mouth open. Sometimes the large, simple, apple-eared farmer could be surprisingly intuitive. Yeah, either that or Grenan was showing his lust and deep dirty secrets openly on his face. Like reading a bloody book with rude lithographs!

Johan was on his feet, now, sword half drawn.

"There it is again. Like a slithering sound."

Both guards drew their swords and Johan opened the hut's door. Outside, the night was still and black and rank. The water's edge from the tannery lake lapped gently against the stained and scummy stone jetty.

Grenan and Johan tumbled from the cosy interior and both men felt suddenly, incredibly, vulnerable. The darkness crept in, like a bat closing its wings. For some reason, both men thought back to their childhoods.

A cold wind blew. It was edged with ice, like a glittering razor.

"I don't like this; not at all," mumbled Johan, sword slippery in his sweating hand. Suddenly the blade fell and clanged on the stone walkway. The sound reverberated across the tannery lake and Grenan almost jumped out of his skin.

"You big dumb bastard!" he hissed, snarling and spitting at Johan as he rounded on him. "You nearly made me shit my pants!"

"I'm sorry, Grenan, really. I didn't mean it."

The slithering came again, louder this time, and suddenly the tannery lake went from still platter, softly lapping, to a frenzy of activity as if a hundred barrels of eels had been suddenly upended into the stinking, rancid depths.

Johan took a step back.

"What is it, Grenan? What is it?"

But before his companion could answer, the water surged up and out, and from the froth leapt figures, twisted and deformed with skin like glistening bark. All along the lake they came, leaping from the waters and Johan and Grenan raised their swords in sudden terror but the seething mass of creatures rolled over them, sharp teeth biting at their flesh, claws slashing. Johan went down an instant before his friend, as teeth tore strips from his face, chewed off his fingers, bit off his cheek, and he was screaming and thrashing as Grenan hit the ground also. Grenan's hands clamped around the neck of one of the creatures, which stank worse than a rotting fish corpse, and for a moment he stared into glistening dark eyes filled with insanity and hate. The creature thrashed, surprisingly strong despite its twisted physique and odd broken image, but then another was alongside it, long curved black claws sinking into Grenan's head and he screamed suddenly as intense pain crashed through him, and he let go of the creature atop him, which surged forward, fangs burrowing into his throat. Blood bubbled into his mouth and he felt himself being eaten, slick gore running down over his chest as his hands slapped helplessly at the creatures, then at the ground, until an attacker chewed off his fingers.

With both guards still and silent and half eaten, the elf rats suddenly paused, almost as one: a gently seething mass of perhaps three hundred, maybe more, hidden in the gloom. Then their heads turned as if controlled by some central hub, a hive mind, and they looked up the long, straight street that led deep into the huge fortress city of Vagan, the War Capital. Ancient cobbles gleamed with ice. Huge buildings, edifices displaying centuries of proud heritage, theatres, civic buildings, clan houses, trade centres, museums of Vagandrak history; all stood, massive and dark and edged with icing sugar, like a picture postcard.

The elf rats started to walk, and hobble, and crawl, and slither up the street: deep into the heart of Vagan.

Belton lounged back in his chair, polished boots up the rough-sawn desk, his brass brandy hip flask in his right hand despite being on duty at the Southern Gate Guard Barracks, and feeling the warm glow of fatherhood in his head and heart and soul, seeping through him like some incredible infusion of Belief. Three days old, she was, little Mia, and as beautiful as any carving of an angel on any church or holy place, not just in the Capital City of Drakerath, but in any damn city in the whole of Vagandrak!

Tiny, she was, with pink-white skin, her fingers so small they couldn't even grasp Belton's stubby, guard's finger. A spiky shock of rich black hair, a scrunched up face that was so cute it made Belton want to be sick with love, sporting a little turned up nose and little toes that wiggled whenever she squawked.

Belton knew he was in love, truly in love, and for the first time. He loved his wife, yes, but this was heart-breaking love, fill your soul full of warm honey and float along the rest of your life to the Halls of the Gods-type love. This was a love you would kill for. This was a love you would die for, no questions asked: a long hard jump into the Pit.

Belton took another slug, and peered out of the barred window. The braziers and torches flickered wildly, and snow was falling once again, giving the nearby houses and paved walkways a ghostly, ethereal ambience.

It was quiet out there, especially at this ungodly hour. What sane person would walk the streets in such foul weather?

Belton snuggled further under his wool cloak, which he'd draped across his shoulders, and unconsciously stretched his free hand towards the small log burner where flames crackled softly.

Mia. Mia!

He took a hefty hit of brandy, and peered out into the snow.

It had been a fear-laden time, for sure: his wife clutching his hand until he thought she would break his fingers, the midwife down between her legs, face calm, words soothing. And then the words he would never forget for the rest of his life. "She's crowning, push now, Salina, push *now*!"

Within moments it was over, a bawling little white-pink bundle that the midwife passed to Belton with a smile. "Here's your daughter, soldier. Hold her with care."

And Belton had stood, big bad gruff Belton, the man who'd bettered Two Trees at the annual South Guards' Wrestling Tournament, breaking the man's leg; the soldier who had no fear and absolutely refused to back down. The man who'd head-butted Big Jim, breaking his nose when none said it could be done. The man who'd horse-whipped the whiskey-smuggler Abdel the Beard, taking the skin off his back. Well, there Belton had stood, grinning like the village idiot and gazing down into the amazing face of his amazing baby girl as if he was a child himself. Thinking about it now, with a few slugs of brandy in his belly, Belton realised he had probably forgotten how to smile. Now, his new baby had taught him that simple pleasure in life, and he realised, as he rocked the chair back, legs creaking, that not *everyone* in the world was a cynical bastard, not *everybody* was greedy and selfish and hateful. Not everybody deserved to be extinguished in a pit of fire. No. There were some positives to life, some good things. And for many, many years Belton had forgotten all about the good things.

Feeling suddenly melancholy, and realising maybe he shouldn't really be drinking brandy on duty, Belton stood and moved to the rough-plank door. He opened it and chilled air rushed in, destroying the cosiness of the barrack room. The street was deserted, as he would have expected at this time during the middle of the night. He shivered. It felt like somebody had walked over his grave and, frowning, he realised his life as a soldier was done. Done and gone and buried. He'd fought at Desekra

Fortress against the mud-orcs; he'd nearly died a score of times. But now, he realised, he had a little baby girl to look after, to bring up in the cold cruel world, and a massive responsibility shifted and lay across his shoulders like a heavy leather cloak. What would little Mia do if Daddy got killed in a stupid pointless battle? Who would be there to look after her?

He pocketed his brandy. No.

It was time to finish this life of soldiering. Time to put it behind him.

And do what? mocked a sardonic part of his consciousness.

He smiled. That didn't matter.

Belton would find a way. He always did.

To the left, two cats shrieked as they came flying from the gloom of a darkened alley. They crouched in the middle of the road facing one other, hissing, each with a paw raised threateningly, ears back, fangs displayed.

Belton grinned.

Nature of the fucking beast, he thought.

The cats attacked, an insanely fast scrabbling of claws as tufts of fur flew. And then... Belton blinked, turning right, as at least a hundred figures drifted and limped down the street from gates now twisted from their hinges. A blast of... *something* hit Belton, a warm wind, filled with the scent of... of pine? Like a pine forest after heavy rain. And Belton staggered, eyes wide, staring at the creatures filling the street, moving past him, ignoring him... until he drew his sword, mouth suddenly dry because this... *this* was not a fucking good place to be, and he had to get back in, grab the bell, sound the alarm–

"Atta–" he started to scream as three of the creatures detached from the flood and launched at him. He grunted, side-stepping, sword hacking down to chop into a creature's neck. The iron blade bit deep, crunching through bone and flesh, but the creature seemed to shrug off the wound and came on, claws slashing for him, pushing past his own considerable strength like a root easing through the cracks in a stone wall and it all happened so fast, panic splashed across him and he felt fangs puncture his neck, biting – no *chewing, burrowing* – into him. He started to punch the beast as the other two bit into his arms, and with legs kicking he was dragged out and away from the barracks, into the throng of creatures that, in the sudden panic and chaos of thrashing, seemed to have the faces of elongated rats...

Belton lay on the cobbles, gasping, blood bubbling on his lips.

The creatures had moved on. Past him. He needed to ring the bell.

His hand came up to try and stem the flow of blood at his neck, and with horror he realised all his fingers had been chewed off. Only his thumb remained, his whole hand looking misshapen and strange and frightening.

I'm going to die.

The concept arrived suddenly, completely formed, and a shiver racked his body. He could feel the thump of his heart. Felt it slowing.

No, he thought. *No!*

Who would look after Mia?

And he pictured the beautiful babe in his arms, her little scrunched up face, that little upturned nose.

And silver tears glistened on his cheeks.

Chalandra was having a very bad dream. Dressed in her white wedding dress, the one she'd never had a chance to wear, she walked through never-ending fields of black poppies. She stopped, knelt, plucked one – and recoiled as she realised the centre of the flower was the screaming face of a man, face writhing, teeth gnashing. She strained to push herself away from the flower, and although she could gain distance at arm's length, she could not force her fingers to open; could not drop the abomination.

She awoke with a start, the taste of last night's liquor bad on her tongue, sour against her teeth. Her daughter, Torney, stood in the doorway, a figure of shadows highlighted against the background of lantern light.

"Mummy? I'm frightened."

"Tush. Come here, child."

Torney padded forward, bare feet slapping naked floorboards. Chalandra held back the covers and Torney climbed in, snuggling up to the warmth of her mother, head tucked neatly under Chalandra's chin as the woman stroked her girl's long, luscious hair.

"It's dark, Mummy."

"Yes, Torn. It's still night. There's no need to be scared of the dark."

"I had a dream, Mummy."

"That's okay. I had a dream as well."

"Was it a bad dream, Mummy?" The girl lifted her head a little, eyes searching.

"Yes, Torn."

"What was it about?"

Imagining the screaming face in the flower, Chalandra gave a little shudder. "I don't remember, dear. Now shush. It's time to go back to sleep. I have to get up early to help at the market, remember?"

"But it's dark, Mummy."

"Yes, dear. I know that."

There was a long pause.

"Do monsters live in the dark, Mummy?"

"No, Torney. There are no monsters."

"But I saw the monsters!"

"In your dream? That's fine as well, my sweet. They can't hurt you when they're in your dreams. They're just made-up. Shout *go away bad monsters* and they'll disappear. I promise you."

Again, a long pause. Outside, there came a shout on the street. Then a clatter. Chalandra gave a frown and hugged her girl closer to her breast. She would be the first to admit they were not wealthy; especially after what had happened to her husband-to-be, Kaṅda, and the shame that followed.

They lived in one of the poorer districts inside the walled city of Zanne, the most westerly city in Vagandrak. And whilst they had not yet been cast into the Haven, they were still only one-step removed from the happily and misleadingly named *slums*, living above a cobbler's on the edges of the Factory Quarter, as they did. During the night-time hours all kinds of nefarious activities took place below their window, for this street was a thoroughfare between the Haven and the heavily working class Factory Quarter. Acts of sex and the sale of sex. Honey-leaf peddling, consumption, and the hallucinations and violence that often accompanied the leaf. The trade of illegal weapons, or slaves, or children. So it came as no great surprise to Chalandra when she heard a cry, a smash of glass, the crash of impacting weapons or the scream of an unfortunate.

"Go away, bad monsters," whispered Torney, placing her hands over her eyes.

Chalandra smiled grimly. She knew, in her world, in the real world, the monsters were men and women of flesh and blood.

There came a *crack* as something struck the window, and Chalandra's head snapped up. Her eyes grew wide. For there, nose pressed against the glass, there really *was* a monster... twisted and broken, skin more moss and bark than skin and hair. And the head moved back, then slammed forward, crashing through the window and scattering sharp shards of glass across the bare boards of the room.

Chalandra bit off a scream. A scream got you nowhere. A scream was a sign of weakness. A sign didn't crush the evil strong.

"What do you want?" she hissed, as the horribly disfigured monster climbed in and swayed across the room. It had one leg shorter than the other, and limped a little, although this did little to alleviate the horror of the situation.

The lips formed into a horrible snarl, like brown snakes in a vat of fish oil. "Why, my sweetie, simply your obedience," said the creature in a voice that was frighteningly human.

Torney opened her eyes then, and screamed, and tried to scrabble backwards across the bed, *through* her mother.

"There, there, little one, it won't hurt. Much." The creature grinned.

Outside, screams had started to echo up and down the streets of Zanne, reverberating through dark alleys, bouncing from slick iced cobbles and dark patchy flagstones. There came the sounds of battle. Sword against sword. The slap of iron biting flesh. The crash of bodies hitting the ground. Running boots. The splatter of blood. Cackles. Snarls. Whimpers.

Chalandra leapt suddenly from the bed, scooping up a wicked shard of glass from the broken window. It cut into the palm of her hand, drawing blood which seeped, bubbled, then dripped to the bare stained wood.

"Stay back!" she snarled. She risked a glance behind her. "Go, Torney! Flee! Seek help! Seek the City Elders! Tell them you are Kanda's daughter! Tell them what you saw here!"

Torney turned and fled, stopping at the door to turn and watch her mother. Chalandra advanced on the creature which held up its hands. Long, thin strings or wires or, or… or *roots* seemed to surge from the flesh and wrap around Chalandra and enter her through nose and mouth and ears and anus… and she was picked up and spun around like a spider spinning a victim in its web… and then ripped suddenly apart into a hundred segments of bloody, quivering flesh that hit the bare floorboards in crimson cubes and chunks and lumps.

"Mummy!" hissed Torney, an almost silent exhalation of air.

Then she fled, and behind her heard the sounds of cracking bones, chewed flesh, and the slurp of consumed blood.

"Guards stand firm!" bellowed Sergeant Tilla, and everybody obeyed instantly, for no soldier crossed the wrath of Sergeant Tilla without ending up with broken cheekbones, a broken back, or both.

The hundred and fifty guards locked their shields, fifteen wide on the main thoroughfare that ran through the cultural quarter of Vagan, and ten deep to a man. A formidable fighting company, many of the men having fought either the constantly attacking forces of Zakora to the south, or even having fought the bastard mud-orcs. These were not raw recruits. They were seasoned men, hard men, carrying scars of battle, experience and a cynical eye.

And as the elf rats approached up the street in a hobbling, crawling swarm, and Sergeant Tilla bellowed, "Stand steady! Present long spears!", there were more than a few veterans who went weak at the knees, dry in the mouth, with full bladders and a desperate urge to piss.

These were not some enemy army.

Not even mud-orcs.

The rumour had gone round faster than a beautiful whore with syphilis. These were *elf rats*. Fucking *elf rats*. Returned to claim the land as their own; as had their ancestors; as the Dark Legends foretold, despite the words and pictures being banned from schools and libraries and museums. What was the song? "With rewritten histories and a fictional past." The history books belonged to the successors. Victorious kings and their creeping, crawling politician slime, sticking tongues up back crevices for a taste of the spoils.

Elf rats!

"Stand steady, lads!" growled Tilla, giving them strength and backbone. As the great sergeant said in his own words: he hadn't been killed yet after thirty-five years of battle, and he wasn't about to fucking start dying now.

As the elf rat charge increased, so long spears lowered. Tilla gave a bleak smile to himself. He'd seen it a hundred times before. The weight of the charge forcing onwards, then suddenly presenting spears from behind a shield wall; the front of the charge would want to falter, to stop, realising they would be inevitably impaled – but the weight of their comrades, eager for battle, and unable to see the low-held gleaming points of iron, pushed them on and on and on...

But the elf rats did not slow.

They came on, accelerating, snarling and screaming and drooling and brandishing short black iron swords...

"Hold steady!" screamed Tilla, sensing a growing panic in his lads as his own adrenaline burst through him and he revelled in the exhilaration. *Damn.* This is better than sex, he thought, and grinned. His old buddy, Jakko, would have slapped him on the back. *That's because you're not doing it right, sunshine!*

The two lines smashed together and the elf rats threw themselves on spears, impaling themselves and grasping shafts in bloodied, bark-covered claws, holding the spears locked inside their dying bodies to form... *ramps*... which the rest of the charging force climbed and leapt from into the ranks of the City Guards. Swords slashed left and right, iron clashing with iron, as men and elf rat fought in sudden, harsh, closed battle for the first time in centuries. Heads were cut from shoulders, blades skewered torsos and hearts, livers and kidneys, limbs were cut free, men went down screaming, elf rats went down silent and squirming. Elf rat claws and fangs slashed out, bit and drew blood, and many of the City Guards crawled away from the battle scene, bitten and bleeding and *infected*.

It was over in a short time.

Sergeant Tilla was the last to die, finding himself in a swiftly decreasing circle of steel and trusted armour. Old

Kav went down, sword-cut and bitten to fuck. Llandana, the jammiest bastard in the whole of Vagandrak at cards, bone-dice and Fish Wife Rune Poker, had his throat ripped out and staggered around, unable to scream. Unja lost his eyes, and was stabbed by two elf rats simultaneously through the belly. All these things Tilla saw, and fought on grimly, hacking away hands and ducking low, cutting through legs at the knee. The point of his sword skewered lungs and heart and groin arteries. He kept low, moved fast, seemed hardly to touch the enemy but left a devastating bloody massacre in his wake. Until a spear jabbed out, cutting into his side, lifting him a little. He cut backwards, but a sword blade smashed into his clavicle, breaking the bone, cutting flesh. Tilla gritted his teeth, refusing to scream as he went down under another half-dozen hacking swords.

Sergeant Tilla lay on his back, looking up at the sky brightening with a pretty winter dawn. Everything was suddenly quiet. Snow started to fall, big fuzzy flakes that turned the world hazy. To his left he could see the Old Opera House, ramshackle and quaint, kept alive by enthusiasts and run by obsessives. To his right, was Old Ma's Bakery, which in his opinion baked the finest meat and potato pies in the whole of Vagandrak.

He grinned, and there was blood on his teeth.

A figure appeared. He was obviously old and moved with great agony, joints crippled, arthritic – if these creatures could suffer arthritis. He wore a cloak of deep brown, interwoven with thin branches of black wood. He moved to stand before Sergeant Tilla, and he stooped, and stared into Tilla's bright, feverish eyes.

"How many guards do you have, my son?" he asked.

"Who… who *are you*?"

"I am Bazaroth aea Quazaquiel, Sorcerer to the Elf Rat King, Daranganoth," spoke the creature, and pulled a long, silver dagger from beneath his brown robes. "Now answer my question, boy, and your end shall be swift."

Sergeant Tilla cackled, eyes bright, brow narrowing into a frown. "Go on, fuck you, elf rat."

"I can make your ending swift and painless!"

"Fuck off! I want it hard and painful; only that way will I get to hunt your kind in the afterlife. So do your worst, you toxic piece of shit. I welcome every fucking second of it. Welcome it, you *hear*?!" he screamed.

Bazaroth looked up at the elf rats. "Move on. Progress. Kill and conquer. Take the city," he said, and the elf rats moved on over the corpses of the slain city guards. Then he looked down at Sergeant Tilla, with something akin to pity in his ancient, bark-woven face.

His black bark lips seemed to writhe for a moment. Then Bazaroth aea Quazaquiel gave a modest smile.

"Our final moments will be intimate," he said, and seated himself cross-legged beside the wounded body of Sergeant Tilla. "I will give you what you ask for."

It took Drakerath, the capital city of Vagandrak, two days to fall. The fighting was vicious, bloody, and relentless. Finally, the city gates were closed and the city itself descended into silence. Nobody entered. Nobody left.

It took Vagan a little while longer, mainly because of the garrisons of King's Guard stationed in the Keep. But even that, after hours of bloody, relentless fighting, was overrun. Many soldiers were hung by the neck from the city walls, eyes bulging, bowels hanging down beneath their boots like some obscene painting from *The Abattoir Monologues*. Finally, the city gates slammed shut. Huge bolts, wider than a man, were slid into place with grating squeals. And the country's war capital, to all intents and purposes, became a silent, mourning, motionless graveyard.

And Zanne. Zanne was the last to fall. The high black gates – the northern Corpsefield Gate, the eastern Winter Gate, and the southern Royal Gate – all were shut with resounding thuds, like the heavy stone lids slammed on a massive, desolate, sealed stone tomb.

MOLA

Mola sat in a rough wooden chair at a rough wooden table outside his villa, listening to the sway of the trees, his legs warming in the weak sunshine, and thought about the pain. It nagged him worse than any fish woman at the market whom he'd bedded and cast aside. It throbbed inside him, worse than any physical invasion of a blade he'd ever had to deal with – and that number measured quite a few. From bottom to top, his left knee was barely weight-supporting, and was raised with angry purple bruises. His left thigh, from knee to hip, was one huge bruise like a lightning filled sky during a summer storm. His hip, surprisingly, had survived the impact, but under his left tit two ribs were broken and constantly clicking, forcing Mola to adopt a slightly effete posture where he cupped his left wrist under his breast, pressing his ribs to offer some modest external support. Above that, his breast bone also clicked when he moved in any way whatsoever, bringing a curse to his lips from the gentlest of manoeuvres. The back of his shoulder and neck was a mass of throbbing, rigid, humming tendons, a cauldron of intense agonies, a platter of pain that made him grin like an idiot and curse like a sailor. But the final reigning glory was his left shoulder – or more precisely, the *tip* of his shoulder where one major part of the impact had occurred. His physician had called it a possible "rotator cuff injury", and he was glad to have had that told to him, but to Mola it was simply the place that, when pressed even gently, made him squeal like a virgin pig having the sacrificial spit-roast spear thrust up its nethermost. He continually attempted to press that area of his shoulder, searching for some improvement. It made him scream every time. And yet, every single damn day, as if in some perverse search for personal masochism and redemption, he'd probe gently at the shoulder, dancing around the fiery hot area until morbid curiosity finally championed and he dug in a finger. "Aiiieee," was normally the retort, and further curses, which highlighted why he should be doing exactly what his physician advised and bloody resting.

The problem was, Mola wasn't the sort of man to rest easy. That's what happened when you not only trained the fighting dogs for the Red Thumb Gangs, but ran the most lucrative illegal dog-fighting pit in the whole of Vagandrak. Called *The Dogs*, it was a *class* pit. Only the best for Mola's fighting dogs. And if you didn't like it? If you were an awkward motherfucker? Well, you got *fed* to the dogs.

His right hand came over and pressed tentatively at his ribs. Something went *click*. "Son of a bastard's bitch's bastard," he muttered, face scowling, dark shaggy brows meeting in the centre, lank ragged hair tossing about his broad round head. "Fucking horses. Fucking stallions. Fucking wagers!"

"You still sore, boss?"

"Yes, Carrion. I am still fucking sore."

Carrion scrunched up his face. "Well, it's been a whole week, boss."

Mola gave Carrion a look that would have had the little man cut into pieces and fed to the meat-eating fishes of the harbour. Or the eels. Yes. Definitely the eels. They consumed bones more readily than a pen full of hungry pigs.

"I'm just saying," muttered the little man, backing away and exiting the villa's easy room carrying a tray with empty glasses, each stained with a residue of whiskey sweat.

Mola sat, enjoying the rays of the dying sun, for what little enjoyment he could feel. The problem was, and this was a common problem, he'd been drunk. Not drunk as a lord, but certainly drunk as a whore. Drunk was something Mola did well. Hell. Drunk was something Mola fucking *loved*. Not so drunk he couldn't function; oh no. What would be the point of that? But drunk enough to furnish him with… a unique *perspective* in any given situation. Drunk enough to be brave about any situation. Drunk enough to face a blade, or shove a blade into another man's guts. Drunk enough to care – fuck it. To Care with a big C.

Mola felt sour, and bad, and cold. His head felt dark and bad and maudlin. He thought back over long bitter years and remembered better times, the good people he'd known, the good times he'd enjoyed. And he thought about those good times turned sour. He thought about those good people he'd known stabbing him in the back and fucking him over. And he thought about the bad times. Shit. There had been a lot.

"Damn you," he cursed, and wriggled, trying to get comfy.

Carrion entered, and moved slowly to Mola. He handed the man some small white tablets. "Time you took these," he said.

"I don't like to. They addle a man's brain."

"You need the relief," said Carrion, with some sympathy, his compact, dark features contorting.

"Thank you. What would I do without you?"

"Die under the blades of the Red Thumb Gangs?"

"Yes. Thanks for reminding me of that one."

"Do I also need to remind you of the fight?"

"No."

"So the dogs are ready?"

"My dogs are always ready," growled Mola, his own voice more reminiscent of the hounds he trained than any human sound a man should utter. His brows formed into a savage scowl and Carrion closed his mouth with a clack of teeth. He'd worked for Mola for ten years, but knew even that was not enough. Never enough. The Red Thumb Gangs believed they controlled Mola and the dog fighting pit he ran on their behalf; but in reality, Mola was a man apart; the sort of man who nobody truly ran, or owned, or controlled – despite appearances. Mola did not feel fear. He felt pain, yes; every fucker felt pain. But fear? Fear was something that happened to other people.

Mola rocked several times, then managed to gain his feet with only a minimum of rich and inventive swearing. His head snapped round and his small dark eyes pierced Carrion. "What the fuck are you looking at?"

"I was merely contemplating your recently increased elegance."

Mola processed this. "You cheeky little bastard. You want to spend five minutes with Thrasher?"

Carrion smiled a narrow smile and took a step back. "Of course, Mola, I should know better than to poke even the slightest bit of fun at you. You are currently a man *without* a sense of humour."

"Currently? Poke fun at me, cunt, and I'll feed you to the dogs on the next betting match down at the pit. See how long you last against Duchess, Duke and Sarge. Make a fucking bit of fun out of that one whilst they're tearing your thigh muscles from your quivering fucking leg bones."

"Yes, Mola. Sorry, Mola; don't know what came over me."

"It'll be my dogs coming over you, you fucker, if you think you can take the piss out of me!"

Carrion retreated. Mola felt bad. Carrion wasn't a bad man. Problem was, you showed a bit of weakness in this life and every cuntfuck decided they'd take a slice of you for fucking dessert. And Mola wasn't a man who liked having slices taken from him. Not without a bit of raspberry jam on the end of his blade, that was for sure.

"Son of a bitch!" he cursed, making it to the end of the porch. Beyond, he could see his stables. A dog howled, and was quickly silenced. Mola grinned. That was Duke. Or "Big Duke", as Mola liked to call him during fights in *The Dogs*. Thirty-nine pit fights and unbeaten. Problem was, now he could only get shit odds so Mola had taken to travelling with the mutt, pitching him in other cities as an Unnamed. It didn't help that Duke, or Big Duke, carried a fair few scars; but then, Mola was an old dog himself, and had a few tricks up his sleeve. He was currently a dab-hand with a make-up brush.

Clutching his ribs, the modest-sized man hobbled across the well-kept lawns towards the stables. As he approached, they heard him and began to bark, and howl, and keen at his impending arrival. This filled him with a deep pride and love and a fierce warrior calling. And what he loved most about his dogs, and dogs in general, was their unstinting love for Man. No matter how depraved and twisted a fucker was, in the flesh, in the bone, in the mind, the Dog still loved him. Unequivocally. Without forethought. Without judgement. A dog didn't care what colour you were, what sex you were, what deformities you carried, what crimes you had perpetrated. He *committed* to you, and remained loyal to you. And that fucking bonding was stronger than blood. Stronger than fucking family. Hell, Mola had nephews and nieces he'd happily fucking cut up during family get-togethers; cuntfucks whom he wouldn't piss on if they were on fire for their crimes against humanity and stupidity and the basic law of moral righteousness. Cuntfucks who would have been better on a noose, swinging, such was their misguided basic misunderstanding of the way the universe and the stars and shit worked.

Mola tutted to himself, and reached the door to the stables.

Those motherfuckers, he thought.

He leaned against the wood, panting a little bit. The pain in his ribs was still a bastard, jabbing him like a stiletto dagger through the guts. He paused, panting and licking his lips, and looked down into a trough of water.

You're not a pretty man, he thought, eyeing the narrow, pointed features, the brown hair receding to grey at the temples.

Mola was not a big man. He was modest in height, modest in the broadness of his chest, modest in girth. But he was strong, under that modest exterior. Stronger than a farrier. Harder than a labourer. But it only took one look in those hard, uncompromising eyes to know he didn't take no shit. No shit from nobody. Never. Ever. Not once. Not fucking once. Mola was not a big man, but he was a Big Man. He'd stab an evil girlfriend in the belly if she crossed him. He'd slit his best friend's throat over a betrayal. Because he had morals, y'see. And honour. A criminal nobility. He didn't fuck people over, and if you fucked him over then you'd crossed the line, and if you crossed the line, you'd better fucking watch your back.

"Getting old," he muttered to himself, and forced his way forward through pulsing waves of pain and into the cool, calm, pungent area of the stables beyond.

And then, of course, there was that special thing.

The Iron Wolves?

Yes. He was one of the Iron Wolves. Or had been.

And he was special, even in such exalted company.

Special indeed.

His dogs came to him. Each one was big, a wolfhound cross, each with different breeds in various experiments at strength and stamina and ferocity. There was Duchess, the most savage bitch he'd ever met; black and white in patches, her eyes as intelligent as any fucking human he'd ever met. She wasn't the biggest he'd ever bred or fought, but she was clever; damn clever. And he really identified with her, being less than massive himself and recognising a kindred spirit. She was modest in size, but clever and ferocious and unstoppable. Just like Mola.

Duke was a black and tan beast, a huge bruiser of a dog who used brute force and open brutality to savage any opponent. Sarge was another huge dog, black as midnight, with soft fur and raggedy ears and a bite that could practically chew through iron. Finally, there was Thrasher,

smaller than all the others and, Mola thought, probably
insane. He had red eyes and, even for Mola, was a hard
bastard to control in any respect. The damn dog simply
lived to fight. He was a chaos agent for the dog fraternity,
abused, fucked-over, destroyed until he'd chosen to fight
back and stomp on every living fucking creature that stood
between his own existence and the end of the tunnel he
called "Life". Sometimes, when Mola cuddled him – and
Mola liked to cuddle all his dogs, no matter how flea-
bitten, wounded or half-chewed – sometimes, *sometimes*
Thrasher gave him that look which said: *Man, I am going to
chew off your fucking face and enjoy fucking doing it.* And Mola
believed him. Yet it had never come. And Mola loved him
all the same.

Mola moved into the pens, and they were howling
now, and Mola allowed himself to smile. In reality, it was
the only time he smiled. When surrounded by his dogs.
His little violent loves. His psychopathic fur babies.

He opened the gates, and they flooded out and over
him. He rolled around in the fresh straw, wrestling with
each one individually and chastising and swatting muzzles
as dog tempers flared and they occasionally snapped at
one other with a bit too much savagery.

His pains, his aches, his worries: all of them fled when
he was with his dogs.

And as he rubbed ears and muzzles and chests, he said,
"There's a big fight coming, you mangy mutts. I hope
you're all ready."

It was late.

Mola had sat on his veranda as a cool wind filled with
ice blew in from the just-visible walls of Zanne. The fact

that he lived within spitting distance of the city, and yet chose not to accept the sanctuary of her high fortified walls, seemed to rankle a lot of people. Whenever they visited, that was always their first comment:

But why, Mola? Why live out here? Inside the city you would be more protected! More safe!

Protected from what?

Brigands, ruffians, criminals.

You misunderstand the person I am. Those people. The brigands, the ruffians, the criminals: *they need protection from me!*

And he wasn't joking.

There had been a night, after drunken revelry, when thirteen men from the city had ridden out after too much ale and whiskey, looking for trouble. They found Mola asleep, his expansive villa seemingly unprotected. They'd kicked from their horses, stumbling drunk, seeking sport, with maybe some demon raging in their young blood and young veins. Maybe they planned a robbery; maybe they just wanted some relief from the boredom of city life in Zanne.

As Mola told the city guard the morning after, they chose the wrong cunt to fuck with.

It wasn't just his short sword that found flesh and bone so irresistible.

And it hadn't just been his dogs, although he did let them run riot, biting and snapping and chewing; for, once off the leash and protecting their lovingly beloved master.

There had been… something else. Dalgoran's gift.

Only one of the thirteen hellraisers survived, and he'd been a gibbering wreck when they found him, half-naked and half-chewed up, out in the Wilds. Gibbering about fangs and blood red eyes and anarchy.

Well. Mola had no regrets, and bad news like Mola travelled far and fast.

Oh yes.

Carrion had retired, and Mola rested back in his comfy chair. The cold wind didn't bother him at all, instead reminding him of his youth, in the army, in the Wolves, training or fighting skirmishes in the White Lion Mountains, or hunting Zakoran bastards across the plains to the south of the Pass of Splintered Bones during several of the coldest winters known to man.

He rested back. And he closed his eyes. And he dreamt of a time he would be free.

The cough – a delicate, polite cough – brought him round; brought him back to the world of the living and the sober. Drugs tasted bad in his mouth and he cursed himself. Never mix your medicine with alcohol, his physician had warned. Horse shit.

Mola opened his eyes and eyed the six men, three of whom were pointing crossbows at him. He didn't like that. Didn't like waking up to find strange men threatening violence on his unprotected body. It was a basic unfairness. An ignoring of the basic fucking rules. If you were going to fight, put up your fists and fight. Don't fucking hide behind projectile weapons and cowardly numbers.

Mola sighed. "All right. What the fuck do you cunts want?"

Immediately the leader foregrounded himself. He was dapper, smart, dressed in city finery. Tall, elegant, good looking, he had a small, narrow white scar under one eye and Mola immediately recognised him as Tanza, son of one of the high-ranking officials of the Red Thumb Gangs. Mola frowned. Which one? Dudabai, was it? Or Keranda? *Shit.*

So. This was a man not to cross due to lineage and bad parenting. A criminal not to fuck with. A high-flying Red Thumb politician who helped control the city; or at least, the *under*-city.

"Quite rude," said Tanza, stepping forward, polished shoes clacking on the wooden planks of the veranda, and taking a chair, reversing it, sitting, staring at Mola over the soft leather of his deerskin gloves.

"I'm a rude man," said Mola bluntly, sitting up slowly and rubbing a hand down his face. "It could be argued that intruding on a man's estate whilst he's sleeping is also an act of something less than openness. A rudeness of character, shall we say. Are you a rude character, Tanza?"

Tanza reddened a little. "Enough of this. You are in my father's employ. You will listen to what I have to say, and then do exactly what you are told."

"Is that so?" said Mola, slowly, rubbing his stubble with a scraping of raw bristles.

"Oh yes. Or you'll end up with ten crossbow quarrels in your fucking chest."

Mola grunted, moving back slowly, tenderly, pain firing through him. "You have me at an advantage, my dear Tanza. Pray, please do continue."

"My father owns you. He owns your dogs. I'd like to... to borrow them."

Mola snapped forward, his pretence at relaxing forgotten as he surged towards Tanza, his fists clenched.

"*What*?" His brows were furrowed thunder. Then he hissed, and his hand went to his chest and the broken ribs as pain chewed at him.

"I want to borrow your fighting dogs. My friend,

Ebreziel," he gestured vaguely behind him to where one of the perfume-stinking dandies languished with his crossbow, "is getting married. We are off to Renza to paint the town red and fuck every piece of skirt that isn't nailed down by an erect cock. We thought it would be fun to run your dogs in a few, ha ha, illegal dog fights. Win us some pretty silver coin to make the evening yet more favourable."

"Nobody fights my dogs but me," said Mola, quietly. Matter-of-fact.

"We thought, on this occasion, you might make an exception." Tanza smiled. He had won, and he knew it. Who could not bow to the threat of death under the onslaught of many crossbow bolts? And indeed, who could not do what he – *he*, backed by his *dear* father – demanded? One did not cross the Red Thumb Gangs. Nobody. Not the City Watch. Not even the fucking *king*, and that bastard knew it. They all knew it. It was unwritten gospel. Carved in the stone of men's hearts by the witness of atrocities across Vagandrak. Red Thumbs were dominant. The shark in the food chain. And nobody bit the shark. Nobody could.

Mola considered this. He considered his position.

And Carrion chose that moment to enter, stepping through the door with a startled, "Oh!". The Red Thumb dandies whirled, there was a sudden twang and the whine of discharged crossbow quarrel. And a thump, as it entered Carrion's belly. The man folded, dropping to his knees, face ashen as blood pumped out.

"No!" bellowed Mola, leaping forward, heaving the men out of the way to slide on his knees, grabbing Carrion before he toppled fully to the floor. He cradled Carrion's head and his hand moved down the man's body, and came away drenched in blood. Carrion looked up at him, tears in his eyes, confusion in his soul. In his gaze were a million emotions and questions, but more prominent that anything else was the question, "Why?"

"Sorry about that," came the smooth voice of Tanza, and he slapped one of his companions – who was looking sheepish – around the back of the head. "You *idiot*! What were you thinking? No, don't point that fucking thing *at me*! You've just proved you're about as reliable as a sausage-skin child protector!" He turned back to Mola, still cradling the dying, blood-frothing figure of Carrion. "Sorry about that, old man. An itchy trigger finger, has the lad. Should put him down at the ranges for some extra training."

Mola glanced back down to Carrion. The man was trembling, then went suddenly stiff in a spasm of agony. Gently, he relaxed into Mola, blood drooling down his chin. The bolt had clipped the bottom of one lung. He tried to speak, then his chin sank to his chest and the man died in Mola's arms.

Mola eased the dead body of his servant, his friend, to the boards and slowly he stood, and stretched with a wince, and wiped his bloody hands on his pants. Then he turned and looked at Tanza. His face was neutral, an unreadable platter, his small dark eyes without emotion. "So you wanted to borrow the dogs, lad? Follow me."

Tanza grinned, suddenly, like an excited schoolboy, and as he followed Mola out onto the neatly hedged lawn, he said, "Gods! What they say about you is absolutely true!"

"And what's that, lad?" said Mola, without turning.

"That you're a man without emotion. That you're about as cruel as they fucking come. That you're the sort of man you don't turn your back on, for fear of getting a short, sharp dagger in the spine."

"So that's what they say, is it?"

"It is, Mola, it is! Luckily for me, I have the weight of the entire Red Thumb Gangs behind me! Like an army!" He cackled.

Mola said nothing, and they reached the stables. Mola paused, breathing in cool night air. He looked to the dark sky where only a few stars twinkled, sparkling against velvet black.

"There's snow coming," he said, at last.

Inside the stables, there came a yap at the sound of his voice.

Tanza suddenly scowled. "Stop fucking about, old man, let's get in there and get the dogs. This game has gone on for long enough. We need to get on the road, for there's a mighty lot of quim that needs seeing to." He gave a narrow smile and licked his already wet lips.

"As you wish," said Mola, and opened the door, stepping into the gloomy interior. The men crowded in after him, eyes gleaming, eager to see the dogs on which, they hoped, they'd win a pretty amount of coin. After all, Mola was the man to see about dog fighting. Mola was the accepted expert in the field.

The interior, with its segregated stalls, was dimly illuminated by moon and starlight. It possessed a ghostly, ethereal glow. The dogs rustled and Mola strode forward, opening the four nearest gates. "Duchess, Duke, Sarge, Thrasher – this way!"

The four hefty animals trotted from their pens and eyed the newcomers. Tanza felt his mouth go dry with a hint of terror. These dogs were big. *Fucking* big. Not just in height at the shoulders, but in the mass of ridged, solid muscle. You didn't get muscle like that on a man. Men were soft, pampered by civility and society. No. These were primeval. Raw. Savage. Of course, Tanza had seen them fight in the pits – hadn't everybody? But here, now, up close, close enough to smell, to touch! Well. These creatures were something else.

"Shouldn't they," the man coughed, clearing his throat, "you know, have leads? Or something?" Duchess gave a low growl and Mola touched his index finger to her muzzle. She stopped immediately, eyes fixed on him: her Master. Her God.

Mola gave him a withering look, and pointed. On a series of hooks were a variety of rope and leather leads, plus various differing sizes of muzzle – some even made from iron mesh. "Help yourselves, gentlemen. I'll be waiting outside."

Mola strode out, leading the four calm, obedient beasts. His fingers flickered in the moonlight and the dogs sat down in a semi-circle, staring adoringly at him. Behind, the Red Thumb men stumbled half-drunk from the stables carrying a variety of leads and muzzles. Lots of muzzles. Mola counted eight and he repressed a smile. They were being a little over-cautious, he reasoned. But then, they were facing a pack of killers, so maybe they should be!

Tanza stood uneasily, a muzzle in each hand, a lead looped around his neck. In the tavern with a frothing ale in his fist, this had seemed like such a fucking *great* idea. Now, in the moonlit home of a bastard's bastard, maybe it didn't seem too bright. But stubbornness and pride edged through him; he couldn't back down now in front of his dandy bastard friends. He'd look like an idiot! *Tanza, all fucking mouth*, they'd say behind his back. *Talks the talk, but can't stand up with the real men. Scared of a bunch of fucking pooches.*

Tanza glanced at Mola. The old bastard's enjoying this, he thought, before saying, "Here, put the muzzles on them, will you?"

Mola stared at him, dark eyes unreadable. Definitely enjoying it. "I cannot do that, laddie." He grinned then. "They're my fighting dogs. I've never muzzled them in my life. Never have. Never will. They'd... *behave* differently for me, and that would ruin the fights in the pits, which would cost the Red Thumb Gangs a heck of a load of coin. So do me a favour, and don't ask me to do something that compromises your own father's fortune. You want them muzzling? You do it yourself."

Tanza stared at him, mouth working silently for a moment, then he glanced back at his gaggle of followers. They were staring at him slack-jawed like the bunch of village idiots they most definitely were. Tanza cursed, and strode forward towards the biggest dog, Duke. Always take down the biggest first, then the others would follow like yapping little poodles.

"Whoa, lad. I wouldn't do that." Mola's words were edged with real concern.

Tanza froze, mid-stride, in what he realised was a deeply comical pose. He cocked his head towards Mola, and snarled, "And why the fuck not?"

"You've got to muzzle the leader of the pack. Or it'll turn on you, lad. They'll all turn on you."

"Which one's the leader?"

"Duchess. The black and white one."

"What? That *bitch* is the leader of the pack?"

"Aren't they always?" said Mola, quietly, dark eyes glittering.

Tanza turned, and moved – edged – towards the perfectly calm, motionless dog. The bitch was still large for a dog, just not as large as the other, more terrifying beasts. Tanza's hands were slippery as he took the lead from around his neck and attached it to the metal ring on the muzzle he held. He inched closer. Duchess started to pant, but her eyes were on Mola, not Tanza, and she gave no outward sign of aggression.

Tanza stopped, and leaned close. The muzzle seemed ineffectually small and feeble in his hand, like a wooden toy sword in the fist of a gladiator, and he wondered if he cut a comedy picture; like a dwarf trying to ensnare a lion with a bit of rope.

"Er. Good doggie?"

"Duchess," said Mola, quietly, as clouds passed over the moon, chasing rushing shadows across the lawns like escaped ghosts. One of the bitch's ears twitched. "Kill."

With a savage snarl Duchess lunged forward, jaws wide, brushing aside the muzzle and closing over Tanza's hand. There came a crunch, a twist of the head, a shake, then a deeper, snapping crunch and Tanza stumbled back, screaming, his stump waving in the air with a shower of blood droplets spraying across black grass. Duchess, standing broad, hackles raised, fangs bared, growling, chewed the hand, mangling the fingers, as Mola screamed, "Duke! Sarge! Thrasher!" His hand swept towards the men. "Kill them all!"

The dogs snarled and leapt towards the group of men, who back-pedalled frantically. There came the whine of a crossbow, then another, one bolt thudding into the earth, another chewing the wood of the stables, but it was too late and the dogs hammered into the group of milling men and...

...the screams began.

Thrasher bit one man's face off in a shower of blood, paws scrabbling at his chest for purchase as the dog rode him to the ground. Then his fangs lowered, and the screams suddenly stopped as the big dog chewed out his throat. Sarge hit two, bowling them from their feet. They scrabbled for knives and swords as Sarge closed fangs around one man's head, pinning him to the ground, kicking and screaming and punching out at the huge dog. Then there came an almost subtle *pop* and fangs crunched through skull and the man suddenly stopped kicking. The second man lunged, his dagger smacking into Sarge, but Sarge felt no pain and spun, the man losing his grip on the blade which bubbled and welled with blood. Snarling, Sarge surged forward chewing through fingers and hands, shredding the skin of the man's arms and then clamping down on his throat. He screamed and gurgled, as best he could, but Sarge was shaking him like a ragdoll and it only took moments for him to be still, nothing more than a bloody sack of dead, sick flesh. Duke had also leapt, his weight and hefty muscle bearing a man to the ground. A blade deflected from the hard ridges of muscle in his flanks, and his muzzle burrowed deep into the man's chest, snarling, chewing, tearing, as the man kicked and screamed and tried to wrench the dog's head from his meat. But it was no use. Duke was too powerful. Too savage. Too primal.

Tanza was running, clutching his stump to his chest where it bloodied his white cotton shirt with lace ruffs and cuffs and spangled gold glitter fabric. He ran for the tall pines and Mola clicked his fingers. Duchess was there, blood staining her muzzle black in the moonlight.

"Bring him down, girl," said Mola, pointing, and Duchess was gone.

Within several heartbeats Mola heard the squawk, and glancing around himself he pulled free his own dagger, and plunged it through the eye of a squirming man who stiffened, one leg kicking, bowels opening. Then he strode after Duchess. Strode after his bitch.

Entering the trees, total darkness closed like wings.

"Duchess! Lie down!"

Obediently, she lay, glancing back at Mola, seeming to grin beneath the dark towering pines. A wind hissed through the needles high above, making the trees sway. Pine oil and forest detritus assailed Mola's nostrils. He loved it here. In the dark. In the forest. Accepted into the heart of the trees.

"I can pay! I can pay you money! Lots of money! You know I can."

Mola stopped, boots crunching dead pine needles. To his right was a fallen tree, and he crossed and sat down on the trunk, placing his hands on his knees.

Tanza was sitting on the ground, having been bowled over by Duchess. It was a miracle she hadn't torn out his throat, but then she was good like that. Didn't kill unless told to do so. Not like the others. The boys could be a bit… unpredictable. Whereas Duchess had more brains. More obedience.

"Ahhh," sighed Mola, rubbing at his stubbled chin. "What to do. What to do."

"Don't let them kill me! Please! I was only showing off before those stupid idiots. I won't tell anybody what your dogs did. I promise. Won't tell how they..." he shuddered. "Killed my friends." He clutched his bleeding stump to his chest. His shirt and fine coat were nothing more than gore-ruined, bloody fabric.

"You see, laddie, I have this little problem."

"I can help with problems. I'm good like that. My father, Fernaza, he has me work in the gambling dens *sorting out problems*."

"Ahh. Fernaza, is it?" *One of the most powerful, the most feared, the most brutal... clever to slip that little piece of information in. Clever to drop it into conversation right now, just when you think your throat is about to be torn out.*

"Yes, that's my father. If you spare me he will be most pleased. He will reward you! He will see you a rich man."

Mola considered this.

"I think," he said...

"Yes? Yes?"

"I think whichever way this thing goes, your father will seek to make me a very fucking dead man. There'll be no riches for me and my dogs. I think, even for taking your hand, I'd spend an eternity in the torturer's chair."

Mola stood up.

"No, no, I have money!"

"Money doesn't buy you everything, lad. Even for rich spoilt cunts like you."

"I take it back!"

Mola frowned. "Take what back?"

"What I said! I'm sorry. I didn't mean it!"

"About being a man without emotion? As cruel as they fucking come? The sort of man you don't turn your back on, for fear of getting a short, sharp dagger in the spine?"

"Yes. I'm sorry. I retract the insult. You have my hand as vengeance. Please. Let me live." Tears were spilling down Tanza's cheeks and Mola moved closer, then sat on the dead pine needles beside the young man. He sighed.

"I don't like to see a man beg," said Mola. "And those things you said? Well. Fuck it. They were true." He relaxed.

"So you'll let me live? I swear it, *swear it*, my father will never find out. I'll be in your debt. I'll owe you my life. I'll be yours to command. I can get you information. On Red Thumb stashes, more coin than you could carry with a cart. Ten carts! It's yours. I'll help you. We can rob the Red Thumbs together!" He laughed insanely, eyes moist, his breath panting like the stink of a rank lion.

"The problem is," said Mola, carefully, "that your words *were true*. I am a man without emotion. Most of the time. I am as cruel as they fucking come – especially to my enemies. And you, dear boy, are surely one of my enemies. And I am the man you don't turn your back on – or more precisely, I'm the sort of man you don't take for a fucking fool. And you've pissed on me for long enough."

Mola rocked back, and stood.

"No!" wailed Tanza. "No! You can't! My father will have you killed!"

"Duchess?"

A tiny whine. Total focus. Complete obedience.

"Silence him."

Duchess went to work, and as Mola strode out of the forest, clutching his damaged ribs with a frown, to survey the handiwork of the other dogs, he muttered to himself, "He'll have me killed? Yeah, well I knew about that already. It's something we'd already established. Now, take your medicine like a good boy. And don't damage my dog's teeth, she'll be needing them."

A LOVING RETRIBUTION

Outside, the wind howled through the trees. Snow was falling heavy. Clouds obscured the moon, and the ancient *Shamathe*, Haleesa, gazed out into the darkness of the thick, oppressive forest. Trees groaned and swayed, pine needles hissing. Distantly, an owl hooted. Behind her sat Lorna, cross-legged, the rounded stumps of her legs resting on the thick wolfskin rug before the fire. A large leather-bound book was balanced on her knees and she was focused, her concentration complete.

Haleesa shivered. Lorna was seven years old, and there was something about the girl which had started to haunt the old woman. It had begun a few mornings ago when Haleesa had been teaching Lorna the basics of illusion...

"Illusions are the simplest and yet the most complex spells a *Shamathe* can cast."

"Why?" The girl's eyes were eager, bright and lusting after knowledge.

"They are the simplest, for they require the least amount of actual physical energy. An illusion is a dance of light, and what the *Shamathe* must do is bend that light, make it show new shapes and new colours which do not really exist. A *Shamathe* is merely redirecting energies which already exist and, for this act, little effort is required."

"Why is it difficult, then?"

"Because the *real* effort comes in the skill, in the manipulation of light. It is like weaving an incredibly complex pattern, at great speed. It requires total concentration and many years of practice."

Lorna nodded, her tiny tongue licking at her scorched lips.

Haleesa closed her eyes and held out her hand with the palm facing up. In it appeared a tiny dragon; the scales glinting brightly. The dragon breathed a tickle of fire against Haleesa's fingers and Lorna moved closer, her eyes fixed not only the dragon, but on the woman who formed the illusion...

Lorna nodded–

And Haleesa felt a shudder rack her body. Lorna had not studied the illusion. She had crept inside Haleesa's mind and studied her technique. Her *mana flow*. The manipulation of light energies. *Hell!*

There was a crash outside, and the illusion was gone. Haleesa rushed to the window and her jaw dropped open. Standing, towering over the trees was a huge, black scaled dragon. Its huge, triangular head swayed left and then right, and falling snow settled along its flanks and folded wings. Flames flickered around its snout and it took a step forward – trees were crushed and snapped like firewood under the incredible weight of its bulk.

"No!" hissed Haleesa in alarm.

The dragon's head dropped, so swiftly Haleesa stumbled backwards as the huge maw loomed towards her, a thick purple tongue flicking within as flames caressed the curved fangs as long as a man's forearm…

Lorna laughed, a tinkling sound, and the maw – and the dragon – vanished.

Haleesa was shaken, stunned into silence.

Now, in the darkness of the cabin, she found that she was suddenly frightened of the child. The realisation of such superior power was deeply unsettling. The girl was a *Shamathe*, but she was also so much more. She showed little emotion, and possessed a quality, a skein within her soul, which Haleesa had never experienced before, and found hard to trace – to understand.

Outside, the wolves sat under the falling snow at the edge of the forest. As Haleesa watched, they settled to the ground, huge shaggy heads resting on wide paws. One started to lick its paws.

Why are they here, she thought.

What do they want with Lorna?

"I called them."

"You called them? How?"

"I felt them, lost in the forest. They were starving. I led them to food."

It was a lie, but Haleesa said nothing. The wolves were more than just thankful animals helped by a mystic child. Lorna had been too young when they first appeared… and their behaviour: it was as if they were protecting her. As if she was their ward.

The morning was fresh and cold and crisp. For days they had been working on Lorna's image: the illusion she would cast of herself in order to walk amongst the people of the tribe. It had been Lorna's idea, sparked by the realisation:

"I want to visit my mother."

Haleesa looked up from where she was repairing a shawl with needle and thread. Then she gazed back down at the item, a slight tremble betraying her worry. "Why now?" She tried to keep her words calm. Tried to think of a reason for Lorna never to visit her mother again.

"I feel it is time," said the seven year-old. She smiled a crooked smile at Haleesa. "My blood-mother has not been near me for three years, now. Will you help me make an image for myself?"

And so they had crafted the illusion from light and once it had been woven into a complex tapestry Haleesa stepped back and stared at the beautiful young girl before her. She was slim, with a gentle rounding of youthful womanhood. Long, luxurious black curls fell down her back to her waist and her face was round, white: unblemished skin and neat, even teeth.

"I feel ugly," said Lorna, suddenly.

Haleesa said nothing. "Does it still pain you to walk?"

"A little," nodded Lorna.

"It will be too far for you," said Haleesa, laying a hand on the girl's shoulder. The flesh felt soft and warm under Haleesa's wrinkled fingers. The illusion was a good one. Perfect, in fact.

"I will survive."

Haleesa took a deep breath, and looked into the intelligent, deep brown eyes before her. "Listen to me, girl. I believe it is a bad idea for you to go to the Palkran Settlement. It will only end in tears."

"Their tears, or my tears?" Lorna cocked her head.

Haleesa shrugged. "I give only advice, child. You take it, or leave it."

Lorna smiled, and placed her own hand on Haleesa's shoulder this time. The old woman felt the gentle squeeze of fingers and again, marvelled at the depth of the illusion. Not only an illusion of light, but a manipulative illusion of the mind.

"I will make my own way in this," said Lorna, gently.

Snow was falling as an exhausted Lorna walked slowly – uneasily – into the Palkran Settlement. Despite the illusion of a perfect body, she still felt great pain in her stumps when she walked for any great distance, and the nagging made the young girl frown as she cast her gaze about.

The few people in the street ignored her as she trudged through the snow, and she finally passed a long row of huts and arrived at the one which had been pointed out by Haleesa years earlier, from the hilltop. Many hours they had spent, seated on that hilltop watching the bustle of activity below. Haleesa had shown Lorna other things, her father, his brother, other people of the village whom Haleesa had delivered in birth or helped, over the years, with their illnesses and their medical problems.

Now, the faces swam before the young girl and she reached the hut and knocked with her pointed stump. The door opened revealing Gwynneth, a young child in her arms, her slim figure accentuated by long flowing skirts.

There was a moment of silence.

"I have come home," said Lorna, softly.

Tears ran suddenly down Gwynneth's face as realisation kicked her in the heart, and she stepped out into the snow, hugging the child before her. She brought Lorna inside, seated her on a chair, and added more fuel to the fire.

"I thought you near dead!" said Gwynneth at last, drying her eyes.

"I was very weak. I have been for a long time. But now… I am better."

"Really? Did Haleesa not accompany you?"

"No."

"You walked all the way through the forest alone?"

"Yes. I am careful, mother. I am safe."

With these words, Gwynneth began to cry once more and she hugged the young boy in her arms tightly to her breast as his wide eyes fixed on his older sister: ogling, spit dribbling down his chin.

"Where is… my sister?" asked Lorna, after a few moments of comfortable silence.

"Out with Sweyn… your father. They are buying bread and vegetables from a trader whose wagon is stuck in the snow. He is selling food cheap – most would be rotten if he waited until the wagon was freed by thaw. He will be *amazed* by this event! By you!"

"Before…" she took a deep breath, "before they come," said Lorna softly, "I must show you something."

Gwynneth nodded, her face frowning with a spark of confusion.

"Show me something? Like what?"

"Do you think me pretty, mother?"

Gwynneth nodded, as she could see the structure of Sweyn's face in the girl's unblemished features.

"I was not born this way. I was born different. But I need to show you. I must show you, for this shell is just an illusion. You are my mother. I need you to know the truth."

"Truth? Illusion? Shell? What do you mean, child?" whispered Gwynneth.

"I will appear fearful to you, mother, but you must see me for who I am. The reality. Only then will I know if you truly love me…"

Lorna breathed deeply, and the illusion fell away.

Gwynneth screamed at the yellow-skinned monster before her, and her young boy snuggled against her breast in an attempt to burrow beneath the shawls, disturbed by this intrusion of sound and increased heart rate.

"This is how I look," said Lorna, sadly. "This is how you created me. How you gave birth to me. How I was *cursed*."

"No!" screamed Gwynneth. "Never! You are no child of mine! Get out, get out of my house!"

The door opened at that moment, revealing Sweyn and the blonde-haired six year-old close behind. The large man's arms were laden with loaves as his eyes fell on Lorna and his face showed a sudden shock and disbelief as realisation bit deep.

Gwynneth was sobbing.

Sweyn leapt into action, dropping his burden of bread and leaping at Lorna, his fist flying, knocking the deformed girl to the ground. His boots thudded with sickening cracks, and taking up a wide pick-handle from the corner of the hut he beat at the stricken figure before him as a sobbing, wailing Gwynneth backed into the gloom of the hut.

"Get out, you monster!" snarled Sweyn.

Lorna crawled to her knees. Blood glistened against her yellow skin. She pointed at him accusingly with a shard of arm bone. "Why do you beat me, father?" she enquired, voice perfectly calm and serene.

"What? Get out, you disgusting creature; get out of my home!" he roared.

Lorna smiled, sadly. "I am what you made me."

The pick-handle whistled, striking Lorna a vicious blow across the forehead and knocking her to the earth. Stooping, despite his loathe to touch the devil, Sweyn grabbed the ragged, blood-stained clothing and dragged Lorna out into the snow.

"What do we do now?" wailed Gwynneth. "Oh, Sweyn, what do we do? Is it really our Lorna?"

Sweyn stared at the unconscious creature before him, where blood soaked in and stained the snow.

"No," he said at last. "This is a dark devil, a demon come to taunt us with memories of our past misery. I will carry it up onto the hill and burn it, so that its evil will no more be spread to good, honest people."

"Shall I tell the Council?"

"Shusht, woman. The Council could do no good... you can see as well as I that this beast is evil. A shape-changer. A devil! Take Suza indoors and I will finish this business."

Gwynneth ushered the blonde-haired child inside and passed out an oil-filled lantern to Sweyn. The door squeaked shut and he was left in the fire-flickering darkness with the creature of darkness. He reached down, hoisted the slim and lightweight being to his shoulder and set off away from the village, his trail marked by a passing circle of lantern amber as he followed a narrow track across the fields and up towards the sacrificial altar sitting squat and ugly atop Grey Hill.

Sweyn's mind was in turmoil...

It is a devil, he thought. A demon of the forest.

It must be burned, destroyed, with nothing left to haunt us.

But what

what if

what if it really is our daughter?

No! screamed his brain. I could never sire something so hideous… so deformed.

He halted, panting under his burden, despite the lack of any real weight. The thing moaned a little and, cursing, Sweyn pushed on. Snow began falling, heavily this time, and he was cold and shivering as he reached the hilltop. He dumped the moaning figure of the deformed girl on the wide stone slab and, without waiting, undid the stopper in the base of the lantern, allowing thick oil to splash across Lorna's clothing. Then, stepping back, he smashed the lantern against Lorna's head and skipped away as flames engulfed the creature, yellow demons dancing through the cloth and flesh and Sweyn, face heavy with sweat and a sudden fear, turned and sprinted down the hillside, away from the burning horror struggling to rise on the altar of ancient stone.

Snow fell.

The Palkran Settlement sat under the weight of darkness. A few people had seen the small fire atop Grey Hill, but none had gone to investigate. Instead, they huddled in the warmth of their homes, and pondered, and slept.

The lonely howl of a wolf drifted through the downfall.

There came a gentle padding of paws.

Followed by a knocking. Raw knuckles on rough-sawn planks.

Sweyn, who had not been able to sleep and was shivering from the cold, pulled on his boots and opened the door to his cabin. Outside stood a vision from recent nightmare… the burned child, naked and terribly scarred by flame, stood with smoking hair and a grim smile touching her forlorn face. Around her sat three huge wolves, their pale yellow eyes fixed on Sweyn.

With a yelp, the man turned to run – but was picked from the floor and hurled across the inside of the cabin with such force that his skull smashed open against the wall, leaving a trail of blood, brain and bone shards smeared indelibly against rough timbers. Sweyn's corpse slumped to the hearth with a sigh of escaping death-air.

Gwynneth screamed.

And Lorna spoke a word of True Power.

Gwynneth's hair and clothes ignited, flames searing up to catch the roof of the cabin. She ran, screaming, towards the door, which thumped shut, and in seconds the whole cabin was ablaze. Other tribesmen rushed from their huts at the sounds of screaming, but the wolves leapt amongst them, tearing at throats and faces and the villagers fled away in panic leaving Lorna and the blazing cabin and the fall of snow completely alone.

Several of the men, having gathered weapons, returned with grim faces and a conviction of duty and honour. Lorna turned her gaze on them. Her lips whispered and lightning crackled in the heavens above, smashing down to pulp the armed men into smears of grease against the ice. Lorna, eyes glowing in the blaze of the roaring cabin, threw wide her arms and yet more fire demons sprang up in other, nearby cabins. The fires quickly spread, dancing from roof to roof, and flames roared and the remaining villagers fled out into the darkness toward deep snow-fields, deeply afraid of the fury-filled demon and its pitiless, attacking wolves.

Lorna turned back to Sweyn and Gwynneth's cabin; but instead of her fury abating, it increased. They had tried to murder her. She disgusted them. Her eyes glowed with an orange light and she strode between the flaming cabins. A child darted left, and one of the wolves leapt upon the little boy, fangs tearing at his throat and head. Tiny fists grappled with the beast but ceased to struggle after three or four heartbeats.

Lorna reached the edge of the Palkran Settlement, her frame a small dark hole against the roaring flames that had swept through every home and sent huge columns of black smoke billowing upwards, cutting through the fresh fallen snow.

She gazed down into the field where most of the tribes-people had gathered, and she felt their cold, and their loathing; their fear, and their hatred. Cold blue eyes hating the unknown. Petty people, she thought. With such limited understanding and emotion.

Her hand raised, and the people started to shiver, breaths pluming, turning blue and purple, becoming rigid with ice.

Lorna's eyes closed. She felt the power within herself, but more: within every living thing around her. Within every rock and tree and flake of snow; within every river and mound of earth and flower and living cell.

The energy of the *elements*.

The power of the Equiem.

Lorna whispered a word, then looked once more at the tribes-people. They were still huddled together in a huge, chilled mass; but as Lorna hobbled closer on her stumps she could see the rimes of ice crystallised on lips, could distinguish the glint of ice in hair and beard, could see the blue-tinge of fresh frozen skin. She moved towards a large man, and touched him with the point of her stump. He shattered, revealing frozen organs and bones and intestine. Lorna wrinkled her nose and turned back to the three wolves, which sat: obedient, patient, waiting.

"Now it is time to visit Haleesa," she said.

The fire had gone out in the cabin's hearth, and the cabin and the world inside nestled in complete and utter darkness. With wolves padding behind her, Lorna walked wearily to the cabin door and pushed it open. Despite her exhaustion, she was wary. She expected violence. Some form of attack.

Instead, Haleesa was seated, facing the door, tears running down her ancient, wrinkled face.

"What have you done, dear child?" she whispered.

"They tried to murder me," said Lorna, bluntly.

"Ahh." A deep sigh. "You abused your powers, and you abused the energies of the *Shamathe*."

"Yes."

They stared at one another for a long time.

"You must leave here," said Haleesa, gently, and with care. "You must leave *me*."

"But, *mother...*"

"I am not your mother. You killed her. Destroyed her. Burned her alive. You have in you a seed of evil, child; and I fear you like I have never feared anything in this world."

Lorna nodded, and turned, her back to Haleesa. But she did not move, and for a long, terrible moment Haleesa thought she was going to feel the wrath and hate of the frighteningly powerful young girl.

Instead, Lorna spoke.

"Let me leave you one gift," said Lorna, her words so soft that they went almost unheard over the moaning of the wind in the trees, the ice in the skies.

Lorna walked away, the three wolves at her heels, and she disappeared into the forest.

Haleesa frowned, and stood. The movement was fluid, and she turned, wondering at the release of pain in her arthritic hip. Has she healed me, thought the old *Shamathe*. Has she removed my terrible pain?

She knelt, adding twigs and a few logs to the almost extinguished fire. Soon, she had blown flames into life and watched the flickering demon devouring the wood. And then she noticed her hand – the skin was smooth, white, unblemished. She gasped, her hands coming up to her face to feel that all the wrinkles had gone. Haleesa rushed to a cupboard on the wall and pulled free a polished bronze pan – and gazed at her distorted reflection, and could see that her youth had returned.

Stripping herself of clothing, Haleesa gazed down at her naked limbs. She was slim, supple, beautiful. Her long legs were straight and powerful, her hips wide and good for childbirth. She felt her hair – rich and luxuriant, reaching below the nape of her neck. It had returned to its full, deep redness.

She ran to the door of the cabin, and stood naked under the falling snow.

The cold did not touch her.

"It is a gift I do not want!" she screamed at the forest. "I do not want it!"

Her echoes were dulled by the snow, and Haleesa fell to her knees, weeping into her hands.

The old man came to her.

"You can make an offer?"

"Yes."

"You can cure her?"

"Yes."

"I don't know what to do. I am… lost."

"I know."

Haleesa stared at the man, with his finery and his uniform, with his haughty regal features, with his inherent nobility and his promise of honour and good things to come. She allowed hope to burn a little candle in her soul. And she wondered if she was a fool.

"She killed her mother. Her father. Her sister."

"I know this, also."

"But you can still help her?"

"I know of her deformities. I also know of her… great power. I believe I can channel her. I believe I can focus her. I believe I can make her good."

"And you think I fucking believe you?" hissed Haleesa suddenly, glaring at the middle-aged man. "You think I'd entrust a wounded human being into your charge? A child so powerful you could use her for very great evil?"

The man seemed to consider this. "Yes," he said. "I think you would."

"Why?"

"You have had enough of hiding the lie. What I can do… it is magick. Real magick, not petty illusion. I can heal her, Leesa. Heal the child. Make her whole again. Make her pure again. Make her *care* again."

"You are sure of this?" She dared to believe.

"I swear to you. By all the gods. By the Seven Sisters. By the Powers of the Equiem. By the twisted energies of the old gods: the bad gods, the twisted gods."

"Then do so. With my blessing. But protect her. Nurture her. Love her."

He smiled, and bowed his head. He reached out, and touched Haleesa's old woman's young flesh. He stroked her cheek, and stared into her eyes, and she found that she believed him.

"I will do so," said General Dalgoran. "You can trust in me."

THE BOX

The cave was surreal. Dark and wondrous, a volcanic space, a forced pressure chamber of igneous creation, organic construction, chaotic revelation. Dropping down from a high platform, Kiki stood for a moment just enjoying the experience. She'd never experienced anything quite like it.

"Amazing," said Dek, coming up beside her.

"So you like this sort of shit?" She stared at him, head cocked to one side. "I thought you'd be more interested in, you know, cock-fighting, and bear-baiting, that type of machismo horse shit. Not some fucking rock formations which look kind of nice." She smiled to take the sting out of her words.

"I love the thought; the concept. Volcanic insanity. All that hot, pressurised, molten rock forcing itself through the ground. I kind of empathise. That's how my mind feels just before a fight."

They moved on, emerging onto another ledge, which wound around the massive cavern containing the iron box; containing the hidden, ancient prison belonging to King Yoon. And, after what seemed like hours, they dropped to the floor and approached the sheer, vast wall of iron. It was a damn sight bigger up close. Vast, towering, mammoth. It made the Iron Wolves look up; and up, and up, straining their necks.

Kiki glanced back, and both Narnok and Dek gave her a nod.

They unsheathed swords, and Trista and Zastarte followed suit, producing their own weapons.

Kiki stepped forward, glanced up once more at the sheer iron wall, then inserted a key into the lock. Then she tried another. And another. On the seventh attempt, there came a deep, heavy *click*, and a sound like a pendulum swinging somewhere far above, deep within the heart of this huge metal box.

"It would appear we are in," said Kiki.

Narnok tugged Yoon's lead. "Come on, you back-stabbing mad-arse bastard. Let's see what you're hiding."

The door swung open, and the Iron Wolves were greeted by a short corridor with blank iron walls. They stepped in, moved down to a black iron gate which swung open easily under Kiki's touch.

They were in a vast chamber, the ceiling soaring off high above. It was lined with cells on four levels with balconies, opening out to, and overlooking, a central space. The whole place was filled with rust and shadows. Along the walls tiny orange globes lit the space, but not enough to banish demons and shadows. Each level's balcony was lined with ornate iron barriers, presumably to stop prisoners falling to their deaths. Rust clung to each surface like a new lover.

Narnok whistled, single eye lifting, scanning the high walls around the exterior of the huge space. "There must be, what? Five hundred cells? This is some bloody prison, I'll give you that, Yoon."

"It is an unused unit," said Yoon, quietly.

"Yeah, right," snapped Kiki.

They moved forward, and stopped suddenly as soldiers drifted from the edges of the huge chamber, like ghosts emerging from a darkened tomb. They walked with elegance; each man was tall, bearing pale white skin and dark crimson eyes. Each man was startlingly similar to his comrade, sporting long white hair dropping to shoulders, and each of a similar slim, athletic build, wearing the same dark clothing, the same black armour, archaic and inlaid with silver runes.

Kiki lifted her sword, eyes scanning left and right; then spinning slowly on her heel as she realised these warriors had also emerged from behind, stepping free of hidden alcoves in the darkness. There were twenty of them, at Kiki's count. They moved forward until they formed a circle around the Iron Wolves.

"Who's your leader?" she snapped. "Show yourself."

"We have no leader," said one man, stepping forward, "but I will act as our Voice. You are intruders here. You must leave this place."

"Or else what, lad?" growled Narnok, hefting his double-bladed axe with obvious threat; a promise of oblivion.

"We will force you to leave," said the delicate, pale-faced warrior, and drew his sword with a sibilant hiss. The weapon was long, black and etched with silver runes that glittered. The blade was nicked in several places hinting at experience in battle. And the fact the warrior was not cowed by the demon-like visage of Narnok, with his one missing eye and criss-cross of terrible scars, showed either very great bravery, or a considerable amount of stupidity.

"We have your king," said Kiki, and smiled slowly. Narnok gave a tug on the leash and Yoon stumbled forward, where he dropped to his knees. Then his head came up, and his dark eyes were gleaming like the oil in his dark curls.

"Don't listen to them," snarled Yoon, voice ringing out "kill them all!", before Narnok back-handed him across the mouth, smashing the king aside where he lay, stunned like a clubbed fish on the cold smooth stone.

Kiki stared around her at the twenty armed warriors. Their faces were impassive, even at this mistreatment of the king. *Their king?* She gave a little internal shrug. She licked her lips. "Let me explain how this can play out. This bastard," she gestured, "is hiding something here. All we want to do is have a little look around. Then we'll be on our way."

The *Voice* of the pale-skinned soldiers gave a narrow-lipped smile. "We cannot let you explore this place, Kiki of the Iron Wolves. Take my word for it, there is nothing – nothing at all – of interest to you here. This old prison is an empty shell. It contains no surprises."

"We *are* going to look around, you fuckers," growled Narnok, and Kiki flashed him an annoyed glance.

"I would like to avoid bloodshed," she said, smiling at the man. "*Your* bloodshed. Now stand down your men."

"I will not."

"So be it," said Kiki, and advanced.

The twenty warriors drew blades, and without cries, without expression, in complete silence, they suddenly attacked. The Iron Wolves kicked apart, forming a tight circle within the enemy circle, each covering the other's backs. The first warrior reached Kiki, sword slamming down; her own blade parried with a shower of sparks and she dropped her shoulder, punching him in the groin; then an uppercut to the chin; she deflected the blade of a second soldier and ploughed her sword through the first's eye. The blade lodged for a moment in the eye socket as he screamed, a sudden loud wail that broke the stillness of the ancient iron prison, but Kiki twisted her wrist and the blade unhooked from bone and withdrew, mashed brains painting the iron tip.

Narnok hacked his axe down, crashing through a sword-thrust and smashing the clavicle of the charging warrior. As the man went down, so Narnok followed, axe swinging overhead to cleave his skull in two straight down the centre. A warrior crashed into him, but literally bounced off the large man and Narnok grinned through his mask of scars. "Surprised, fucker?"

The chamber became a sudden, whirling blur of swords and charges, of clashing steel and chaos. As ever, Trista and Prince Zastarte fought as a team, practically back to back, blades licking out, piercing, stabbing, deflecting blows intended for one another. In battle they were a team, despite their mutual loathing. They were a fighting unit of unsurpassed skill.

Dek fought with mechanical savagery and no remorse. A veteran of the fighting pits, he was used to long duels with fists, helves or blade, and this was no different. He did not think: there are twenty warriors ranged against us. He simply considered: how long will it take to kill the twenty warriors ranged against us? He fought with fists and boots and head as much as his blade, and he was a savage opponent. Three pale-skinned warriors charged him, and he ducked a vertical slice intended to remove his head, dropped to one knee, thrust his sword tip into a groin slicing the femoral artery with a sudden gush of... white blood. He gasped, but twitched right as a blade tried to skewer his face, and rammed his left fist into the man's testicles, feeling them compress under the weight and power of his hefty blow. The warrior went down squirming and Dek palmed a long knife from his left boot with the same hand and hammered the weapon down into the man's eye, as he parried a sword thrust with his blade, dropping his sword suddenly to slash at his attacker's legs. The blade went in behind a knee guard, cutting through skin and twisting, popping the kneecap open. White blood oozed free. It was like gutting a fish. The man screamed, grabbing at Dek's sword, but the long dagger punched out, through the man's screaming mouth, silencing him.

Kiki fought with elegance: a dancer, a sword in each hand, whirling and spinning. She felled one warrior with a backhand cut, landed lightly, twisted to the left as a straight thrust came past her, then elbowed the attacker in the face. Blood gushed from his nose like cream, but he did not scream. His boot lashed out, hooking Kiki's leg and pulling back. She hit the ground on her back with air exploding from her lungs, then rolled fast as his blade smashed down, clanging from stone. He leapt at her head, both boots stomping as she rolled again, and Kiki deflected a series of hard, fast blows, each one jarring her arm, each one a micro second slower than the last, as showers of sparks rained down on her. And she felt it. A weakening. This warrior was good. No. He was exceptional. Their blades clashed again, but Kiki was struggling and he knew it; he had her. She could see his crimson eyes gleaming, teeth bared, white blood glistening on his chin from his crooked nose. His blade caught her shoulder, piercing flesh, and she gasped, and growled, and felt an awesome, massive power well up within her… then Dek was there, looming from behind, blade cutting out to remove the warrior's head. The man's cadaver toppled, neck stump gushing blood, and Dek hauled her to her feet. He grinned at her.

"Thanks," she breathed, as they spun, back to back, and eyed the remaining enemy warriors.

Narnok faced off against a white-skinned fighter, who was spinning his sword with expert proficiency, a whirl of steel, feinting left and right and watching with care as Narnok's axe blades shifted in anticipation of attack. Studying him. Then he leapt forward, and Narnok batted away the blade and jabbed the butterfly tips towards the man's eyes, but he was too fast, taking a step back, sword reversing, parallel to his forearm as he lunged, tried a horizontal slash. Again, Narnok's axe batted the blade up this time, his boot coming up to front-kick the warrior in the chest, knocking him back. With a sudden scream, Yoon leapt on Narnok's back, looping the leash around the big man's throat. The weight carried Narnok crashing and stumbling back, grunting as Yoon's fingers raked at his eyes then pulled tighter on the stranglehold. The enemy swordsman leapt to the attack, and Narnok barely deflected the mad slashing blade as he staggered under the weight of his king attempting strangulation. "You bastard!" he choked, and slammed his head back but Yoon was waiting for it and twisted his own head aside. The swordsman came on again, and with a mighty effort Narnok's butterfly blades described a glittering figure of eight keeping the warrior at bay. Again and again he tried to slam his head back, but Yoon was a wily bastard. What he needed to do was drop his axe, whirl and throttle the king, but the warrior before him smashed that possibility into horse shit and the ghost of a smile on the man's lips infuriated Narnok beyond belief. He was turning purple, neck bulging, veins standing out like cables as the rope he'd used to tame Yoon became his garrotte. Suddenly, Trista was there behind the enemy warrior, and her sword hacked down diagonally, cutting into his neck. He spun, as white blood pumped out, and his sword licked out, but Trista stepped back, knocking the blade aside before ramming her own weapon through his mouth. Her eyes met with Narnok's for a second, then the big axeman threw down his axe, reached behind himself, and slammed both palms against Yoon's head. The king howled, dropping from Narnok's back, and Narnok turned, pulling the rope free from about his throat, his eyes murderous. He lurched forward, fist cracking into Yoon's face: two blows, then three, and the king went down with a broken nose and split eye, unconscious.

Narnok looked around. The fighting had stopped.

They'd killed them all. Corpses littered the stone floor of the abandoned prison.

"Is everybody all right?" said Kiki, hand to her shoulder where blood was seeping out. Zastarte twirled his sword.

"I am, my sweet little darling."

"I'm not fucking all right!" growled Narnok, still flushed red, huge rope burns circling his throat. He grabbed up his axe. He turned, and advanced on Yoon, intention obvious.

"No!" snapped Kiki.

"Backstabbing motherfucker has it coming," said Narnok, hefting the weapon. His single eye met Kiki's gaze and she gave a little shake of her head.

"Not here. Not like this."

"He has it coming!"

"And he *will* be punished. But we might need him. So *not yet*. And that's an order, soldier."

The Iron Wolves checked themselves over, and Dek moved through the dead warriors with his dagger, making sure none were faking it. Then, he circled the huge chamber, sword at the ready, poking his nose into the alcoves from which the warriors had emerged. He shouted back from the far end, voice reverberating hollow and metallic, "It's all clear."

"I have a question," said Narnok. He'd been busy tying the unconscious Yoon up good and tight, and dragging him away from the pile of corpses.

"Huh?" said Kiki. She'd removed her jerkin and shirt, wincing at the shoulder wound. It wasn't too deep and didn't affect the mobility of her shoulder or arm; but it still stung like a scorpion strike.

"You'll need stitches in that."

"Yeah. Later. When we stop." She rummaged in her pack, pulling free a small jar. In it sat a stinking yellow paste, and, using her index finger, she applied it to the wound. "What's bothering you, axeman?"

"Their blood. It's white. What the hell is that all about?"

"I saw something similar, once before. Far to the north, near the White Lion Mountains. I was hitched up with a mercenary squad; we found a man crucified on a lightning blasted oak. Tied up he was, and they'd hammered nine-inch nails through his wrists and ankles, and branded his forehead with some kind of religious symbol. He'd bled white. We thought it was candle wax at first, some part of a strange, superstitious ritual, but one of the lads took a knife out, cut open the dead man's calf muscle. Fresh dead he was, not even hard yet. He oozed white blood. We all slept with one eye open that night."

"Well, I ain't ever seen anything like it," said Narnok. "It ain't natural, it ain't."

"They're a race of creatures," said Trista, settling her pack on her back. "They look human, like us; but they're not."

"What are they, then?"

Trista shrugged. "Damned if I know. But I know they're hard to kill. We did well."

"That's cos we're the Iron Wolves," grinned Narnok lop-sidedly. Then he glanced at Trista. "Thanks for that. Back then. With Yoon."

She gave a nod. "Not a problem, axeman."

"If I were prettier, I'd give you a kiss."

"Yeah. Well, don't get too many ideas. Most men who kiss me seem to end up dead."

"I remember," said Narnok, voice suddenly sober. "Nothing like seeing an old soldier friend with a knife in his spine to remind me what a terrible, deadly black widow you really are." He smiled. "Still, lass. Glad you're on my side." He gave a cough. "Let's head up there, check out the cells. I reckon we'll find whatever Yoon is hiding pretty easy."

"Let's see," said Kiki. "You lead the way."

The stairs were steep, made of iron grilles, and Narnok led with Kiki and Dek close behind with weapons drawn and ready. Zastarte and Trista stayed behind to guard the entrance to the prison. As Narnok so eloquently put it, "I don't like no fucking back-entrance surprises."

You're not going to like this, whispered the ghost of Suza in Kiki's mind. Kiki's mouth felt suddenly sour and her mind spun a little. She took deep breaths and gripped the rusted handrail tight. It felt suddenly insubstantial; as if she grasped at smoke rings and felt herself tumbling, gazing down a long dark shaft made of black glass with perfectly smooth sides leading deep into an eternity well.

Go on. Fall, bitch. Die, bitch. You'll enjoy it.

And then Dek was there, iron grip on her bicep, clasping her tight. She turned, and looked into his questioning eyes, and smiled.

"I'm fine. Honestly. I'm well."

"Keep it together, Keeks. Now's not the time to be craving the honey-leaf."

She gave a curt nod, and carried on up the iron steps. Suza nestled in the back of her mind like a small black toad on a corrupt and poisoned lily-pad. Squatting. Silent. Watching. *Watching.*

They reached the top of the ornate iron stairs and stood on the high walkway. Narnok glanced down. Zastarte gave him a thumbs-up sign. Zastarte was grinning. This was positively his *type* of desecrated dungeon tomb; Narnok snarled something crude in a different language.

"I'm not liking this," said Kiki, slowly, and twirled one of her swords thoughtfully. "There could be a hundred soldiers up here; or an army of the insane."

"No," Dek shook his head, and rubbed his beard. "Yoon's hiding something. Protecting something. It's not men. And it can't be treasure, despite the bastard squandering the country's wealth on his *Tower of the Moon* horse shit. He still has enough gold in his harems to sink a war trireme. Come on. Time to search."

The cold stale air, with its metallic stink and hint of old oil, became infused with another aroma. Something bad. Decay. Corruption. They wrinkled their noses in distaste; except Dek, whose nose had been broken so many times in the Red Thumb Fighting Pits aroma was simply something that happened to other people.

Narnok moved to the first cell grate, which was half open. He peered into a narrow, confined space. There was an old wooden bed pallet, rotten, black and broken; an iron pot; and various sections of angular metal, rusted through: chunks of anomalous iron, littering the floor as if scattered like broken dice. He looked back. "Odd."

They moved down the row of cells, the walkway stretching off into the gloom. Each had an open grate, black, rusted; some closed and locked solid, some open allowing entry – not that they wanted to investigate. This place had an oppressive atmosphere, dark and brooding; home of many an evil past action.

"How are you doing up there?" Zastarte's voice boomed through the large space: metallic, and sounding positively chirpy.

"I swear," muttered Narnok, "it's like the woman-torturing bastard has just come home." Then he shouted, "Nothing of worth!"

They continued, checking down the long row of dark cells, peering into centuries-old spaces, many filled with strange angular chunks of rusted iron. Kiki stepped forward into one space, and hefted an almost triangular shape. As she held it, she felt something *move* inside the iron object, and there was a tiny *click*. She dropped it with a *thunk* and stepped hurriedly away.

"What was that?" said Dek.

"I don't know. But it was mechanical, and I'm not going to stand here and let it chop off my hands. Torture instruments, is what I'm thinking. Which makes this place even more savage than I first thought. Is that what Yoon's been doing down here in secret? Something cruel and illegal that would turn the entire population of Vagandrak – finally and openly – against him, resulting in a forced and necessary abdication?"

"Let's carry on," said Dek, grimly, and they moved to the next set of iron stairs.

These were even more degraded, and shook alarmingly, flakes of rust cascading down as the three Iron Wolves ascended, one by one, to the second level. Narnok caused the worst scare, for the big axeman was no effete showman like Zastarte, and he was pale and sweating when he reached the top. He peered over the ornate barrier, taking care not to lean too hard on the old metal.

"That's a big drop for a big man like me."

"Come on," said Dek. "There's a lot of cells and I'm starting to feel an urgent need to get out of this place. I wouldn't ever say I'm a claustrophobic man, but this place has a certain effect on a person. Like it's supposed to, I suppose."

One by one they cleared the cells, finding nothing but old rotten wood, rusting implements and more of the strange, randomly shaped chunks of iron. At the end of the row of seventy or so chambers, they climbed the third set of shaking, rust-infected stairs to the third level. Half-way down this, Kiki started to get a sinking feeling in her heart. Were they being dicks? Maybe Yoon *hadn't* been using this place for secret torture sessions, or to horde some terrible machine he wanted to keep secret from his generals and the politicians of Vagandrak. Doubt wormed into Kiki's mind, into her breast, and she licked her lips, ran her hand through her bobbed, brown hair. Shit. *Shit.*

They climbed to the uppermost level, Narnok now lagging behind. He was still pale, clammy, and Kiki turned. "Go back down, Big Man."

"Eh? What? *Why?*"

"Some people are fine with heights. But this is…" she peered over the barrier, taking care not to touch its rusting swirls and curves, "a long way up on unsteady walkways that could collapse at any second. You're the heaviest of the three of us. And…"

"Yeah?" he snarled, teeth bared, clutching his axe tight to his chest as if the great twin-bladed weapon of dark iron could protect him from a long fall onto a hard stone floor.

"Some people," she said, gently, "deal much better with heights than others."

"I fought mud-orcs on the high edge ridges in the Mountains of Skarandos. I skewered an attacking mangy lion on a narrow path four thousand feet up in the White Lion Mountains, letting it charge onto my spear then casting it down onto the steep icy slopes where it disappeared into mist and stone. I stood watch in the ice on the high towers of Vagan Fortress, with no guard rails and only slippery black stone under my boots waiting to piss me over the edge. Don't try and say I'm scared of heights, Kiki, my dear."

She looked at the terror in his eyes, and gave a single nod. "I was just wondering if Yoon had awoken. Maybe your knots weren't so good. Maybe, even now, the slimy little fucker is crawling towards a unworthy escape, wriggling his way to freedom; then he can gather his elite soldiers and hunt us down like a, aha, a pack of *wolves*."

Narnok scratched his chin. "You think so?"

"I think one of us should go and check."

There was a moment of silence. Down in the vast chamber, there came a scraping sound. Narnok looked into Kiki's eyes.

"I can go and check, if you like." He gave a deep cough. "As you say. Yoon's a wily bastard. Could be he's on the move."

"You go," said Kiki. "I doubt there's anything up here anyway. We'll check these last cells and follow you down. Only be a couple of minutes."

"Yes, yes," said Narnok gruffly, and moved carefully back to the shaking stairs, slowly, hands spreading out a little as if he might drop to his knees at any moment. As he began the descent, he glanced back at Kiki and gave a little smile of thanks. And then he was gone. And Kiki and Dek were alone.

"Just me and you," said Dek, and stepped a little closer. Kiki shivered, and looked up into his brutal face, with its minor scars, buckled nose and bad tattoos. Their eyes met, and they shared a moment, searching one another. There was history there. So much history. Battle, and war. Loving, and hate. Lying on blankets under a winter moon, naked, entwined, kissing, his tongue on her breasts, his gentle questing hand sliding between her squirming wet thighs...

"No."

"Yes."

"No!" She grabbed his arm. Relaxed her grip a little. Softened. Smiled. "Not now. Now, we do this. Afterwards…"

"Yes?" A gentility that was almost alien for the large tattooed pit-fighter.

"Afterwards, we can talk."

"Oh?"

"And *then* we can fuck."

He bared his teeth, a cross between a smile and a grimace. "You lead the way, then, Captain. I'll be right behind you."

"Yeah. I bet you will."

Here, the cells were different. They weren't so much cells, as had been witnessed on the lower three floors, than large, open rooms with a variety of chains and leather straps and buckles and wooden racks and *devices*. The first three rooms held terrible instruments of torture. Chairs with spikes, racks with spikes, and nails, and rusted blades, instruments to stretch a man, ripping his arms and legs free of their bloodied sockets, benches with nozzles for poisons and acids to direct into eyes and ears and anus; chairs to impale a woman through the quim with a curved cutting blade on a pendulum; all manners of torture were catered for. All the evil imaginings of a horde of insane pain-seekers and scream-merchants.

Kiki analysed it all with a low-level disgust, a snarl on her lips, a dangerous glint in her eye. "I don't even dare to dream about the shit that's gone on here, Dek. I don't dare to dream."

"There's a nobility with a blade. Even in death. But this… this is sick. It reminds me of Zastarte."

"Yeah, well, there's a cunt who's going to burn in the Chaos Halls, if we're honest about it. Come on. Let's get this prick tease finished, then get the fuck out of here. I feel sick to the core of my being." She gave a narrow little smile. "Sick to the core of my cancerous heart."

They moved down the rooms, each filled with a history of ancient depravity. It was halfway down the row of seventy cells that they stopped. From inside the next cell came the sound of rustling. And the sound of weeping.

Dek and Kiki shared a momentary glance.

"A woman?" mouthed Dek.

Kiki gave a quick shake of her head. "No. Something else."

They came to the door. The chamber was in darkness. But streams of light came in, diagonally, from a shattered roof. Hardly enough to see by. But enough to see the prisoner. He, or she, or *it*, was staked out on a thick-beamed machine of black wood, tensioned iron bands like folded layers, and stone-block feet. The figure was strapped down with tight, thick leather straps, and brass buckles gleamed. Here, there was no rust, no decay, no entropy. Trays had been placed under the rack to catch the blood. A small brazier burned in the corner of the room, providing another source of dancing shadows.

With swords aloft, eyes scanning, Dek and Kiki entered the chamber, fully alert. They cleared the room like professionals, ignoring the obvious, focusing instead on the subliminal, until they were sure they were alone. Then Dek half guarded the portal, half stared in disbelief upon the figure strapped to the rack as Kiki moved forward, slowly, carefully, eyes wide, mouth open, and stopped abruptly before the mewling, weeping, tortured thing.

"You're an elf rat," she said, gently, words little more than an exhalation of disbelief. It was not a question, but a statement of fact.

It was naked, as far as anything which had skin reminiscent of bark and moss and grass could ever appear naked. It was tall, much taller than a human – over seven feet in height, with narrow bony limbs that hinted at being branches, covered in skin that hinted at being the corrugated bark of an ancient oak. The head was over-large for the body, with bright yellow eyes too large for the oval face, and hairless except for patches of beard, grey-green and tufted. Long fingers were like talons, with black fingernails sharp as razors at the end of every finger. The creature was twisted, irrelevant to the torture-rack on which it was broken, legs and arms of differing lengths, spine jutting out near the centre, its trunk twisted a little and not quite straight with the pelvis. The yellow eyes fixed on Kiki, and there was pleading in their depths, and a tongue the colour of heartwood slipped out and moistened lips that were black and rough and hard.

"You poor, poor thing," said Kiki, stepping in close.

"Wait!" snapped Dek, in a strangled tone. He rushed over. "It's a fucking *elf rat*."

"I can see." Kiki's voice was stone.

"They're *poisoned*," said Dek.

"So we are led to believe in twisted children's fantasy tales. How do you know? How do you really *fucking know*, Dek? This creature has been held here by Yoon. The bastard's been torturing it for information; that much is obvious. So? The torturer wasn't frightened of becoming infected – correct?"

"Go slow, Kiki. It's not always what it seems." Dek's words were ominous. Kiki gave a swift nod.

She positioned herself. "You can hear me?"

Hands lifted, stopped by the leather straps. The head nodded, turned, eyes fixed on her eyes and they seemed... old. Ancient. Older than Time.

"It's... it's okay, we're going to cut you down. This shit will stop for you, can you understand me?"

Again, the creature nodded, and Kiki realised she was scrunching up her nose at the stench. It was shit, but mixed with rotting old leaves, the aroma of the compost pile. The stink of dead things left too long without burial.

Kiki stepped forward, drawing her knife, and sawed slowly through the leather bonds around the creature's ankles. The leather came away wet, with blood, or sweat, she did not know. The long, angular legs kicked for a moment, freed, then were still. Kiki busied herself with the wrist restraints, and finally a thick band of leather around the creature's neck. She had to get in close for that. She could smell its breath: intimate, like rotten old earth freshly dug up. And see the teeth. White and grey, curved slightly, like thorns. She took care with the neck leather, no need to cut the creature's throat with her hurried razor strokes. When it was free, she stood back, and it did not move, although its large yellow eyes followed her.

"You can get down. You are released," said Kiki.

For a long time the elf rat did not move, and then it toppled from the rack and squatted on hands and knees, coughing up vomit, sharp claws raking the iron floor of the cell. Then, gradually, its head lifted and it fixed on Kiki, and then Dek, as if memorising their faces: imprinting them to an eternal root memory buried deep in soil and rock and Time.

"I thought nobody would ever come," it said, and its voice was gentle, like the whispering of trees in a strong breeze: leaves brushing against one another, sibilant and gentle and mesmeric.

"It was a coincidence, believe me," said Kiki.

"Nothing in this life is coincidence; all roots lead to the heartwood." The creature gave a grim smile. "You are of Vagandrak?" It was flexing its long fingers, looking down at its black claws, and Kiki knew enough about body language to take several steps back, sword lifting a little, involuntarily, so she had a defence of solid iron between them.

The elf rat smiled, as if sensing her sudden change of mood.

"As you say," snapped Dek, stepping in. "What we need to know, is if you're friend or foe. Shall I cut your fucking head free right now, or let you live? You were imprisoned here, and we've freed you, whatever fucking race you are." He spat on the ground. "I reckon that means you owe us."

The elf rat considered this and rose to its feet, weirdly, smoothly, jacking itself up as if the muscles were hydraulic. It towered over Kiki and Dek, and looked down at them, still flexing long black talons.

"I apologise. One forgets one's manners when strapped to a torture implement and forced to endure..." it calculated, "more than a whole *year* of indignity and torture." It forced a smile to its bark face, which looked wrong, and bared its thorn-like teeth. "I am Sameska. As you say. An elf rat. A part of your legends, I do believe. A part of your dark mythology."

"Yoon imprisoned you?" said Kiki.

The elf rat tilted its head slightly, and gave a long, slow, lazy blink. "I do not know this Yoon. My bane has been the white-haired demons. The fucking *krazanz*." It spat, and rolled its head lazily, as if releasing tension from strung-out, tensioned neck muscles. Then it gave a little moan, and dropped to its knees, and collapsed on its chest, and lay there, whimpering.

Kiki rushed forward. Dek was more restrained.

Kiki knelt, touched the elf rat. "You are injured?"

"I am less than whole," the creature managed, simpering. "They have done their worst to me. Burned me, cut me, sent energies pulsing through my heartwood. They seek answers, but I do not have the questions."

"Can you walk?"

"No."

There came a subtle feeling, then, to Kiki. A *trembling*. As *Shamathe*, she understood the energies involved. The balance of earth and soil and fire and water. "Help me," she said, glancing up at Dek, and together they stooped and lifted the wounded, degraded, tortured elf rat. It whimpered. *He* whimpered. Legs scrabbled, and they half-carried the feeble creature onto the crumbling iron walkway – away from the torture cell.

"How did you get here?" said Dek, lowering his shoulder.

"I was a scout," said Sameska. "For my people, in Zalazar, beyond the White Lion Mountains. I was watching the army. But I didn't realise they had their experts watching me. They crept around me. Hunted me. Captured me. And then it became... a whirlwind. And then an eternity." The creature stumbled into silence.

Kiki and Dek spent the best part of ten minutes escorting the wounded, tortured creature down the rickety iron steps, shaking and trembling, whining sometimes in a voice that was half skittering, wind-blown leaves, half creak of thick timbers. It was a truly bizarre experience, and several times their eyes met behind the tortured beast, which towered over them by a good head, and yet seemed to weigh so little, like chopped kindling.

Finally, as they descended the final steps, they heard raised voices, and as they reached the stone floor they found Narnok, Trista and Zastarte arguing over the cringing figure of Yoon near the portal by which they'd entered. Yoon had yet more marks on his face, and a bloody lip, and it was immediately apparent Narnok had not forgiven him for the earlier strangulation whilst in the midst of battle. Zastarte looked calm and cool as ever, with only the fact that his white ruffs were stained with dirt a sign he'd been removed from his natural existence of parties, wine, drugs and easy-to-seduce women. Trista, on the other hand, had a hard look in her eye and a hand on the hilt of her narrow sword. She looked like a woman not about to take any shit, even from a huge axeman like Narnok.

As Kiki and Dek approached with the limping creature, Sameska, draped heavily across both their shoulders, the others looked up and their words froze in the air like so much dragon smoke. As they got closer, so Yoon's arm raised, finger pointing a long, painted, cracked digit at the creature. "No!" he wailed. "*Noooo*, you cannot set it free, it will poison us all!"

At the same time, Sameska focused on Yoon's face through his obvious waves of pain, and suddenly started to back-peddle as if attempting to get away. To flee. "Not him, not him! He is my torturer, the bringer of pain and death! He has taunted me, burned and stuck blades in my flesh these last long months. The others are bad, but him, that bastard, he is a purity of evil!"

The Iron Wolves looked from one to the other, and Dek and Kiki fought the elf rat until it sat back, suddenly, on its rump. Yoon was grappling, as if for a blade, but there was no blade there and he howled again, a primal fear in his eyes. Then his head snapped to Kiki, his gaze burning into her. "You fucking *fool*, do you even understand what you're dealing with here? This is a fucking *elf rat*! It will poison you, bring decay and terrible disease and death to us all!"

"Ha!" boomed Narnok, scowling. "What horse shit. The elf rats are nothing but dark shadows in children's stories, dreamt up to put the fear of the gods into their happy, terrified little hearts."

"If that's the case," snarled Yoon, head flailing wildly, finger jabbing at the creature, "then what the fuck is that?"

They all stared at the creature sitting on the floor making a soft whining sound. He stared right back. Then spoke softly. With a great gentility, despite the warped features, the apparent blend of elf and the forest which, presumably, had spawned it, "Do not listen to the mad king," said Sameska. He gave a little shake of his head. "I am no danger to you. No danger to you at all. There is no poison in me. If there was, how could your... *king* spend many months at my flesh with a blade, and not become infected? No. He seeks to learn my secrets; the secrets of Zalazar. Because he wants our *wealth*." The elf rat spat on the stone floor of the prison – of the torture chamber, which had held him incarcerated for long, bleak, pain-filled months.

Kiki met Dek's gaze, then Narnok, Trista and Zastarte. "We should leave here."

"I bloody agree!" rumbled Narnok, hefting his axe. "It's giving me the creeps. Right down my spine." He shuddered. "We should never have come."

"No." Kiki gave a shake of her head, hair bobbing. "We've learned something valuable. Not only is this bastard," she kicked Yoon, and he yelped, "into shit so deep we'd need a mineshaft to probe his decadent mind, but there's other business afoot in Vagandrak. Other games being played." She glanced at Sameska. "But let's get out of here first. I feel like I need a hot bath."

They travelled long corridors of stone, trod through vast caverns formed by ancient volcanic pressure. Rock gleamed with damp, as if the underground passages suffered night-sweats of fear. Only, finally, when they collapsed in exhaustion and Zastarte set up first watch, did the Iron Wolves fall into dreamless sleeps, motionless as cadavers. Yoon, on the other hand, was tossing and turning on his narrow strip of blanket. His lips murmured constantly, and his hair was lank with sweat and old oil.

Sameska, who was on the opposite side of the chamber, pretended to sleep. In reality, he was elf rat and barely needed it. But he knew it would make his human companions nervous if he sat on his haunches, big yellow eyes staring at them, so he huddled under a blanket provided by the one with the kind eyes. The female. *Kiki. Kikellya Mandasayard. I know you. Have spoken to you through soil and ash, through stone and dust, through bark and sap.* He smiled slowly, in his fake sleep, and for the first time in months summoned the quests. They crept, slowly, from the palms of one hand, and began a tentative crawl across the stone floor of the cavern. Sameska took his time, after all, he didn't want to alert the bastard on watch known as Zastarte. *Now, there is a man with evil eyes. The eyes of a torturer. I know you well.* Sameska shuddered with a moment of bitterness. In Zalazar, to carry out such behaviours against a fellow elf rat would be to summon instant death. But then, it would never happen. *How can you treat your fellow people in such a way? How can you have such disregard for the history and development of your species?*

The quests inched along the rocky ground. Zastarte stood and stamped his feet, rolling his neck and shoulders to ease tension. He glanced sharply to Sameska who froze, the quests nothing more than string-thick roots of dark crimson against the black rock. Very hard to distinguish. Almost impossible, he knew.

Zastarte went back to his theatrical stamping of feet and blowing into hands, and Sameska noticed the man's continual glances at the hard, bitter woman, the one with the golden curls and harsh, unforgiving manner. Trista, they called her. Trista of the Iron Wolves.

Eventually, the quests reached their goal. Yoon turned in his sleep, making a snorting sound, dark curls tumbling over his face. The quests crept through his hair with all the gentility of a lover's tender strokes, until they reached the top of his skull. Then they eased through skin, and through the bone, and gently, into the brain within.

Yoon jerked, but the quests had already administered a local anaesthetic via the teeth in their heads, and then triggered a series of nerves in the brain which allowed

Yoon to sink into a relaxed state of unconsciousness. They moved deeper, easing through tissue and causing the minimal amount of damage.

Then, they stopped.

Feelers sprung from each head, narrow strands almost invisible to the human eye, which spread out through brain tissue, searching.

Back under his blanket, Sameska gave a narrow smile. A nod of the head.

And slowly, the quests began a retreat towards their master.

"Now, I understand," he whispered.

She stood in a forest. Mist curled across a blanket of dead pine needles. Her heart beat a tattoo of panic in her chest. She was unarmed. Naked, without her weapons. She glanced up, sweat on her brow and caressing her top lip, salt in her mouth, fear in her breast and with quivering fingers. *Where was she? Why was she alone?* Confusion smashed her like a helve blow from behind.

She blinked.

There were five shapes up ahead. Tall, just shimmering black shapes in the woodland gloom, their limbs slightly distorted, their heads kinked to one side as if listening for something.

"We have followed you for an eternity," said one of the figures, the voice beautiful, musical, and a part of the forest.

"You are in our dreams," said another.

"Until we kill you," said a third.

"But… you are in my dreams," she whispered, words barely more than an exhalation of fear.

"Not so."

One figure stepped forward. It was a woman. Tall, lithe, powerful. She looked vaguely human, but her eyes were like black glass, the expression on her face one of hate and arrogance. "Fucking human," said the woman, striding towards her. Her movements seemed to drift, like smoke, as if her eyes weren't working properly.

"What do you want?" she said, but the smoke shifted, reappeared closer, shifted again. The figure rang out a peal of brittle laughter, cold and cruel.

"I am Sileath," said the figure. The words came from all directions and none. "And I am here to kill you."

She blinked. And Sileath was there. Close as a lover.

"Welcome to Hell," said Sileath, and slammed the curved blade into Kiki's chest and she was falling, and she was drowning: drowning and choking in an ocean of her own blood.

THE BLEAK

The storm rolled in from the oceans to the north and east. It ploughed over the mountains from all points of the compass. It cast giant shadows over the Crystal Sea, the Elf Rat Lands and the Plague Lands to the southwest. Winter's onslaught had arrived, pushing forward, violating the skies, with towering storm fronts driving across Vagandrak in its entirety and depositing snow, and sleet, and bringing the bitterest cold winds the country had experienced in a century.

A raven, flapping high, flew west over the barren Rokroth Marshes. A light peppering of snow covered the reed beds, the narrow channels of water, and even more narrow pathways, which criss-crossed this treacherous part of the country. Deep in the icy waters, vicious tenta eels and sharp-toothed moranga pike lurked, waiting for an unwary step and plunge; and indeed, waiting for one another.

The raven coughed a cry, dipping its left wing and banking, dropping to lower, slightly warmer currents. To the north squatted the ancient and abandoned Skell Fortress, high black towers like spears, the battlements and their crennellations like so many broken teeth. Deserted, haunted; it was a place not often frequented. It was said men went mad beneath the shadows of its ancient walls.

The raven pumped wings, flowing onwards across Vagandrak. Far to the south a large unit of infantry was camped, fires burning, pennants loyal to King Yoon's Vagan Division flapping wildly in a rush of tempestuous wind blasted from east and south. The raven continued, heading straight for Vagan. The city, with its huge fortified walls loomed on the horizon like a squat beast, a creature of stone and iron. The huge Eastern Gates were shut, black oak and thick iron bars centuries old and scarred from some long forgotten civil war. Usually the gates were open during daylight hours, allowing travellers, merchants, adventurers and soldiers access; it was an anomaly to see them closed, but the raven did not concern itself with such matters.

Its wing beats thudded on, fighting a headwind now, and as it approached the city walls it noted, without consideration, a change in the landscape below. The ground before the city fortifications was always kept clear, of scrub and trees, of market traders and debris. But a hundred feet out some trees did flourish, and now was the time of year for winter blossoms and the glow of evergreen. However, something was subtly changing in the trees. In the pines, in the red cedar and blue spruce, in the silver fir and various vast holly bushes that ranged away from Vagandrak's outer walls; the colours of needles and leaves seemed to have subtly shifted. They had darkened, into deep rich greens, perhaps shot through with another colour, something like blood. And, again, a subtle transformation, the trees were leaning, or bending near their summits. As if sending out tendrils seeking sunlight and changing the direction of growth.

The raven gave a caw, ragged and bleak, foregrounding the utter, total silence that drifted up from the city of Vagan like inverted snowflakes. The glossy black bird spread its wings and soared over the fortified walls. There were no guards there. No pikemen, no archers, no infantry standing watch. The braziers were cold and silent and full of black, damp ashes. A chilled ice-wind snapped along the deserted battlements, like an angry little dog.

And over, swooping down into the city. Streets were silent. Cobbles gleamed with ice. Market stalls stood empty with tarpaulins cracking and snapping in the wind. Windows were dark and without light. Not a single chimney pumped out smoke. The War Capital of Vagandrak was a ghost town; an abandoned realm; a city of the dead.

The raven flapped towards the Palace of the Autumn Stars, Yoon's own private and personal estate at the heart of Vagandrak. Over yet more perimeter walls, across marble walkways and past sculpted gardens, and on to a vast architectural indulgence of fanned, curved, pure white marble steps which were dominated by huge bronze doors.

The raven cawed again, and dropped, black eyes fixing on a figure seated on the steps. The creature, for he was not a man, looked up sharply at the approach and lifted his arm, twisted and deformed, to create a perch.

The King of the Elf Rats, Daranganoth, smiled a smile

of thorns and, leaning towards the black eyes of the raven, which appeared glassy and dead, whispered, "Tell me what you've learned about the traitor."

They called him *Pockets*, on account of his superbly light touch and the ability to lift purse, watch or coin from minister, clerk or whore without capture. He was twelve years old, with dark eyes and a cynical expression far beyond his years and earned, in the majority, from being abandoned by a honey-leaf addicted mother at the age of six and having to learn to feed himself, fight his corner against the larger, more vicious street urchins, and basically *survive* in a nasty, cruel world of poverty which showed no mercy to a kid down on his luck. And Pockets had been down on his luck right from the start.

The main reason for Pockets' survival was his intelligence. He was bright beyond the ken of your average orphan or youthful street vagabond. He'd started with simple theft, usually from the markets where the mass of people made it easy to slip in and out, and, indeed, *beneath* the market stalls where there was always a plethora of fallen fruit and veg, the odd crust of a pie or half-eaten sausage roll. By the age of eight he had a room with another two orphans up by the tanneries where the slums provided plenty of condemned housing – apparently unsafe to occupy, but with a bit of love and care to the broken roof tiles, provided a reasonably comfortable, dry, rent-free accommodation which kept the snow and biting wind from skinny, underfed bones.

By the age of nine Pockets was running his own gang, their crimes escalating until they were staging robberies on carriages during the dead of night, and breaking into jewellers and watchmakers. He had contacts throughout the city of Zanne, and further afield, where he could fence marked stolen merchandise away from the eyes of the makers. He even had a couple of contacts in Rokroth, although had never visited himself. He preferred to stay in the city he loved and loathed, having an expert knowledge of every street and alley, walkway, slum, bridge and palace. From the Corpse Fields to the gloomy, frightening streets of the Haven where even the City Watch hardly dared tread, Pockets was a smiling, happy character with lots of friends and even more enemies, but who knew his place in the great scheme of things and was willing to get on with life after the shit card he'd been dealt by an uncaring God. A boy makes his own luck, Pockets thought nearly every morning when he first opened his eyes after yet another dreamless sleep – Pockets did not dream – and it was a philosophy that had seen him survive this far; survive *and* prosper.

However. Something had changed.

Pockets had begun, just like his mother before him, to experience the properties of the honey-leaf, that illegal, bitter and most joyous of leaves. Whether smoked, placed under the tongue and sucked, or increasingly formed into concentrated little cubes and swallowed, Pockets and some of his fellow gang members had been *experimenting*. The previous night, if indeed it *had* been the previous night, had been the heaviest session yet and it had allowed Pockets to – whilst not *dream* exactly – to at least experience some forms of colour and flashing wild imagery during that long, coma-like experience other people called sleep.

Now, as he lay on his low pallet bed with cold winter light peeping between cracks in the old wooden shutters, he tried to decide exactly *what* was different. And then it hit him worse than his pounding head, and the bitter dregs nestling in his mouth like so many unwanted tea leaves. Outside, the streets of the Haven were *silent*.

Slowly, and with a groan, Pockets rolled over and fought with his blanket for a moment. He rubbed at weary, bloodshot eyes that had no place in the head of a boy of twelve, and searched the room for his companions in leaf experimentation, Jona, Ranz and Solimpsapa. Incredibly, considering the amount of leaf they'd ingested, all three beds were empty. Indeed, the blankets were pulled back as if they'd not even been slept in at all.

What happened last night? Did I come home alone?

Who was I with?

Where did I go?

The previous evening was a blur to Pockets, and he had simple, vague outlines of memories, of dancing through fresh snowfall, laughing into the scratching claws of the wind, an intention for mischief. But that was the last image in his mind. Kicking up flurries of snow.

Why was it so damn quiet outside?

There should have been shouts and bustle and laughter. Only twenty footsteps from his front door was Midwives Market, so called because, apparently in long-gone poorer times, back during the Bad Old Days, it was common for a so-called midwife to steal a newborn babe and sell it to the highest bidder, whether that be into slavery, to parents who could not sire their own, or to horrible characters who wanted them for personal pursuits. Now, the market was much more respectable – in as far as *anything* in the Haven could be considered respectable – and dealt in simple pies, vegetables, loaves of bread; and sometimes stolen merchandise and property.

There should have been noise. A *lot* of noise.

Pockets rolled from his bed and eased open the shutter a fraction. Outside, cold grey light made him squint against the honey-leaf dregs, and his dry-bark tongue roamed around his bitter mouth with a hint of regret. But then, it makes you dream again, so how can there be any regret? He peered down at the blackened, cracked cobbles. A smattering of icing snow clung to them, powdered and fresh. Pockets frowned. There were no footprints. *No* footprints?

He pulled on some tattered trousers and a thick jumper, shivering at the chill in the room. The reality was he could afford the grandest, richest livery from the finest tailors in the city of Zanne; his money hoard was now quite exceptional thanks to his *light fingered approach*. But to dress in the manner he could afford would be not only to destroy his anonymity, but ironically, to place him in the firing line of other vagabonds and pick-pockets in the city.

Still frowning, Pockets stepped down the rickety staircase and opened the door a crack. A cold breeze caressed him, along with the silence. Distantly, a dog barked. Then, fell suddenly to quiet. It did not bark again.

Pockets stepped out into the snow, and walked swiftly along Market Street, but before he reached Market Square, which was anything but a square, he ducked left down Cracked Skull Alley, narrow and winding, with the buildings to either side having shifted on weak foundations so they leaned together high above, where they'd been propped apart with hefty iron beams to halt any more progress. It made the alley dark, foreboding, and treacherous unless you knew the right people. Pockets knew *all* the right people.

He stopped, and listened to the silence again. He moved to the nearest house and, cupping his hands to the glass, tried to peer in through the grime and cracked panels. Inside, nothing looked out of the ordinary. But there were no people present.

Pockets trotted down Cracked Skull Alley, pausing at the junction between Quimspike and Groper's Lane. It was still silent, still eerie and deserted – a spirit town. But here, now, there were marks in the newly fallen snow. Looking left and right, Pockets moved warily to the scuffled marks. Footprints approached down the centre of Quimspike, quite far apart and smudged. Somebody running? Then the marks turned suddenly into a series of sweeping crescents. Pockets searched around the centre of the marks, which seemed to suggest a struggle. There were no other prints. It was as if the person had simply... vanished. No tracks led away.

Pockets straightened. A very, very bad feeling sank through him and he glanced around again, as if searching for an enemy, or at least some sign of life. It was instinct that kicked him back a step as the creature landed in front of him with a thud; a split second earlier and it would have landed atop him. Pockets caught a glimpse of skin like bark, and deep black eyes and teeth like thorns, and he spun, skidding, to accelerate into a spin... but a cluster of thin tentacles shot out, wrapping around his waist, his legs, his arms, and he was pulled back suddenly with a shriek and gasped as the ground rushed away and he was launched upwards, body screaming, then tugged into the dark black upper stories of a four storey house – where the elf rats were waiting for him.

The Iron Pike Palace, Vagandrak. A vast monolith of marble and iron, a beautiful sculpted edifice towering ten stories up and dominating the centre of the country's War Capital.

Up polished iron steps, gleaming under a winter sun. Black and white tiles spread out in patterned arcs, under ornately carved stone arches and balconies and sculptures that belonged more in a cathedral than Yoon's War Palace. Rushing through the throne room, it was dominated by vast statues depicting former Kings and Queens of Vagandrak, and a series of ten thrones stood lining the far wall on a raised dais of granite. Now, the vast, high-ceilinged chamber was dominated by a gathering of elf rats. There were several hundred, standing silently around a central space. In this defined area stood four acolytes of Bazaroth aea Quazaquiel, Sorcerer to the Elf Rat King Daranganoth, swaying, each with quests like long white roots connected to a central, locked down figure. Masketh, Captain of the Royal Guards, lay pinned to the floor, face red with shouting curses and struggling against the thin, wavering strands.

Bazaroth appeared at the huge arch that defined the entrance to the palace throne room; a hushed silence spread through the elf rats, and all heads turned, tracking the sorcerer as he shuffled forward, staff clacking on the marble tiles, to eventually stand, staring down at the tense, snarling figure of Masketh with spittle on his lips and hate – and fear – in his eyes.

"You humans are more resilient than I would have given you credit for." Bazaroth smiled, his face wrinkling and corrugating like some monster from childhood's darkest dreams. "Many are hiding. But they cannot hide for long."

"Scum!" snarled Masketh. "Why did you come here? What do you want, you filthy, poisoned rat bastards? You're not even supposed to exist! What dark sorcery is this?"

"An interesting perspective," said Bazaroth, gaze fixed on Masketh. "A shame your ancestors felt a need to erase us from the history books; from your history, specifically. Other cultures, the jungle tribes of Jugenda, for example, see fit to give us some credit for the building of their ancient civilisations. But you," and now a dark gleam was in Bazaroth's eyes, "not only do you seek to exterminate us, driving us from lands we nurtured for ten thousand years; hunting us like common vermin; exterminating our menfolk, our females and our children. Then you have the *fucking temerity* to delete us from history altogether." He'd leaned forward during his exposition, but now straightened, or straightened as much as one so old and bent and broken and crippled *could* straighten.

"You are childhood nightmares, nothing more," said Masketh. "This is some black magick. Evil sorcery. We will fight you, and we will defeat you."

"Your race's answer to everything," sighed Bazaroth. "The law of the sword and the axe. Conquest by blood and death and slaughter." His face grew a little tighter. "By genocide," he said, quietly. "Do you feel guilty for the crimes of your ancestors? But then, of course you do not. You have no idea of the atrocities of which I speak. The dark deeds carried out underneath the ground in vast torture chambers. The mass exterminations. The burial pits filled with oil and corpses, then igniting with vast explosions, flames roaring up into the clouds like huge mushrooms of blinding white energy, a terrible rage, an all-consuming fire, eating flesh and eyes and bone." Bazaroth was panting, one hand raised, lifting his twisted hardwood staff. Then it hammered against the palace floor, and a thick marble tile cracked. His eyes narrowed. "Do you feel guilty, Masketh?"

"Fuck you, elf rat scum."

Bazaroth aea Quazaquiel smiled, and made a swift gesture. From behind, through the crowd, two elf rats dragged a struggling woman. She was slim, dark-haired, pretty. Her blue dress was torn and blood lay indelible on nose and chin and shins. She was barefoot, hair tangled, eyes just a little wild. She stopped struggling the minute she saw Masketh, and from his trembling lips there came a tiny, "No."

"Masketh. I think you recognise Shaela. Shaela, I think you, too, recognise your loving husband, Masketh. He's the Captain of the Royal Guards, you know." Bazaroth was moving, hobbling forward, his staff clacking on the polished floor of the throne room until he was close to the woman who recoiled in absolute terror. Bazaroth grinned at her, teeth like dark thorns tipped with blood. He glanced back at Masketh, still pinned to the floor but struggling now with an intensity that was almost frightening; as if he might split himself in two in the act of trying to escape.

"Please," said Masketh, halting his struggle suddenly in the realisation that he would never break the root-bonds of the acolytes. "Please. Don't hurt her. Please. I'll do anything!"

"Tell me where Yoon's wife, Tryaella de Franck, is hiding. This palace is a warren of hidden rooms and escape tunnels; she has taken Yoon's three little bastards and flown their rich little nest. Where have they gone?"

Masketh suddenly paled.

"I don't know," he whispered.

"You do know!"

"No, such important information is kept from me!"

"Horse shit!" roared Bazaroth. "You are *captain*. One of your roles is that of protector of the *queen* and Yoon's spindly little fucking offspring. You will tell us where they are, or we will rip Shaela apart!" Already the quests were squirming from Bazaroth's gnarled hands, thrashing like a fist of oiled snakes as they lurched and writhed across the air space between him and the suddenly cringing, squirming, wailing woman...

The seething mass of thrashing root strands paused in front of Shaela's face and she went suddenly rigid, as if struck by a bolt of high magick energy, and her eyes were fixed on those seething roots, which bunched as if into a giant fist ready to punch a hole through her teeth and down into the gurgling stomach beyond. Her scream of panic started almost beyond the range of human hearing, dropping in pitch until Masketh coughed, and with tears streaming down his face yelled, "Stop! Stop, please; I'll tell you. I'll show you where the queen has fled."

"Where?" Bazaroth's head turned and fixed on Masketh. His eyes were older than the forests and mountains of Vagandrak. Masketh felt a chill wind blow through his soul, tolling a bell that signalled an End of Days.

"Let me up," he panted, sweat staining his clothing, lank in his hair, rolling down his forehead, dripping into his eyes. "There is a chamber, I will show you. I will take you there. But please, do not hurt my wife."

Bazaroth nodded, and Masketh was released. Shaela was tossed in his direction and they crumpled together like crushed flowers, hands and arms clamping one another as they fell into an embrace, and sank to their knees, sobbing at one another.

Bazaroth made an impatient, clucking sound. "Your sentiment is touching, *humans*, but if you are not on your feet in three seconds and showing me what I want to know, then my original offer of tearing you limb from bloody, shredded limb still stands. One. Two..."

Both Masketh and Shaela scrambled to their feet, still clinging to one another like drowning lovers. Their eyes were wide. Masketh's understanding sank in slowly, and he lurched into motion, dragging a limp-limbed Shaela with him. They moved across the throne room, into a series of large, high-arched corridors with high plaster carvings of kings and queens from ancient history. Limping, staff clacking, Bazaroth snarled at many of those depictions in unfavourable remembrance. Some of them had been responsible for driving the elf rats from Vagandrak in the first place.

Down long corridors they travelled, Shaela sobbing, Masketh attempting to calm her, until they came to a mammoth, redwood panelled library, rising up with ornate black iron spiral staircases to three balconies above, revealing towering stacks of books, not just in their thousands, but tens of thousands. The smell of leather and polish was strong, until Bazaroth brought his own elf rat stench; a mixture of woodland decomposition and... a metallic something, underlying, like a half-buried cat corpse half eaten by maggots.

"There." Masketh pointed.

Bazaroth limped forward, and whacked his staff against a dark panel in a wall of similar panels. There came a hollow thud. Quests wormed from his opened hand, surging from his palm. They wrapped around the panel and wrenched it free with a tearing of wood and iron brackets. There was a *twang*, as of heavy released springs.

Bazaroth smiled, and stepped disjointedly into the darkness of the tunnel beyond.

General Namash, a huge, hulking elf rat warrior with skin like dark oak and fists like tree stumps, pushed forward through the acolytes who had followed the sorcerer. "Bazaroth!" he barked, and the wizened old sorcerer turned.

"Yes, General?"

"What about those?" he pointed to the two shivering humans who had betrayed their queen.

"Feed them to the Tree Stalkers," Bazaroth whispered, eyes gleaming.

WHITE WORLD

The mountains of Skarandos were huge, a vast range of towering grey and black peaks, some nearly ten thousand feet in height and perpetually capped in snow, both at summits and in great rivers of ice down their flanks. They bordered the southwest realm of Vagandrak, running all the way from the Plague Ocean, where glittering metallic waters lapped at shores of fused sand and tainted rocks, a vast crescent of dragon's teeth curving up to the western Salt Plains, the inhospitable desert of salt that bordered Vagandrak to the west, and which had never been successfully crossed. Or at least, not by anybody who could tell the tale. The Mountains of Skarandos were broken by just one natural pathway through their mass – the Pass of Splintered Bones, and guarded at the southern end of the pass by the mighty vast walls of Desekra Fortress, built from stones mined from the very mountains themselves.

Now, snow was falling heavily across Vagandrak, and the land seemed to have sunk into a surreal grey witch-light. Mist drifted in thick patches, and silence was heavy at the foot of the Mountains of Skarandos on their northern flanks, where various huge peaks stood as enormous black guardians, like serrated pike teeth, with rocks the size of houses at their splayed toes and steep, stocky, unwelcoming feet.

There were caves along the feet of that mountain wall, surrounded by a million scattered rocks. Many were shallow, carved by rushing spring melt water, cold from the upper slopes. Some went deeper, but were far too cold, damp and bleak for any kind of reasonable habitation. Now, as snow fell and mist drifted in icy curtains, a face appeared. It was a face that had once been carved by the razors of a savage torturer, a face with only one good eye that worked, the other having been burned out by acid and an unflinching hand. There was tufted stubble on that face in uneven patches, thanks to the criss-cross scarring, and a bleak look to the single eye to match the savage, lifeless scenery, a cynical snarl on scarred lips to make even the most optimistic man look at his own life and future prospects with caution. *This could fucking happen to you*, that face seemed to say. *I was handsome, once. I was happy, once. And then some cunt with an agenda took a razor to my face; took his time, he did. Left me as a proper Pretty Boy. And you know what? You put your foot wrong in this life; you disrespect the wrong people, you fuck over the wrong criminal gangs, and this could happen to you.*

After all... it happened to me.

Narnok stepped from the cave and stopped, head lifted a little as if sniffing the air. He carried his huge axe in one fist, and in the other a length of rope, which he tugged viciously and with some little joy. King Yoon came stumbling from the darkness, blinking rapidly and coughing up phlegm, which he spat. The noise seemed deafening in the midst of the mist, the snow and the boulders.

"Looks clear to me," rumbled Narnok, and stepped down the slope sending rocks tumbling, skittering, clattering.

Trista and Zastarte came next, also blinking but taking deep, exaggerated breaths, glad to be out of the tunnels; glad to be out of the dark. Next came Sameska, lifting his long fingers up to cover his eyes like bars. He limped into the open and stood, lips working noiselessly, nostrils quivering; a tiny keening sound came from deep within him. He was free of his imprisonment. Free of King Yoon's torture cell. For now.

Finally, wary of the elf rat in their company, Dek and Kiki brought up the rear, hands never straying far from sword or knife and looking around themselves, gazing with long years of wariness at the many places an ambush could lurk.

"You think Yoon's soldiers know about this exit?" said Zastarte, taking several steps forward, his neat boots causing nothing but a stirring of pebbles. He frowned in annoyance, noticing the scuffs on the leather. "That just won't do," he muttered.

"Well, they're not here yet, lad," rumbled Narnok.

"There's always time," said Yoon, smoothly, and shook back his hair. Despite his bindings, despite the accumulated filth from days spent under the mountains, despite the dried blood in his nostrils, he set back his shoulders and lifted his head high, eyes challenging. Yoon had a natural haughtiness, an arrogance born of an entire life pampered, an entire world which bowed to do his will.

Narnok laughed, and cuffed him round the ear. "Well, if they show now, lad, we'll give them a fucking good run for their money."

Now it was Yoon who smiled, despite the blow. "Indeed you will. And later, when I have your head on a spike mounted at floor level in one of my many palaces, I will often use you as a latrine as I piss in your bloody eye and gormless slack mouth."

Narnok's smile fell and his axe came up.

"No!" snapped Kiki, stepping forward. She glanced around. "No time for this. It will be night soon. We need to find some shelter."

They marched north through the vast army of boulders, Sameska limping in their midst, an oddly silent member of their group. As they walked, Kiki watched him constantly, the wonder in her eyes at such an unusual creature marred only slightly by the horror stories told to all children about the elf rats during stormy nights after they'd broken crockery during washing up chores.

If you've been a bad girl, they will crawl through the city sewers, crawl up the wall of your house like a slow-moving ivy creeper, and step into your bedroom.

What will they do then, Mam?

Then, it's time for the elf rat to eat naughty little girls with teeth like thorns and hands like brambles!

With an early night darkness fast descending, Narnok spied the edges of woodland and they angled north and east, leaving the plain of huge boulders behind, and wandered across snow laden moorland peppered with rocks and streams. The woods were silent, dark, enclosing, and as the weary party crept under boughs covered in snow, Narnok leading the way, the distant howl of a wolf came like a strangled cry from the north. It dropped off, gradually, into silence, and the Iron Wolves exchanged glances.

"I think we should build a fire," said Dek, glancing north. He was a big man, powerful: a brutal pit fighter. But he knew the reality of starving wolves in winter. Knew their cunning, and knew their savagery. The lonesome howl was not a good omen.

"I agree," said Kiki, quietly.

They moved under the high canopy of leafless oak and ash, and towering pines that swayed softly, snow trickling down like stray sugar. They found a dry place where the snow had not managed to intrude. Narnok dragged three fallen logs into a rough "U" shape, and gathered some rocks in which to build a fire. Sameska sank gratefully to the ground, rough face pale, exhaustion etched like acid into his eyes and movements. The others gathered wood whilst Narnok tied Yoon to a nearby tree trunk by his throat and arms, which were bound behind his back. Yoon sank to the ground, leashed and pale and with eyes full of absolute hate.

"You will die for this, you big ugly fucker."

Narnok rumbled laughter at him, and moved back to the ring of rocks, dumping his pack and pulling free a reasonably sized cooking pot and various utensils, including salt. The pot was black from old use, and he'd picked it up in the storeroom back under the Mountains of Skarandos. He turned it over in his hands, inspecting the quality of the brazing, the old blackened aspect, which spoke of many a fine meal around a hearty campfire. For some reason, the pot cheered Narnok and he was still gazing at the item as Zastarte returned, arms full of kindling.

Zastarte stopped. "Nice of you to help us out, old horse."

"I was just looking at this pot," said Narnok.

"It's a pot," said Zastarte, dumping his load of wood.

"Yeah, but I was just thinking about its history." He looked up, single eye fixing on the dandy.

"Its history," replied Zastarte, voice dry, and level. "The history of a pot?"

"Yeah. You know! Like what kind of life it's led, all the meals it could have cooked and people it entertained. The life of the pot!" He saw Zastarte's face. "It's fucking life, all right? If it could have told some fucking stories, all right?"

"Were there some, you know, mushrooms inside this pot of yours?" said Zastarte. "Big purple and yellow ones? Did you taste one?"

"Hey, fuck off, so-called Prince. I know what I'm talking about."

"Well, I'm glad somebody does. Now, light the fire, there's a good goat. Some of us have serious hunger cramps."

After a bit of fighting with damp kindling, Dek took over from a grumbling, mumbling, bad-tempered Narnok. He had a baby blaze going in minutes, and a roaring fire within fifteen. Narnok was still mumbling and cursing as they added dried beef to the pot, and Trista returned with wild onions and mushrooms (along with a quip from Zastarte: "Hey, now we can all start talking to the pot!", followed by, "I'll fucking cook you in the pot, you dandy bastard!")

As night fell, and another lonely, distant wolf called to the cloud-covered moon, so the fire was roaring and the stew in the pot smelled just fine. They sat around on the logs Narnok had dragged, all except Yoon, who stayed by the tree to which he was shackled, mumbling to himself, cursing them: cursing the Iron Wolves.

Trista ladled stew into wooden bowls, and they ate in silence, all except Sameska who refused the food with a simple hand wave. "I cannot eat meat," came his gentle, lulling voice. "None of my kind eat meat."

"What do you exist on then, lad?"

"We have various ways of feeding," said Sameska, glancing up with his large, yellow eyes, almost shyly. "We eat what the tree provides; be that moss, or fallen leaves and pine needles, or wild mushrooms and onions, chestnuts, acorns, the seeds of the tree."

"Never trust a man who doesn't eat meat," rumbled Narnok, scratching heartily at his crotch. "They're all fucking spineless, weak-kneed and lily-livered. Yellow as a fucking yellow chicken, they are. And I bet you a flagon of whiskey piss…" he gesticulated with his spoon, almost, but not quite, in Zastarte's direction.

"Go on, old goat," smiled Zastarte, taking the bait.

"I *bet* a man who doesn't eat meat, does some of that young boy fancying, I'd wager."

"What does that mean?" said Zastarte.

"You know. Fiddling with boys. Young men. Whatever." He took another hearty bite of stew-softened beef.

"Fiddling? You mean some kind of cheating out of his honestly earned inheritance during a bad game of cards?"

"Noo-*ooo*, you horse dick. Fiddling. You know. Hands down shorts, fingers up the arse, that sort of man-love-man-love-boy ridiculousness." Narnok sat back and licked his spoon, his long red tongue easily equal to that of any horse.

"Don't go there," muttered Kiki, glancing up.

"So then," and he was smiling broadly, "are you telling me," Zastarte said, watching in increasing horror as

Narnok's tongue threatened to swamp the utensil, "that you've never, ever, used that big red flapping tongue of yours to pleasure a man?"

Narnok choked, tongue sucked back in quicker than a striking adder and almost dragging the spoon with it.

Zastarte pressed his advantage. "Are you telling me a Big Man like yourself has never had the joy of taking a cock between his teeth, and sucking another man to the point of pleasurable explosion? Feeling it swell and pump against your tongue, feeling that hot honey squirt into your mouth..."

"Stop!" roared Narnok, stumbling forward, his spoon striking Zastarte on the nose. "Just shut your mouth now! Before I go and get Old Faithful and carve you a new fucking throat smile. I know you're just doing it to wind me up, and yes, you get a reaction from me every time. All I want you to know, *fucker*, is don't tar me with your own man-loving cock, right?"

Zastarte considered this, head to one side. "Narnok, my good man? Don't knock it, until you have tried it."

Narnok scowled. "I thought you cheated the wives of wealthy civil servants, dignitaries and politicians out of their wedding vows, orgasms and jewels, in that particular order"

"I did. I *do*. But that doesn't mean to say I don't enjoy lying with a pretty boy once in a while."

Narnok stared back at him. It was a hard, unforgiving stare. The kind of stare that had seen ten big men back down in a tavern brawl. The kind of stare that sent screeching mud-orcs reeling. The kind of stare Narnok used before using his axe to cut a bastard from crown to crotch in a slippery puddle of his own fucking necrotic bowels.

"You don't."

"I do."

"You fucking don't."

"I fucking do. And fucking enjoy the fucking."

"So… you stick it, you know, up there."

"Yes," smiled Zastarte, finishing his stew and lounging back with ease, hands behind his head. "It can be tight, I'll warrant you, and a little oil helps. But that tightness, Narnok, that clenching around your cock… reminds you of that first hot quim, that first desperation *is she going to let me, is she going to let me, fingers in, hot and slippery, then pushing inside with absolute disbelief at getting that far and her not pushing you away like all the others with a cheeky giggle and a harder than usual playful slap that isn't really a playful slap, but a very fucking real warning she'll go and get her dad and five brothers to break your fucking arms.* It's like that, Narn, all over again. Just close your eyes and enjoy it."

"I… I don't think I could do that. To another man, I mean. I mean, it's just wrong, right? I mean… it's the wrong hole, ain't it? That's a hole for pushing out with, not pulling in with." He stared around, and Kiki and Dek burst out laughing. Trista had a twinkle in her eye, and only Sameska stayed still, head tilted slightly to one side, his confusion obvious.

Narnok growled, but Kiki leapt across to him, firing Zastarte a warning shot harder than iron to *shut the fuck up*. Her hand touched Narnok's lightly, and she looked into his good eye. She gave a little shake of her head, and said, "Don't let him do it to you again. It's warm here by the fire. Don't go storming off."

"Well." Narnok ruffled his feathers, then leaned sideways, addressing Zastarte around Kiki's protective bulk. "You put your little man sausage near me, lover boy, and I'll cut the little prick clean off. Now *that* is Narnok's promise."

"Point taken," smiled Zastarte.

Kiki patted Narnok, and slipped him a small silver flask. "Whiskey. It's Dek's. Don't drink it all. This is dangerous country and these are dangerous times; I still need you focused, axeman."

"Sure thing, Captain."

They bantered around the fire for a while, laughing; the oppression of battle, and the threat of being hung by the very people they were protecting, followed by days under the mountains in oppressive tunnel systems, finally easing from them like garlic through pores, and drifting gradually away. Sameska stayed, sat quietly watching, whilst Yoon crouched against the tree trunk, face in a dark scowl, obviously deeply annoyed by the Iron Wolves' improving mood.

Narnok got up, cut a chunk of bread and cheese using his skinning knife, and carried them over to Yoon. "Here you go, lad. Don't want you starving on us. After all, you're the king of *all Vagandrak, whoooo*!" He was grinning. Dek's whiskey had hit a soft spot.

Yoon took the food and ate it quickly. Then his dark eyes sought out Narnok's orb of iron. "You really don't understand, do you?"

"I think I understand perfectly," said Narnok, and Kiki and Dek came up behind him.

"No, no, no." Yoon shook his head, long dark curls moving about his shoulders and the rich embroidery of his soiled jacket. "You've kidnapped the king. You are guilty of *treason*. I condemned you to *death*."

"Yeah, you back-stabbing cunt," snapped Narnok. "We fucking fought for you, we saved the wall at Desekra against the mud-orcs, against that bitch-queen Orlana; we offer up our lives on a plate and you fucking try and hang us! Some king you turned out to be."

"It was... necessary," said Yoon, stiffly. "I had greater plans with Orlana, and you got in the way. The point is, my friendly little Narnok One-Eye and his band of incredibly stupid mercenary *cunts*, the point *is* that the elf rat over there who you have so happily rescued from my secret prison, is helping to plan an invasion of Vagandrak; I was in discussions with Orlana. She did not want to conquer Vagandrak. She simply wanted passage to the Plague Lands and our little fortress stood in the way. I was in negotiations to open the gates and provide passage, and you came stumbling along and ruined everything! Now, you have committed the most vile treason and, get this *Iron fucking Wolves*, put the country in far more peril than it was already."

"That is so much horse shit," said Kiki, finally. "Orlana's mud-orcs were slaughtering our people. Your men. *Your soldiers*. There were no talks to begin with. No groups of politicians sat around in war council trying to prevent war. Orlana the Horse Lady came and attacked the fortress. It was that simple. Now you're trying to twist it because some other game was being played."

Yoon looked sly for just a moment. It was a glint in his dark eyes that hinted at, despite his veritable insanity, a cunning that ran deeper than any twisted politician.

"The elf rats plan to attack," he said, gently. He pointed at Sameska, who looked suddenly vulnerable and terribly, terribly frightened. "That bastard is an elf rat spy for

Daranganoth, the Elf Rat Ring. This will be the war, Iron Wolves. *This* will be the battle to end all battles. They will pour like a plague from their lands in the far northeast, Zalazar, beyond the White Lion Mountains. And when they come, it will be a flood. When they come, none shall stand in their path."

"And you know this?" said Kiki.

"Tortured it out of that little quivering bastard," said Yoon, gesturing to Sameska.

Suddenly the elf rat, snarling and spitting, scrambled across the logs and leapt at Yoon, claws raking for the King's eyes. Narnok interposed himself, serious and big and holding his double-headed axe like he meant business. Dek and Kiki grabbed at Sameska, then swayed back as blackthorn claws like razors slashed towards their throats.

"You liar!" snarled Sameska, filled with a fury so huge he was shaking like an earthquake. "LIAR! You people, you humans, you drove our race from Vagandrak thousands of years ago, and then deleted us from your history books, erased us, so it appeared we had not even existed! Your ancestors hunted us, killed us, hundreds of thousands of elves were slaughtered and the poor remains driven into the White Lion Mountains to die in the ice and snow. But we found our way through treacherous passes, many thousands more dying of cold or tumbling down into the bottomless valleys filled with ice and blood." Now, Sameska backed away from Yoon and Narnok. Kiki had her sword out, Dek his hands splayed wide as if trying to pacify a hot-headed fist fight. Sameska looked around, and no longer was he a weak and tortured individual; now, suddenly, in the blink of an eye, he appeared incredibly powerful, containing the strength of root and heartwood, sap flowing through his twisted veins. Sameska may have been tortured by Yoon, but he had not been broken. Not by a very long bow-shot.

"Kill it," croaked Yoon, suddenly full of panic. "You must kill it!" he screeched.

"You forced us into the place of poison, away from our Heart Trees, away from the Motherwood." Sameska was hissing and spitting. "In Zalazar the land is poisoned beyond repair. It is a terrible, haunted, evil place." And Kiki realised the elf rat was addressing her, large yellow eyes almost pleading. "We were forced to join with the twisted, blackened, poisoned and poisonous trees just to survive; an elf is connected to the earth by more than blood and bone. You should know this, *Shamathe*..."

Kiki gasped.

And then Sameska turned and with incredible agility, incredible strength, bounded across the camp. Trista and Zastarte had weapons drawn, formed a wall, but in a blur Sameska was beyond them, both Iron Wolves knocked back, whirling around, Zastarte gasping, sword cutting out at something that was no longer there.

Silence fell like ash. The fire crackled. A log shifted, making a banging sound.

Yoon gave a low, deep laugh. "You've done it now. You're like a group of lively village idiots, re-enacting a tragedy in the village square for your supper and a hard bed and even harder fuck with the local syphilitic whore. But the only tragedy is *your* lack of understanding of the real fucking world. The only tragedy, my hopeless friends, is that you're allowed to continue. Thankfully, when Captain Dokta sorts his shit out and arrives, we can offer you thanks on behalf of the slaughtered people of Vagandrak."

"Big words for a little man, tied up," said Narnok, moving close.

Yoon tried to back away, seeing murderous intent in Narnok's single iron eye, but the tree was in the way. Kiki appeared at the axeman's side and gave the monarch a bleak smile.

"When Dokta arrives, we'll be waiting for him. No matter how many men he brings. My guess is he'll travel light and fast in the hope of catching up, intercepting us. It will be a pleasure, King Yoon, I assure you. But for now, I really do suggest you keep your flapping, pessimistic mouth shut. Or maybe next time, I won't intervene when Narnok here wants to smash out all your fucking teeth in an attempt to silence you."

Everybody slept. Kiki lay awake, staring up at the pines high above and the occasional flake of snow that penetrated their dense canopy. Dek and Narnok followed Sameska's trail into the woods, but soon lost the wood elf; the wood elf *rat*. As Dek so eloquently put it, "He's a fucking *elf*. Bonded to the trees and the heartwood. How will we find him in here?" Kiki felt reasonably safe. She had a funny feeling Sameska contained an incredible power, possibly similar to the *Shamathe* power she herself carried, which... could be unleashed... when a need for massive destruction was at hand.

Kiki shivered, but not through the cold.

The elf rats plan to attack... This will be the war, Iron Wolves. This will be the battle to end all battles. They will pour like a plague from their lands in the far northeast, Zalazar, beyond the White Lion Mountains. And when they come, it will be a flood. When they come, none shall stand in their path.

She rolled from beneath the thin blanket and, grabbing a makeshift poker, a wood with a pointed, blackened end, she stoked the embers of the fire and tossed on another couple of logs. Soon, heat was blossoming from the burning wood. It crackled softly, glowed like an old friend in an alcoholic embrace. Kiki warmed herself for a while, but the chill in her soul was nothing that an external heat source could ever cure. She glanced over at Yoon, and spat into the fire. The bastard was still keeping facts to himself. Still playing his *xazenga* cards close to his chest in the hope of cleaning up across the whole game board. Well. Kiki didn't care for his fucking politics. She didn't care for his kingship. And maybe, just maybe, for the first time in Vagandrak history, it was time to put his wife – the queen – on the fucking throne.

Kiki stood and stretched, a long, feline movement, then moved away from the campfire. Away from the flames, it was suddenly, deeply cold and she gave a shiver from the core of her body. And then he was there, wrapping a blanket around her. She said nothing, and as he placed the blanket around her shoulders he stayed there for a few moments, holding it in place, sharing his body heat.

Kiki walked a few more steps out into the dark, and the snow cool of the forest. Long shadows danced. The blacks were blacker than ink. The scent of pine was strong, mesmerising. Like a drug.

"How do you feel?"

She turned, and stared up into Dek's face. To some, she knew, he was nothing more than a brutal thug. After the Iron Wolves had folded, after the glory and the honour and the prizes, Dek had bounced from meaningless dockland job to meaningless warehouse job. Finally, an argument led to a fight outside a tavern, the Fighting Cocks, and after a short brutal bout where Dek demolished the resident bare-knuckle champion, the landlord of the Fighting Cocks had come up with a proposition. Now, a renowned pit fighter – huge, heavily muscled, with small dark eyes and a head that constantly lost a fight with a razor – Dek was scarred and badly tattooed in places, with some of his tattoos received after drunken sessions, and some even only half-finished. His carcass was not one that inspired instant respect; well, not as much as his scarred knuckles and the natural broad shoulders, narrow hips and easy gait of the born fighter. But to Kiki, *to Kiki*, he was so much more. So much deeper than a fucked-up pit fighter with no family, a history of betrayal and nowhere to go. And, worst (or best) of all, she knew he loved her. Through and through. Right down to the core. He loved her like no other human being on this miserable fucking planet had ever loved her before.

"Dek," she said.

"Let me just hold you a while."

"That's… good. Yeah."

They stayed like that, his arms around her from behind, his chin nuzzled into her neck. She sensed him inhaling her musk. The scent of her hair. She grinned. Now *that's* not been washed in a long time. Still probably had mud-orc blood and brains lodged in the matted strands from Desekra's walls before…

before.

She blinked, and it was gone. The *Shamathe*. The powers of the Equiem. Dark magick. Old magick.

He reached up, took hold of her shoulders with surprising tenderness for one so brutal. He turned her around to face him, and she was looking down.

"Kiki."

"Yes, Dek?"

"I have something to say."

"Will I like it?"

"Probably not... I love you."

Kiki paused, and his hand came up, finger pressing against her lips. "I know I've told you that before. And I know I was a bad man. I know I did terrible things. Not just killing your friend that time, although I was drunk and she fucking deserved it, the carping fish bitch; but... the other things. The women. The woman. Narnok's wife. I know I had you. I know you were mine, body and soul. I know I was sucked into a web of deceit and lies and violence; set up like a piece of cheese in the centre of a steel-fanged rat trap. I took the bait, like the weak fuck I am. And I suffered the consequences. We all did."

"Dek..."

"No. Wait. Let me speak. I fucked up. I was more stupid than the village idiot after ten pints of Old Bowel Rot. And I suffered. You suffered. We all suffered. But I'm a different man now, and I'm a different man living a different life. We live in dangerous, violent times, in a time of change, of upheaval, of battle, and of war. Back there in the Prison Box, when we faced down those white-skinned bastards... well. I was proud to have you by my side. But I was ashamed. Ashamed you didn't know the deep roots of my love for you. I can live with dying, Kiki. But I can't live with dying until you know how I feel."

She lifted her head and stared into his dark eyes. "I know," she said, gently.

"I betrayed you. But I am not that person any longer. I am yours, body and soul, forever, until we die, until we are condemned to the Chaos Halls and tortured for eternity. But I am yours." He took her hand and kissed her skin. "Yours, Kiki. Until the stars die."

Kiki leaned up, and kissed him on the cheek.

"That's a nice fuck-off." He grinned.

"Not at all."

"Then what is it?"

"You could have just asked me for sex. It's… been a long time."

"This isn't about sex," he said.

"I know," she said, and punched him playfully on the arm.

Dek stared into her eyes. "What are you saying, Kiki?"

"I'm saying I love you, Dek. I always have. I always will. I can still hate you for betraying me. I can hate you for betraying Narnok. I can hate you for fucking his wife, for sticking your tongue into her cunt and her groaning her way to orgasm… but hate only gets you so far. And you know what, mate? Love gets you further."

Dek leaned down, and touched his lips to Kiki's. She responded, and they stood in the cold, snow-bound forest, enjoying the gentility of a kiss that should have belonged on the lips of lovers two decades younger. Then Kiki took Dek's hand, and led him out into the forest, and under random beams of moonlight, removed her clothing to stand naked before him.

Dek groaned, a low animal sound, and he stepped forward, but her hand pressed against his chest.

"I've shown you mine. Now it's your turn."

Dek undressed in a frenzy and, naked, his cock huge and eager, stepped in towards her. He licked lips dry with nerves and gave a little laugh.

"What is it?" she said, moving in close, hands touching his skin, head dipping, teeth biting him just a little.

"I can face down the biggest fucking mud-orc in the world, and not feel as much fear as this. This, now."

Kiki lifted her head, features softened by strands of moonlight. "There's nothing to be afraid of here," she said, and guided him towards the soft, cool, welcoming forest carpet.

ZANNE

They travelled north. The snow had stopped. A biting wind filled with ice needles drove into them, making each man and woman lower their heads, wishing for hats and gloves as they pushed onwards towards the nearest city on Dek's battered, tattered map: Zanne.

"I fucking hate Zanne," mumbled Narnok.

"Why's that, axeman?" asked Dek, genuinely interested.

"It reminds me of worse days. It reminds me of bad days."

"Such as?"

"Maybe I don't want to talk about it." Narnok threw Dek a scowl.

"Come on, Narnok. We're old friends. Maybe I'm here to help."

"What, liked you helped fuck my wife? Like you helped split us up? Liked you helped channel her towards a friendly torturer who removed my eye and fucked up my face? I've seen enough of your help to last me a lifetime, Dek. Why don't you fuck off and grease up your new and yet old pussy. I'm sure she's enjoying it. Sure sounded like it out in the forest last night."

Dek's jaw clamped shut, and he cut sideways, leaving Narnok walking alone and tugging along the uncomplaining figure of King Yoon behind, like a dog on a leash.

"Trouble?" said Kiki, smiling until she received no response.

"Nothing I can't deal with."

"Is he moaning about his wife again?"

"Oh yes."

"He'll never get over it, Dek. Something you're going to have to learn to live with. You betrayed him. He hates you for it. Can't blame the man for that."

"It wasn't my fault," said Dek.

"Have you heard yourself? Did your cock force itself inside her quim? Did she drug you and rape you?"

"No. All right. It was my fault. I was weak."

"We're all weak," said Kiki, remembering the lure of the honey-leaf and the need to slit a person's throat just to get that bitter sweet drug under her tongue. Nothing mattered anymore. Not people. Not family. Not friends. Although in all honesty, her family were shit and dead. Especially Suza. Especially *that* bitch. Kiki shuddered. The lure of the honey-leaf was still strong; and yet she had passed away from the physical addiction. General Dalgoran had helped her with that. Helped her *overcome* that, God bless his suicide-soul. And she realised, now, with a gradual understanding, that the addiction was not in the chemical, not in the drug in her blood. It was in her head. In her mind. And even without the need for chemical stimulant – even *without* the need to take the shit to feel normal again – it was still there. Gods. The honey-leaf was still there like a long lost bastard brother coming back to regain his shitty undeserved inheritance.

Still there. Always would be. Would haunt her until her dying day. Would *ensnare her* until her dying day; or at least, until the day it forced her to die.

Forever gone. Forever lost. Forever loved.

Kiki found tears on her cheeks, and she wiped them away, and Dek asked her if she was okay, and she wiped that away as well. Some things you had to suffer on your own. Some things weren't for fucking sharing.

"Look at that," said Narnok, and they stopped, snow stuck to their boots, the sun hanging bloated and orange and low in a bleak winter sky streaked with blood.

"What?"

And then they all stared.

It was a copse of trees, presumably oak. But each one was twisted and blackened. As if the whole woodland had been strafed with a series of rapid lightning blasts in some unholy storm from angry and belligerent gods.

"That's unusual," said Trista, taking an uncertain step forward. She stopped when Narnok placed his hand on her shoulder.

"Leave it."

"What's wrong?"

"They are wrong. Those trees. Look, they've not been struck by lightning. Some of the leaves are still green. Some of the ends of branches are still... living. It's as if they've been poisoned and it's worked its way through them from the inside out."

Kiki approached, but stopped short. The snow had melted around the base of the trees, and a thick, black tar was seeping up through the soil. It smelled rancid, corrupt, and Kiki backed away. "We need to get away from this place."

"What caused it?" said Narnok.

"I don't know. I've never seen anything like that in my entire life."

"It begins," said Yoon, smiling up from under dark curls.

"What does?" said Kiki, jaw tight, muscles rigid in her cheeks giving her a stern look: the look of the Captain of the Iron Wolves.

"The pollution. I told you. The elf rats are coming. And you just let one of the most important ones escape. What was he? Sorcerer? Acolyte? Spy for the Elf Rat King?" Yoon shook his head. "I had him ready to spill his information. It took a lot of work. A lot of effort with blade and fire. But we'd damn near broken him. You waded in with your misguided sense of justice, of right and wrong. Tell that to the children you find crucified on twisted oaks like *those*."

Kiki turned away, and Narnok gave Yoon a slap to silence him, but his words bit home and Kiki rubbed at weary eyes and placed her hand against her chest, where she felt the echo of her second heart.

They marched throughout the day, stopping mid-afternoon for a swift meal of dried beef. The landscape was rolling hills, white under the fresh snow, and there were few houses this far out from the high-walled protection of the city of Zanne.

They found an old crofter's cabin nestled between two hills, built from rough logs and containing nothing more than two pallet beds with rough blankets, a rough-sawn pine table and crude stools. As was the tradition in the Vagandrak wilds, a fire had already been laid in the grate and Narnok discovered a generous wood store covered by waterproof tarpaulin at the rear of the cabin. It began snowing again, and as darkness fell they soon had the fire roaring and Zastarte cooked them a fine broth using barley, onions and chicken stock. As the others gradually fell asleep after a hard day of marching, Dek and Kiki sat at the table and, by the light of the fire, studied Dek's old map.

"How far, do you reckon?"

"Another day. We'll reach Zanne by nightfall, or shortly afterwards. I'm looking forward to a hot bath, a foaming ale and a night away from that snoring bastard." He gestured towards Narnok.

"What are we going to do about this elf rat, Sameska?"

Dek shrugged. "Not much we can do, Keeks. I still think our bastard monarch is holding out on us – and don't buy into his guilt trip. We did what we thought was right. And let's be honest, torturing that creature should never have been an option. We should have left that shit behind in the dark ages. A good clean battle, yes; extracting information using fire and blade? Evil acts by evil men, Kiki."

"You always did have an honourable soul, Dek."

"I try to be a good man." Kiki stared into the dark eyes, studied the tattoos and the huge scarred knuckles, from breaking bones in the fighting pits. "But people keep bringing me their aggravation. All I want is a simple life. A wife. Children." He sighed, staring into her eyes. "But the horse shit keeps on coming. I suppose that's just the way it is."

"When we get to Zanne, we're going to have to do something with Yoon. We can't be dragging him around the whole country."

"I suggest imprisonment. But what then?"

"We need to get control of the army, and reinforce Desekra Fortress. I still think that bitch Orlana will be back. I have this strange feeling in my bones."

"I wanted to ask you something."

"Yes?" The flames from the fire made her face glow, her dark eyes glitter. She smiled at Dek, and reached across, putting her hand on his. "You can ask me anything."

"That thing you did. Back at Desekra."

The smile faltered on Kiki's face, and she took a deep breath. "You've all been good to me. I expected a thousand questions after I..." She rubbed wearily at her face.

"Kiki. What was it you actually *did*?"

"I thought I was dying. I had a growth, according to surgeons, beside my heart. Too close to operate. I was going to die. What the medical professionals didn't realise was that it wasn't a growth; it was my second heart; the heart of the *Shamathe*."

"Dark magick?"

"Not dark magick. Just magick. The energies of the planet, Dek. The energy, the *mana* contained within every rock and tree and mountain. A *Shamathe* doesn't create or destroy, they channel energy, or change the state of matter using channels and procedures defined by the ancient Equiem. It's extremely difficult to explain. Like golden filaments that run through the world, Dek. And back there at Desekra during the attack by the mud-orcs, when it became clear we could not destroy Orlana, even under the influence of our curse, then I followed the threads, sought guidance from the Equiem deep down within the earth. I found the warren of mines from when the fortress itself was built. Many were man-made excavations, but many were natural, formed by high-pressure underwater streams and rivers coming down from high up in the Mountains of Skarandos. I created a shift, began to build the energies contained deep down in those caves and mines. Have you ever seen that game of skill storytellers often play in taverns after the storytelling is done? The little wooden blocks, all stacked in complicated patterns, and people have to remove one at a time until the whole thing collapses? Well that's all I did. I explored, I found the right leverage and I redirected energy. An incredible amount of energy, I grant you. But it brought the whole fucking system down, and sucked the mud-orcs and Orlana down with it."

"So you are *Shamathe*. You control the energies of the Equiem?"

"Yes." Her voice was soft and she took both his hands across the table. "But sometimes, it just isn't there. Most of the time, I control nothing. I can see nothing. Do nothing. If anything, Dek, *it* controls me. I feel like a puppet doing another's bidding." She fell silent for a few moments. "Right here and now, I could not summon the collapse like I did at Desekra. I close my eyes and search and the power simply isn't within me. So don't be afraid, Dek. Don't think I'll suddenly send fireballs hurtling from the heavens to fry you into a soup." She smiled, but her eyes were hard. Concerned.

"I am not frightened," said Dek softly.

"This power inside me. This… *thing* that is from somewhere else. It doesn't make me different to any other woman, Dek. I still think and feel and love the same. I'm still here for you."

"I was lucky to find you." He lifted her hands and kissed them.

"It's good to be back with you, Dek. Let's keep it right this time, yeah?"

Dek nodded, averting his eyes, but then looking back with renewed strength. "Yes, my love," he said.

After leaving the cabin how they found it, with a freshly laid fire in the grate, they pushed another hard march over steep, undulating hills that fell away from the Mountains of Skarandos like great rolling waves. Sometimes there were narrow stone paths to follow, but most of the time the landscape was rough, tall winter grass, often buried under snow, and harsh drops down to fast flowing streams filled with icy melt water. Narnok complained about his cold ears, his cold fingers and toes, and the burden of dragging a silent and bleak Yoon after him. Dek offered to take the leash, but Narnok gave him a withering look as if to say: boy, you haven't got the technique, I have; I'm the one in charge of our stinking king, and that's simply the way it's going to remain.

Trista walked in permanent, icy silence, her cold eyes constantly scanning for signs of the enemy. But then, she'd be the first to agree with any comments about her being an ice queen; it was an image she reinforced at every opportunity. In contrast, Prince Zastarte was in fine form, quipping about the sway of Trista's buttocks and their comparison to a particularly fine donkey he had once ridden. Her sword was out faster than the flush to her cheeks, and Zastarte had to dance away from its flashing tip.

They pushed hard, and by nightfall saw the distant, looming black walls of Zanne. Most cities in Vagandrak had some kind of fortification, which spoke of the countries' often violent, bloody history and various civil wars and uprisings against the monarchy. There were battlements, low crenellations for archer fire, but nothing like the scale of the massive Desekra Fortress, which had been built, essentially, as an impossible barrier for any enemy to overcome.

Zanne was, to all intents and purposes, an unwelcoming city no matter which direction a person approached. And despite the dreary black walls, which could sometimes be seen decorated by the corpses of noose-hung criminals, it also had a powerful and not too complimentary reputation to contend with. Zanne was not only a drug haven for honey-leaf smugglers, peddlers and addicted users who felt they could partake with impunity, despite the honey-leaf being illegal under Vagandrak law and outlawed by the Church; it was also a city almost wholly run by the Red Thumb Gangs, and indeed, an uneasy truce existed within those high black walls between the gang's members and the City Watch and King's Guard. The western quarter, known as the Haven, was an area where the Watch and the Guards did not venture, by mutual consent. The Barrier Road, as it was known, was heavily patrolled – but everything west of that was given over to the Red Thumbs on the understanding they kept the rest of the city relatively free of their presence. In reality, it didn't work as smoothly as that, for many Red Thumbs operated independently of the core Lodge, but it gave the Guards and Watch reason to be exceptionally brutal when a Red Thumb was caught robbing a merchant or politician in the more civilised east and south quadrants of the city.

The Iron Wolves, with Yoon in tow, closed on the southern Royal Gate as the gloomy grey sky gradually turned to black. To the west, a dying sun stuttered like a burned out candle allowing a few violet rays to wash the curve of the planet. After that, darkness seeped in and night fell like a crossbow-shot dove.

Dek was the first to call a halt, Kiki next to him, and the others followed. The walls were close now, huge and towering. Dek looked up, head tilted to one side, frowning.

"What is it?" said Kiki.

"Last time I visited this armpit of a city, it was a damn sight noisier."

"Eh, lad?" boomed Narnok, staring at the pit fighter.

"Quiet, Narn. There's something wrong."

"Nothing wrong I can see, lad. What are you moaning about? Come on, let's get inside – Yoon wrapped in a blanket so no bastard spots him – and see if there isn't a soft bed, hot bath water and good flagon of whiskey to be found."

"Wait," said Dek, and turned to them all. "Does that sound like the bustling hum of a city to you?"

The Iron Wolves stood in a line, silent now, heads cocked, *listening*. The wind breathed a soft low moan. Snow scurried across the road leading to the Royal Gates. An ominous silence seemed to roll towards them, and they realised Dek was right. Zanne was a big place, with tens of thousands of inhabitants. There should have been shouts, chatter, laughter from taverns. The low-level *hum* of a city closing down for a winter's night. But instead, it was eerie and desolate.

"The gates are shut," observed Kiki. "Is that standard procedure come nightfall?"

"I… don't know," said Dek. "Last time I was here, they had huge lit braziers outside the gates. Beacons to guide weary travellers home. Look." He pointed to where two huge iron drums stood, one each side of the closed iron and oak gate. "No fire, though."

"Maybe the Fire Master is drunk?" grinned Narnok.

"No," said Dek. "This is something else. Let us approach in silence, and see if we can gain entry."

They moved forward, drawing weapons, slowly, each footstep a tentative test of the ground as if they feared it might open up and swallow them. Something was deeply wrong. A chord was playing out of tune in their collective Iron Wolf souls.

Darkness tumbled down around them.

Approaching the gate, Kiki reached out, pushed hard. They were locked and barred from the inside. She glanced left and right, then up around the huge iron arch which emanated cold and the stink of old fish oil. There were no levers, no handles or winches, and no inspection hole in the gate. Just oak and iron, black and unbending. Like a big *fuck off.*

"Look at that," said Narnok, voice curiously subdued as if the huge silent walls of the city of Zanne had sucked away some of his life-force; some of his natural, huge lung volume. He trotted forward and fingered a small vine that was crawling its way up the edge of the arch. Only this vine wasn't green, and hadn't been immediately noticeable. It was black. The black of the abyss. And each leaf was curiously shaped, bent and curled, as if fighting itself. Distorted. Twisted. Deviant.

"There's nobody home," said Zastarte, voice soft and light and musical. His narrow blade was steady in his hand, but Kiki saw the fear in his eyes. This whole situation was odd. Just deeply wrong.

Narnok lifted his hands, and cupped them to his mouth. Kiki slapped them away with a fast audible *slap* that left Narnok standing in shock, eyes wide and falling quickly to a thunderous scowl on his savagely scarred face.

"What you do that for?" he snarled.

"No shouting," hissed Kiki. "You want to fucking announce us to every man and his cunt? Keep your mouth shut and your hellos to yourself. This ain't a fucking reunion for old soldiers. This is odd, Narnok."

"We need to find another way in," said Trista. "Find out why they're locked down. Is it something to do with this bastard being kidnapped?" She kicked Yoon, but he did not respond. "Hey? Hey you? Is this what happens when a king of the realm gets kidnapped by the fuckers he tried to hang? Do they lock down the cities and search them from wall to wall, arsehole to scrotum?"

Yoon looked at Trista, then slowly and deliberately, spat on the ground.

"I think we should just bang on the door," said Narnok.

"Try not to think, sweetie." Trista patted him on the shoulder. "Leave that to the pretty ones."

"Hey, fuck you, bitch…" but Kiki was there, a flash of sudden movement, both hands on his shoulders, face on, braced against him, staring into his good eye and shaking her head with a narrow smile.

"No, Narnok. Not here. Not now. Control yourself. We need you. *I* need you obeying orders, soldier."

Narnok considered this. Then said, "Yes, Captain."

"I know a way in." They turned and looked at Dek, and he seemed suddenly sheepish. "Last time I was here, was for a pit fight. Against a big rabid bastard, Black Horse Jonny they called him. Dirty bastard. Teeth, nails, ripping off of bollocks. He thought it was all fair. Well. I did him good."

"What did you do to him?"

Dek inspected his dirt-encrusted fingernails, and gave a little cough. "I killed him. Didn't mean to. Just a fight, after all, right? A fight for money. Would never want to kill a man for that, would I?" He looked up. Everybody was staring at him impassively.

"Go on," said Kiki.

"Delivered this right hook, broke his fucking neck. He must have had a weak spine or something. I broke his neck and he lay there screaming something rotten. Couldn't shut him up, we couldn't. And then the City Watch came flooding in and we had to do a runner, and I was teamed up with Bad Grolf and Lazy Wilf, and they led me down into the sewers. Showed me a way out of the city." Dek looked up, then back over his shoulder. "There's an air vent, over that way somewhere. We had to smash a lock, but we got out of Zanne and headed for fucking Drakerath where a pit fighter can lose himself in anonymity and whiskey."

"Can you find it?"

"Sure, as long as you don't mind getting covered in shit."

"Sometimes," said Kiki, softly, "it feels like my whole life is covered in shit."

Dek led them out into the darkness. It began to snow again, and the Iron Wolves were chilled to the bone and beyond. They stood around like useless idiots as Dek searched, occasionally glancing back at the dark, silent walls of the dark, silent city. Trista herself shivered to the centre of her being.

Something bad in there, whispered a voice in her soul. Something real bad.

After an hour, with the others fanning out to help, they found the narrow aperture of which Dek had spoken. It had a thick metal grille, barely big enough for an adult to squeeze through, which was jealously guarded by a thick padlock that, under Dek's expert hands, felt substantial indeed.

"Narnok, need your brute force here."

Narnok puffed out his chest and, dropping to his belly, took a hold on the thick iron. "It's a big one," he said.

"I bet that's what all the boys say," grinned Zastarte.

Narnok threw him an evil glare, lost in the darkness.

Snow tumbled down, and the world was silent and dark and cool. Narnok took hold of the padlock in both hands and squeezed and pulled and tore; but it would not come apart. He tried again and again, but it was just too strong, even for his mighty muscles. Finally, exasperated, he stood up and snapped at Dek, "Give me your jerkin."

"Why?"

"Just do it."

"No, fuck off, it's freezing. Use your own jerkin."

Mumbling and cursing, a red-faced Narnok struggled out of his thick fur and wrapped it around the gleaming double heads of his axe. "I'm sorry, baby," he whispered, kissing the blades, "you were meant for more noble tasks than this," and hoisting the weapon above his head, he brought it down with consummate skill and murderous rage. The padlock held. Again he hammered his axe into the iron, and again, and again. Until, under the tenth blow, there came a massive dull metallic *crack* and Narnok grinned around like a toddler winning a pissing contest.

"Done it," he said.

Dek scrambled down, and threw aside the mangled block of iron. Then he strained, and with a squealing of rusted hinges, the grate came up. He looked up, grinning, then saw the serious looks on their faces, and the smile dropped.

"Who's first?"

"You are fools," said King Yoon, sombrely. He was kneeling in the snow, staring forlornly at the ground.

"Shut that maggot up," snapped Kiki.

"You do not know what lies beyond!" wailed King Yoon, suddenly grabbing the rope around his throat and trying desperately to scramble backwards. "You will all die! You will all be doomed!"

"You know what?" snapped Kiki, suddenly. "I've had enough of this fucking horse shit." She advanced on Yoon and he crawled back fast, hands and boots kicking up snow. But he wasn't fast enough and Kiki loomed over him, a snarl on her lips, hate in her iron dark eyes. Her intentions seemed obvious and even Trista tensed, licking her lips, eyes growing just that little bit wider.

"No," said Yoon, lifting his hands. "No!"

"Is that what Sameska said when you came at him with razors and fire?" snarled Kiki, all femininity suddenly gone, all slipping away in anger and a rage which highlighted just *why* she had earned the rank of captain in this, the greatest elite force ever created by the Kings and Queens of Vagandrak.

"No, please," whimpered the King, and for a long, long drawn out minute it seemed as if his will had been broken; stretched out like a piece of elastic, getting thinner and thinner and thinner until, at last, finally, with one short, sharp action, it snapped and left the mind within the shell, a broken fucking useless thing.

Kiki's sword hacked down, and cut through the rope.

King Yoon stared at her, slack jawed and useless.

"Go on," she said. "Fuck off. I can't look at you any longer."

"Don't let him *go*," snapped Narnok.

"Yes, I *will* let him go. He's no use to us. He's just a fucking embuggerance; he saps morale, and let's be honest, who hasn't wondered, if he got free, would we all wake up dead with a dagger in the kidneys? No. He can fuck off with this promise." She fixed her iron gaze on the King; on *her* king. "Yoon." She lowered herself, and delivered an awesome stinging slap that rocked his head from east to west. "Yoon!"

"Yes. *yes*?" He gazed up at her, eyes as wide as if he'd spent a month on the honey-leaf.

"Go on. Go away. And if I ever see you again, I will put my sword through your guts."

"I can go?"

"Yes. Go."

Silently, Yoon rose. He stared at Kiki for a long time, and for a moment she thought he would launch himself at her. Then his features softened.

"Do you know what's in there?" he said, softly, words little more than a chill winter breeze. "Inside the city?"

"Yes. I think so." Kiki's face was impassive. Carved from stone.

King Yoon's eyes glittered with a sudden, burning intelligence. "If this thing is truly happening, Kiki, Kikellya Mandasayard, Captain of the Iron Wolves – if we are both right, *if* the darkness has come to overshadow Vagandrak with evil, then there's only one thing you can do. Sameska told me things, back in the Box. About the elf rats, their history, their heritage, their *magick*. About their homeland beyond Zalazar. Kiki. Deep within the Mountains of the Moon there is a place, a fortress born of elf rat sorcery; this place is known as the White Towers. And inside the White Towers lies the Elf Heart. That, my girl, is the only thing that can save us when the elf rats come back..." and then he turned, and with the severed piece of rope flapping around his throat, scuttled off into the darkness, limping away into the snow, into the chill blizzard. Into a wilderness full of hungry wolves.

"He may die out there," said Trista, voice soft. "In fact, I'm pretty sure he *will* die out there."

"Fuck him. He asked for it. Because he'll fucking die if he stays here," promised Kiki. Then she turned to Dek. "Soldier. You seem to know the way. We need to get inside that city. We need to find out what the hell is going on."

Dek saluted her, with a grin. "Iron Wolves. Follow me, into the city. Zanne waits for us with a big smile and open arms."

"Open bowels, more like," snorted Zastarte.

"Yeah, that as well," said Dek, and, with a step, dropped down into the darkness of the sewer outlet.

They moved through the darkness.

The sewers of Zanne were old. Ancient. Far older than the exterior walls suggested, and harking back to a different time, an older world when a different race ruled not just Zanne, but Vagandrak in its entirety. The walls were fashioned from uneven black bricks, crumbling in many places, and the Iron Wolves passed beneath high brick arches, ornate in an industrial fashion, displaying unexpected pride from previous architects and builders.

After all, why have ornate and decorative sewers? But these sewer tunnels contained a brutal kind of art. Urban; filled with decay; strangely decadent, and dark, and beautiful.

Not so the stench. The sewers were still operational, and Narnok mouthed his disgust loud and long, whining until Kiki hissed at him to be quiet. Zastarte sprayed a little perfume on a silk handkerchief and held it over his mouth, cursing the sewage ruining his finely tailored trousers. The rest just waded in grim silence.

The elf rats, whispered the words in Kiki's mind. Who are they? Where do they come from? Are they as old as they claim? Were they really driven out by Vagandrak's people of old? King Yoon's ancestors? Had they come back now for vengeance? To reclaim their land? Or was it something more sinister they planned?

"There's something up ahead," said Dek, slowing his pace. The water – the *sewage* – was knee deep and stank like something horrid. Dek coughed as he spoke, almost vomiting, as thankfully *unidentifiable* lumps bumped against his knees.

They stopped as a group, squinting into the gloom, silent, staying their movements, swords held poised and ready. Narnok's twin axe blades glinted like evil demon butterflies.

The tunnels were narrow, narrow enough so that only two could walk abreast and would probably be hampered, and hamper one another, in a combat situation. *Probably*. Kiki grinned at that, a baring of skull teeth in a face drawn and tense. She had thought the weight loss was because of the cancer in her chest, a tumour near her heart; but that was now so much horse shit. *That* fucking abomination was her *Shamathe* heart. Her second heart. Beating with a second rhythm; like an echo. Like a… dark twin.

Hello, whispered Suza, sliding into Kiki's mind like a corrupt cock into her quim. She shivered violently and felt suddenly sick to her core. The shudder came from the centre of her being, working its way outwards, gradually, carefully, and making sure she felt it through every single atom of her being.

What do you want?

I want to help. Suza sounded… odd. And Kiki could remember her pouting, fake pretty features scrunched up, lips enlarged as if ready to deliver a big kiss. Hell, she'd taken enough boyfriends from Kiki. The self-centred, *notice me,* bitch. But did that come before or after the fire? Kiki frowned, metaphorically, in the cave of her own mind. It was all so foggy and jumbled. All so confusing. Because… *because* Kiki thought Suza was only a child when she died.

I want to help you remember.

I already remember.

I want you to remember more, *you fucking whore. You wouldn't give me the time of day when my own fucking baby was on the chopping block and I suffered, suffered worse than I can ever remember; I had trauma, you evil cunt, trauma like you could never* fucking believe! The last was delivered in a sudden pitch-raised scream that Kiki had not anticipated, and she winced, as if physically slapped.

You made that up, Suza. You were never with child.

I had a fucking baby! And it nearly died. It did die. And if it didn't die, then it fucking should have. She started to sob, head held low and cupped in hands wet with tears, too many tears; eternal tears. With Suza there were always tears. Always bloody tears. It was something you got used to.

You said you want to help. How?

I will help. I will help you, Kiki, help you overcome the problems you are about to face.

Problems?

The elf rats.

Kiki felt herself go just that little bit cold.

What do you know about the elf rats?

Suza paused. Kiki felt the hiatus, and it blew like a cold wind over a grave she had yet to inhabit. Dead roses rustled in the breeze, their scent gone, their stems brown and lifeless. Kiki looked up slowly, and saw Suza, the sun to her back, her face in shadow like it always had been. It was as if she wasn't human. Had never been human. Like she was the blackened side of a coin. Like she was a bad dream, made flesh and real.

They are old, said Suza, voice low, gravelled, and for the first time in Kiki's memory she seemed... unsure. Nervous. As if she was spilling some great secret that could dump her in a world of shit. Ironic. She was dead. What could be worse than that?

That hardly qualifies as news.

They have come back.

Again, Suza, you ain't fucking surprising me...

Shut up!

The screech rent the air like steel talons down a blackboard. Kiki winced behind the bars of her own caged skull. She ducked a little, as if imagining hurled projectiles. She wondered about her own sanity, and the fragility of her mortality.

Silence followed.

Kiki blinked in her reality, in the dark tunnel following Dek who was just a few steps ahead of her. She could taste copper. She must have bitten her tongue. She would have preferred the honey-leaf. That bitter-sweet drug crushed delicately under her tongue, tasting vaguely of lemon and cinnamon and *something else altogether more alien*. And then the head rush, and the pulsing in her veins and heart and head and womb. All parts joined together by the thumping pleasure that welled through a person, like wild surf storming a beach.

They're coming, said Suza. There was a hint of joy in her voice.

Kiki blinked, still remembering the honey-leaf. Oh gods, it had been so long and she missed it, missed it worse than her dead fucking mother and father, missed it worse than the best ever hot hard sex, driving, pushing her hard to a thumping, thrusting, slick orgasm. She missed it. Missed it more than life.

Hmm? What?

They're coming, grinned Suza through her dead white skull features, through eyes with maggots crawling deep and wriggling in rotting sockets; grinning, teeth dropping out, fingers clacking impatiently against her coffin lid as she drummed them, drummed them repeatedly as she waited to be buried and laid to rest.

Who's coming?

But it was too late. They were already there.

They swarmed down the sewer in the gloom, surging through sewage, and they carried no weapons, but their fingers were long talons sharp as any razor. Kiki recognised them in that half-light, in the gloom from distant memories and ancient fairytales, and a distant, faded association with Sameska that had been all too brief; all too brief because she hadn't learned half enough, hadn't learned a hundredth of what she really, truly needed to know.

They'll kill you, you know, grinned Suza.

And then Dek was screaming, and Narnok was bellowing, and Kiki came slowly into bubbling consciousness as if rising from a deep dark pool. Dek was staring at her, hard eyes, his sword lifted in a defensive position, and she looked up fast to see the elf rats storming towards them through the narrow tunnel, sewage splashing and surging up the walls...

"Glad to have you back... at last!" snapped Dek, on the verge of panic.

"You should have woken me sooner," smiled Kiki, sliding free both short swords as the first wave of elf rats hit them in the narrow tunnel confines.

"Let me through!" bellowed Narnok, but it was too late, the tunnels too narrow, and Kiki and Dek were shoulder to shoulder in the gloom.

Claws raked for Kiki's face and she swayed, sword lashing out. It thumped, cutting the hand free at the wrist which splashed into the water. She saw a dark skinned face, ridged and twisted to one side as if roots grew through cheek to temple. Wide bright white eyes loomed at her and she took a step back, lowering her left sword and as the elf rat came on, despite its severed hand; thrust the blade up into its belly, the second blade hacking down through its clavicle with a crunch. She half expected the creature to be made of wood, for her blades to have no penetration; but the creature was flesh and blood, and the sharp honed steel bit deep and savage and the elf rat stumbled forward, deflating, going down under the sewage. Dek blocked a blow on his forearm, turned the block into a right-hand overhead punch to the face, then slammed his blade down vertically. It chopped the elf rat from shoulder to breast, cleaving it open. A second blow saw its head cut free in a shower of dark crimson.

If the narrow tunnel meant the other Iron Wolves could not join the battle, so it rendered the same restrictions on the attacking elf rats. They were snarling, rabid, savage, clawing at one another to get to the Iron Wolves as Kiki and Dek took down two more with hacks and cuts, and the bodies started to pile up, making it harder for the elf rats to advance, presenting stumbling blocks as Dek and Kiki took more steps backwards.

Trista unslung her bow, notched an arrow and let fly. It whistled past Dek's ear and took a snarling elf rat through the eye. It looked stunned for a moment, black fletch quivering beside its nose, and then it collapsed.

Dek glanced back. "Be fucking careful with that thing!" he yelled.

"I'm accurate, nine times out of ten," she smiled sweetly, face shadowed and eerie in the gloomy tunnel half-light.

More elf rats, clawing over one another. These had knives and swords, and for the first time the clash of steel rang out in the tunnel. Kiki, blocked an overhead swing, stuck her left blade through the elf rat's throat in a quick thrust that left it choking, clawing on its own opened windpipe. Then she was attacking the next even before that dead one went under the shit, a fast hammer blow to the face with the hilt, and a diagonal slash from high right to low left, slapping through the elf rat's leg to cut it free just above the knee and sending it crashing sideways into a comrade, stunned, as Dek removed its head.

Trista sent two more arrows flashing down the tunnel in quick succession, and two more elf rats went down with steel barbs in their eyes.

An elf rat blocked both Kiki's blades with its own and front-kicked her. She stumbled back and the elf rat leapt at her, almost *on* her but Narnok was there, towering over it as his great battle-axe swung, removing the elf-rat's head and missing Dek by a thumb's breadth. Dek flinched sideways and snarled something incomprehensible at Narnok, who grinned and strode forward, great axe slamming through the three remaining elf rats in a figure of eight that removed two heads, followed by a final overhead slam that split the creature from crown to crotch in a bloody spray that cut the fucking thing clean in half. As its insides spilled noisily into the sewage, a sudden silence filled the tunnel, broken only by the lapping of water and faeces and dead elf rats against the crumbling black bricks.

"What were they guarding?" breathed Dek.

"Entrance to the city," said Kiki, face crooked. "Question is, did any more of the bastards hear our little lover's tiff?"

The Iron Wolves stood, listening. The minutes stretched out, then Kiki said, voice very low, "Nobody speaks from now on." The others nodded, and moved warily forward, clambering over the twisted faces of dead elf rats, boots pushing them down into the slime.

They moved down the tunnel with care, trying not to splash or create too many waves.

They found the one-legged elf rat a hundred yards on, mouth just above the surface of the sewage, spluttering as it dragged itself forward with surprising speed – no-doubt to warn more of its kind.

"Let me deal with this," rumbled Narnok.

"Oh no," said Kiki, placing a hand against the huge warrior's chest. "You stay right there." She caught up with the elf rat and leaned the tip of one sword against the nape of its neck. It rolled over, looking up at her, eyes gleaming, a twisted smile on twisted lips reminiscent of bark. And then it started to laugh, and a chill crept into Kiki's soul.

"Going to warn others of your kind?" she said, voice low.

"Yes." The elf rat nodded.

"Are there many?"

"A few," said the elf rat, voice slurred, breath coming in short, sharp pants. Then a dagger lunged up from the sewage and Kiki's sword slammed down, knocking it aside.

"Who is your leader?"

"The sorcerer, Bazaroth aea Quazaquiel, and General Namash, led the forces of Daranganoth. Our king." The elf rat's voice was a low, rasping crawl. It spoke slowly, forming each word with care, as if unused to the language. "Human bitch, and I can tell you are a bitch because of the piss and semen stench between your legs, toxic and barren even through this smell of human shit." It smiled. "Bitch. You *are* going to die." Its gaze flickered to the rest of the Iron Wolves. "You are *all* going to die." It launched itself at her, claws raking for her legs, long fangs like thorns trying to tear at her juicy, succulent thighs and Kiki stumbled back, her sword plunging down through the open snarling maw. A few teeth snapped. Blood pooled around the tip of her sword. The elf rat gagged, and choked, and died.

"I'm thinking, maybe to continue is perhaps not the best choice of action," said Dek, slowly.

"Horse cock," snapped Narnok, striding forward. "Tis nothing but hot words from a defeated enemy. Ignore it. Look how we bested them! They are like wheat beneath the shafts of our iron and steel."

"We need to find out what's going on," said Kiki. And without further word, she stepped past the bobbing corpse and headed further into the eerie underworld beneath the city of Zanne.

They came to a set of steps guarded by a thick iron portal, which had been forcibly wrenched and twisted, like straws bent and broken by an angry child. Zastarte touched the thick iron bars, twisted out of shape, and ran his finger along the cold iron with a low whistle. "No human hands did this."

"Come on."

They mounted black brick steps and stopped, smelling the night air. Kiki peered above the ground, looking quickly about. The night was dark, thick snow clouds filling the sky and blocking out the light of the constellations. No lanterns or brands had been lit. Highly irregular in any city, where every king, prince, guardian, watchman and politician had to at least *appear like* they cared about citizen safety after dark, no matter what they felt inside their own money-grabbing cock-greasing back-stabbing petty little minds.

Kiki spied a nearby building, two stories, industrial, towering soot-smeared red brick, long and low. She moved from the sewer steps and darted for the doorway, a blank metal plate, and pushed it open, peering inside. The others followed, and they all stepped into a massive open space filled with benches and odd shapes in the darkness.

A few shafts of light fell in through windows protected by steel mesh. Trista closed the door behind them, and they stood still, waiting to get a sense for their surroundings.

"Oh no," said Dek, and looked to Kiki, although he could not see her features.

"What's that smell?" said Trista, nostrils twitching. "It's... sweet. But bitter. What is it?"

"The honey-leaf," said Dek, quietly.

"This is an illegal processing plant," said Narnok, moving forward to a bench. His hands moved over implements in the darkness. We must have come out in the Haven."

"What's the Haven?"

"The slums," said Dek. "The shittiest of shit holes narrow alleys and dark taverns where evil bastards plan their dark deeds. A place where even the City Watch won't tread. They leave it in the hands of the Red Thumb Gangs."

"Ahh," said Narnok, rubbing his short, patchy beard with the tip of his thumb. "I'm not well liked by them bastards."

"Me neither," said Dek.

"I, also, am not in their good books," smiled Kiki, weakly. "Seems like we've all been busy making friends. Come on. Let's get up to the roof, see if we can work out what's going on."

They moved with care through the honey-leaf processing factory, the smell prickling nostrils and making them all feel just a little bit sick. All except Kiki. Kiki felt her eyes widening a little, felt her nostrils flaring, her heartbeat – her *twin* heartbeats – quicken. As they walked along a floor littered with trip-hazards, she trailed her hand along a low bench filled with many small, intricate machines used for drying and compressing the plant leaves. And other machines used for mixing resins and pastes, to create cubes, and what were known in the trade as *coins*, little round pieces of dried paste honey-leaf which could be sat under the tongue and allowed to dissolve for a long period of time; even after one had lost consciousness.

Kiki's hand trailed along the benches as they headed for a set of cheap iron stairs leading to the roof.

And Kiki could not help herself.

They crouched by a low parapet. Behind was a steep, sloping slate roof bordered by rusted iron railings. A cold breeze blew, ruffling hair and chilling exposed skin. The wind offered a knife-bite of winter. It spoke of ice, and frost, and death.

"What's that?" said Narnok, pointing.

"A tree," said Dek. "A big old oak, but it's…"

"Twisted, broken. As if struck by lightning."

"Yes."

They peered some more, looking off over the Haven, the warren of slums, of narrow streets and tightly compacted houses, many of which, even in this poor light, could be seen to be in massive disrepair. Some were half fallen down ruins, abandoned, some simply skeletal structures of torched wood where nobody had bothered to rebuild or repair after a savagery of fire.

"There's a lot of plant life in the streets," said Narnok. "Look. All them shrubs and young saplings growing up. I wouldn't expect that. Not here, and now."

"Again, they're all twisted and broken," pointed out Dek.

"Aren't elves supposed to be linked to trees? So the old stories go."

"Maybe they're growing their own?" said Dek, his words highlighting his unease.

Their gazes turned north, across the Haven, and then northeast towards Zanne Keep, the massive, hulking black cube at the centre of the city which acted as both King Yoon's palace and citadel in these parts; and also as his War Council. Twin towers rose up in the sky, like thick black fingers, and the huge edifice was surrounded by an expanse of wildly tropical gardens which, even from this distance, looked more like a jungle of the far south than anything from northern climes.

"The Gardens of the Winter Moon," murmured Kiki.

"You know them?"

"I was there, once. As a child." She licked her lips, gaze sweeping south. "There's nobody here," she said. No people. No fires. No smoke from chimneys. No sounds other than those we make."

Even as the last syllable left her lips, movement caught their eyes. A young girl, some scruffy barefoot street urchin with long matted hair and a soot-smudged face, was running in a panic along the black cobbles of the Haven. She couldn't have been more than ten years old. And they *blinked* as they realised she was being pursued. The elf rats, perhaps ten of them, were running on all fours like cats. Several bounced onto walls and doors, running along the vertical surfaces for a few steps before hitting the cobbles again with claws clacking.

"No," hissed Narnok, and moved to stand.

Kiki grabbed his shoulder, but he shrugged her off. "You, you fuckers! Leave her be!" he bellowed down into the snow-laden street. The other Iron Wolves froze, faces in rictus grins of disbelief, then they all stood and drew their weapons.

The elf rats didn't even glance up. They pounced, were on the young girl. Her screams pierced through the city night, cutting like glass. Tearing sounds came, and her screams rose to a wail as Narnok, snarling, ran back into the processing plant and pounded down the metal staircase making the whole thing shudder in its rusted frame, brackets vibrating free of stone with showers of dust. The other Wolves followed, and Narnok kicked the door from its hinges and charged out into the snowy street, hefting his double-headed axe, eye alight with fury.

The girl was in pieces against the icy cobbles. Her arms and legs had been pulled free of the body trunk, and lay several feet away in different directions. Blood had pumped out, more blood than Narnok would have believed possible from a child, along with straggled strands of tendons and veins. Her face was locked in a mask of incredible pain, eyes open and glassy and staring at the sky. Snow started to fall: a gentle, delicate shower tumbling, and snowflakes touched her face and blood-spattered lips, and suddenly the world was a very still, serene place.

Narnok strode forward with great speed for such a big man. His axe came up and slammed into the back of the nearest elf rat, severing its spine and pitching it forward into other, still feeding, creatures. Heads snapped round, but Narnok was in them, amongst them. The axe sang left, cutting a head free, then right, lodging in an elf rat's chest. One turned and leapt at Narnok, snarling, fangs open wide in a face made of bark with long ears swept back and black eyes glittering with feral ferocity, but the world seemed to drop into a dream and Narnok's left hand snapped up, fist catching the elf rat under the chin with a thunderous blow as he tugged his axe free with his right hand, and the great weapon followed the punch and split the elf rat's head down the centre like a ripe melon spilling out brain slop and brain shards, like so many rotten seeds. Then, the Iron Wolves were there, swords smashing and cutting, Zastarte's rapier darting in to skewer a brain, Trista's bowstring touching her cheek as she released three shafts in quick succession and two elf rats were punched from their feet, scrabbling at deeply embedded barbed heads as Dek fell on them, his long sword slamming into chests and throats.

The Iron Wolves stood in a circle of elf rat corpses, and looked about, turning, searching for more enemies.

"You put us all at risk," snapped Kiki, suddenly, catching Narnok's eye.

"I don't need your fucking permission," growled the big axeman. "You don't like it, fuck off and let me do my own thing. But I ain't standing by and watching little girls get tore apart."

"You could have compromised our..."

"What?" sneered Narnok. "Our mission? We haven't *got* a fucking mission. Dalgoran is dead. Yoon wants us dead. We're not the Iron Wolves any longer, Kiki. Don't you get it? We're fucking outlaws. Well, you wanted to know what was going on in the city. It's clear as summer sunshine. Zanne is overrun with elf rats. So what you gonna fucking do about it now, woman?"

"Er, Narnok?" said Dek, voice low, eyes looking past the big warrior.

"Don't you start getting involved, pit fighter, just cos she's your new bitch and rides the end of your cock like a drunk whore after a big payout!"

"No, Narn, you *dick! Look*!"

Narnok turned. There were elf rats, advancing slowly, and in silence, down the street.

"How many's that, do you reckon?" scowled Narnok.

"I reckon that's about a hundred," said Dek, starting to back away, licking his lips, catching the eyes of the others as they formed into a ragged line.

"More this way," said Zastarte, words crisp and fast.

From the other end of the street, around the corner, they came. Ten, twenty, thirty, then their numbers were lost in the ranks of the elf rats, each one different, walking, hobbling, limping, with twisted spines and humps and distortions, with black vines like external veins winding around arms and legs, with heads squashed to one side or disfigured beyond the realms of any disfigured humanity the Iron Wolves had ever witnessed.

"Fifty at least," said Trista, her eyes darting from one to another to another, as their unit shifted, from line to circle, as they now faced two fronts.

A high-pitched keening sound went up in the air, so high it made the Iron Wolves flinch and it was taken up by the others until they all raised their elf rat snouts to the sky and shrieked and ululated, throats quivering before they dropped to all fours, like a huge mass of wolves...

...and charged down the cobbles in attack.

OLD EVIL

It was like the old days. It was like the bad days. It was like the days of blood, the weeks of slaughter, the months of bloodshed, skirmishes, the battles, the war, the fucking mud-orcs scaling the walls of Desekra Fortress guarding the Pass of Splintered Bones at the foot of the Mountains of Skarandos, twenty years ago under the onslaught of Morkagoth the Sorcerer, then, like history repeating itself, the return of a bad old penny, mud-orcs once more summoned from the Oram Mud Pits by Orlana the Horse Lady to wreak havoc and bloody terror across the world, alongside their twisted, deviated horse brethren, the splice...

The world and sanity dropped and tumbled into a swirling pit of chaos. For each and every member of the Iron Wolves, the whole world slowed to a blur as not just adrenalin kicked in, but the curse that flowed through their veins, normally a background sluggish drug, but now kicked into full violence, a full *flow*, which gave them a special edge, which made them what they were.

The elf rats leapt forward, a swarm, a plague, and the Iron Wolves lifted weapons and took them on – full in the face. Kiki felt the game kicked into another realm. Fighting with two swords, the blades became a glittering dark blur under the falling snow, slashing left and right, each following the other in crazy arcs of death leaving behind spinning bloody droplets as heads, arms and legs were cut from trunks; as throats were slit, bellies opened, eyes cut out. A sword slashed by her, she swayed, elbowed the attacker in the face, right blade sliding into another's groin to cut the major artery, first blade back-handing an attacker across the eyes, right-hand sword hacking into a head, front kick to a third attacker's chest, then leaping forward, boots on him, sword plunging down through his mouth as she ducked another sword slash and rammed her sword hilt into his teeth, snapping them with bone crunches. She landed atop the thrashing figure, everything crazy chaos about her. Dek fought with his savage pit-fighting aggression, long sword a whirling frenzy of iron, bludgeoning as much as it was cutting, and his fists, feet and broad forehead delivering hefty thumps and crashes. Narnok's twin-headed axe was a demon, glittering and singing, and the huge axeman seemed to pull off impossible feats with the weapon, slashing and cutting, reverse cuts, feints, twisting the butterfly blades to lock swords, snapping them as if they were a child's wooden playthings. Trista moved with a cool grace, sabre and long knife flashing about her as she spun and danced, elegantly avoiding enemy strikes. And Zastarte, similar to Trista in his technique, a dainty touch from a master swordsman who relied on delicate skill and accuracy rather than any brute force. The tip of his blade was a razor always opening just the right amount of flesh to maim or kill, but never threatening to lodge in bone or sinew. His was a daintiness, like a tight-rope walker, and his slim build and athletic grace made him a formidable opponent. But more, *more* than the individual warriors they all undoubtedly were, they gelled into the perfect fighting unit, unconsciously covering one another's backs, cutting hands wielding swords before a blow could be delivered, stabbing out the eyes of a comrade's opponent, creating a whirlwind circle of iron and steel and razor death for any who stepped within killing range of the collective of dazzling blades.

However, the Iron Wolves were not perfect.

A narrow thrust caught Kiki along the ribs, and she felt skin part – that old hot sting and bite of steel – felt warmth rush down her side before her short sword cut up into the elf rat's groin and removed his cock and balls. He grunted, eyes wide, and Kiki's second blade crashed into his face, flat-first, sending him stumbling back into the attacking mass. An elf rat leapt at Dek, boots first, both crashing into the pit-fighter's face and breaking his nose – but even as the elf rat was still in the horizontal, boots against Dek's cracking cartilage, so Narnok's great axe slammed down cutting the elf rat clean in half at the waist and leaving two wriggling sections of body squirming in a sudden open flood of bloody entrails. Zastarte took a cut to his cheek, and stopped, stunned, for the first time ever receiving a facial wound. Horror slammed through him and Trista had to skewer his attacker and slam her fist into his chest. "Fucking fight, you idiot!"

"But… my face!" Horror.

"They'll be cutting off your fucking head next!" she screamed. "*Fight*!" But even as the words left her spitting lips, so the elf rats suddenly pulled back in a circle of snarling fangs, slashing claws, gleaming eyes; they left a huge ring of dead in their wake, and the Iron Wolves moved closer, shoulder to shoulder, panting, snarling, preparing themselves for another attack...

"Wait!" The word was a command.

The Iron Wolves watched with narrowed, suspicious eyes as an old, bent, broken figure hobbled through the horde of elf rats. The way they parted, with nobody touching him, many heads bowing in reverence, spoke of this creature's power or standing. His face illuminated his great age, and his rough brown robes were interwoven with brown and black branches. His head came up, surveying the Iron Wolves as he leaned heavily on his gnarled staff, which was taller than his own bent frame.

"I am Bazaroth aea Quazaquiel," he intoned, and from his right hand there was a sense of thrashing snakes in shadows.

In one fluid motion, Trista pulled free her bow, notched an arrow and sent the shaft plunging into Bazaroth's eye with a thud that sent the ancient sorcerer stumbling back. The Iron Wolves ran for it, sprinting over corpses and hitting the line of elf rats as a wedge with the mighty Narnok at its point, axe cleaving through bodies with sickening crunches... and then they broke free and charged down the street, sliding on ice. They reached the corner of Blackleg Alley, but were charged by a squad of elf rats who appeared from the gloom. Their attackers ploughed into their midst with a burst of amazing speed and aggression, curved fangs snarling.

Kiki, Dek and Zastarte were hammered back into a narrow alley by the elf rat charge, fighting a sudden retreat, swords clashing against swords and long spears as fifteen elf rats charged them, falling down on the cobbles with crushed skulls and skewered eyes, but still coming on, still snarling and spitting...

"There's too many!" screamed Kiki, swords a blur, narrowly missing having her own head removed by a horizontal slash from a pitted black blade. She ducked and spun, sword piercing an elf rat through the guts.

"Back!" snapped Dek. "We have to fall back." Suddenly, they turned and ran, searching for an alley they could cut through to rejoin Narnok and Trista. But the winding cobbles took them south, then arced to the right with only left exits leading further south towards the Royal Gate. Before they knew it, they were in the heart of the Haven again, only a hundred feet from the pursuing elf rats.

"Down there!" pointed Dek.

"Narnok and Trista?"

"No, it's the tunnel that led us into Zanne."

"We can't leave them," said Kiki, eyes gleaming.

"We need a confined space to fight. There's too fucking many of them, Kiki!"

Kiki nodded, and they sprinted back towards the black brick steps leading down into the sewer tunnels under Zanne. And with only a sharp backward glance, plunged down into the darkness, the sewage, and the unholy stink...

Back at the corner, the larger section of this split elf rat squad focused on Narnok, swarming around the axeman as his blades cleaved left and right, splattering brains and cutting heads from shoulders. Trista fought close by with increasing frenzy, her cool and poise now gone. Their group had been split, and the two of them were on their own. A much more worrying prospect now, considering the numbers ranged against them.

Suddenly, the elf rats fell back – and parted.

Trista was panting, curled blonde hair lank with sweat and getting in her eyes. She brushed it away, glanced at Narnok who grinned at her with his terrible scarred face and single narrowed eye. He didn't seem out of breath and she wanted to curse him, to shout *you fucking got us into this, you horse dick, trying to save that little girl,* but she didn't have the breath left in her. Instead, she scowled, then gestured up the street.

From the corner of an alley strode a huge elf rat, easily two heads taller than Narnok, and much wider at the shoulders. He carried a mighty hammer of oak and iron, with thick banding and brass studs the size of a man's fist. He was limping slightly, one leg longer than the other, and was bald, his skin coarse and grey, his eyes red like berries in a face that was oval, and smooth, like old polished ash.

This creature, this giant amongst elf rats, accelerated suddenly at Narnok who gazed up, mouth actually open, as the huge hammer raised above the elf rat's head and it leapt at him; Narnok side-stepped, axe lashing out to be batted aside by a forearm brace forged from iron. Sparks flew. The hammer thundered against the cobbles, making the whole street seem to shake and cracking ten of the rounded stones. Narnok staggered, then leapt back as the hammer was jerked into a horizontal strike that nearly crushed him against a wall. Instead, it completely removed the edge of a brick house and bricks toppled out like rock-fall, the house groaning as it sagged on old rotten timbers. Narnok's axe came up in both hands, and he backed away, the elf rats lumbering around and grinning at him, some with evil curved fangs as long as a man's forearm.

The huge hammer swung again, and Narnok felt the rush of displaced air as he dodged, and struck out with his own weapon. Again, the axe was blocked against steel-shod braces, and the elf rat dived forward, a sudden movement, and a heavy fist blow slammed into Narnok's chest, accelerating the big axeman backwards, axe skittering across the ground, spinning, as he landed, then rolled, and finally slid to a stop. He looked up, thunder in his face, and spat on the cobbles under his chin. He climbed slowly to his feet, clutching his side where he felt at least two ribs broken. He could not breathe and gasped in little pockets of air, like a child taking medicine. The elf rat strode towards him, swinging the hammer, intention clear. He was going to crush Narnok like a bug.

Narnok limped towards his axe, and the elf rat gave a deep, booming laugh, increasing its pace. The huge hammer swung up as Narnok staggered, almost falling, fingers stretching for his axe... and then everything seemed to happen so fast it was a blur, and the hammer swung around but Narnok tripped, sprawling, fingers curling around the haft as the elf rat's hammer thundered close-by over his head and Narnok curled into a ball as the elf rat skidded past, and the butterfly blades lashed out, razor steel slicing through ankle tendons with tiny popping sounds, hamstringing the huge creature.

The elf rat roared as his tendons were cut, and went down on one knee, twisting, hand going to the injury at the back of its ankle as Narnok rolled free of hammer range, stood, glanced around. Trista was in the doorway to an old factory, beckoning him, as he limped to the huge elf rat and slammed his axe in a massive overhead blow – and into its head. He tugged the blade free, front-kicked the elf rat – still howling, still not dead – onto its back, huge hammer slipping from twitching fingers with a meaty clang, then limped as fast as he could to the doorway, slipping into the dark huge space beyond. Trista slammed the portal and turned a huge key in the lock, then started dragging some large chests from nearby as Narnok leaned against the wall, wheezing.

"Bloody help then, you big oaf!" she snapped, grunting and dragging a second battered chest of old, stained wood. It scraped and squealed across ancient, warped floorboards.

"I… don't think I can," said Narnok, mouth forming an "O".

"Is this the Big Man brought low by a single punch?" snapped Trista.

Narnok met her gaze, and her mouth clacked shut. Narnok was hurt, and hurting bad. He smiled gently and gave a small nod. "There's always somebody bigger and tougher. First rule of life. But you know what? I don't think I ever found him, until now."

Trista dragged various extra chests and heavy boxes of old, rusted tools and bolts, piling them high, sweat beading on brow and upper lip. When she was satisfied, she moved to Narnok, hand on his shoulder.

"What are your injuries, old man?"

He gave another smile, and decided not to point out he was only two years Trista's senior. "He broke my fucking ribs with that punch. Two. Maybe three. And cracked a couple of others. Maybe even cracked my sternum. It fucking hurts to breathe. I doubt I can run."

"Anything else?"

"I have a fucking bad headache, but I'm suspecting that's more to do with the situation and the lack of a fine drop of brandy," growled the axeman. He jacked himself off the wall, hissing through clenched teeth.

"Spit," said Trista.

"Eh, lass?"

"*Spit*. There, on the floor. We need to know if a lung is punctured by your rattling ribs."

Narnok spat, but it was white.

Trista nodded. "Good. Can't have you running around gurgling on your own claret. You'd slow us down."

Narnok threw her a nasty sideways glare. "Nice to see you care." He spat again, just to be sure. "Still. Come on. We need to get moving. Get out of here. Those bastards will be through that door real soon."

"Agreed. But we move slow, and we move quiet. Stealth is our ally."

Narnok nodded, hefted his mighty axe, and winced like a broken child. Then he gestured for Trista to lead the way, and limped along after her, his left arm cradled under his ribcage, pressing tight as if to hold it in place. He found it helped. A little.

They moved through the gloom. Huge machines smelling of old bad oil loomed through the half-light.

"What is this place?" whispered Narnok.

"I've no idea. But it stinks bad, Narn."

"We need to find Kiki and the others."

"They headed south," said Trista, with a twitch at the corner of her mouth.

"Oh no," said Narnok. "Don't be thinking fucking thoughts like that, bitch. They didn't abandon us. They did what they had to do. We was cut in half by a wedge, right?

They went one way, we went the other. It's the law of the jungle. The shit of battle. It's what happens time and again, and you just deal with it, and get on with it. We're here together, and we look after each other *now*. Right?"

"Right, Narnok," said Trista, curiously submissive in the gloom. He squinted. That wasn't like her. He'd expected an argument.

They continued in silence, the huge, disused factory gradually giving way to a warehouse with a vaulted ceiling containing high steel walkways and thick chimneys, which reared up, disappearing through the roof. Water dripped down, slowly, rhythmically, in a hundred separate locations. And weak shafts of moonlight came through a broken roof at random intervals. Old engine oil sat as a low-level undercurrent to their twitching nostrils, mixed with a fresh breeze and smell of snow, and something else; something like the scent of a forest, but just that little bit corrupt.

"Old leaves," said Narnok, eventually.

"What?"

"The smell. It's old leaves."

Trista stared at him. "If you say so."

They journeyed on, through a huge complex of warehouse buildings that led to smaller and smaller buildings, all linked, all deserted and filled with ancient machinery, worn and battered crates and boxes. The place was damp and cold, seeping into their bones after a prolonged period.

"I hate it here," said Trista, rubbing her cheek and leaving a dark smudge. "I want to go back outside."

"It's safer in here," said Narnok, pausing and leaning against a wall. Trista stared at him, and understanding settled across her shoulders like ash from a forest fire, infusing her mind like a poultice, and she *understood*. Narnok was injured worse than he liked to admit. And Narnok was the rock-solid backbone, the indisputable solid iron core of the Iron Wolves. But he was weaker, now. He was injured. Battered. And he recognised in himself that he had bent, just a little. He had not just taken a physical beating, he had taken a mental one, too. Once, he had waded amongst the enemy, cutting heads and limbs free, Godlike, seemingly untouchable; the odd scratch, the odd flesh wound, but leaving a trail of fucking corpses wide as a river. This encounter with the elf rats had shaken him up. Taught him a bit of humility. Taught him a bit of mortality. And, well, that could never be a bad thing.

"Come on," said Trista, gently, and they passed through more silent buildings.

Outside, distantly, presumably beyond the walls of Zanne, a wolf howled. Narnok and Trista exchanged glances.

"They'll get out," said Narnok.

"Kiki, Dek and Zastarte?"

He nodded.

"Then we need to get out as well."

"We need to reach the sewer."

They climbed various ramps and ladders, heading in what they thought was the right direction through the linked, deserted old factory buildings. Finally, they came to a door that led out onto a ledge.

Dawn was breaking, yellow fingers crawling over the horizon like a claw over a cracked egg.

They eased themselves towards a rusted iron barrier, Narnok grunting in pain, and peered over. Trista thought, *that's not like Narnok. Hurting so much. So brittle, now.*

Something has crumbled inside him. Something has broken. Like corrupt clockwork in a smashed watch.

Light raced across the city of Zanne. The many elf rats out in the street lifted their heads, as if relishing the winter sunlight; taking it into themselves, absorbing the positive energy. Feeding on it, like a tree welcoming life and light.

"There," said Trista, pointing.

It was Bazaroth aea Quazaquiel, who had briefly introduced himself to the Iron Wolves. Briefly. Far too briefly. He was talking to the crowd of elf rats, gesticulating wildly. Trista's shaft was still embedded in his eye. The small, bent, ancient sorcerer seemed not to notice. Then, an elf rat in the crowd pointed and made various comments. There came a long pause, where Bazaroth simply stared, saying nothing.

The old sorcerer reached up, and pulled the arrow from his eye socket. There was a distant little *schlup*. Bazaroth threw the arrow down in disgust, and faced the elf rats, mouth working wildly, words drifting like so much distant campfire smoke.

Narnok slumped to the ground and placed his back against the low wall.

"Narn? Are you well?" Trista knelt by the huge axeman.

Slowly, his eyes closed and he slumped to the side. Trista saw blood leaking out onto the old bricks.

"Shit," she snarled, and ripped open his jerkin. Not only were there huge purple bruises up his side and across his chest, there was a knife wound in his abdomen. Blood was oozing out, running down his flesh, dripping to the old bricks. "Oh, you stupid, stupid fucker," she said.

Below, the elf rats roared, and several waved swords and spears in the air. Bazaroth seemed unconcerned that he'd recently taken Trista's arrow in his eye socket. The old cunt. She returned to Narnok, now slumped sideways and unconscious. She tried to move him, but he was damn well too heavy. Grunting, she dragged him a little, rolled him onto his back. By the gods, he fucking weighed an awful lot. Like his bones were made from solid iron. Or calcified stone.

She tore open his jerkin and shirt, and observed the wound proper.

"Oh, Narnok," she said, and quickly checked the rest of his huge, bloody carcass for serious cuts. "You should have told me sooner."

In the streets below, deep in the Haven, the elf rats dispersed. Distantly, Trista could see the stone steps from which they had emerged from their sewer entry.

Now, between her and Narnok and the steps, there must have been five hundred elf rats. They were out in force thanks to the Iron Wolves' violent incursion. Patrolling the streets. Searching for the living. Searching for more Vagandrak *humans*.

Shit.

Shit.

And as the sun rose over Zanne, so Trista pulled free a small medical pack, and licking the end of a white thread, fed it on the third attempt through the eye of a curved needle.

"I'll make you good again, Big Man. You see if I don't," she said.

Narnok walked along the winding road under the broad spread of old oak trees. It had been raining, but now the sun was out, sparkling through wet leaves and playing patterns of shadow across the smooth black surface.

Narnok's strides were long, and strong, and he felt powerful and filled with youth; with a raw power he hadn't felt in… *decades*. He stopped by a pear tree and, reaching up, twisted two ripe fruits, biting into one, sweet juice running down into his beard. He carried on walking, up the winding road to his large white house, and as he came close, so she stood in the doorway, back arched, lips pouting, radiating beauty in a stunning display that left Narnok's mouth dry and knees weak and cock hard.

"Katuna," he breathed, pear juice sweet on his lips, and he quickened his pace, for it had been a long time, and she giggled at his approach, dark eyes flashing, head tossing back her mane of long, black curls.

He reached her trembling, animal figure, and lifting his hand, gently stroked a finger across her olive skin. "Katuna, I missed you," rumbled the warrior, Hero of the War of Zakora, the Axeman of Splintered Bones, Axe Master of Desekra; and Katuna made a noise, half purr, half mewl, and threw her arms around his neck, stretching up a little, kissing him with those full sensuous red lips. Her tongue darted in just a little, a tease, and he groaned as her hand dropped and stroked his inner thigh.

Narnok bent and scooped her up. She gave a giggle, arms draped around his neck, fingers dangling, kissing him on the lips and cheeks and forehead as he strode inside the house, back kicking the door shut. He started for the bedroom, but only made it to halfway up the stairs before they were ripping at one another's clothes in passion. And then he held her, and he was inside her, and the whole world was a warm good safe haven, and the rest of the world – the battles, the army, cruelty, monsters – all of it melted away as they made love and he smelled

the musk of her olive skin and he was there again, where
he belonged, back with his wonderful wife Katuna.

Narnok propped himself up on one elbow and gazed down
at his sleeping wife. She was beautiful without compare,
and in sleep her features had softened; no longer did
she have the tiny scowl of concentration that sometimes
betrayed the gears of her massively over-active working
mind. Now, she was not thinking. Now, she was sleeping
– softened, honey, cream – and Narnok's eyes travelled
down her face to where the silk sheets had slipped down a
little, revealing her fabulous rounded breasts. He reached
out, fingers caressing the velvet skin. She murmured in
her sleep, and gradually her eyes opened and she smiled
and reached for him, and they made love for the fourth
time in as many hours.

She was propped up on fat pillows, an ornate silver bowl in
her lap filled with fruit from the orchard. She'd giggled as
Narnok ran out into the dark and the cold, wearing nothing
but her semi-transparent gown with gold-edged trim,
showing off his hairy legs nicely, and now pear juice ran
down her chin and leaning forward, Narnok licked it free.

"Are you well, my love?" she asked, concern showing
in her eyes.

"I had a dream."

"Not a good dream?" She pouted with those full red
lips, glistening, kissed by juice.

"Not a good dream at all," said Narnok, scowling.

"Oh my love, take those dirty scowls away."

"I cannot. For it has come back to me in all its
magnificent glory."

"I will kiss it away, then" And she was straddling him, one leg on either side, kissing his eyebrows until he laughed and she swayed above him, sucking her thumb, then her index finger, then her middle finger.

"You are so strong, and hard," she said.

"Ye gods woman, is there no end to your stamina?"

"Not on this night," she said, rubbing herself close.

"Well, being the gentleman I am, it would be uncouth to leave you so dissatisfied."

"Show me," she growled, her gyrations getting stronger.

And he took her in his arms and kissed her.

Daylight burned his eyes through gauze curtains. Narnok groaned, as the previous night's brandy kicked him in the skull like an irate donkey called Mary. He rolled over, and Katuna was standing, fully dressed, a dark look on her face.

"Kat?" he said, softly.

"That's him. Fuck him up."

And she stepped aside revealing big men with helves and iron bars, and they beat down on him and he roared, lurching from the bed, but there were six of them and they hammered him down to the expensive carpets, green with gold and crimson swirls, and he remembered picking those carpets with Katuna, remembered moaning about their extortionate price, remembered her kissing him, pouting; and he remembering giving in to her.

You can afford it, she'd said.

And now he was paying the price.

And awoke tied to a chair in a torture cellar. Ahh. I remember this bit. Ahh. This is my favourite fucking bit!

The bit with the razor blades, the bit with the acid, the bit where they burn my eye out...

Xavier stepped close, but that was impossible because Narnok had killed him, watched the sharp steel push in, heard his screams and his bubbling as blood rushed through him and spilled out onto the stone flags like so much Vagandrak Red.

"Welcome home, Narnok," said Xavier, and grinned his skeletal grin in that old pointed face full of wrinkles beneath a bald head and piercing eyes of fevered evil. "I've waited for this moment for a long time," cackled the old torturer. "I dreamt about it so hard I actually ejaculated in my trews."

"Well live it up, fucker; this is a dream. I killed you." Narnok gave him a full teeth grin. "I killed you deader than a dead corpse, fucker."

"Really?" Xavier raised his eyebrows, a movement accentuated by the fact he was bald and had more exposed forehead to illustrate the facial gesture.

"Yeah, really, so fuck off."

Katuna stepped forward then, and swam into Narnok's vision. His mind was still spinning from the beating, and he thought he had broken ribs and... what felt like a knife wound. He stared up at her, and she smiled, like she was his old friend, like she was his... wife.

"Yeah, bitch?"

"Don't be like that, Narnok. We both know this was a business transaction from the start. We both know I was far too good looking, too beautiful, too sexy, too sensual, too delicate, too smart, *ever* to hook up with a brutal savage fuck-up like you. It's only your money I was after. We both knew that at the altar. You may have chosen to gloss over the facts in whatever way aids your libido, like those fat pig-ugly politicians you see with twenty year-old beauties on their arms; like those famous playwrights you witness in the city, riddled and crippled with gonorrhoea but sporting some sexy young lady who thinks they'll be the next Emily Zanzibane. That's just the way it is. Quim chases money. And you got your money's worth for my quim, *dear*. All you need to do now, *bastard*, is hand it over. Or Xavier here will scar you up bad. Put out both your eyes. Cut off your cock. You get the vivid picture."

She stepped back, smiling.

Narnok grinned, and Xavier and Katuna shared a quick glance. "Well," said the big axeman, spitting blood at his feet on the stone flags, "what *youse fuckers* need to understand is that this already happened, and this whole barrel of horse shit is nothing but a dream. So do your fucking worst, then I can wake up and get on with my life."

Even as he was speaking, Xavier was nodding to a character out of sight, and pulling on thick black leather gloves, the sort of gloves Narnok had seen down at the docks used to handle dangerous snakes and spiders and scorpions. The phial in Xavier's hands was steaming softly, just a hint, like sweet tea just gone off the boil; but there was nothing sweet in that glass bottle.

And Narnok transferred his gaze to Xavier. His eyes were fevered, fanatical once more. Sweat beaded his upper lip, which he licked with a quick fish tongue.

And then he leapt, and was upon Narnok, and the acid was poured into the man's left eye, and then poured into his right eye, and he was screaming and thrashing as the burning flowed into his face, into his eyes – sweet GODS into his fucking brain – like some molten metal, and burned him all the way down into oblivion and down beyond into his heart and core as Katuna laughed, her laughter pealing and beautiful and cold as the distant stars, as the acid flowed down *down* into his fucking soul.

Narnok came awake to a cool breeze. He gave a little gasp, a sharp intake of breath, and looked around quickly. He could see. Sweet Mother of the Seven Sisters, he could still see! His hands came up to his face, and he felt the heavy scar tissue delivered by the razor blade of the dead Xavier. And Narnok groaned, and hung his head, and allowed the pain from the ribs and knife wound to pulse through him.

"You all right, Big Man?" Trista knelt beside him. It was night. Somewhere out in the city of Zanne, something burned. Narnok could see the reflection of flames in Trista's eyes and he realised, groggy and disorientated as he was, that they had moved location. Now, there was a lean-to roof above them. Some kind of balcony, but well sheltered. He also realised he was covered with two blankets.

"They took my eyes," he said.

"You've still got one good one, mate."

"That's like the finest stallion stud, with only one good ball."

"Which means *he'd still have one.*"

"Working at half complement, so to speak," moaned Narnok.

"I'd rather be half than nothing at all. Bad dream, axeman?"

"Yeah. Real bad dream."

"About the bitch?"

"About *my wife.*"

"That's what I said." Trista grinned.

Narnok pulled himself up a little, and half turned, wincing. "Did you have to stitch me up?"

"Yeah."

"Thanks."

"Don't mention it. You can do it for me sometime."

Narnok considered making a joke about stitching up Trista's mouth, but thought better of it. She had that mean look in her eye again. "How long have I been out?"

"Three days."

"*Days*?"

"You lost a lot of blood. Some elf rat scum got you with a knife."

"Yeah. I… remember."

He reached up again and touched his heavily scarred face. Trista realised, with a start, that there were tears on Narnok's cheek. They glinted in the reflection of the distant fire.

"What's the matter?" She reached out. Touched his arm.

"In the dream, I had my face again. In my dream, I had two good eyes. It was before Xavier, and Katuna's betrayal, and all the rancid horse shit that followed. I was the old Narnok. The full and proper Narnok; the Narnok women actually wanted to sleep with and bear his children."

"You are a good man," she said.

"Yeah, but would you fuck me? No. I didn't think so. It gets so lonely, Trista, you know? Do you know how it feels to be utterly and totally alone? Fuck it, it's not even about the sex. It's about… companionship. It's about having a woman who cares for you, who loves you, who is there for you, to tend your wounds and cradle your crying baby face."

"I'm here for you," said Trista, and tears were on her own cheeks.

"But you don't love me?"

"No," said Trista, grinning. "But if it's any consolation, I don't love anybody. I'd as soon put a knife through a man's throat than take his cock in my mouth. So you're ahead of the pack, my friend."

Narnok took a deep breath, and grinned himself. "Ahead of the pack," he said. "That's the place I like to be." He scratched at his chin, and winced. He'd taken a battering, for sure. "Heard anything from Kiki? Dek? Zast?"

"No."

"No? I thought not."

"They've abandoned us."

"They had no choice, little lady. Like us. Backs to the wall. Feet in the fire." He lifted himself a little, turning again. He could hear the fire now, for it had spread. "What's burning down there? I feel like I've been out of the game for too long. Damn knife wound."

"Over there." Trista gestured vaguely. "Some buildings. Some trees." She looked at him. "Shit."

"Trees? You mean the twisted black trees we saw growing in courtyards and gardens and that?"

"Yes."

"Can you see where?"

"Over by the museum. Between the Gardens of the Winter Moon and the Haven."

"You know what that means, don't you, Trista, my little honey-pot filled with random scorpion stings?"

"Not really, Narnok. No."

"It's the trees. The trees are the key. These are fucking elf rats, *right?* They're linked to trees – elves are linked to trees. According to legend. It's part of their physiology, whatever the fuck that is. The elf rats are growing their own spirits, their own bonding trunks, or whatever it is they do with them. Damn odd if you ask me. But the point is, *somebody else knows this*. And they're burning the trees. Burning the elf rats' *lifeblood*. Teaching them a damn bloody lesson."

"So we have allies?" said Trista.

"All we have to do is find them."

"And you think they'll help us escape?"

"I think they'll help us fight this scourge!"

Trista considered this. "That's what I was afraid of," she said, words a whisper.

They had to wait another two days whilst Narnok regained his strength. Trista went on little scouting missions and found water and food, which they ate cold, huddled together for warmth. Out in Zanne, fires still burned. Somebody was on a mission to fuck up the elf rats good.

Finally, when Narnok felt strong enough, they gathered together their meagre possessions and headed down through the building.

It was dawn. At ground level, they could see plumes of black smoke rising into the sky. They travelled deserted streets laden with snow, moving slow, keeping to the walls, avoiding the Haven and sticking to the richer, eastern side of town.

At one point, curiosity overcame Narnok, and he kicked down a door to a narrow, two bedroom terraced house that leaned alarmingly to the left, defying gravity, or so it seemed. Its timbers were ancient and screamed that it was one of the more authentic, original buildings in

Zanne. Part of its heritage. Part of its culture, despite the city's fall from recent grace.

The house interior was gloomy, filled with a chaos of upturned chests and furniture. There was a smell, and the smell was bad. No. *Fucking bad*. Narnok wrinkled his nose and moved through the lower floor, coming to a back bedroom.

Inside the squalid depths, something moved and groaned in a bed of grey, shit-stained sheets.

"Hello there? Are you well?" said Narnok, feeling the words were redundant; feeling stupid in his urgent sudden need to explore this urban interior. After all, how could something so squalid and shit-stinking possibly be well?

The figure groaned in its personal bed of pain, and thrashed beneath the sheets. The smell of corruption was excessive. Something large, and jagged, a bit like a scorpion claw, emerged from a ragged hole in the sheets and started to make a cutting motion in Narnok's general direction.

"I think we should leave," said Trista, voice ragged and muffled, mouth covered with a torn strip of linen which she'd dampened with her canteen, and held fervently in place lest she catch some terrible affliction.

"Yeah. Maybe you're right."

They stumbled out into the grey daylight. It had started to snow again, huge tumbling flakes, romantic in another time, another world. The stench of bad, burned wood drifted to them on the breeze. It was choking and vile.

"This way," said Narnok, limping ahead.

Trista glanced back at the corruption and shadows within the house. What happened to you people, she thought, uneasily, idly, shivering as she did so. Then she followed Narnok, her sword drawn and close to, her body tense and ready for combat. She'd never been more ready. Never.

"*Halt*!" boomed the deep, bass-heavy voice. What made it more terrifying were the accompanying ripples of bestial growls that joined the words from the gloom of the museum arch; as if the shadowy figure wreathed in darkness commanded an army of slavering monsters ready to charge and leap and tear out throats in their animal hatred. Maybe he did. "*Halt*!" Take one more step and you *will DIE*!"

"A little melodramatic," muttered Narnok, turning so his injured ribs were to the rear of any prospective combat; protected, so to speak. He lifted his axe. Light from a rack of thick, sputtering candles gleamed iron eyes from the blades, and reflected dancing patterns across the marble tiled floor of the museum interior.

"We saw your fires," said Narnok. "We saw you burning the trees of the elf rats. Figured you were out to smash them. We wanted a part of that. Reckoned you might need some help. Obviously, if you don't need our help, then we'll fuck off, like."

There came a long, contemplative silence. Narnok exchanged low, slow glances with Trista. If this thing went bad, which sometimes these things did, there was going to be yet more violence. And Narnok, despite appearances, was not in the best shape for a fight.

They waited at the behest of the madman in the shadows, surrounded by his low growls, dogs probably, hopefully, and wondered what the next move would be.

Like a game of chess, although without the logic, and with swords and axes as a bright bloody attack. So. Not *really* like a game of chess at all, then, although Narnok would like to register some element of tactics, somewhere, whether he deserved them or not.

"You going to speak then, man, or what? We saw you burning the trees. Figured you might like some help against the scourge of the occupying elf rats. If not, that's fine, mate. We can go toss off to some other psychopath's nightmare."

"Narnok?" Soft words. A confused question. An imagined tilt of the head.

"Aye, that's me. Narnok of the Axe. Hero of Desekra Fortress and Splintered Bones, not that it means a flying bucket of horse shit anymore."

"Narnok? *Narnok?*"

"Yeah yeah, bastard, don't wear it out. Am I supposed to know you, or something?"

The figure stepped forward through flickering candlelight. Above him, statues and busts stared down with eyes of reflected flame, severe and uncompromising and condescending. Their disgust at his half-breed looks seeped through Narnok's bones, and he felt just that little bit crushed. Like a man teaching at a premiere university when he intrinsically knew he had no right to be there, either by virtue of solid working class roots, by virtue of a limited, stilted, narrowed intelligence, or by virtue of achieving his position by cheating his damn way inside.

Narnok squinted, leaning forward a little.

"Do I know you?"

"Oh, you know me all right," said the figure, voice quite neutral. Narnok gave a shiver, for he could not quite decide whether this man was friend or foe, and the sounds of the growling had increased in pitch and ferocity, as if the man barely controlled a platoon of rabid werewolves on a leash.

Narnok shivered.

"So? What's your name, *friend*?" said Narnok, unhooking his axe and sliding it into a combat position with infinite ease, but all the time displaying a smile, a fake smile, a smile that had hooked blank-eyed whores, a fake grin that had pacified brain-dead politicians intent on furthering their own money and career. As, indeed, they all were.

"My name," said the man, taking several steps forward until the firelight illuminated his narrow, wiry, powerful torso, "is Mola. I think you know me well, Narnok of the Axe, Hero of Desekra's Latrine, Warrior of His Own Dog-dick Ego."

"Indeed I do," growled Narnok. "I think you owe me a goodly sum of money, by all the gods!"

"Bollocks! That's the other way round," boomed Mola. Lots of growling. The scrabbling of claws on stone.

"Is that Duke and Duchess? Sarge and Thrasher?"

"Yes, it is, Narnok of the Axe. And I think they can smell your ripe blood. And fine blood it is, I am sure, when spilt on the rugs and flags of this brooding mausoleum, on account of serious and large debts unpaid."

"Well, Mola of the Dogs, I can't say I'm overly fond of your fucking mangy, flea-bitten mutts, so if you want to let them loose, by the gods, we'll see how their fangs fare against my sharpened axe blades." His words echoed from high vaulted marble ceilings. His words reverberated from stone alcoves, and statues, and plinths containing scenes of the Great Depression. Ancient kings and gods and whores stared down at him, stony-eyed, uncaring, merciless.

"Think I might just do that," said Mola, and there came a sound of scraping leather on leather. "After all. You were the bastard who let me down."

"Ha! Don't remember that!" snapped Narnok. "Remember you sticking it up my arse plenty, though." He smiled a long, low, lizard smile. "Lots and lots. Especially at Skell Docks when we played the dice."

"Let's sort it, then, axeman."

"As you wish."

"You're *really* going to fight him over an unpaid debt?" hissed Trista in disbelief.

"Aye? What's the problem with that?"

There came a *snap* of leather, and a frantic snarling and scrabbling of claws on stone. From the gloom, from the horror show, came four terrifying beasts; each was a huge creature, much bigger than a dog had any right to be and stacked with heavy ridges of muscle. Mola's hounds were vicious, feral and powerful beyond the vision of any normal, canine animal. Like wolves, thought Narnok, with a bitter smile. "Wild, rabid, untrained wolves..."

"I'm with you," snapped Trista, narrow blade gleaming, protecting Narnok's weakened side.

"That's okay," said Narnok, slipping into a light-headed, almost surreal otherworld of impending combat – as the beasts charged at him, snarling and drooling.

Because he knew; *knew* he had to do it.

He had to kill Mola's dogs. Then kill Mola.

Then find the force behind the enemy in Zanne.

And kill them, as well.

Kill Mola...

Once, he was your best friend...

Narnok's face went hard. Harder than stone. Harder than granite. Slammed shut like a portcullis when the enemy breached the bridge.

"So be it," he rumbled, lifting his axe to meet the charge.

GAME OF SOULS

Kiki, Dek and Zastarte pounded down black brick steps, splashed into the sewage and ran on through the darkness. Elf rats pursued them into the gloom, and as the Iron Wolves came to a sharp bend they suddenly waited, whirling about, weapons at the ready. The elf rats came at them in the near total blackness, like monsters from some child's horror story painted by insane artists high on the honey-leaf. Suddenly, Kiki and Dek leapt to the attack, swords blurring, cutting through flesh with thumps like a butcher cleaving chunks of beef. Blood spattered up the brick walls. Droplets rained down in sewage. Screams echoed from bricks, cutting back and forth, reverberating squeals more animal than human. With savagery and no mercy, Dek and Kiki waded forward, no longer appearing human, their faces seeming to shimmer as Kiki reached down, into the bricks of the ancient tunnel, and felt the energy there, felt the *mana*, and her twin heart beat faster, pumping blood and energy around her veins. Their faces seemed to lengthen, shimmering in a gloomy silvery half-light; lengthened, into muzzles…

And they were fighting with blades, but now with slashing claws, and the elf rats fell back dismayed, their distorted faces with tree-like bulges and bark displacements twisted even more into the grotesque of the deviated elf rat. Suddenly, Dek howled a howl so feral, so savage, it tore through the sewer tunnels and broke the morale of the charging elf rats. They turned as one unit and fled back down through the sewage, boots and claws splashing.

Lights flickered from somewhere high above; some access shaft, some kind of methane release pipe. It flickered on Kiki and Dek and they lowered their faces, which were blurring, shifting, and looked nothing more than perfectly...

human.

"Let's go," growled Dek in a voice so low it could have almost been torn from the throat of a wolf.

They ran, despite their injuries, despite their fatigue and battle cramps. They fled back down the sewers, aware that at any moment hundreds more elf rats could flood in and overwhelm them. They were beaten back, they knew. And even worse, they'd lost Narnok and Trista back there; and the thought hung heavy in their hearts, and in their souls.

Dawn had broken when they emerged from the evil gash in the earth, and they stood breathing deeply on a plain of rolling hills, a wicked wind slashing across them, biting like pike teeth. They looked at each other, each marked with congealed blood and the flowers of recent bruises, and each bearing a weariness that went bone deep.

"Come on," said Kiki, coughing out exhaustion like a rock.

"Where the hell to?" snapped Zastarte, whirling on her, his blade up, gore covered, battered, but segments still gleaming. "We've got to go back. We have to find another way in. We have to rescue Trista... and Narnok."

"They don't need no rescuing, lad," said Dek, placing a hand on Zastarte's shoulder.

"And who made you our fucking Captain?" snarled Zastarte in the dull grey light.

"I understand your pain," said Dek. "You have... feelings, for Trista. You're worried about her. But we need to... to regroup. To rest. To think. To plan."

"No," hissed Zastarte, glaring at Dek; but his teeth clacked shut.

"Dek's right. We're no use to anybody like this. We need to rest and plan. Come on." Kiki started off across the snow, each footstep leaden and weary.

"Where are you going?"

"I know a family who live a few miles from here. They have a farmhouse with a welcoming fire and, I hope above all else, fresh baked bread, butter and a spot of red wine. Hot water would be an incredible bonus."

Dek and Zastarte glanced at Kiki's retreating back, then over at the high black walls of Zanne; shut down, closed down, silent and ominous.

"Don't think we're leaving her," said Zastarte, fire in his eyes, "because we're *not*."

"Nobody is thinking that, lad," said Dek, gently, and guided the distraught figure of Zastarte after Kiki, whilst all time thinking, I knew it, deep down in my heart and soul, I knew it – but didn't quite believe it. I knew this bastard was capable of some kind of love for something other than his own lustful pleasures, his hard cock and the gleaming gold in his purse; but imagine choosing here, and now, this place, this time, to fall in love with the most savage, man-hating, ball-slicing back-stabbing bitch in the whole of Vagandrak? Not just bad luck, my friend, but an emotion just about ready to get you cut down in an instant.

Dek followed Zastarte, his nose and ribs throbbing, the cold wind biting him like a merciless wolf.

The farmhouse, a large white building backed by cobbled yards and five generous barns, was deserted, and there was evidence the occupants had left in a hurry. The front door was half open and snow had piled through into the hallway. Kiki shouted out a few greetings, but there came no answer. The kitchen had items strewn over table and floor, and Kiki bent, lifting a fallen chair and placing it on the flagstone floor with a clack.

"They left in a hurry," observed Dek.

"I wonder where they went?" said Zastarte, who had calmed down considerably and seemed to have withdrawn into himself, almost in the sulky state of a child who didn't get what he wanted.

"Maybe they saw the elf rats invading the city," said Kiki, and turned, kicking the snow from the hallway so she could shut the door and throw across a few bolts.

"We need to check through the rooms," said Dek. "Make sure everywhere is clear."

Kiki nodded, and they moved as a unit carefully through the house. Upstairs, there were several chests half full of clothes; obviously intended for departure, but things must have got worse, and worse fast.

In one room, a collection of children's dolls and teddy bears were spilled on the floor and Kiki stooped, lifting one little ragdoll and stroking the soft hair. She carried it with her as they clomped back down the wooden, uncarpeted stairs.

"At least we can get some sleep," said Dek, rubbing his exhausted eyes.

Kiki nodded.

"Can we light a fire, is the question that burns me?" said Zastarte. "I could do with a hot bath and a hot sweet drink. I'm beginning to stink like a charnel house. Maybe you peasants don't mind the dried blood and elf rat brainslop, but I certainly do."

Zastarte went for wood from the woodshed as Dek used kindling to light a fire in a great iron stove. He rooted through the cupboards and larder, and although many of the supplies had been taken, he found plenty that they could use; two half pigs, cured and salted; onions; potatoes; carrots; some dried and salted fish; some stale loaves of black bread. "This'll soften nicely in stew," mumbled Dek, returning with laden arms to the kitchen. Kiki had filled several large brass pans with water from an outside barrel, cracking the icy surface with the hilt of one short sword.

Zastarte appeared, arms laden with wood, and with Dek they piled the black iron range high and soon watched fireflies dancing up the iron pipe. Both men stepped outside, looking up at the chimney where smoke poured free.

"Well, every fucker will know we're here, now," said Zastarte, words clipped.

Dek shrugged, and rolled his shoulders. "You know what? That's a risk I'm willing to take."

Kiki appeared. "Who's doing the cooking? I'm damned if you think I'm doing it, just because I'm the only woman present."

"I'll do it," said Zastarte, grinning. "I'm sick of eating your tough beef slop. I'll cook you a meal fit for any princess. As long as you get busy filling that bath with nice hot water. I actually think I've got entrails in my hair. Can you believe that? Fucking *entrails*. In my fucking *hair*."

"Maybe you need to hack it off. It's looking a bit feminine," said Dek.

Zastarte gave him a withering look and the gentlest of nods. "What? And end up with it looking like *that*?" He gestured. "I'll take my chances with the entrails, if it's all the same to you. But on a more positive note, I found something else when I was looking for the woodshed."

"Such as?"

"Horses," said the dandy. "Live horses."

"Much better than dead horses, I think," snorted Dek.

"Well, I was actually considering them in a food sense. Fresh meat. After all, we wouldn't be needing them for a journey – because we're heading back into Zanne to find Narnok and Trista, aren't we?"

Kiki and Dek exchanged a quick glance, which Zastarte noted. He scowled, eyes narrowing, licking his lips and baring his teeth. "I'll go and prepare us something to eat whilst you two ponder the impending terrible deaths of our abandoned friends. I just want you to be aware that if anything happens to Trista…"

"Yeah?" said Dek, eyes dangerous, hand on the hilt of his long sword.

Zastarte grinned. "Then watch your back."

Kiki reclined in the hot water, scrubbing at her skin with a block of soap. It felt amazing. It felt *more* than amazing. An orgasm that lasted over and over and over. The simple, basic premise of washing sweat and gore and crap from her skin until she emerged, scrubbed and pink and... feeling like a woman again. Dek was waiting for her. He grabbed her round the waist, held her naked, but she slapped him in the chest with the heel of her hand. "Get off me you oaf – you *stink*!"

"Ha, you didn't say that the other night in the forest!"

"That's because we *both* stank. Get in the bath and get rid of that filth. Look, you're covered in elf rat gore. It's disgusting!"

"Wait for me, my lady," he grinned.

"I'll be downstairs, helping Zastarte with the food."

She moved through to a bedroom, coarse towel wrapped around her, and rummaged through Beth's old clothes. Beth. *Beth*. I wonder where you are, Lady of the House? I hope you are well, and that you and Old Skern and the Little Ones are safe. I hope you headed away from this madness. I hope the evil in Zanne didn't suck you in and tear you down.

Beth's clothes fit reasonably well, and Kiki dressed in tight-fitting leggings and a cool cotton shirt of white. She pulled on a thick lambs-wool jumper, and found some soft leather boots, handmade and uneven, but wonderfully comfortable.

Stepping lightly down the stairs, she found Zastarte frying onions and garlic in butter. He glanced at her, but his face was a mask; unreadable.

"Would you like me to help?"

"No."

"Have I upset you?"

"I heard you. Upstairs, with Dek."

"Meaning?"

Zastarte turned on her. "If it was Dek we'd left behind there, in Zanne, we'd already be on the fucking march, searching for another way in, looking to help our old war comrades. We've been through a lot together, Kiki, and I know you well, but this turn of events is beneath you. We have *abandoned them*. Can't you see that? Left them to fucking die under the claws of the elf rats."

"No." Her face went hard. "We were separated beyond our control. Narnok and Trista are both incredibly competent soldiers; warriors. They *are* alive, Zast, and you know it, and I bloody know it too."

"But *how* do you know?" he said, almost pleading.

"I am the Heart of the Wolves. You know I only want the best for all of us. And I would crawl over broken glass and a million dead enemies to rescue a single one of you." She took hold of Zastarte's shoulders. "You *know* that, Zast. You fucking *know it*."

"And what about Yoon?"

"What about him?"

"About what he said. About Sameska. About Zalazar. About *the White Towers and the Elf Heart*?"

"That's a different discussion," said Kiki, gently, eyes locked to Zastarte. "But trust me, my friend, when I tell you we're not going rushing off on some fool's errand on random information given by some lunatic like Yoon. Narnok is a brother to me, and yes, Trista is a sister to me. You are my *family*. The *Iron Wolves* are in my blood. By the Seven Sisters. You *are* my blood."

Zastarte ladled out the onions and garlic – which smelled amazing – and added dried beef, tomatoes and water from a boiling pan, which he then stirred idly as he returned the pan to the hot plate of the wood-burning range. "You want to know what's ironic?" He barked a short laugh. "*I* believe him. Believe that mad fuck, Yoon. I think what he said is true. It was like a prediction, Kiki. A vision of the future; like he *knew* the fucking elf rats were going to invade Vagandrak." He stumbled into silence, stirring the bubbling broth.

"Let's eat, and sleep, and regain our strength," said Kiki, wincing as Dek's stitches pulled tight in her side. "Trista will be all right. I promise."

"Yes," nodded Zastarte, and listened to Kiki move away, back up the stairs, to the encompassing arms of her lover.

Nobody saw the tears running down his cheeks.

She ran her hands through the curled hair on Dek's chest, and lowered herself onto his throbbing, erect cock. It eased inside her, an inch at a time, and she closed her eyes, throwing her head back, chewing her lower lip. His hands found hers, their fingers interlocking, and she pushed down on him with every beat of her heart, every *th-thump* of her twin hearts. And as they fucked long into the dark hours of the night, the world and battle and Vagandrak, everything fell away in that basic farmhouse bedroom, lit by candlelight; everything fell away, slow swirling like oil down a sink hole. And even as Kiki felt herself rising to climax, and her eyes flickered open to see Dek writhing beneath her, his teeth gritted, face beautiful in this moment despite his absolute lack of beauty, she felt their union, their symbiotic power, the rush of blood through veins, and she came with a long low moan and felt him come inside her, felt his hot rush and his total utter abandon, and then she collapsed on him, rolled to his side, snuggled into his cuddle, one hand on his heaving chest as his panting quickly receded and he turned to look at her.

"You're beautiful, my lady," he said, eyes earnest and bright.

"Fuck off. You've got what you want, you don't need to mock me."

"I'm serious." He jacked himself up on one elbow. "I've never seen you look more beautiful. You look…" he stroked her red-flushed cheek, "*radiant*."

"I bet you say that to all the girls," she said, snuggling against him again. Outside, wind and ice needles drove against the windows, howling. The storm had returned with a vengeance.

"Yeah. And they all believe it."

"Bastard." She punched him in the bicep.

"Ouch. That hurt."

"Want me to kiss it better?"

"So soon?"

"I'm a hard woman to please," she said, stroking his sex-warm flesh.

"Go on then. Kiss it better," he said; and she did.

An undulating, snow-filled plain.

Trees surrounded the edges, tall and thick and foreboding. Creatures watched from the dark places. They were wolves. She could sense they were wolves. She could smell the blood on their muzzles. Smell the need in them. The lust for the kill.

Five figures walked towards her, boots crunching in the snow. They halted. She could see them more clearly now.

"We have come for you, Kiki, Captain of the Iron Wolves."

Kiki drew both her swords.

"At least tell me who you are, before I fucking kill you."

"We are the Tree Stalkers," said a tall, beautiful figure. His limbs were slightly twisted, his eyes black like molten glass. "And I am Aeoxir. Remember it well." He charged, and Kiki's swords attacked in a blur of steel. But he was too fast, sweeping past her, hardly shifting to avoid her clumsy strokes. She felt both her belly and throat part under soft whispers of razor steel. Watched in disbelief as her blood pattered to the crisp white snow, and felt the *shift* as her bowels spilled from her opened abdomen...

She hit the ground with a grunt, which spat blood before her disbelieving eyes.

And, as shadows fell over her, she closed her eyes and her mouth filled with warm blood and she remembered how hot the blade had been; the one that cut across her throat.

Dek slept, and Kiki stared at the ceiling, shivering. There were cracks in the plaster running diagonally between the beams. She wondered if Old Skern knew. She wondered if Beth was still alive, and she pictured the woman's round, happy face, remembering the time at the Cider Fayre when they'd both got stinking drunk and Old Skern had had to bring them back to this very farmhouse in a cart. She realised tears were on her cheeks. *Gods be with you and your family, Beth*, she thought.

And she thought about Aeoxir.

Thought about the chilling ice of the razor across her throat.

Beth? Old Skern? Like you give a flying fucking barrel of horse shit. Suza sidled into the dark recesses of Kiki's mind, and Kiki felt herself sigh internally. And yet she could see Suza, hazy, as if through a veil and standing in the corner of a fire-scorched room.

What do you want?

I want nothing you haven't already given me.

Well fuck off, then, thought Kiki. *I'm tired of your… presence.*

You're tired? That amuses me greatly, sister of mine. Because if you're tired, then you're weary, and if you're weary, you've had enough of the world and, hopefully, you'll soon be hanging from a noose tied by those delicate, pretty little fingers of yours. Oh how pretty they are, long and white and tapered; the nails could do with a bit of a manicure, but that's, as we all know, because you like to play hard and rough with all the soldier boys.

Haven't you got something better to do?

Of course. Always have. But sometimes, it's fun to poke shit at you, you useless, pointless excretion.

Kiki smiled to herself, and rolled from the bed. She glanced down at Dek. Gods, if he knew the shit that went on inside my head. Surely he'd think I was…

Crazy, agreed Suza.

Do I have no secrets from you, bitch?

None at all. She felt, more than saw, Suza smile in the blackened room. But she *felt* it. The lies. The *fake*.

You're lying, realised Kiki. *You know some things, but others are a distant dream from when you were alive.*

Horse shit!

No, I am right. In the same way you can no longer experience the amazing sensation of a man's huge cock inside you, bringing you to a slick, fast, hard, mind-blowing realm of fucking ecstasy, so you can no longer see into my thoughts, or into my heart. Something's changed, hasn't it, Suza? That's why you're here. You want something, bitch.

I want nothing! The scream almost blew Kiki's brain out through her ears with its random suddenness and terrible ferocity. No human vocal cords should have been able to make a sound like that; but then, this was not a sound in the air, but a pulse of power, or magick, in the mind.

The world seemed to blend, to merge, and Kiki was in that fire-blackened room. Above her, fire ravaged timbers creaked, bowed, barely able to support the roof. Through ragged gaps she saw a sky so black it was a bottomless chasm. There were no stars. Around her, the walls had been kissed and devoured by flame, and yet still stood, carbon-smeared stone proud and solid and refusing to buckle. But the worst thing was the stench, the absolute terrible fucking *stench* of the fire. It was more than woodsmoke, more than warm ashes; it was scorched flesh, pig flesh, human flesh, rich and ripe with bubbling fat and the sickly sweet aroma of over-cooked baby meat. Kiki nearly gagged, but forced herself into some semblance of civility and sanity and her head came up and she saw the dark, blackened face of Suza.

"Welcome to my world," said Suza.

"I came invited?"

"Of course not. You are a fucking intruder."

Suza took a step forward. Her clothes were melted rags. Every inch of her skin was blackened, dry, cracked. Her hair was crisp dry stalks. Her fingernails had burned free. Only her eyes held colour, and they were dark, glittering, and filled with a purity of hate directed straight at Kiki.

"You brought me here," said Kiki, frowning, unsure.

"You brought yourself here. You stepped across the threshold. I want you to leave."

Kiki smiled, then, a long, slow smile. "*You* want me to leave?"

"Fucking leave, fucking bitch," snapped Suza, taking another quick step forward. Her hands curled into claws. "Before I take out your eyes."

"Relax, sister," soothed Kiki, but she changed her position with infinite subtlety, awaiting the attack, making herself better placed to defend. "I'm not here to ruin your day. Or your life. Not like you seem to try and ruin mine!"

"I show you things; I keep it real," snarled Suza.

Kiki laughed, a laugh filled with mockery. "Oh do fuck off. You torture me for your own personal amusement; you cause me pain to exact some kind of petty retribution for the pain you suffered at my hands. Well, I'm sorry, Suza. If I could take it back, I would. If I could change the past, I would. But I cannot. Are we going to play this silly, petty game for the rest of our existence?"

"Until the day you die," spat Suza, so full of hate it filled her to the brim.

Kiki felt her own anger fire through her like acid, and she stalked forward as Suza raised her hands, palms outwards.

"I'm sick of this game. Release me from this place! And leave me alone!"

"I've come to warn you," said Suza.

"Yeah? Horse shit!"

"No, really… when you step back into your own world, into your own time; Sameska the elf rat is even now sneaking through the kitchen of the farmhouse. I don't know if his intentions are murder, or help; but I do know the elf rats must be halted."

Kiki stopped, scowling, and glanced over her shoulder. "Back there? Now?"

"Yes."

"Why the fuck would you warn me?"

"Because the elf rats are a scourge on our land." Then she smiled. "Even worse than the fucking *Shamathe*."

Kiki gave a nod, turned, and felt herself *squash* through an invisible barrier. Then she was back, and Dek was snoring softly, and she grabbed one of her short swords and, naked, hair swaying to her shoulders, moved to the stairwell and listened.

All was silent.

She trod carefully, one step at a time, shivering a little. They'd allowed the kitchen range to extinguish, and the winter cold was fighting a winning battle against the insulated warmth of the borrowed home.

Sameska was seated in a rounded comfort chair, head tilted to one side, watching as Kiki approached through the doorway. He had his narrow bony limbs crossed before him, long fingers like talons submissive in his lap in a non-threatening way. Kiki met that gaze, met those bright yellow eyes, those large eyes in the oval face with skin like bark, deeply grooved and marked, almost like tattoos of wood grain, and she smiled gently, walking forward, grabbing a blanket from another chair and wrapping it around her shoulders for modesty. She seated herself opposite Sameska on a wide couch, and crossed her legs, arranging her blanket discreetly, sword across her lap.

"You came back," she said, finally.

"Yes."

"Why?"

"Because of you, Kiki." He looked at her, almost shyly. "Because of your past. Because you were born… *different.*"

Kiki blinked. Her breath eased out like oiled smoke. "How could you know that?"

"You are *Shamathe*. I am an elf, dear lady. Born of the earth and the trees. Us rats, us *elf rats,* are not so different from your kind."

Kiki considered this. "I cannot control my powers," she said, eventually. "They are available to me only on occasion; and even then, they are so terrible I feel like a tiny fishing boat lost at high sea in a raging storm. Does that make sense?"

"Yes," said Sameska, gently. "You lost your control when you submitted to Dalgoran's curse, the curse that infected all of the Iron Wolves. In fact, do you realise the curse relied on your *Shamathe* ability? No, I did not think you understood the magick which governs you all. General Dalgoran was a wily one. He mined you like they mine for gold; used *you,* as a binding tool to hold the Iron Wolves together; to give them strength. If you die, Kiki, you all die." He whispered the last few words, and Kiki felt a terrible chill run through her soul. Her hackles rose on the back of her neck and she felt herself drop into the chilly embrace of understanding.

"Thank you for *sharing* that information. I will keep it to heart. But there is another reason you have come."

"Yes."

"You need our help?"

"Very observant, Kiki. But it will involve very great danger, for no personal gain."

"We have friends, trapped in the city of Zanne. Indeed, they are trapped by *your kind*. By elf rats. We watched hordes of elf rats stampeding through the streets, hunting down survivors, pulling children limb from limb."

Sameska gave a nod, and Kiki was surprised to see tears running down his cheeks. "There are some of, as you say, *my kind*, who have sunk very low indeed. But your friends are safe; for now."

"How do you know?"

Sameska closed his eyes. "I can find my way there, through the roots of every tree and holly bush and blade of grass. The big one with the axe, and the ice-eyed woman of cold beauty, they fought their way free and escaped into an old factory. The woman of ice stitched the big man's wounds. They are safe. For now."

"This is true? *True?*"

"Yes. I do not lie."

"But your deviated people invade our lands and murder our fucking children."

"Yes. The situation is far more dire than you could ever imagine. Daranganoth, the elf rat king, has ordered his armies out of Zalazar to annihilate your kind, in return for the genocide and poisoning visited on our people centuries earlier by the lineage of King Yoon, and King Tarek before him. Their bloodline has been condemned by Daranganoth. Extermination is his aim. He is a king filled with bitterness, hate, and a singular lack of mercy."

"These armies – they are in Zanne? Now? They are in our cities?"

"No," said Sameska, softly. "Those are just *the Flood*. Sent in advance with the elf rat sorcerer, Bazaroth aea Quazaquiel, to take key strategic points across Vagandrak; to take the cities and religious places, where our stones are buried. General Namash is here, also, with a scouting force; the real armies are on their way, and when they come they will hunt down every one of King Yoon's battalions and smash them in bloody war. Your men will have nowhere to turn; nowhere to find food and shelter and weapons. They would have to lay siege to their own cities. An ironic reversal. And they would be broken."

"What do you want us to do?" Kiki could not keep the sneer of cynicism from her voice.

"King Yoon was correct when he told you of Zalazar, when he spoke about the White Towers. And I know they have been in your dreams these long months... have they not?"

Kiki nodded, sneer tumbling from her face to be replaced by the images from her dreams; from her nightmares.

"You must travel there, find the Elf Heart. And either bring it back to Zanne, bring it home to *me*. Or destroy it, if you can. We will be purified. The elf rats will regain their nobility, their kindness, their humility, and their sense of civilisation."

Kiki stared at Sameska for a long, long time. "I could ask if it was a trap, but that would be pointless. I believe that you are far more powerful than anyone could imagine. Am I right, Sameska? I believe what you're saying is true; however, what I want to know is, why don't *you* do it?"

Sameska smiled, then. "That is one of the great ironies. If an elf rat touches the Elf Heart, they turn to ash. If you like, it is *our curse*, visited upon us by the ancient magickers and *Shamathe*s of Vagandrak. The only people who can save us, return us to some semblance of civilisation, are those very people who exterminated us. The Elf Heart is not our creation, Kikellya Mandasayard; it is yours. This was a way the magickers protected themselves."

"Finally, Sameska, tell me: what do *you* get out of this?" Her eyes held those of the elf rat, and they sat in silence for long moments.

"Can you not see, *Shamathe*? Can you not read my thoughts?"

And Kiki could see past burning moorlands and fire-filled citadels, a great battle raging. Two brothers at war to be the ruling leader of the land of Zalazar. On the one side, leading massive armies of mounted elf rats on twisted horse beasts from horror came Daranganoth, mighty, barrel-chested, twisted out of all recognition; and on the other side, leading battalions of elf rat soldiers in silver and black armour came... Sameska. Two brothers. Fighting to be... king.

Kiki gasped. "You want to rule?"

"I want my people back," said Sameska, "but more, I want diplomacy, I want society, I want civilisation. I do *not* want war and retribution. I do not want fucking carnage."

"Why not?" snarled Kiki. "What makes you so different?"

"Because we can exist together in this world, Kikellya. If not in Vagandrak, then in Zalazar – or in other places. I see my brothers and sisters being slaughtered, and I am tired of the death, exhausted by slaughter. I want peace, Kiki. And you, and your Iron Wolves, can help save not just Vagandrak, but the elf rats from your darkest legends. You can put right what is wrong. You can make good the evil of Vagandrak's past."

Kiki placed her chin on her fist and stared hard at Sameska. There came a sound from behind, and Zastarte glided into the room. His sword was out, glittering alongside his eyes. He was staring at Sameska, and then turned to Kiki.

"You heard that?"

"Yes."

"How much?"

"Enough."

"And your thoughts?"

Zastarte weighed up his response, then snapped at Sameska. "For some reason which is unfathomable, I actually fucking believe this twisted pile of shit. And if he can prove to me, *prove to me*, that Trista – and Narnok, obviously – are still alive in Zanne, and if he can assure me Trista – and Narnok, obviously – aren't about to be viciously slaughtered, then I agree to accompany you, Kikellya," he grinned, then, "on this madcap fool's fucking errand to save not just our own world, but those of our ancient enemies who are now toxic deviations polluting our land with their poisonous trees." He smiled broadly. "How *do* we keep getting into these rancid piles of staggered horse shit?"

"We need to talk to Dek. Go get him."

"That's all right. Dek's already here," said the big man, easing himself from the gloom of the corridor.

"You were both there the whole time?" said Kiki.

Dek nodded. "Let's call it protection; backup for the Little Lady." He gave her a wink.

"I have one more thing to say, before I leave for the snow and the poison seeping into your land, into your trees. You may have noticed them already? The toxicity of Zalazar is making its way here through root and bedrock and river and leyline; it could be surmised King Daranganoth is intent on making your slaughter a one-way process." He smiled, teeth like thorns.

"Speak," said Kiki, all too aware that the presence of

Zastarte and Dek with weapons drawn, two of the most evil, lethal bastards she knew, had done nothing to even make Sameska stutter. He was indeed an elf rat without fear; or one of the best poker players Kiki had ever come across in a lifetime of gambling in shit-holes and Red Thumb gambling dens.

"There is a great threat to you, Kiki, and to you alone. They are aware of you. They have been sent for you. They may even have appeared in your dreams."

Kiki felt goose bumps crawling up and down her arms.

"What are you talking about?"

"Tree Stalkers."

A cold silence met Sameska's words, as they all tried to digest the name, and indeed, the concept it represented.

"Tree Stalkers?" said Dek, eventually.

"They are our natural killers. Our elite. The nightmares that stalk children's dreams. The reality that rips out throats and spines in the dead of night. These are King Daranganoth's elite. His special killers. His shadows in the dark. They are patient, and they are merciless, and they are deadly. They will come for you in your sleep. Always in your sleep. They will send in their quests..."

"Quests?"

"Thin roots which come from their hands, they can crawl inside your brain through ears and nose and mouth and rip your head apart with a simple tug. Failing that, they will face you in battle. They are fast, and deadly. Beyond the understanding of mortal man."

"I'm pretty fucking deadly myself," growled Dek.

Sameska threw him such a look that Dek went cold inside.

"You will know them when you see them," said Sameska, "and they will hunt you through Vagandrak to take your souls back to the Dark Places; back to the Toxic City. First there is Ugrak, brutal, primitive, he is basic and simple but so, so strong. Try chopping down a five hundred year oak with a hand axe. That is Ugrak. Then comes Aeoxir, a thief of shadows, covert in every word and action and deed. His intelligence is legendary. He plays life and death as if it is a board game; and he is always the winner. His special skill is that he can merge with the trees. Become completely invisible. Become a part of the woodland. Then, there is Ffaefel, incredibly tall and thin and elegant. It is said he sleeps with other males, and young boys, and slits their throats after copulation. That is his ejaculation: the bringing of death. There is Sileath, the only female of the group. She is like smoke, dark smoke inhaled through a drug pipe. She will intoxicate your mind and get in close and deliver a blade to the heart. It is why she was born. Why she was twisted. Why she was trained.

"And finally, there is Villiboch – a warrior and archer beyond compare. He is the leader of the group, and without doubt the most deadly elf rat ever to walk the lands of Zalazar. He has bested more than two hundred contenders in single combat. Most matches – and these were against the most deadly swordsmen and warriors in our lands – most matches last less than a minute. I have seen this amoral bastard fight; and he is like nothing on the face of our decadent planet."

Sameska trailed off into silence, and looked away, and then back at Dek, then Zastarte, and finally Kiki. "It is unfair of me to ask you to do this thing. I know how large are the risks, and I know the probable outcome. And yet I must ask you. It is not something I can physically accomplish myself."

"So what will you do here?" said Kiki.

"I will work at bringing down Daranganoth from the inside. I will do my utmost to slay his primary weapon."

"Primary weapon?" Zastarte raised his eyebrows.

"The elf rat sorcerer, Bazaroth aea Quazaquiel. He is dangerous beyond belief."

"How will you do that?" said Kiki, voice low and level.

"I will find Narnok and Trista," said Sameska, with a smile of sharp, slightly twisted thorns. "And I will help rally the rebels inside the city – ready for your triumphant return with the Elf Heart. Either that, or its destruction."

Sleep came easily to Dek. He snored the snore of a pig, and Kiki was annoyed at first, and then grinned to herself. Better the snore of a pig, than the utter total silence of loneliness, she tried to convince herself. It was a hard fight to win.

She lay on her back, the blankets warm around her, cosy, pondering the words of Sameska. A long journey. Hunted. Battles. War. But then, wasn't that a description of her entire fucking life? Not for her the chance to settle down, find the right man, marry, have children. Raise those children with love and education and understanding.

But why? *Why not?*

It was in her hand before she even realised, and slowly she placed the stolen *honey-leaf* coin from the Zanne processing plant under her tongue. The reaction was almost automatic, a reflex instinctive rather than learned. The hard coin softened, and slowly crumbled, and gradually melted. It tasted bitter. And yet the bitterness was like an old, welcome friend. A fine whiskey. A perfect steak. The passionate kiss from a perfect partner on New Year.

The honey-leaf crumbled under Kiki's tongue, and Kiki crumbled into the honey-leaf.

And it felt good.

It felt right.

And nothing, nothing, could ever be the same again.

Can you control it?

Hell yes!

Really?

No, not really.

So. Can you control it?

What the fuck do you think?

Do you want to control it?

Sometimes, I'm beyond giving a fuck. Sometimes, I wonder what death will be like. I'm tired of the fight. I'm tired of the struggle. Sometimes — sometimes — I wonder what it would be like to simply lie down, and go to sleep, and stay asleep. Forever. No more waking up into pain and anguish and battle. No more messing about with the pain that is life.

Do you think that's normal?

Who gives a fuck? And what's normal, anyway? I know what I feel, and I know what I want.

And what do you want?

I want another honey-leaf.

Do you think Dek will value your new path?

Fuck him.

Really?

No, not really.

So you respect him?

More than anybody.

This will torture him.

Maybe.

So you have no *respect for him.*

Of course I do. Of course! I love him. I love him more than words can say. I've come a long way through the shit, and he's my guiding light; my moral beacon.

So… why are you doing this, then?

Because I can.

Really?

Because I want to.

Do you really want to?

I cannot help myself.

And do you want help to escape?

No. Fuck the help.

So you enjoy the drug?

I need the drug.

You enjoy the pain?

Kiki blinked in the candlelight, and ran her hand down Dek's flank. *Fuck yes; pain is what tells you you're still alive.*

RED THUMBS

The four huge dogs – Duchess, Duke, Sarge and the monster from Hell that was Thrasher – charged with scrabbling claws across polished marble leaving trails of saliva. At the last minute, Narnok turned and heaved Trista to one side, grabbed a nearby chair and leapt up onto the long feasting table, boots scarring the highly polished surface. Duchess came first, and the heavy wood clubbed her down. She rolled, yelping to one side, and came up fast. Then the other dogs were there and Narnok laid into them, the chair smashing into pieces in his fists. Thuds echoed out as Narnok beat all four dogs from the air like a batsman playing Heart Ball, and they fell, yelping, rolling, and Narnok's eyes found Mola and the two men exchanged a moment and Mola knew, *knew* Narnok was playing the kind man, the kind soul, and suddenly he threw down the sticks and hefted his axe and it was no longer a game. Mola had had his chance, and Narnok had given him an opportunity, but now, if he didn't call them off, real blood would be spilt…

Narnok readied himself with his axe. In truth, he loved dogs, and it hurt him to beat even these huge shaggy brutes with a club. But this was no game and they'd drag him down and tear him apart given half the chance. Narnok was under no delusions as to their ferocity. It was just... he remembered his puppy. And he fucking loved puppies.

"*Dogs*!" roared Mola. "*Down*!"

Three turned to stare at him, almost in disbelief. Only Duchess obeyed immediately for she loved him without question. She was a good bitch.

"*Down* you fucking disobedient wretches!" stormed Mola, stamping forward, and all four dogs lay at his feet, gazing up at him, and competing for his love.

Slowly, Mola lifted his gaze to Narnok, who stepped down onto a chair, then to the floor, axe easy by his side but there just in case he needed it; for man *or* beast.

"You're a lucky man," growled Narnok.

"How's that?"

"I don't like killing dogs. So I let them live. Men, on the other hand," he smiled a grim smile, "that's a different story."

"Point taken, Narn. Point taken."

There came an awkward silence, and Trista stepped forward looking both men up and down. She tutted, and stroked her chin.

"You still owe me that money, though," said Mola.

"I agree. This changes nothing. You ripped me off, you bastard."

"Gentlemen, gentlemen," hissed Trista, her own eyes flashing dangerous and she glanced between them. "This is, and I say it with absolute sincerity, *fucking insane*. There's a horde of deviant elf rats out there just dying to rip you apart. If you feel the need for some fucking aggravation, just step outside the front door of this museum."

Mola shrugged.

Narnok turned and looked away.

The dogs growled on the floor.

"Shake hands," said Trista.

"Eh?" snarled Narnok.

"Over my dead body," growled Mola.

"I can fucking arrange that," snapped Narnok.

"Stop, stop, stop," said Trista in exasperation. "What is it with you two? It wasn't like this back in the day, was it? I would have remembered. Then stabbed you both through the heart when you were asleep." She smiled, grimly, and they both realised it wasn't just a figure of speech; she actually, really, actually meant it.

"Bardok? What's going on there?" The voice was lazy, casual, sensuous, authoritative. It drifted like woodsmoke from the rear of the museum hall, where deep shadows lay, where tall sculptures cast esoteric images on the marble and the matt white walls.

"*Bardok*?" hissed Narnok. "What game is being played?"

Mola's eyes went wide. "Play the game, horse dick, or we'll all be dead."

"Eh?"

"Explain," whispered Trista.

"These are the Red Thumbs," said Mola, waggling his eyebrows in what would have been an amusing gesture if it hadn't been for the raw terror the simple name the "Red Thumbs" was capable of conjuring. "*Play along*, Narnok. They fucking hate the Iron Wolves. I mean, *fucking hate them*."

"Not as much as they hate me," muttered Narnok. "I've, er, had some dealings with them in the past."

"What kind of dealings?"

"I killed some of them."

"*Which* some of them?" Mola's eyes were even wider, now.

"Er. Some important some of them."

"Fuck."

"Time to leave?"

"Just play it cool."

"I'm a hard man to hide."

"It's too late to run."

A shadow detached from the other shadows at the back of the museum hall. It drifted forward, casually, with an air of natural grace one might associate with decadent royalty, or maybe a natural, drunken warrior.

He was tall, and dashingly handsome. He wore his dark hair long to the nape of his neck, his face was finely chiselled – a square jaw, handsome humour lines, piercing blue eyes – broad shoulders, narrow hips, a natural swagger that spoke of confidence and conquest and arrogance. He carried narrow curved swords on each hip, and knives at boot, thigh, hip and chest, which spoke of profession in real combat. These weren't ornaments. This almost-dandy was a killer.

"Randaman," said Mola, turning and nodding. "Found these here people wandering. Thought I'd check they weren't… you know. The diseased. The twisted. The… *elves*."

"Of course." Randaman strode forward, and Narnok noted he kept a certain distance from the axe and swords on display. He was experienced. His every movement screamed it. Narnok immediately despised him. Randaman reminded Narnok of all those ale-house male whores, those smooth charmers who took the virginity of innocent young farm girls and left them to rot with a baby to feed; he reminded Narnok of the slime who ran the gambling pits, making money from the needy and the desperate in society; but most of all, Narnok despised him because he simply *looked like a cunt.* Thus, he kept his mouth shut and let Trista do the talking. After all, she had blonde curls and a figure to die for. What competition an old soldier with scars for a face?

Randaman took careful, wary stock of Narnok. This man was no fool. He saw the experience laid out in the chips and metal-scars on the axe blades. Then his eyes, only a cursory scan to begin with, fell fully upon the beauty that was Trista. Yes, she hadn't washed in a while, and had been involved in various battles leaving bloody stains on clothing and face and hair, and she was filled with exhaustion and pain and fear, which laid itself out across her grey face like a pastel painting. But there was no disguising a goddess. And Trista was the most beautiful of them all; as many a man had found, to his peril. And indeed, his terminal curiosity.

"Lady?" said Randaman.

"That sounded like a question," purred Trista, turning to keep up with his traversal. The turn made her head and body turn against itself, and the image was intoxicating. "You think, maybe, I am not a lady?"

"Oh no; no, no, I am certain to the nth degree that you are fully a woman, and indeed, one of the most incredible women I have ever witnessed."

"I haven't heard that one before," smiled Trista, although it was an ice-cold smile and her eyes were diamonds trapped in ice for a million years.

"Come now." Randaman stopped his dandy's waltz. Narnok nearly puked with the theatricality of it all. "No need to be modest. Not here. Not in this company." He smiled a heart-winning smile which Trista returned. She'd seen it all before. On a million fake advertisements for love.

"I'm not being modest," she said. "We're just trying to stay alive. Out there... out there..."

Narnok noted how she turned her voice a little. Now, she was a desperate princess in need of rescue. Narnok grinned through his remaining teeth. Fuck, he thought. How did you get so fucking cynical? But then, people – and cunts – kept proving him right. Once, the world used to be a pleasant place filled with people willing to help one another. Now, it was a charnel pit filled with death and scum and shit.

Yeah? Why did you fight at Desekra Fortress then?

For the money and the fame, bitch. Always for the money and the glory.

"You have come a long way?" asked Randaman. Trista looked at Mola, who kept his face straight and neutral. No help there. Mola was playing the solo game. Mola was simply looking after his own base survival.

"We've been holidaying with a rich uncle at the foot of the Mountains of Skarandos," lied Trista smoothly. She'd had a lifetime of practice. "We were there a month. Then we travelled north to Zanne, and... the whole city was locked down. Screams came from within. It was terrifying!" She played the fraught virgin with expertise, despite hints to the contrary. No woman of Trista's age or beauty was a virgin. Well. Not often. Still, Randaman was sucked in and you could see it in his eyes, in his face, in his stance. He was intoxicated by Trista. Body, heart and soul. He wanted in. Inside. In that warm place. They all did, till they felt the reverse fuck; the slide of cold iron into their hearts and throats. A double penetration. Who fucks who?

"These are dangerous times," nodded Randaman. "You… you should come with us. For protection. For safety."

Narnok snorted a laugh. Randaman slid his gaze to the huge axeman; a sideways shift. "Something amusing you, pretty boy?" he snapped.

Narnok cooled himself, and turned full on to Randaman. Just to show him exactly what he was fucking with. "I recognise," said Narnok, slowly, as if addressing a simpleton, "that my face resembles a steak dinner after the dogs have chewed it. However, the one thing no cunt can ever take from me is my pride. The last man who called me *pretty boy* in puerile sarcasm," Narnok considered this for a few moments, hand across his chin and lips as if solving some great conundrum, "well, lad," he growled, "I cut him in half with my axe. And I fucking mean *in half*. From the top of his skull, to his dangling slack ball sack. A dissection of skin and meat and fat and bone, a neat cut of organs and bowel and bloody shit. As I sat around the fire that night, with the lads, picking bits of sliced bollock from the chips in my axe-blades, I asked myself a question – *is there a time when you'll grow up, and stop taking needless offence from the pointless hot-air of yapping idiots?* And you know what my answer to myself was? It was a fucking *no*, lad. Because if you ain't got no self-respect, then what have you got in this shit, pointless life?"

Randaman stared at Narnok impassively for a few moments. Then he gave a beaming smile. He took a small step forward and patted Narnok on the shoulder. "I like you, Big Guy. You've got a fucking good sense of humour. You can stay."

"Oh. So you're letting me then, are you?"

"Yeah."

"And what makes you think I won't just lop off your grinning fucking head and stay anyway?"

Randaman gestured, almost languorously, to the darkened, hidden balconies lining both sides of the chamber. "Archers," he said, and gave a sick little smile. "I'm sorry. You need to come with me or we'll cut you down like rabid dogs in the street." The smile stretched a little wider; like a cat that was pleased with itself, licking cream from its whiskers.

"And there I was, thinking you were a gentleman," said Trista, tossing him a haughty look.

"Alas, dear love! These savage times force us into modes of address one would not normally embrace. I eschew all forms of antagonistic behaviour. Truly, I do. But as you have seen for yourself outside," he gestured broadly, and his voice hardened. "We have to protect ourselves."

"We'll come with you," said Narnok, brows furrowed above his heavy facial scarring, "but we keep our weapons."

"You are hardly in a position to barter, dear boy."

"That's the deal," said Narnok, frowning. "Else I'll cut you down now and take my fucking chances with the arrows."

"You think you could?" Randaman's eyes were narrowed.

"You know I could," growled Narnok, with a smile.

There was a moment of intense tension, then Randaman suddenly relaxed and stepped forward, slapping Narnok on the arm. "Of course, no worries, old timer. No need to be so grumpy about the whole show! Now, if you'd like to follow me," and he turned, whilst Narnok was still blinking and grumbling and favouring the tight stitches, and Randaman offered his arm to Trista.

She linked with him, surprising even herself, and they walked down the ornate marble hall, connecting with long flowing corridors lined with rich oil paintings depicting the violent past of Vagandrak and its outlying cities, towers and lands; they moved past display cabinets filled with all manner of antiquity, Narnok shuffling along in his battered boots, his eye dark, the other empty socket itching him like a bastard.

Some of the archers padded down carpeted stairs leading from the deeply shadowed upper balconies, falling in behind Narnok and Trista. Narnok turned and stared at them. They were clad in black cotton, more like assassins than the kinds of archers Narnok knew, and they kept their notched bows *not-quite* pointing at the huge axeman.

Mola, with his growling dogs now on leads, came bellowing and snarling through the midst of the archers until he walked alongside Narnok, who gave him a curious sideways glare. Mola grinned at him, then winced.

"You suffering?"

"Aye. Chucked from a horse. Broke some ribs and my collarbone."

"That pain suits you."

"And you! What's that? Sword wound?"

"Dagger, I think. Or maybe claws. It was a big battle. Hell, lots of big battles. I'm starting to think my whole life has just become one big battle, and I'm starting to get a little tired. Maybe I should become an onion farmer. Or something."

"I know how you feel," said Mola, rolling his neck and shoulders. Duchess took that moment to growl and snap at something that was apparently invisible, and Mola hauled her back with a snarl. "DUCHESS! DOWN!"

"I'm not sure who's leading who," grinned Narnok, suddenly. He burst into laughter, and Trista glanced behind, from where Randaman was explaining the ancestry of an encased and particularly fine set of pearl earrings hanging on a carved wooden head. "I knew, if I ever met you again, you'd still be hanging around with a bunch of dogs."

"Well, that's the thing about dogs," said Mola, and it was his turn to smile. "They're a damn sight more loving, more *trustworthy*, than any woman." His eyes were gleaming. "How's your wife, Narn? You married that fine filly, didn't you? Kahuna. Black curls. Flashing dangerous eyes, if ever I saw them on a woman."

"Katuna," corrected Narnok. And stared at Mola, smile frozen; then dropping from his face like a widow's veil. "Not with her anymore," he mumbled.

"Seen Dek recently?"

"Oh yeah," said Narnok, eyes gleaming. "Me and Dek had a good little chat, we did."

"He still alive?"

"So you *did* hear, then. Grak's Balls! Is there *any bastard* on this continent who hasn't heard of my fucking woes?"

"You're an Iron Wolf, mate," said Mola. "We're worse than any gaggle of fish wives."

The wide, plush corridor suddenly expanded into a vast exhibition room filled with all manner of artefacts, tapestries, even ancient carriages used by a procession of royalty and preserved, here, gleaming in reds and blacks and golds. Narnok glanced up at the vaulted ceiling, a criss-cross of white arches with intricate paintings mastered within, and giving the chamber an even more regal aspect. Huge pillars supported the high arches, and Narnok's gaze swept around the chamber, and the history of the realm, coming to stop at a makeshift camp that had been erected *here*, inside the vast museum's main exhibition hall.

"Odd place to camp," said Narnok, stepping forward.

Randaman shook his head. "Not at all. We have access to food and wine from the museum's stores, we have almost unlimited weaponry," his arm swept towards the military quarter of the museum hall where all manner of suits of armour, pikes and spears and long swords, from a multitude of historic periods, sat on display, alongside some heavy ballistae and siege engines towering up towards the high arched roof. "If we need them. Come and meet the gang."

"The gang?" said Trista.

Randaman gave a nod, eyes glittering. "Yes. The Red Thumb Gang."

Trista, Narnok and Mola exchanged a glance, then followed Randaman. As they approached, the talking stopped. There were about thirty present and Narnok's eyes swiftly swept over the group, searching for notable figures in the Red Thumb hierarchy; he had a few enemies, and his entire body was tense, and quivering, until he realised nobody recognised him.

Slowly, Narnok released a slow breath and glanced sideways at Mola, who gave a noncommittal shrug.

"We have some new... survivors," said Randaman, smiling and gesturing. "Here, we have the delectable Trista, travelling with... I'm sorry, Big Man, I didn't actually ask you your name?"

"Narn," muttered Narnok softly. "Old buddy of Bardok here. Go way back. Ducking and diving. You know."

"I'm sure that I do not," said Randaman. "However. Let us give some proper, formal introductions."

The Red Thumb gang members had sat up a little, from where they centred around a central camp area for serving food. They were like a group of big cats, following a feeding frenzy. Full, and lazy, but idly curious about the next kill. A small fire burned in a controlled ring of rocks. On this, a pan of something sweet-smelling bubbled and Narnok found his nostrils twitching. By all the gods, I'm fucking hungry, he realised, but then turned his attention back to the group of killers. His eyes swept them and he shivered. These were the scum of Zanne underground, if truth be told; the largest, singular gathering of cut-throats, back-stabbers, jewel thieves, coach robbers, rapists and murderers known (or probably, unknown) to modern Vagandrak. And here they were, lazy as lords, full on the spoils of the conquered city. Narnok felt suddenly sick.

"…a fine meal," Randaman was prattling. He gestured with a flourish that was really starting to get on Narnok's nerves. He glanced at Mola, who was feigning disinterest as his huge dogs sat, panting at his feet. "Now, then, for the benefit of our new, er, *guests*, first we have Badograk! Badograk, stand up and say hello!"

Badograk rose ponderously to his feet. He was easily as big as Narnok, his arms huge rolls of muscle. He had black eyes, stubble and a shaved head. He carried a large battle-axe in one thick-fingered paw, and he watched Narnok with unflinching interest. Narnok knew exactly what the Red Thumb gang member was thinking; it was an appraisal. A weighing up. Almost, a challenge. The man couldn't help it. Narnok knew; he was doing it himself.

"And that, there, is Veila." A slim, athletic woman sat perched on her pack. She was pretty, lithe, and very feminine. Her hair was long, and black, and knotted into a braid that fell down between her well-defined shoulder blades. She wore surprisingly little for a warrior, a revealing of too much flesh for Narnok's liking, and she had pointless high boots made more for cavalry. She nodded towards Narnok.

"Scar-face," she said, and flashed him a smile with small white teeth.

Narnok felt himself reddening, and ground his teeth, saying nothing. *Was she mocking him? Toying with him? He wouldn't take it, just fucking wouldn't take it* and he felt his temper rise immediately and he gripped the haft of his axe tight as his temper started to boil when Trista stepped forward, her hand resting lightly on his forearm, and he glanced down at her beautiful, sculpted face with its gorgeous blonde curls, and her smile said: don't worry, we'll kill them all, afterwards. He smiled. And relaxed.

"Over there is Shafta." A young lad sat, rocking back on a chair. He wore the clothes of a young ruffian, all browns and blacks, dark colours to help him blend with the night shadows. His clothing was threadbare, his hair a tangled mop of brown, but his blue eyes were bright and intelligent and the steel of two long knives glinted at his belt. He couldn't have been more than thirteen, yet he nodded at the newcomers, as if from one equal to another.

"Dag Da," gestured Randaman, to a wild-haired woman with skin the colour of ebony. She wore an array of random armour pieces, they were later to discover had been taken from those she slew, and her long bony fingers held a staff, each end of which was finished with long, razor-sharp spear heads. Her eyes were deep brown, large in her rounded, almost plump, face; but there was no mercy there, just a long fall into oblivion clutching your own excised entrails.

Randaman went through the rest of the group, and Narnok and Trista were polite, as the Red Thumbs weighed them up, and they in turn considered these cut-throat vagabonds who had somehow clubbed together and survived the worst excesses of the elf rat takeover of the city.

Randaman gestured them forwards, and they sat, were offered a bowl of sweet stew cooked by Dag Da, who watched their faces intently. Narnok wolfed his food down with a large spoon, and Trista picked daintily through as the black woman's intense gaze watched closely for any sign of dissent.

"Fabulous!" boomed Narnok, finishing his plate and smacking his lips. He looked over at Dag Da. "You're a damn fine cook, woman. I've not tasted anything like that since the campaign south in Oram, beyond the Plague Lands."

"I am satisfied, then," said Dag Da, voice curiously soft. And she smiled, with both lips and eyes, and Narnok felt like he'd made a new friend.

Shafta, who'd sidled over, nudged the big man.

"Yes, lad? What is it?"

"Well, axeman, if you hadn't liked her cooking – Dag Da's, that is – she would have cut your throat. Probably when you slept."

Narnok stared at the young boy. "You serious?"

"Aye."

"Nice company you're keeping."

Shafta stared at him, with deadly serious eyes. "It's a sign of the times," he said, without a sliver of humour.

The Red Thumbs were idly sharpening swords, and seemed relaxed. Randaman asked Narnok and Trista a few more questions, and seemed satisfied with Narnok's answers; he'd been in the army, then dishonourably discharged after felling an officer with a hefty right hook. Randaman liked that bit. They all did.

Outside, night fell. It was easy to tell, because sections of the ceiling had globes of opaque glass and they saw the fast-fading light.

"Tell me what you saw out there," said Randaman, sitting cross-legged on a blanket. Behind him sparkled a case full of diamonds. Surprisingly, his band of cut-throats had chosen not to loot it and Narnok pointed this out. Randaman shrugged. "I could take those any day of the week for the last three years. Where's the challenge in taking them now?"

"So you see theft as a challenge?" rumbled Narnok.

"Of course. It's a game."

"Tell that to the robbed."

"Oh, Narn, don't be so stuck-up," said Trista with a tinkling laugh, and brushed a stray blonde curl from her face. Randaman looked at her every move; enraptured, just a little.

"*So*, how did you come by the museum? Bardok says you did a lot of fighting out there. Got cornered by the elf rats and had to fight your way free. Is that true? We don't see many who'd survive a horde like was on the streets yesterday."

Narnok shrugged. "We don't die easy," he said. "We came up through the sewers. We was staying with my uncle south, amidst the foothills of the Skarandos. Thought we'd come looking for warmth and pleasure during the winter months; the Skarandos is no place for fun during the harsh, weak blizzard months. Just snow and chopping bastard wood. I'd have more fun fucking my sister."

Randaman nodded in understanding.

"So we trek north, no drama, and arrive at Zanne. Everything's quiet, and dark, like. No answer at the gates. I was once chased by the City Watch here after a pub brawl, had to make a quick exit, went out through the sewers so I didn't get my head coshed. Through the tunnels, and out down a long pipe. I smelt like shit, but at least avoided three years at His Majesty's pleasure in Breakneck Prison. Ha ha."

"Ahh, yes, Yoon's Severe Policies." Randaman gave a bleak smile. "Brought in hanging for us lot," he said, with a lean and narrow smile.

Narnok bit off the words before they escaped past his lips: hanging's too fucking good for you lot.

"Breakneck Prison?" Trista raised her eyebrows. She actually looked interested.

"Aye," rumbled Narnok. "To the north of here, beyond Zanne Keep and the Gardens of the Winter Moon. It borders the Factory Quarter. Big ugly long building, it is, letting the factory workers gaze on it day and night, reminding them where they'll end up if they're bad little boys and girls."

"Yes. I've done my time there." Randaman gave a cough, and looked around at the group. "In fact, most of us have."

Narnok frowned. "Are there men and women still in there? That'd be a good fighting body, if we could get them out."

Randaman scratched his chin. "Not sure, old boy. It's locked down worse than the city gates. Silent in there, it is. No signs of life. A few of the Red Thumbs have circled it, looking for survivors. Want to bring them back here."

"Really?" said Narnok.

"A good fighter's a good fighter, especially when the odds are stacked against you." Randaman gave him a bleak smile, and suddenly Narnok saw beyond the mask. Yes, he was a dandy, a powerful sub-leader, perhaps, answerable only to the Red Thumb Gangs' higher echelons. But here, and now, the world and Zanne, this *enclosed* and sectioned off little microcosm, had become a level playing field. It was no longer City Guards versus the Red Thumb Gangs. Suddenly, a new and powerful adversary had been tossed into the mix; one that seemed to kill indiscriminately. Suddenly, enemies were now friends as they worked against a common foe – a common foe that was, seemingly, unstoppable.

"After we came out the sewers," said Narnok, carefully, "we ended up in this big fight with these elf rat bastards. And there was this one, old he was, they moved out of his way as if he was a king or a wizard…"

"I put an arrow through his eye," said Trista, softly. "But he seemed unperturbed by a good Vagandrak shaft in his brain." She gave a grim smile.

"A wizard," said Narnok again, his eye widening. "By the name of Beza… Baza…"

"Bazaroth," said Randaman. "Bazaroth aea Quazaquiel. He is one of their ancient order, and personal sorcerer to the elf rat king, Daranganoth."

"So he's leading the elf rats, here?"

Randaman shrugged. "We have seen him from afar. It certainly appears that way, although there is another, more military in his bearing. We have heard the name Namash, and he is referred to as a general. Who knows how these creatures operate?"

"Well, I propose a plan," said Narnok, grinning. Something touched his cheek, an insect, or a drift of dust. He rubbed at the scar tissue there.

"And what would that be?"

"These rats in charge, they will be holed up at Zanne Keep. It's central, it's fortified; if I know Yoon, he'd have it stitched up tighter than a back-handed jewellery robbery by the City Watch."

"And you propose?"

"We take the Keep."

"What?"

"You heard, Randaman."

Randaman glanced at Mola, his smile widening with incredulity. "You hear that, Mola? Does that sound like a good plan to you?"

Again, something touched the back of Narnok's neck and he glanced up. A drift of dust came down through the pale gloom from the massive, high arches.

It took a second or two for realisation to sink in, and by then the Red Thumbs had mobilised, leaping to their feet with drawn weapons. From the shadows around the gathering edged archers with drawn bows, arrows pointed at Narnok, Trista, Mola and the growling, throbbing dogs. One word. One tiny word…

"Don't even think about it," muttered Narnok, loosening the strap on his axe. Randaman saw the tiny movement.

"You bring that blade up, old horse, and it'll be *your* turn for an arrow through the eye. Your good eye, that is. Just think on that. Even if you survived, and Veila over there is an incredible archer, trust me on this, well – you'd be *completely* blind. How would that suit you, Narnok?"

Narnok relaxed into an easy smile, whilst Trista and Mola were still tense beside him.

"That's okay, Randaman. Well done." He clapped his heavy hands with a pendulous rhythm. "Good bit o' detective work, that. But if I'm honest, we're all in this shit together. Killing us would be stupid when you think how many of that horde out there we could take down between us. Now listen. The plan to take Zanne Keep is a cracking one." Narnok stared with his single orb into the piercing blue eyes of the handsome Red Thumb gang member before him. "I know a secret way in," he said, smiling with scarred lips. "We can do this. Kill the sorcerer, and the general, hold the fortification until Yoon's army gets here to put a spiked boot up the fucking arses of these invading elf rats."

"There's a problem," said Randaman.

"Oh yeah?"

"Yes, Narnok of the Axe, Narnok of the Iron Wolves. A very *large* problem."

Badograk growled, and Narnok watched him move to one side in his peripheral vision. A figure in a dark cape stepped forward from the shadows of the museum interior. He was tall and slender, with pale skin and a light scar under one eye. He seemed *vaguely* familiar.

"Hello, Narnok," he said, moving into the light.

Weapons bristled. There were a few coughs.

"Do I know you?" snapped Narnok.

Distantly, there were several creaks, and cracking noises. Muffled. Like breaking tinder.

"I'm not sure," said the man, moving yet closer, then circling Narnok with an arrogance and confidence he should not have possessed. "But you knew my cousin."

Narnok went cold; his muscles tensed, ready for the impending battle.

"My name," said the tall, gaunt figure, finally standing still and turning to face Narnok, face to face, his eyes searching Narnok's single orb, "is Faltor Gan." He allowed the words to sink in. "I am one of the three ruling Lords of the Red Thumb Gangs."

"Lords, is it, now?" snapped Narnok, staring back, hard.

"I believe you knew my cousin, Narnok of the Axe. He was called Galtos Gan," said Faltor, quietly.

"Don't know what you're fucking talking about."

"No, no, I think you do. Really. Truthfully. You knew him. He paid a visit to your fine whorehouse, up past the Rokroth Marshes in that shit-hole some people call Kantarok. You murdered him, tipped him into the river. Surely you recall that simple, single event?"

"The only thing simple," growled Narnok, eye shining, hand tight on axe-haft, "was your cousin's fucking brain. He threatened my girls with a knife. Got violent, like. Had to be taught a lesson."

"But... *murder*, Narnok? Come on. Surely he didn't deserve to *die*?"

"Aye, well, things got out of hand. I didn't mean it to go that far. But when it did, it did. So say your fucking piece, and get it out."

Faltor Gan took a step closer, inside Narnok's axe range. Brave. He was confident, pale face unreadable, eyes watching Narnok closely. When the attack came it was swift and massively unexpected; Faltor slid a little curved dagger from the sleeve of his leather coat, and despite his leanness he moved with lightning speed, dagger slamming up under Narnok's chin where it would have hooked him like a fish and carved out his throat. But Narnok had been ready, and despite Faltor's speed, was not exactly a fat waddling bartender himself. He swayed, a subtle movement and the little curved blade nicked Narnok's chin. He dropped his axe, stepping in yet closer, arms encircling Faltor in a bear-hug, great flat forehead slamming Faltor's nose. There was a crack and a spray of blood, but no scream. Faltor was harder than that. Much harder.

"No," whispered Trista, and suddenly Narnok glanced up. The archers had closed in; shafts were aimed at his face.

"Let him go, axeman," hissed Veila, eyes narrowed. And Narnok knew; he *knew*. The shaft could skewer him before he took down the Red Thumb *Lord*. Before he ended the feud before it really began.

Narnok opened his mouth to speak, but a deafening roar suddenly blasted through the museum, rocking them all, and the whole ceiling seemed to collapse inwards from the shadowy dark heights above. The museum shook, as if in the throes of an earthquake, and from the darkness on unreeling ropes like thin spooled tree roots, dropping fast from high above amidst the tumbling debris, the plaster and the dust, came the elf rats… a hundred, at least, dropping with blades between crooked teeth and eyes alight with a quest for blood and vengeance and death.

SALTEARTH

Fingers of light crept over the horizon in radiating waves, weary grey beacons dragging in the unwilling dawn. Horses stamped the icy cobbles, four mounts taken from Beth's stable. Each gelding was seventeen hands and a fine specimen, with good teeth and recent shoes. Well trained, Kiki thought, they were creatures more bred for war than the simple workings of a farm, but she said nothing, kept her words to herself. Zastarte had gathered several packs with supplies, which they tied to the saddle of the fourth animal, also to be used as a spare mount in case of an accident, or if one beast went lame.

Sameska stood in the courtyard, head bowed, staring down at the ice. And then he looked up, his spindly limbs lifting, his fingers spreading in what Kiki realised was a wave of farewell.

Kiki looked back at Dek and Zastarte. Dek – large, broad, stoic – grinned a bare-toothed grin. Zastarte gave a single nod, and Kiki realised how much he was tearing himself apart inside. *Damn. He really does love Trista. But does the ice bitch even realise?*

"Yah!" She dug heels to flank, and spurred the gelding forward across the cobbles. Iron hooves clattered, and Dek and Zastarte followed, and they were away, out into the snow, into the wilds and the biting headwind, filled with needles.

Kiki rode ahead, scouting with keen eyes. She felt good. More alive than alive. And yet she could taste the bitter taste of the honey-leaf, and she knew; knew it was a fucking con trick. The Leaf gave, and the Leaf took away. Just like *everything in life*. And as you advanced, it took away more than it gave, in a progressive ballet of abuse and self-deception. And she knew this. Her intelligence spoke the words to her in a nagging cycle. And she listened. By all the gods, she listened.

Cold wind hissed, stirring the snow in circles.

The road was narrow, heading north, and at the top of a large hill by an upthrust of jagged rocks, Kiki suddenly reined in her mount, which struggled for a moment, head fighting the reins, until she got the creature under control. She turned, and looked back, and could see the distant city of Zanne. From here, it looked like a high-walled cube. Matt black. Locked down. Silent. Motionless.

"It looks wrong," said Dek, reining in his own mount. "Too quiet. Too deserted."

"I hope Trista is all right," said Zastarte.

Dek reached over, and punched him in the chest, a not inconsiderable blow. "What's the matter, you become a lovesick fool now, or what?"

"I have my moments," said Zastarte, primly.

"Last I heard, you were burning bitches in your cellar dungeon."

Silence rolled over them, and Zastarte looked away. "Maybe I am a different person now," he said, voice barely more than a whisper.

"Yeah? Well, what changed you, man?"

Zastarte stared at him. "Maybe that noose around my neck had something to do with it. One starts to realise one's own mortality when the King of Vagandrak desires you dead."

Kiki slapped Dek across the back of the head, and he scowled and turned to her. *What?* said that stare. *What the fuck did I do wrong now?*

"She's a warrior princess," smiled Kiki. "Her and Narnok; well, they'll kill any enemy bastard that gets in their path. You know they will. They're both survivors. We survived Desekra — twice. We survived Orlana, the bitch. And this is just another blip on the vellum scrolls of history. We *will* fucking kill and conquer. We will kill and conquer."

Zastarte bowed his head. "Yes, Captain."

They rode north, through ice and snow. The wind cut at them like knives. It was a bitter wind, full of mournful songs and sorrow and needle blades. Kiki welcomed it, for it kept her awake, and aware, and alive.

The day was a blur of snow and ice, and they camped in a hollow of rocks where a few sparse trees offered some shelter. Dek built a fire, but it was a pitiless, weak-willed effort; more to inspire morale than to provide any real heat in this plunging, desperate temperature. Its flames seemed completely devoid of warmth, or joy, and all three Iron Wolves huddled beneath furs and blankets, scanning the night sky for signs of more snow and each wondering, in different ways, what the future held for them. Snow seemed to have crept into the most improbable of places. Down boots and into socks, beneath shirts and up sleeves. It was a bastard snow. Intent on bleaching life and body heat.

"So, you love her?" said Kiki, after Dek had laid out his bed and snored into the fire.

"I... don't know." Zastarte gave her a quick glance, a tight smile, then looked away. "For a long time I hated her. I think. She was so... arrogant. She could have any man she wanted, back in the *good old days*. But she never wanted me. Eventually, I came to realise that she was killing, actually fucking *killing* any man who crossed her; any man who fucked her. Until she found her true love. The man who married her. Then betrayed her. And caused a hundred wedded brides to lose their lives."

Kiki gave a short laugh.

Zastarte nodded.

"Yeah. I know. Fucked up, isn't it?"

"I think we all are, in our own way," said Kiki.

"But recently, recently... well. I don't know."

"You want to love her, but you fear she will kill you?"

Zastarte snorted a laugh. "You think I fear death, Captain? After all I've been through? After all the shit I've endured? No. Death is a welcome release. A welcome release when it comes. Just like a long sleep. But... I think my biggest fear is that I may have missed out on something major in my life. I thought I was in love, many, many times. You'd slide fingers into quim, feel that slick warm honey that meant they wanted you, welcomed you, and that would be the end of the game. You'd won. The bet was done. You had that quim ready and fucking begging, because, after all," he gave a weak grin, "we're all animals, right? And it's the nature of the beast to fuck and reproduce."

"So why fuck men then?"

Zastarte gave a sideways grin. "That's a different story," he said.

"And? I suppose this is the part where you had an epiphany?"

"Not at all. This is the bit where I started to go mad. I'd kidnap young women from well-to-do families. Usually fuck the mother first, because there's many a fifty year-old who has a husband grown content on his money and lands and privileges, and is too busy drinking the port and brandy and not giving Lady Whatshername her weekly slick spice of life; fuck the mother, create a shield, take the daughter. Fuck her. Sometimes. But this went beyond sex. This was about…"

"What was it about?" said Kiki, softly.

Zastarte sighed. "I despised them."

"The women?"

"Hell no! Not the women. The people. The fucking people. All of them. There's so much self-righteousness. So much self-importance. So much arrogance. So much fake pride and feeling and self-fucking-love and pathetic puking self-pity; they feel they're better than everybody else when the only thing that's true and right is that we're all born from the shit and the slime, and we're all going back to the shit and the slime. Society creates a fake veneer. People think they're better than others. Looking down on their neighbours and friends and family. They think they're more… deserving. Richer. Cleverer. More educated. Higher social standing. But you know what, Kiki, and I mean this with all sincerity, from a hundred lessons learned in my little dungeon, when little rich boys and little rich girls learned, oh how they fucking learned, to leave behind their arrogance and wealth and social standing and fucking focus, FOCUS on the important things in life – like how to stay alive. Well, they were learning. And I was learning. About nature. Human nature. About the nature of the beast and oh, how that beast has changed. And I realised. We have to go back to basics. We have to regress. We have to lose the fake icing sugar coating of society and civilisation – and make it real again."

"You want us to regress?"

"Is it really a regression? Ha. Well. Yes. Whatever. Ironic, that's me, a creature of the King's Court, a creature of lace and perfume and alcohol and oral sex; a beast of the hedonistic virtues of court and parties and afterplay; ironic that such as me would want to return to simple virtues. Home baked bread. A warm hearth. Children. Education."

Kiki considered this.

"So, Prince Zastarte, it took the torture of innocent people with blade and fire, to make you realise you wanted to be a part of the human race again?"

Zastarte faced her, and with absolutely no irony or sarcasm, gave a single nod. "Yes."

"And you fell in love?"

"I fell in love with our species. I'll rephrase that. I *refound* love with our species. And then I started to watch Trista, and to learn about *her*, and to understand what she was, and what she carried. And I knew that if it worked then I could make her happy. I could take two negative, self-despising, downtrodden bastards – and turn them into a positive force for progression and harmony."

"And you believe that?"

"With all my heart."

"And you think Trista will reciprocate your love?"

Zastarte grinned, and some of his old humour and anarchy and chaos returned. Bizarrely, Kiki was pleased to witness it so.

"Maybe. One day. Or I'll die trying."

"You'll die trying?"

Zastarte gave a nod. "Most definitely."

The morning was a cold bleak grey bastard.

They rode, suffering the cold and the pain of the saddle. They suffered the cutting bite of the wind. And as miles and miles passed under iron shod hooves, so the cold ate into them, and wore them down, and worried them like an unworthy, scabby dog. They camped again in a dead forest, then a night later in a ring of rocks as a howling wind like a raped banshee screeched and howled amongst the stones, making them cover their ears lest they suffer permanent damage.

On the next morn, after an hour of weary riding and still heading north of Zanne, they reached the edge of the Salt Plains.

Dek dismounted, and knelt on one knee, touching the line of sizzling snow that greeted them. He looked left, and right, where the zig-zagging line of bubbling snowmelt careered away, offering a very distinct borderline.

Dek glanced back at Kiki, and raised his eyebrows.

Kiki shrugged.

"It's the salt," said Zastarte.

"Eh?"

"No ice or snow can survive here. It's a desert of salt. We used to come here on manoeuvres."

"You *did?*"

"Aye. Didn't you?"

"Nah. I knew the fuckers in charge of the rotas. We made sure we spent most of the time whoring, gambling, or having nice easy rides through Tulska Forest. Why the fuck would we want to come to this desolate, harsh, life-bleaching shit hole?"

"To *train*?" said Zastarte, in moderate disbelief.

"Nah. That's bollocks. Harsh environment? Ha! It's all about your state of mind."

Now it was Zastarte's turn to smile. "All right then, *pit fighter.* I'm looking forward to seeing your state of mind over the next few days when the salt kicks in."

Dek shrugged. "I've been through worse," he rumbled. "We'll see."

Bizarrely, as they now travelled, despite the icy, biting wind, the hard-packed salt landscape radiated a little heat, as if it were some kind of battery that had stored energy all summer and was now releasing it to combat the dropping temperatures. Despite the hard-packed nature of the earth, a solid white crust, the wind still managed to kick up biting dust, which proved to be even more invasive than the snow of previous hours. It got into boots and sock and trews; it got into the creases of joints and acted as an abrasive. Within hours, all the Iron Wolves were starting to curse inventively.

And then Dek, who was riding point, hauled up his mount. He'd dampened a rag – an old torn shirt – and tied it around the gelding's nostrils to protect it from the wind-blown salt. The beast gave a muffled whinny, fighting his command for a few moments, and then settled down. Dek stared at the vision before him.

"Gods," he said, stroking his stubble.

"The Ships," nodded Zastarte.

"Eh, lad?"

"The Ships," said Zastarte, as if that, indeed, was enough.

All three stared for a long time at the huge, rearing edifice which emerged from the salt plain, like a rearing, storm-tossed vessel trapped in a sudden ice-freeze. It speared towards the sky like a lance, and was vast, bigger than ten houses; bigger than fifty. The whole edifice was a scarred matt black, as if the diagonal *"ship"* was cast from a huge single block of black iron, and yet showed no rust. Huge icicles hung from the prow, high up against the chilled grey sky, and formed long glittering stalactites from gantries and decks. Both ice and wind-blown salt had etched weird concentric patterns into the surface of this ancient, shipwrecked vessel; if indeed, it was a vessel.

Dek tilted his head. "That's just weird," he said, finally.

"I see images in the patterns; old lovers. Distant cousins. Lost aunties." Zastarte's face showed pain, his eyes narrowing.

"Aren't they one and the same thing?"

Zastarte flashed him a dirty look. "Dick."

Dek shrugged, and looked to Kiki. "I suggest we ride on. This place feels like, well, a cross between a fucking mausoleum and a supernatural tableau from beyond the grave. It gives me the creeps."

"You?" Kiki fixed him with a stern stare. "Lord of the Fighting Pits, frightened by a big black lump of immobile iron?"

"Get fucked. You're taking the piss."

"You're giving it away."

"Must be the effect of this place. Tell me we're moving on."

"Night's closing in."

"Kiki." Serious. "This realm is haunted."

"No. This realm is savage, and could murder us if we don't find shelter. Look down there, near the base. There are what look like caves. They may even be tunnels that lead inside."

Dek stared at her, aghast. "You cannot seriously be thinking about going *inside* that thing?" His eyes travelled from the wide squat base, where ridges of iron ploughed beneath the rolling salt dunes, slowly, up the great sweeping flanks to the almost pointed pinnacle. At regular intervals, running away at odd disjointed angles, were what looked like decks with rails. He could see, now, why Zastarte had called it a ship. But how the hell did it get here? And how, in the name of the Seven Sisters, had it ended up with half its arse under the ground? And don't get him started on how they made iron float. It was impossible...

He shivered. "I say we cut west, cut out this shit, suffer the marshes and swamps."

"No. We stay. We endure. We survive. Then we head east, after Renza."

"Ah yes, *another* godforsaken shit-hole."

It was Kiki's turn to shrug, and she dug in heels, cantered her horse forward. The iron edifice loomed above her, getting bigger, and bigger, and bigger, until it finally seemed to block out the sky. Her nostrils twitched, and she could smell something tangy and metallic, and the bad smell of old oil. The wind made little mournful sounds, each one the tiny sigh of a pleasured woman. Kiki tilted her head, listened, and the sighs became a song at the same time random and yet synchronised. It was beautiful, and it was terrible, and it was almost indescribably eerie.

She dismounted, and heard Dek and Zastarte dismount behind her. The horses seemed strangely calm, and they hobbled the creatures, moving towards one of the round black openings. Without thinking, Kiki drew her short sword and glanced back, past Dek and Zastarte, over the rolling salt dunes, which stirred, gently, disturbed by the wind and constantly moving.

Dek and Zastarte drew their own weapons, and the three Iron Wolves moved into the gloomy opening, their faces grim.

It was a short tunnel, with a floor that sloped upwards and which kinked in the middle, leading to a cubic room of magnificent intricacy. It was dry and unmolested by the elements, save for a small scattering of salt at the entrance, and its lack of molestation was probably due to the upward slope. Kiki stopped so fast Dek bumped into her, and they all gazed about, eyes wide. The interior surface, every single millimetre, was covered in an array of brass pipes and valves, dials and wheels, a thousand different tiny mechanisms connected to other pipes and funnels and dials. They covered the entirety of all the walls, even the ceiling, each metal polished surface gleaming. Kiki cast about, but could see no other entrance or exit from the room.

"There are no doors," observed Zastarte.

"This can't be it," rumbled Dek. "The exterior is vast!"

Kiki shrugged. "Matters little. It's a place to shelter."

"This is amazing." Dek stood, staring around like a child in the world's largest sweet shop. "Truly amazing. It's like nothing I've ever seen."

Kiki frowned. "I feel like we're inside a machine."

"Maybe we are," said Zastarte, voice soft.

Kiki snorted, and headed back to the short corridor. The others followed her, and watched the swirling, violent clouds moving across the sky. They towered, and formed columns, and howled in the distance.

"What the fuck am I looking at?" snapped Dek.

"A storm to end all storms," said Zastarte.

"A big one, then?"

"Oh yes."

They covered the horses' muzzles with damp cloths and brought them, stomping and agitated, into the tunnel, as huge yellow bruises lined the horizon. Distantly, banshees wailed, and Kiki stood as Dek and Zastarte went to cook supper. She watched demons dancing through the sky. She watched Sky Gods pissing on the realm of mortal man.

"Come on," she muttered, eyes wide. "Bring it on."

"That's a bad situation," observed Zastarte. "I've seen desert storms like this before, during training. They can leave hundreds dead."

"That's the desert," said Kiki.

"This is extremely similar."

"We shall see."

The storm came in fast, howling like demons across the salt dunes. The blast slammed against the hull of the ship with animal ferocity, screaming metallic wails and squirting up the tunnel like an ocean wave breaking down a barrier.

Kiki was the last to retreat, backing up past the horses, which stood subdued, ears flat against long skulls, hooves stamping, voices stressed with low growls and whinnies. Kiki watched the salt come smashing in, and retreated towards the brass room and the others, and their prison cell of tiny machines. The sloped floor hurt her ankles when she walked, and the gleam of the brass was annoying. It was too neat. Too perfect. A machine room from a different age; now derelict, defunct. Beautiful and impressive, yes, but nothing more than a pretty ornament. Ultimately, useless.

Dek was sat in the middle of the sloping floor. He leaned back on his pack against a bank of vertical gleaming pipes. He scowled at Kiki. "This is bad shit going down."

"Relax."

"And what if the storm lasts a month? In the desert they do, sometimes. People die from lack of water. How much bloody water have we got?"

"Not enough for a month," said Kiki.

"Exactly."

"Relax. One day at a time."

They slept. And they awoke. And outside, the storm still howled, raging. Dek and Zastarte went down to the entrance but were driven immediately back. There was a definite reason the Salt Plains were uninhabited. They were uninhabitable. And this sort of natural shit proved the point beyond any sort of doubt.

"So why are we here?" said Zastarte.

"It's the quickest way," said Kiki.

"Not if this storm lasts a fucking month, it isn't," he said.

"Exactly."

"Then Narnok and Trista will die."

"As will we."

They all stared at one another.

"An act of Nature," said Dek, voice sombre.

"Collateral damage is the phrase," said Kiki.

"I ain't ever going to be fucking collateral," snapped Dek. "I go out kicking and screaming and killing every fucking bastard in the immediate vicinity."

"Amen to that," said Zastarte.

"We have to wait. It's the only way. A natural order of things."

Dek put his chin on his fist and sighed.

"Tell me about her."

"Why?"

"I'll tell you about my dad, if you tell me about your sister."

A pause, just a little longer than usual. Then Kiki nodded. "We've got fuck all else to do."

"What do you want to know?"

"What did he do? For a living?"

"He was a career soldier, at first. Later, a docker. Worked down on the docks organising the teams who loaded and unloaded ships. Freight. Cargo. His name was Kedd. Him and Mum met when he was in the army, way back. He'd been captured, then dug a tunnel with nine others and escaped. They were picked up by a scouting squad from Desekra; Vagandrak men."

"So where was he from?"

"Far east. You never would have heard of it. Gave me an accent and a name that wasn't local."

"You have problems at school?"

Dek grinned. "Yeah. But. They learned fast, those Vagandrak fucks; no offence intended."

"None taken," said Kiki. "So you were beaten?"

"Nah. I was expelled. A lot. No bugger could stand against me, and yet there was always some cocky fucker trying it on. It is the nature of men. Of boys. Boys will be boys. All that horse shit. I remember, one day I was at home, peeling potatoes for Mam, and there's this knock on the door. Three little shits wanting a slice of the new boy. So out I goes, and my best friend Callum is there, and he says, 'Gods, you're brave Dek' but I shrugged it off because I wasn't being brave, it was just a job that had to be done. And so we squared up, this absolute nasty, spineless little turd called Heeley. We waded in, I knocked his jaw to the other side of his face, then his mates jumped on my back. That was a fucking learning curve, I tell you. Taught me a lot about back-stabbing bastards. Taught me a lot about *people*. Because that's what *people* are like. Out for themselves. Out to win. Out to conquer. Out to fuck over the weak with force of arms."

"What happened to them?"

"All right, I broke Heeley's jaw and cheek and shoulder, although I had to stamp on him three fucking times to make that work; then I killed Webber. Drove a shard of glass through his fucking heart. Had a lot of problems over that one. In the end, it helped they came to find me. It helped they came looking for me. It helped they'd attacked. I got away with a lot because of that. Self-defence. Obviously, I never told them I stamped the bitch, but hey, that's all fair in love and war because the Law is a bitch and the Law favours the rich." He smiled, a smile very much without humour.

Silence followed for a while. Outside, the storm howled.

"So then," he said. "Tell me about your sister."

"Nice try, Dek. Was that *really* a story about your father?"

Silence.

"Well?"

"No."

"So, that's not a fair trade then, is it? Come on. Spill it."

Dek considered this, and Kiki saw it in his face. The raw animal energy to say *fuck you. I won't tell you anything; why should I? This is my damn life, not yours.* But then something buckled, something cracked, and Dek looked down at the ground with its brass pipes and dials and intricacy.

"Talk about your father."

"I don't see why I should."

"I think it might help you."

"Really?" Sudden animal ferocity. "You fucking reckon, do you?"

Kiki stared at him. He subsided.

"Sorry." His words were mumbled. "Don't know what came over me."

"We're not in the Red Thumb Fighting Pits now, Dek." She smiled, to take the sting out of her words. She took his hand – his large, scarred hand, more like a shovel with bony ridges in all reality – and she squeezed it hard.

"I've never told anybody before."

"That's all right." She looked up at him in the surreal witch-light of the surreal chamber, deep within the bowels of an alien salt-ship.

"Kedd was a hard man. His father had been a hard man before him. It wasn't so much that he beat me, but he did whack me whenever I was bad – and that was all the time. I was always breaking stuff, smashing stuff, even down to furniture. And I was naughty. Fighting – that you know about, but it didn't bother Dad that much. There was this one time down at the Dead Dog Tavern, I was with Dad because we'd been to market and Dad's on his stool with a soothing pint of ale, and I'm sat in the corner, keeping quiet like, 'cos they didn't like kids in the taverns, then, and a landlord could get into a whole lot of trouble with the Watch. But Dad was a regular, knew the landlord, Big Pete, and even though Dad was well known as somebody you didn't tangle with – you only had to look at the size of his fists and the bent and broken nose from scuffles in his youth, and later, from boxing in the army – well, he wasn't a trouble maker and Big Pete allowed him a lot of leeway. So I'm sat there, with a bowl of dried pork strips to keep me quiet and not tell Mam we'd stopped off at the Dead Dog, when a man known as Boxing Buttley, big as a horse he was, and about as clever, comes over. Had a few too many ales, he had, accuses Dad of staring at his wife's arse. Dad smiles at him, cool as anything, and says the only reason he'd stare at an arse that big would be to wonder how the fuck she could squeeze it through the door. Buttley stares at him, gawping, mouth flapping, until he worked out the insult. Throws a right and Dad just… kind of twitches, the slightest movement, and Buttley misses, spins and crashes to the floor. Everybody laughs, until Buttley gets up and glares around with his small piggy eyes. He was a mean bastard, and well known to be a mean bastard, him and his brothers."

"What happened next?"

Dek pulled a flask from beneath his jerkin, and unscrewed the cap. He offered it to Kiki, who took it and knocked back a large slug. She choked, and coughed, red in the face, eyes streaming, and handed it back.

"Rancid fish oil?"

"Rokroth Marsh Fire."

Kiki spat on the ground. "Of course it is. I should have known that taste... anywhere. Dek, they make it from fucking eels."

"*Fucking* eels?"

She smacked his arm. "You know what I mean."

"I ain't told no one this story before." He took a hefty swig. Then another. Then a third. He grinned at Kiki, and she could see the fire ignite his eyes from the inside. They glowed like dragon eggs. They glittered beautiful, like stolen diamonds.

Outside, the wind howled like a spear-stuck pig. Salt pattered against the walls of the ship; it sounded like distant snow.

"Yeah, you already said that." She leaned forward and kissed his cheek. "It's OK. I'm here to listen. I'm here to help. I'm here to care. I'm here to *love you*, Dek."

He nodded. "I know, Keeks. I know."

"Go on then. Boxing Buttley."

"Launches himself at Dad, and there's me with a dried pork strip to my mouth and holding my breath. This time, Dad kicks back off the stool and they set to like nothing I've ever seen. Boxing Buttley had his name for a reason, but Dad fucking pulverised him. Broke his nose and both cheekbones and one arm and his ankle. Left him whimpering on the floor like a little child. Then Dad stamps on his chest, breaking his sternum. I can still remember the cracking sound." He gave a little shudder.

Kiki frowned. "Dek, you've done much worse than that. I've seen you!"

"Yeah. I know. But that was war. This was a pub brawl."

"Dek, I've *still* fucking seen you do much worse than that."

Dek considered this. "You reckon?"

"Oh, I know!"

"Well. Dad goes back to his ale, and the landlord brings out an ice-pack for his right fist because it was swollen something horrid. I carry on munching on my pig snacks, and ten minutes later the door opens and these five big fuckers come marching in, each one a bruiser and a brother to Boxing Buttley. *'We're looking for some cunt called Kedd,'* says the biggest one, and man, was he big. A head taller than my father. But then, as I learned that day, doesn't matter how fucking big you are – sometimes, you'll just never be big enough. Dad stands up and lamps him one, knocks the so-called hard cunt out with one right hook to the temple. The others wade in, and Dad just stands there like a fucking… machine! It's like he's untouchable, and within about a minute he destroys them all. Utterly smashes them to the Chaos Halls. Then, he coolly finishes his ale, nods at the landlord, and walks through the hushed men of the tavern like he was a god. It was the most incredible thing I ever saw. Then we gets outside, and on the way home he gives me this big talk about how fighting is wrong, and you should always talk your way free of problems, and how Mam will be really pissed with him and it's not good to bring possible future trouble down on your family. And all I'm thinking is, 'Fuck, my dad is the hardest man in the world! He'll never die! He's indestructible and could even fight the mountains and win!' because that's the sort of hero worship bullshit a twelve year-old boy has for his dad."

Dek lowered his head, rubbed his stubbled, weary face with both hands. Kiki squeezed his hand again. "What happened next?"

"The next day, down at the docks, they were unloading massive freighter crates using high cranes and steel cables.

The Buttleys turn up in force looking for my dad, there's ten of them this time, cousins with clubs and iron bars. But it was too late."

"What was too late?"

"They were too late. He was already dead. A steel cable snapped, and a huge crate – big as a house – fell on Dad and three other men, killed them instantly. Crushed them. They sent one of the office managers to tell us. She was very sympathetic. But it still couldn't stop my mother's wails. Or stop my hate. Some reason, I blamed the Buttleys. Like, I don't know, like it was their fault. If they'd left Dad alone, none of it would have happened."

"Didn't stop you though, did it?"

"Eh?"

"Logical thought and reason. Didn't stop you hunting them down. Fighting them? Beating them into a bloody pulp? All of them?"

Dek gave her an odd look: sideways, confused, admiring. He shrugged. "That's another story for another day. I told you about my dad. How he died. And that wrenched my heart from my chest and left it dangling on a hook for any shark to come and have a nibble on. I changed that day. I became a *bad person* that day."

"You're not a bad person, Dek. Never have been, never will be."

He gave a little shrug. "It feels like it, a lot of the time. And there's a lot of people out there with healed broken bones and bad memories who think I deserve to die. And there's a lot of dead people waiting for me beyond the threshold of death; waiting with helves and iron bars, just waiting for me to step my little foot over the barrier. Then *whack*. Time for some serious retribution. Ha ha."

Kiki leaned forward, and wrapped her arms around his massive frame. She couldn't reach all the way around, but he got the idea.

"Your turn," he said, and looked up at her.

"Ha. I knew you were going to say that." And then the smile fell by gradients, and she looked into Dek's eyes, at the love there, at the caring, and something gave a little shiver inside. "You want to know about my sister, Suza. But by telling you about Suza, I have to tell you something else. Something about my childhood. Something... terrible."

"We all carry ghosts," said Dek, gently.

"This is... different. It's about the way I was born; born, that is, to be a *Shamathe*. It's about the way I was born, and the way I was treated. It's about how magick then... shaped me. Changed me. Healed me. But it's a terrifying story for me to tell..."

"Why?" and Dek was there, and tears were rolling down her cheeks.

She looked up at him, looked into his face. "Because I'm afraid you'll leave me when you know," she said.

"I'll never leave you. Ever." Hard words. And final.

Kiki gave a nod, but Dek could tell she didn't believe him.

"What is it, Keeks? What's so bad you think I could ever lose you again? Because you're fucking wrong. I'll love you till the stars burn out. Love you until the sun dies and falls from the heavens. I'm yours, baby. I'm yours forever."

"I was born... different," said Kiki, slowly, refusing to look up. "The first sounds of the midwife were a sharp intake of horrified fear. I..."

And then the horses started screaming.

Zastarte rolled awake, sword out with a hiss, and Kiki and Dek drew weapons and ran down the short tunnel, pausing carefully at the turn. The horses were rearing and stamping in the short space of tunnel, and Kiki leapt forward, grabbing reins, calming them down. Outside, the wind and the salt storm were shrieking, but it seemed to have lessened; grown calmer.

The three Iron Wolves advanced down the tunnel.

Outside, the sky was black, and salt whipped about, forming patterns in the air from the gusting violence.

"Still too harsh to travel through," growled Dek.

"What upset the horses?" Kiki glanced back at him.

He shrugged.

Then Zastarte pointed. "What… is that?"

They stared through the gloom, where the salt danced above the hard-packed plain and rolling dunes.

And it was Dek who said it.

"Holy Mother, where the fuck did *those* come from?"

Out on the salt plains, before the mammoth, trapped ship, there were *statues* formed from salt. Kiki stepped out, sword raised, looking about. Dek followed with Zastarte, and they moved to the massive salt statues, arrayed like some artist's gallery, vast, towering sculptures which had not been there just a few hours before.

Suddenly, the storm dropped. It was binary. Gone, in an instant; as if simply switched off.

Kiki stepped forward a few more paces, neck straining, taking a deep breath, and staring up at the vast figures which now surrounded her. There were men and women, regal in bearing, and the detail in the salt figures was incredible, as if they'd been meticulously carved from ice. And they seemed to *gleam*, as if polished.

"I don't fucking understand," growled Dek, spinning slowly around, long sword before him, face writhing with uncertainty and primal fear.

"The storm has carved these figures for us," said Zastarte, and grinned. "Maybe it's a gift from the gods of the salt desert?"

"Or maybe a warning," said Kiki, gesturing to the bloated figure of something horrific.

Suddenly, the salt surged beneath them and around them, and many of the sculpted figures collapsed in great crumbling heaps. The salt beneath their boots became fluid, and all three collapsed to their knees, and felt as if they were sinking. Waves of salt rolled around them, and mocking laughter echoed through the bleak blackness of the night.

The Iron Wolves, whispered the hiss of the salt. Waves rolled around them as if they were standing on an ocean, and suddenly they were sucked down deeper, up to their thighs. Dek lashed around with his long sword, but a swirling tendril made from salt granules leapt up like a thrashing tentacle, and took it from him like a sweet from a young child; and he was stranded, weaponless, teeth bared in a grin of horror.

"What's happening, Kiki?" he yelled above the hiss and whirl of salt and wind. "I don't like this!" He thrashed around, but the salt sucked him in deeper. He was up to his waist now. They all were. It was like sinking sand. Lethal.

"Keep still," yelled Kiki. "Stop all movement!"

They stopped struggling, and the remnants of the storm seemed to fall. Salt pattered to the ground. Everything was terribly still, and silent. In the tunnel to the ship, they could hear the frightened whinnies of their horses; but eventually, even they were quiet. Silence rolled across the world like a great veil of ash.

"What now?" growled Zastarte.

"Wait," said Kiki, holding up one finger.

"I don't want to die like this," whimpered Dek. "I want to die with a fucking sword in my hand!"

"*Shhh*!"

Kiki turned her head, looking about her. Around half of the sculpted figures remained, towering ten and twenty feet in height. And then she turned to look straight ahead, due to some primitive intuition, and particles of salt started to jiggle and vibrate before her eyes. She opened her mouth as if to speak, but there came a sudden uprush, a wave of salt gushing towards her like a tidal wave and she lifted hands to protect her face, protect her eyes, but it halted, hanging there, spinning, turning like a mini maelstrom, and twisting, finally, into a huge face. It was the face of a woman, hanging in the air and made from gently spinning particles. Silence fell. And the face smiled.

Kiki, hissed the salt.

"Yes?" she said, mouth dry, a great and terrible fear worming into her heart, which suddenly dropped, like a black stone down a bottomless well.

It is your time, sister of the Shamathe. *I do not wish to do this. Truly, sister of my heart. But unfortunately in life, we have to do those things that are the most painful for us. Say farewell to your friends. It is time for you to merge with the Salt Plains of Eternity…*

THE KEEP

Narnok thrust Faltor Gan away from him with incredible
force, kicking back as a snarling elf rat landed right before
him and the great, double-headed axe swept up with a
song of chaos, cutting into the creature's chest with a
thud and a shower of blood. It howled, claws slashing
for Narnok's face, and the whole world plummeted into
a madness of elf rats landing, weapons slashing out, claws
raking at eyes and faces. Narnok drew a knife and stuck
it in the howling elf rat's guts as another flew at him, a
sword smashing for his head. He swayed back, dragging
his axe with him, and kicked out, but the creature came
on, dropping its sword and lunging with both twisted
arms outstretched, dark, gleaming claws scrabbling for his
throat and flexing. His axe sang, slamming in a horizontal
strike that left two clawed hands twitching on the marble.
A second return strike cut the head free. Narnok searched
out Trista. She was fighting with Mola, the two Iron
Wolves back to back. An elf rat leapt at them, but Veila
sent a shaft through its open, screaming mouth and it was
punched back, twisting, limbs flailing in a diagonal kick.
Narnok roared and leapt forward, cleaving two elf rats in

half as he waded towards Trista and Mola, and they parted for him, so they formed a trio of bristling steel. "*Dogs to me!*" roared Mola, and the beasts, snarling and chewing, muzzles red and black with blood and gore, returned to their master, great jaws fastening on elf rats along the way.

"We need to get out of here!" yelled Narnok.

"No shit," snapped Mola.

"To the doors!" shouted Trista above the sudden din of battle, and they began cutting themselves a path through the gloom-laden charnel house, Mola's vicious bastard dogs forming a spearhead of snapping teeth and iron jaws as they forced their way forward. They saw Badograk, with his two-handed axe, and Narnok called to him, but before he could turn, the heavily-muscled fighter went down with three elf rats on his back. Their claws gouged his eyes, tore out his throat and they bore him like a dying bull to the ground where a curved black blade lifted, and hacked down, cutting his head free. Trista saw Shafta, fighting bravely, both knives covered in blood. But as he backed away, an elf rat loomed behind him, jaws suddenly wide, wider than they had any right to be. They clamped down on the young lad's head and he screamed as he was picked up, legs thrashing up into the air, knives clattering to the hard marble floor.

They made the double doorway, panting, covered in elf rat blood, and were joined by Veila, now out of shafts and fighting with a curved silver sabre, by Dag Da, and then by Faltor Gan. "Follow me," said Faltor, his pale face speckled with black droplets, both fists drenched in gore.

"And why should we?"

He faced Narnok, and gave a narrow smile. "You were right, axeman. We need to stick together against the common enemy. Against these…" he savoured the words, "*elf rats.*"

"And how do I know I can trust you not to stick a knife in my back?"

Faltor grinned then. "Because, my belligerent friend, I heard what you said about taking Zanne Keep and slaughtering General Namash, and that sorcerer bastard, Bazaroth."

"Ha! We'd need an army," snorted Narnok, and cut his axe through a charging elf rat, showering them all with blood.

Faltor wiped glistening droplets from his face, and said, "You know that Breakneck Prison you were talking about?"

"Yeah?"

"Well, I found out where the prisoners went. They'd been digging a tunnel, and when Zanne was invaded, overrun, they killed what few guards remained and broke out. A good few hundred of them. All hardened criminals, wondering what the *fuck* was going on, and trapped in an old iron works."

"You think they'll fight for us?"

"Not for us," smiled Faltor, grimly. "But they might just fight for me."

There were sixteen of them left, survivors from the museum, plus Mola's dogs, which had been wounded by slashing claws, but didn't seem to display any feelings of pain. Panting, they ran alongside their wiry master, who winced occasionally at his snapped clavicle and clicking ribs, but tried not to show it. The streets were dark and mostly deserted. The survivors hugged the walls of buildings, moving mostly in single file, Faltor Gan leading the way. They passed twisted, blackened trees, which grew out from beneath paving stones, pushing the heavy slabs of stone upwards and away and making the roads uneven, buckled. Some of the toxic trees were even growing up through the walls of buildings, and had pushed out bricks and supporting pillars, causing walls to sag, and roofs to collapse. The whole city of Zanne had an air of despondency; of bleakness, and poison, and emptiness. A cold wind blasted down the snow-filled streets. The air smelled of oil fire, of rotting vegetation, of despair.

Their boots crunched on snow and they stopped when Faltor held up a hand, still crusted in blood. Narnok shouldered his way to the front and poked Faltor in the ribs. "You'd better be right."

"You'd better shut up."

"Or what?"

An elf rat leapt from a roof, bearing down on Narnok who twitched, mighty shoulders rolling, axe flashing up and cleaving the creature damn near in half. There came a sound like rope unravelling as bowels and internal organs plopped and slopped to the snow, followed by the thud of the body.

"Or that," said Faltor, and Narnok gave a sombre nod. "I see what you mean."

They reached the edge of the Hanging Square as the moon emerged from behind heavy, swirling clouds. Cold wind drifted powdered salt across the bleak space, which was dominated at the far end by the Hanging Oak, an ancient, some reckoned *thousand year-old*, tree of magnificent stature, its lower boughs wider than a horse and carriage, its huge frame a dominating and threatening shape.

"I've seen a few friends hanged on that bastard," said Faltor Gan, and spat on the floor between his bloodstained boots.

"I reckon they probably deserved it," observed Narnok, voice impassive.

Faltor slid him a sly look, sideways, and then returned it to the Hanging Oak. The tree creaked in the distance, as if recognising one it longed to see dance between its very own branches.

"You notice no evil has seeped through its branches, turning them black and twisting them out of shape?" Faltor gave a nasty, narrow grin. "That's because The Hanging Oak is already steeped in evil; it's already a pit leading straight down to the Furnace, and filled with the screaming souls of evil demons." He spat again, rubbing his mouth with the back of his hand.

"Well," said Narnok, "I still reckon you thieving shit-bags deserve what you get. A long jump with a short rope." He gave a nasty smile. "I probably put a few of you there myself, when I worked these streets with Dalgoran; cleaning up when the City Watch didn't have the bollocks, so to speak."

They moved across iced black cobbles. The Hanging Square was surrounded by high buildings of old, scarred stone; civic blocks; another museum; various offices for the hundreds of clerics who attended King Yoon; large trees acted as a modest screen between the windows of these many majestic edifices and The Hanging Square itself, which was used for markets on Thursdays and Saturdays, and occasionally – in olden days – had been the central meeting point for artists, bohemians and protestors. In the days before Yoon ordered his King's Guard to cut the heads from the shoulders of such people.

It was eerily quiet.

"Look," said Trista, the surrounding trees had indeed taken on a blackened, twisted countenance, although not to the extent they'd witnessed further south in the city of Zanne.

"It does not bode well," said Narnok, grimly.

Trista moved with the group, alert, the taste of fear in her mouth. She was unused to being frightened, for it was not an emotion that had touched her in many years; not since her business with her *husband*. His face flashed into her mind and she spat on the iced cobbles under her boots. That bastard, she thought. She remembered their wedding night. It had been amazing. And then afterwards… afterwards…

Tears ran down Trista's face, and she glanced around to see if anybody had noticed. How bizarre, she thought, to bring this back, here and now, amidst this chaos, amidst this promise of death.

Well, didn't you bring the promise of death to so many others, you murderous bitch?

Yes, yes, but those asleep on their wedding night had found a perfection of existence; it was the pinnacle of what they would ever achieve. To die then, at that moment, in perfect, blissful happiness, could only immortalise the moment.

You killed them to satisfy your own need for revenge.

No, I killed them out of love.

Trista, my darling, you killed them out of rage.

"You okay, Lady?" Randaman had dropped back, his movements sleek and athletic, and reminding Trista of Zastarte. *Prince Zastarte*. Yeah right, or so he told all those slack-legged young women he wanted to bed.

"I have… felt better." She rubbed at her eyes, and Randaman caught the movement. Smiled, a caring smile.

He reached out and patted her shoulder, and Trista had to force herself not to remove his hand at the wrist. He saw the containment, and slowly took back his hand.

"I apologise if I offend. I meant only to reassure you. You fight with some of the best in the city; and yes, we might be criminals," his face broke into a handsome grin, "but we're hardened criminals, despite the rugged good looks."

"I… am sorry." Trista was unused to apologising. It felt somehow *wrong*.

"You are a beautiful woman, Trista. I wish we had met during happier times."

Trista was used to receiving compliments. Many of the young men who petitioned her ended up dead. But this felt somehow strange, and a new feeling crawled inside her as she realised, horse shit, she realised she was attracted to Randaman.

Where did that come from?

Just where the *fuck* did that come from?

Her eyes narrowed and she opened her mouth to put down his compliment, when he suddenly swung away and she realised they were passing beneath the massive boughs of The Hanging Oak.

Trista looked up. The ancient oak creaked, massive boughs shifting. The upper reaches were lined with snow, giving the tree a slightly jolly look. From a distance. Which was massively at odds with the purpose it was now used for, by the law-makers of Zanne.

"I wonder how many people have died here?" she said, and glanced at the floor, as if expecting to see blood seeping up and out from the roots; as if the great oak had spent the last hundred years absorbing the fluids of its victims as they swung, either strangling or with broken necks, and was now willing to regurgitate that stored-up life-force for her visual entertainment...

"Fucking lots," said Narnok, rounding on her. He pointed with his axe. "We had a garrison headquarters over yonder. Every day we'd look out and take bets on whether it'd be a neck-snapper or a slow strangulation. Ahh, the fun we had watching bad criminals die."

"How could you be sure they were all criminals?"

Narnok shrugged. "Well, you had to trust in the judges, didn't you? I'm sure they got it right. Most of the time."

"How fucking incredibly unfair," snapped Trista. "What about all the times they got it wrong?"

"Tough luck?" shrugged Narnok.

"Yeah, tell that to the wives and the children."

"Oh, we saw a good few women hang as well," said Narnok, grinning. "Not so many children, though."

"Well that makes it completely all right," said Trista.

"Equal rights for all, that's what I always subscribe to," said Narnok gruffly.

They moved again through the shadows, boots crunching snow. They left the Hanging Square behind, and stopped in a narrow alley between two four-storey white stone buildings with arches high overhead, and fancy carvings of gargoyles, long tongues curled out, pointed teeth promising pain.

"It's up this way," said Faltor Gan, "but my scouts have reported a lot more elf rat activity. We'd better be careful. We've had it lucky so far."

The warriors readied weapons, or readied them *more*, and they padded down the narrow alleyway. Now they could smell smoke, and as they reached the end of the alley they could see another tree burning.

"The Red Thumbs have gone to work again," said Faltor.

"Under your instruction?" enquired Narnok.

"Aye. We have several hundred throughout Zanne; or we *did* have. I do not know how many survive, but we learned pretty fast that burning the blackened, twisted trees hurt the damn elf rats a whole lot."

"Does it kill them?"

"Horribly," said Faltor Gan, with a grin. "Only problem is, the trees don't burn easy when they turn. You need an awful lot of lantern oil to get one started. Unfortunately, by that point you've usually been discovered."

"How do they die, when you burn the trees to which they're… connected?"

"They catch fire, from the inside out. Die writhing."

"Isn't it quicker just to cut their damn heads off?" snapped Narnok.

"Well at the moment, they're proving themselves to be quite… formidable," said Faltor, quietly. He smiled. "We must forge ahead. Our city, indeed, our *Vagandrak* won't save itself."

"And there's me thinking all you Red Thumb thieving, lying, back-stabbing, scumbag, horse-shit bastards were just in it for the money, and the whore sex." Narnok's single mad eye was challenging.

"Not at all," said Randaman, coming up fast from behind and slapping Narnok on the back. It did little to rock the big axeman. It was like slapping a bull. "But we *need* equilibrium. These elf rats are messing everything up. There's no point bloody *killing everybody;* if everybody is *dead,* or twisting into horrible deformed tree creature things like the elf rats themselves, being taken over by some toxic tree plague, then, well, there's no rich people left, is there? So who do we rob?"

"You could simply loot the houses of the dead and diseased," said Narnok, voice and eyes cold.

"Ha! Where's the fun in that?"

There were several burning trees, but no sign of elf rats. The survivors of the museum battle ran across a wide road, heading into a maze of dark alleys that led, weaving, in a northerly direction towards Zanne's high outer walls.

The condition of the buildings got worse and worse the further they moved away from the southern and central quarters of Zanne, and into the Factory Quarter. Here, the streets were narrower, with hundreds of buildings on shallow foundations and leaning gradually in one direction or another. Many had blackened or stained exteriors, from the furnaces, with oils and great machines and chemicals used in some of the larger factories, tanneries and slaughter houses. Everywhere, windows were smashed or boarded up. Some buildings had been daubed with slogans, with several quite offensive towards King Yoon. He was not exactly what you could call a *People's King*.

They passed various huge walls and windowless buildings, vast factories of various purposes, everything from forging armour and weapons for the king's armies to making smocks and cloaks and boots for peasants and noblemen. The grime and lack of pride in the Factory Quarter was self evident; even from before the elf rats had plagued and plundered the area.

The group moved, stealthy and slow, through a maze of narrow corridors, stepping carefully over dead rats and litter, and the occasional dead body. Faltor Gan gestured with his right hand, *up ahead*, but did not speak. The rest followed, weapons gleaming in the gloom, until they came to a massive rectangular block which could only be identified as a factory because of one huge chimney stack, to the rear, which rose above the city like a dark spear.

Faltor stopped by a thick iron door, and looked carefully around. Then he gave a complicated series of taps, and the portal opened with surprising smoothness and silence, on oiled hinges, and the Iron Wolves and the Red Thumbs entered in single file, Mola muttering calming words to his dogs, who were growling with menace, hackles raised and fangs bared, in a perpetual mask of hatred and threat.

Trista found herself channelled into a series of long, narrow corridors, and then out into a vast dark space where a cool breeze soothed her and a smell of fish oil and mud invaded her nostrils. Massive, towering machines surrounded her, exuding cold and the oil stench. All around were stacks of metal slabs, and bins filled with screws and bolts, shavings and irregularly shaped off-cuts of iron. There were huge tubs filled with black oil, rancid and stinking, and the ground was uneven and littered with more metal debris. They passed long workbenches filled with tools, hammers and files, and intricate looking devices for threading nuts and bolts. All the hammers had black handles, the wood ingrained with dark oil. Trista found the whole place utterly desolating, the antithesis of the large ballrooms and gala functions where she felt she really belonged; the sort of place to meet newly married couples, and slit their throats afterwards whilst they slept.

The factory was a grim place and, Narnok imagined, not much more fun than the Breakneck Prison, which awaited if you didn't work here and couldn't pay your taxes. Damned if you did, damned if you didn't. Narnok gave a nasty grin. How he loved the way the world worked.

Suddenly, the corridors of machines opened into a large central space. Lounging around the outsides were perhaps fifty large men, some still wearing their prison overalls. Many had shaved heads, some bushy beards, all had the piercing looks of men you did not fuck with. Narnok stopped dead, eyes sweeping the group, searching out old enemies. He'd decided, in this situation, if there was going to be any trouble he was going to instigate it; chop off a few heads, nip the problem in the bud, so to speak. Many men met his one-eyed stare, unperturbed by the snarls and the heavily scarred face from a torturer's wet dream. Some turned away. Thankfully, there were none Narnok knew – or at least, none he remembered – and Trista put her hand on his arm and made a soothing sound. "Calm down, Narnok."

"I just ain't a fan of this crowd. I'm a soldier, is all. Not a prison bird."

"Soldiers end up in prison as well, Narn," she said, not unkindly.

"Well, I don't know any."

"What about Black Jake? He cut his wife's throat."

"All right, I'll give you Black Jake. But he was a bastard through and through."

"And what about Rebecca the Whore? She started off in the bloody King's Guard, Narnok. Ended up infecting various married high ranking officers; got herself locked away for crimes against the military High Command."

"Yes yes, I'll give you Rebecca the Whore as well…"

"And there was Maggot Boy Memm, who…"

"*You've made your point*," snapped Narnok, and coughed, watching Faltor Gan move to three of the large men – presumably, those in charge of this happy little bunch

– and shake hands, then share an embrace, as between brothers who loved one another.

The Iron Wolves stepped forward, Narnok, then Trista, then Mola with his dogs straining at their leashes, growling and begging to be allowed to chew out throats. Narnok stared at the men ranged before him, hard men, tattooed and ragged and beaten; but still proud.

"So, what we got here, then?" said Narnok.

Faltor Gan introduced Breakneck Prison's finest. "This is Bones, Meatboy, Darkdog and Cunt."

Narnok raised a single eyebrow. "Cunt? Really?"

The large slab grunted, and nodded.

"May one ask *why*?"

"Cos I'm a real cunt, ain't I?"

"Ahh. Of course you are."

Faltor grinned at Narnok. "Hard men, for sure. Just the kind we need for assaulting Zanne Keep, don't you think?"

Narnok looked around the hardened bunch. At the cheap harsh weapons, jagged and chipped. At the bad tattoos, the shaved heads, the hard muscles, the grim demeanours. He smiled. "I reckon this is about as good as it gets," he said.

Clouds covered the moon. Another fall of snow made the ground soft and slippery. They ran in groups of ten, down narrow alleys, across iced cobbles, across frozen ridges of corrugated mud. Various Red Thumbs had cut a hole in the rear wall of the Gardens of the Winter Moon several nights earlier; more as a bolt hole whilst they were on their travels burning black trees, than any real attempt to *assault* the Keep. Zanne Keep. Eight stories high, a massive slick black cube with six towers riding its highest walls. Now, however, the temporary portal, a respite from fighting the elf rats, afforded the Iron Wolves, the Red Thumbs and the recently escaped prisoners of Breakneck Prison, a handy back door. They slid through the gap quickly, whilst lookouts with swords and daggers kept fearful watch. And then they were beyond the high wall and inside the gardens themselves.

Zanne Keep was buried deep within ten acres of walled, private garden; or more precisely, the Gardens of the Winter Moon. These had been a distant project of a distant relative of King Yoon; great-great-*great-great*-grandfather, or something. He'd never bothered to find out. Quite an explorer, this ancient relative had scoured the modern world for flora and fauna, his servants bringing back tubs of shrubs and ferns and trees and flowers from many and varied distant climes; from Oram and Parissia, from Falanor and Zakora, no land went un-raped by the distant relative's urgent need for a vast variety of plants never before witnessed by the nobility of Zanne, and indeed, Vagandrak.

Now, the resultant forest of exotica was something to both see and inhale, and was – or had been – carefully tended by an army of gardeners numbering near fifty. Alas, the gardeners were gone, and even here the symptoms of the city's invasion could be seen. Huge green ferns were black and sagging at their bases. Flowers once colourful were deflated and withered. Grass looked scorched and limp. The Gardens of the Winter Moon were a victim of the poison in the land, the toxicity of the invading elf rats.

The group moved slowly through the vegetation, on edge lest it carried hidden assassins, elf rats with bows, warriors with blood-dripping swords. But there was nobody waiting. No elf rats leapt out, snarling and aiming for disembowelment. Narnok was frowning constantly; it simply didn't feel right.

Zanne Keep reared above them as they came through the trees and shrubs, ferns and withered flowers. It was vast and black, dominating the area, the walls formed from huge blocks and offering only scant handholds in the cracks.

Narnok looked up at the sheer expanse. "That's one hell of a fucking climb," he said, hissing, and wondering in his heart if he could really make it. He was a big lad, heavy, and fingertips could only support so much mass. It was one thing to talk about it, in some fire-warmed hall after a couple of honeyed ales; but another to put a broken neck on the line if he slipped on the damn icy wall because he had two left feet and gammy ribs. "Damn."

"What about my dogs?" said Mola, looking around at the others. "My dogs can't possibly climb up that."

"Leave them behind," said Faltor Gan, face impassive.

"I... I wouldn't like to be leaving them at the mercy of these elf rats."

"They've fought the elf rats before and survived," said Randaman. "They are hard and vicious indeed."

"Yeah, but... but we were together. Like a pack. If I leave them, and something terrible happens, something where I could have given my life to save them..."

"You love those mangy mutts so much?" barked Narnok. Then he saw the tortured look on Mola's face. He grinned. "Yeah. I expect you do. Why doesn't Mola wait here, guard the ropes so to speak. That way he can shout and scream if trouble comes forcing in from behind. A rearward entry." He said it with a straight face.

"Whatever you think best, axeman," said Randaman, voice smooth, and turned his attention to the treacherous climb. "We're going to need some psychopath to go first. I reckon at least half these men couldn't make a climb like that." He looked around himself. There was a surplus of bulk and heavy boots. "Probably more." Fighting, yes. Heavy infantry, yes. Treacherous wall climbs in the dead of night? He'd brought the wrong crew.

"I'll do it," said Trista, stepping forward, breath smoking. "Who's got the rope? I'll climb up, tie onto something, toss it down."

Veila, also, stepped forward. "I'll climb with you." Trista eyes scanned the lithe fighter, who had at least put some more realistic clothing on since their hours together in the museum. Still, the wool coat clung to her incredible athletic figure like a second skin.

"You don't need to do that."

"I may be of some help." She flashed Trista a bright smile, all white teeth and pretty lips.

"As I said, I work well alone."

"You don't have a choice in this, sweetie." Trista looked to Faltor Gan, and saw the man watching her with a strange expression. Then he smiled.

"Veila is simply offering assistance. She is a fabulous climber; the best thief in the Vagandrak Red Thumbs – and by that, I mean across the whole of country."

"You mean you have fucking competitions in this?" snapped Trista, taking a proffered coil of rope from Narnok and looping it over one shoulder, then settling the thick band against her hip. She watched Veila do the same with a second coil. "Not taking no, eh?" She gave a skull grin. "Well, let's get to it, bitch. It'll be nice having some company when we fall from a great height and crack open our skulls like rotten eggs."

Trista moved to the great smooth wall, and placed both hands against the surface. It was terribly cold, an ice sink that had readily absorbed the winter. She wanted to pull on thin leather gloves, but knew they would impede her progress; perhaps condemn her. She felt for the edges of the first block, then hauled herself up, right arm extending upwards to find the next crack, pulling her up again with a jerk, her toes edging neatly onto the top of the first. To her right, Veila did the same, and they began the long, long, cold climb upwards; towards the velvet sky, and a yellow moon half covered by black, ominous clouds.

Within a minute, Trista's fingers were aching, her toenails painful in her thin boots. She glanced up, pausing for a moment, breath steaming ahead of her to spread across the black wall. *This is fun, my dear.*

Yeah. Almost as much fun as killing a newlywed.

Well, if I fall I'm sure there's a few of those waiting in their smart suits and white gowns on the other side of the door leading to the Chaos Halls. I bet there's a few with axes to grind.

You talk too much. Focus on the climb.

And she did. She powered upwards, from edge to edge, block to block. She found ice and her fingers slipped and she hung for a moment by one set of fingertips, turning slowly like a pig on a spit. A grin fastened on her face. *I think it's time to fucking die,* she realised, before gently swinging herself back around and finding purchase – just as her other finger gave in.

Veila came level with her, and her face was lathered with sweat. "But damn, my fingertips are killing me."

"Mine too."

"Guess what?"

"Yeah?"

"I broke a fucking nail."

Trista bit back a peal of laughter, and looked into Veila's bright eyes, and realised suddenly she liked the woman. Liked her a lot. That was a novelty. An event that was bloody unique. "You're not married, are you?"

"No. Why?"

"No reason." Trista gave a cold smile. "I suppose it's too late to turn back?" she said, frowning.

Veila glanced down. The Iron Wolves, Red Thumbs and escaped prison inmates were distant toy figures surrounded by a cacophony of winter shrubbery. Lots of faces were turned upwards, watching their progress; little white and black circles as random shafts of moonlight illuminated them, before plunging back into a heavy, foreboding darkness.

"I think there's a few relying on us," said Veila.

"That there are."

"You like Randaman, don't you?"

Trista looked into Veila's eyes, into her face, and realised the woman was a lot younger than she'd first realised. Put a sword in her hand, call her a killer, bathe her in enemy blood and suddenly the youth falls away, and decades of experience show in lines around the eyes; in the demons glittering in tear-filled orbs.

"Yeah. I like him. He's a regular party animal."

"I like him a lot, as well," said Veila.

Trista smiled. "Well, I have one piece of advice."

"Which is?"

"Don't fucking marry him."

"Why not?"

Trista's eyes drifted, distant. Then she smiled. *"Because everything always falls apart,"* she whispered. And then she was off, climbing again, hauling herself elegantly and painfully up the vast vertical wall of black stones and slick ice.

Beneath, the gardens fell away, now, and stopping, panting again, Trista could see far off over the walls that surrounded the Gardens of the Winter Moon. The Royal Walk stretched off, arrow-straight, towards the Royal Gate at the south. Casting about, she could see the many thousands of elegant buildings of Lily Gardens, unofficially known as the "Rich Quarter", which itself was dominated by the South Palace. She cast her gaze to the other side of the Royal Walk, with its trees – many now twisted and misshapen, even from this distance, and great gardens filled with glistening white moonflowers, until she came to Haven Church and the cowering, squatting, black-mass bulk of the Haven itself: the slums. The homes of the less than fortunate.

"Quite a sight," said Veila.

"Yeah."

A cool wind stirred across the two women, gazing out from their high vantage point. Up here, it was silent as death. They could see distant fires, which were suddenly extinguished. Darkness flooded back in, like ink into a well.

"This is a war," said Veila, her own breath flowering like ice white petals.

"No." Trista gave a small shake of her head. "This is just a battle; there's a war to come."

"You think there will be more elf rats?"

Trista fixed her gaze on Veila. "Many more," she said, shivering.

The rest of the climb was made in silence and, reaching the summit, Trista slowed her movements, anticipating enemies on the other side of the lip. Her fingers found purchase on the slippery rim of stone, and she pulled free a dagger, placed it between her teeth, and with great care eased her eyes over the ledge.

Nothing. Deserted. Cold, the wind howling mournfully between carved gargoyles, with a large drop to various sloping and flat roofs beneath.

Trista's boot found purchase and she squatted, reaching back to grab Veila's hand, wrist to wrist. She hauled the younger woman up and they both crouched, balanced on the precarious ledge, the whole of Zanne falling away behind them, the plain spreading off beyond laden heavy with snow, and distantly, when the moonlight shone just right, the faraway and mighty peaks of the Mountains of Skarandos.

They both leapt down onto a sloping, iced roof. The entire roof at the top of Zanne Keep was a massively complex array of perhaps a hundred separate interlocking roofs; there were slats and spars, vertical sections rising up with lean-aways and stone joists and other sections jutting free at seemingly irregular and random angles. It was a mess of badly added architecture.

"I thought it would be flat," said Veila.

Trista nodded, and dropped down onto another angular ledge. Veila followed, as Trista peered around, searching for enemies. Nothing.

Trista turned, to head back and drop the rope. Veila placed a hand on her arm. Trista gazed at her, a question in her eyes.

"Don't trust Randaman. Or Faltor Gan."

"I don't trust anybody."

"You can trust me…"

"Why?"

Veila stepped in a little closer. "Isn't it obvious?"

Trista paused, and blinked, and laughed. "You've picked a fine time to declare your undying love for me, woman."

"Not undying love. Just lust."

Trista met her gaze, then leaned forward and their lips met, a gentle brushing, then Trista pulled away. "Maybe later," she said, voice husky. And thought: As long as you don't fall in love with me, child. For my heart is given to another. And she doesn't even realise it. And as they rut under the stars, his cock deep inside her, bringing her wailing with clenching hands to a cat-clawing orgasm; that should be me. That should be fucking me.

I miss you, Kiki. Always have. Always will.

She leapt back to the wall, and looped her rope around a solid protrusion of stone. She stepped up onto the precipice and allowed the rope to uncoil as it fell. It hit the ground with a distant *thump* and Narnok pulled it tight, giving several tugs. To one side Veila was doing the same thing, but she was gone for Trista, everything was gone as she gazed out with tears on her cheeks, stared at the vast expanse of space before her – and thought very seriously about jumping. A long cool fall. Instant release.

To float through the sky for an eternity. There will be no pain. There will be no hate, any more. No hate, or anger, or grief or love. Mostly though, it's the hate.

"Whoa," said Veila, grabbing Trista's arm. A blade flashed by her throat, and soberly, Trista sheathed the blade.

"You nearly lost your windpipe," she said, throat husky.

"I… I thought you were about to fall."

Trista glanced down, where men were busy climbing and sweating and cursing. Then she smiled across at Veila, and released a deep breath.

"I fell a long time ago," she said.

They moved through an intricate maze of corridors. Narnok had visited many years before, but he'd drunk a damn lot of whiskey in the intervening years and his dim memories were nothing but lost shadows.

Again, they had weapons out, but there were no signs of the enemy. Of the elf rats. The tension was killing them.

"There must be guards here," whispered Narnok as they stopped at a balcony which overlooked a huge hall, with a patterned red and black tiled floor far below. Moonlight spilled from skylights far up, giving the room a bleached, ghostly look. He shivered.

"Unless you were all wrong," pointed out Trista, "and this Bazaroth sorcerer bastard and his pet general prefer to live in the sewers."

"I'm not wrong," said Narnok. "It's pride. It fucks with a man's brain. If he's in charge, he takes over the biggest, the best, the most dominant place of residence; it's just the way it is, and I don't give no rabbit's fart what race or type of creature you are; if we'd been invaded by queer, tap-dancing dragons wearing top-hats and breathing cabbage fire, they'd still come here for their centre of command."

They descended wide carpeted stairs. There were blood stains, and further signs of struggle. Overturned suits of armour. Sword-hacked tapestries. Several broken vases, the shards scattered across mosaic tiles like bone knuckles in an abandoned game.

"There," said Veila, stepping in front of Trista, almost

protectively, and pointing. It was a body. A corpse. But a corpse that was...

"What am I actually *looking* at?" said Trista, moving forward, wary.

"Don't touch it." Randaman was there, his hand on her elbow. "We've seen this before, on a few occasions out in the city."

The body, a heavily bearded, broad-shouldered man, was pale-white of face, eyes closed, blood at the corners of his mouth and trickling into his grey-streaked beard. It appeared he had been wrapped in vines, or roots; around and around, almost forming a cocoon of yellow strands. But the worst bit was the wrist-thick bunch of strands that were forced into his mouth, so that his head was pushed back, mouth forming a silent "O".

Narnok shivered. "By the Seven Sisters, that's no way to die."

"I knew him," said Randaman. "Poor bastard. He was butler to King Yoon."

"Shall I hack off his head?" said Trista.

"Best leave him be," said Randaman, and his own face was pale. "Leave him in peace. He looks like he's earned it."

The large group moved on through the gloom, weapons at the ready, and despite their hardcore nature, many made the sign of the protective cross and prayed to any gods that might be listening to see them cross over in some manner of dignity, with some form of humanity. Because this fight was long from done. In many ways, it felt like it was just beginning.

Through endless corridors they moved, and came across more bodies wrapped tight in vines or roots, their mouths open in silent screams, and stuffed full of the damned sprouting things. The temperature dropped. No fires roared in hearths, and the Keep was suffering the worst excesses of winter.

Passing another body, Trista shivered violently. "They look so alive," she said, glancing at the dead woman. She couldn't have been more than twenty, and a bulge hinted at late pregnancy. "What's happened to them all?"

"Only the elf rats can tell us that," growled Narnok. "And, hopefully, this sorcerer bastard."

"You really think we'll find him here?"

"I know we will," said Narnok, face grim.

By the stairs, beside a mosaic floor scattered with broken shards of vase, the butler to King Yoon lay, rigid, encased in roots, eyes shut, blood in his beard. Suddenly, his eyes flared open, and he started to thrash – but quickly calmed. There came slapping, whipping sounds, and the roots that entwined him loosened, flowed from him and all around him, emanating now from the portal that was his engorged mouth. Slowly, he climbed to his knees, all the while the hundred or so strands thrashing and quivering about his head and face and shoulders and torso. He walked, woodenly, down the corridor and stopped beside another body – where a similar thing was happening. A teenage girl this time, with blood in her eyes. She climbed unsteadily to her feet, the roots from her open maw quivering around her face and head with tiny whipping, slapping sounds.

These two moved off, almost silent, into the gloom.

And were soon joined by many others.

The endless corridors, with their straights and curves and twists and corners, led, inevitably, to the central throne

room. There, King Yoon's Central Zanne Throne stood
on a raised dais at the head of a huge, magnificent hall.
Normally, huge fires would have roared in hearths to east
and west, but as Narnok, Faltor Gan and Randaman led
the large group of ex-prison fighting men and women
from the shadows, the hall in its entirety was gloomy,
cool and still. A single figure sat on the throne of King
Yoon. It was Bazaroth aea Quazaquiel, the elf rat sorcerer;
ancient and twisted, his body enshrouded in brown robes
interwoven with roots from his Heart Tree, his dark eyes,
from a face of twisted bark, fixed on the group. He had his
chin on his fist, and he was quite obviously waiting.

The group moved warily into the hall, weapons
bristling, searching for other enemies. But all was quiet;
all was still.

"Come forward," said Bazaroth, his voice both low and
yet carrying the distance.

Narnok, Randaman and Faltor Gan led the way, striding
purposefully towards this commanding elf rat.

"Where is General Namash?" snapped Faltor Gan as
they grew close.

Bazaroth gestured idly with his hand. "He is charged
with bringing the armies south. Even now, they will have
crossed the White Lion Mountains; they are a force that
cannot be stopped."

They were standing before the throne now, and
closing fast. Narnok noted that the hall's outskirts were
lined with the dead, cocooned, as they had seen bodies
throughout their journey into the bowels of Zanne Keep;
and something prickled his scalp with the wrongness of it
all. It was like they were being kept as trophies. Or... or
because they still had some use? Narnok tapped Trista on

the shoulder, and gestured, and she nodded. Her face was drawn with fear. This wasn't like her, but then, they were now facing a sorcerer who had taken an arrow in the eye – one that had surely pierced his skull and brain. And yet here he sat, smiling and breathing and *living*.

As if reading her thoughts, Bazaroth turned his attention on Trista. "I am linked to my Heart Tree," he said, gently, explaining a new concept to a child. "You must destroy my heart to destroy me, and she lies far away back in Zalazar. Where your ancestors banished us. Where your ancestors sent us to die."

"Not my ancestors," said Trista, eyes narrowing.

Suddenly, from the shadows there came movement and the men and women readied themselves; the cocooned bodies were moving, thrashing in a sudden frenzy of activity, the roots which emerged from their mouths whipping and snapping about like so many snapped tendons – and they rose, a hundred of them rose, and Narnok's arm came back with his huge battle axe, readying the throw that would surely split Bazaroth in half – as Faltor Gan's dagger appeared in his fist, tip touching Narnok's throat and drawing blood.

Narnok gave a sharp gasp of pain, and halted, axe above him, his eye widening.

"You betray us?" he growled.

"Sorry, Narnok of the Iron Wolves. This has been a long time in planning."

"What, this meeting?"

"The invasion, you oaf," smiled Faltor Gan.

The monsters created by the elf rats shuffled forward, their limbs moving woodenly as if controlled by another; and the men and women formed a circle of bristling steel, back to back, as Narnok stood with Faltor Gan's blade at his throat. And it was going to explode. Explode real fast–

Trista whirled, but the blow dropped her with a groan. She slapped against the floor, cheek on marble, head spinning, tasting blood and a chip of tooth, stunned. She rolled onto her side, looking up through stars, and saw Randaman grinning down at her and patting the flat of his sword.

"Sorry, sweet lips, but it had to be done."

"What are you doing, you crazy fucker?" shrieked Veila, her own sword turning on Randaman but a fist-thick sheath of tentacles vomited from his mouth, writhing and moving until they became the length of an arm – and from Faltor Gan, also, came a retching sound as he disgorged a sheath of tentacles and the two Red Thumbs stepped back from the shocked members of their own group, away from the Iron Wolves and the armed prisoners – to form a protective shield before Bazaroth aea Quazaquiel.

The wizened old sorcerer got to his feet, slowly, and seemingly with great pain. Then his eyes fixed on those before him, as more and more shambling creatures came from the shadows: from the deep halls of the Keep, from the dungeons, from the bedrooms, from the corridors, from the kitchens, each one infused with roots from Bazaroth's very own body. The creatures, possessed humans of the Keep, surrounded the intruders; there were three hundred now, and more were shambling through the high arches and into the hall of Zanne Keep.

"Once, you made slaves of us," said Bazaroth, his voice deep and melodious, and edged with a hissing sound like whispering leaves. "You killed us. You enslaved us. And you drove the remains from Vagandrak – into a place of poison that warped us into what you see before you today."

Narnok helped Trista to her feet, and held her, and they glanced about helplessly.

"Now, you will know fear, and then you will know peace. For you shall all become slaves; slaves to the elf rat hordes."

And with a cacophony of screams and the thrashing sounds of vomited root tentacles, with a rush of hundreds of bodies, the circle charged in...

Narnok's axe lifted, thudding into one skull, then a reverse sweep sent it into a second, slicing tentacles from the face and cutting the head clean in two before the swarm was over him, engulfed him, and both he and Trista went down hard under the crush of many attackers.

GHOSTS

Why, asked Kiki, and released a breath. *Why could you possibly want me to merge with the salt plains?*

Your magick. It is in your blood. From you, I must feed.

I won't go without a fight.

You have already lost.

Really?

Kiki plunged down into herself, and tendrils of energy scattered outwards, searching, questing, and she felt the raw energy of the salt plains spread out around her for hundreds of leagues, beaten by the wind and charged by the sun for millions of years. And she felt the pulse of magick through her veins, and revelled in the sudden glory of the *Equiem.* It was like somebody had opened a door in the air from a vicious, violent storm, and stepped into sunshine. And Kiki stepped through, arms wide open, accepting the raw *mana* of the *Shamathe;* of the land; of the Equiem.

Her eyes flicked open, and she lifted from the salt and she saw the face before her open with an "O" of shock. Kiki leapt, arms outstretched as if diving from a high place into a pool of molten gold, and was sucked suddenly into the slow-spinning maelstrom of the face. It became a thrashing image, and Dek and Zastarte found one another's eyes, and their faces were grim with knowledge of impending death. The giant face was rolling, spinning, no longer a face but a twister of white streaked through with coloured images; as if Kiki and the salt demon had somehow become merged, were one, entwined in some symbiotic form of skin and bone and blood, and the very essence of the crystalline mineral. They spun and flowed and were a merged thing. A creature at war with itself.

Suddenly, the winds dropped. The whole storm literally fell to the salt earth. Above, stars glittered in a deep eternal sky.

Dek and Zastarte breathed fresh air, and slowly clambered from their sucking imprisonment, struggling at first, but managing to pull themselves free, crawling on all fours like dogs. Or wolves.

Dek scouted around, locating his long sword, and both men stood and stared at the large, immobile globe of white that hung, static in the air.

"She's still in there," said Zastarte, in awe.

Dek nodded.

"Is there anything we can do?"

Dek stepped forward, and tentatively touched the surface, yelping and withdrawing his finger with great eagerness.

"Cold?"

"No." He sucked his finger. "Hotter than the lowest boiling level of the Chaos Halls."

"So we wait."

Dek swished his sword from side to side, and glanced around. But the rolling salt plains were deserted. He looked back at the vast slope of the embedded vessel; the upended *ship*. In the tunnel, the horses stood, motionless, ears flat against their skulls.

Dek ground his teeth, and waited.

You have immense power.

Kiki looked around the smooth white walls inside the globe. She smiled. *Yes. Surprised, motherfucker?*

I did not want it to come to this.

But you were willing to kill, and willing to feed.

All life must take other life to survive. It is the nature of things. It is the nature of the Equiem. And you are born of that power, that energy. You draw on it in ignorance, and revel in its fruits; but you did not plant the seeds. I have been here from the beginning. I helped to plant the seeds.

Kiki considered this. *You have changed your position, have you not?*

Yes.

What's your name, demon?

My name is Shaheesh, of the Salt. And I am no demon. I am… how would you understand it? I am the life pulse that beats through the salt flats and the rolling mineral dunes. This is my land. My gateway. I am a guardian, if you will.

Guarding against what?

If Orlana the Changer had succeeded in bringing her army past the walls and gates of Desekra Fortress, you and the people of Vagandrak would have discovered, much to your regret. However, as we fought, as we coupled, I have seen into the deepest reaches of your mind. I am willing to let you go.

That's fucking noble of you. Kiki could not keep the sneer from her tone.

I could crush you, Kiki, if I so wished. You do not understand what I am capable of. Shaheesh seemed to pause, in consideration. *I will let you go because of the elf rats. Because of your mission. Because of your selflessness. As I said, I am a guardian. I am not evil. But I must feed, on occasion. Feed from your kind. From our kind.*

Kiki laughed, but it was a cold laugh. *You have three seconds to release me, or I'm going to rip a hole through the centre of you so big, I could ride a war charger through in full plate mail.*

As you wish.

Kiki landed on her knees in the salt, coughing, and the globe surrounding her fluttered down, drifting apart in a gentle, cool breeze. The dawn was breaking, a cold blue horizon beckoning.

"Kiki!" Dek ran forward, scooped her up, hugged her hard.

"Good morning, Dek." Her boots thudded the salt. There, at her feet, were her short swords and she lifted them, and ran them home into sheaths. "Zastarte. Saddle the horses. We need to leave here... quickly."

"What happened in there?" asked Dek, eyes wide.

"Let's just say we had a little woman to woman chat."

"Was she a demon?"

Kiki frowned, then shook her head. "You know, Dek, I have a horrible feeling she was one of the old gods. The Equiem. Here, from the beginning of time. And guarding against something so terrible, and powerful, we're all better off in our happy little ignorant bubbles."

"Grak's Balls! A goddess? I hope you were polite."

Kiki gave a little cough, and took the reins of her mount, kicking herself up into the saddle. The beast snorted, stamping. It seemed far from happy. "Let's just say I could have been a little more like a lady."

They rode across the salt plains hard and fast, with increasing urgency, pushing their mounts and angling north and east, eager to be free of the rolling, hard-packed landscape. It was bleak, barren, a thoroughly sterile and lifeless land. Kiki and Dek hated it. Zastarte, for all his claims of hedonism and city sex, loved its bleakness.

During a short stop, where the lathered horses had muzzle-bags of oats, Kiki said, "We are only a short way from Junglan. Then we cut east past the Crystal Sea, then on to Skell Forest. Maybe we could reinforce there? I bet there's still some of our old battalion stationed."

"Sounds like a good idea to me," said Dek.

"Unless the elf rats got there first," said Zastarte, and his ominous words were met by contemplative silence.

Eventually, a distant horizon of rocks met their vision, and the salt flats gradually petered out into rocky foothills. A savage side-wind, which had been haunting them with wind chill and salt blast, was suddenly cut, and they slowed their pace, taking deep breaths, feeling at once more relaxed to be away from the threat the Salt Plains offered, yet increasingly frustrated by the pace at which they were crossing the land.

Zastarte, specifically, had withdrawn into long sullen silences, no doubt contemplating Trista's fate, and wondering not just if he'd ever see her again, but even if she lived. He tortured himself with the several and severe ironies of the situation. He'd known her for years, and yet only now decided he was deeply, madly in love with her. And him, Prince Zastarte, who'd said so often and loud how the only woman who could ever ensnare him was one with enough wealth to buy a city. Him, Zastarte, terror of mothers and daughters alike. In fact, the man who liked to see them *burn*.

He shook his head, silent conversations trickling through his mind.

What would he say to Trista when they next met?

And if, *if* he plucked up the courage to proclaim his undying love to this notorious man-hater, would she simply laugh in his face? Or run a dagger through his eye? He gritted his teeth. It was a risk he was willing to take. One he had to take.

They camped that night in a small copse of trees, a wooded hollow where they were protected from the harsh howl of the wind. The snow was more hard packed here, and had fallen lightly, making progress swift. But by Dek's reckoning, they were still a good half day from Junglan.

They arose with the dawn, to find weak winter sunlight penetrating the sky. The sun was a runny fried egg, pale yellow and unappetising – but better than nothing. Kiki lifted her face to it for a while, whilst Dek and Zastarte packed up their temporary camp; then she stuffed her pack with the few possessions she'd bothered to remove, and folded her thick blanket carefully. Her breath streamed like white smoke, and she shivered, turning to watch Dek scrub his pan and tie it to his own pack. He was a stickler for keeping his pan clean; or at least, what Dek considered "clean". She didn't consider a scrub down with a handful of old leaves or a fist of snow really adequate. But then, in this harsh environment, after all the soldiers had been through, she no longer had the energy to complain.

They set off across rolling hills, then dropped into deep lost valleys where shadows piled on shadows, and chilled them. As they climbed the slope out of the third valley, after scouting a small collection of cottages and farmhouses, all deserted, they were pleased to find themselves back in the weak yellow sunshine. They followed a frozen mud road, and as they breached the rise they saw Junglan nestled far below at the base of a steep valley, the slopes rich with pine, ash and sycamores, and a scattering of holly bushes.

They dismounted, and moved to a stand of trees so as not to be silhouetted. After hobbling mounts, Kiki crouched, and watched. From this distance she could pick out tiny homes and the battlements of defensive walls to east and west. The north and south of the city were protected by near-thousand feet cliff walls: vertical jagged stone, grey and impenetrable. She supposed attackers could descend on ropes – damn long ropes – but it would hardly be a charge. No, Junglan was well protected from attack. But then, so had Zanne been.

"Can you see any movement?" Dek crouched beside her, chewing on a chunk of black bread, his eyes fixed on the distant city beyond the steep slope of snow-peppered forest. He tore a piece free and handed it to her. She took it in silence, chewed in thought.

"No," she said, eventually.

"Me neither. Those walls should be manned. Come on."

"Where to?"

"We should go and investigate."

"You think?"

He moved in close, swift, his arm around her waist, pulling her in to him. He kissed her, and she was taken by the suddenness of the gesture. When they separated, she was laughing.

"What was that for?"

"Nothing. Get your shit together. We're going in."

"Listen to Mr Independent-I'm-In-Charge Boss Man all of a sudden."

He winked. "That's what love does to you." And then he was gone, and Kiki paled, and she remembered what she needed to tell him, remembered what she had to tell him; about the change. The Beginning. And the End. Shit. *Shit.*

Dek led the way, bristling with energy, hopeful there would be a tavern, a hot bath and a frothing ale waiting for them in Junglan. The roadway was better kept here, and edged with large cubes of stone. It had to be, for it was damn steep, despite its worming, S-formation switchbacks that carried a traveller down the steep slopes. From the corner of her eye Kiki noted several guard towers above the road at strategic positions; they were squat, brooding looking things, and currently unmanned. They had to be, for no challenges were issued. And anybody who'd ever travelled with Dek, with his tattoos, his scars and his bad attitude, knew he was a man who always brought questions from bureaucrats in authority. It's just the way it was.

On the steep descent towards the western city gates, they heard it. A distant moaning, like the wind. And then a scream. They glanced at one another, and Kiki bit her lip. "Oh no," she said.

"Could just be another young dandy getting robbed at knifepoint," said Dek, glancing at Zastarte.

"Or some big bruiser with horse shit for brains getting his nose broken for the tenth much-deserved time."

Dek gave a grin, all teeth, and they continued down the steep slope.

They came to the final guard tower, before the city gates themselves. It was built from large black stones, finely crafted by a master stonemason. Around the tower the trees had been cleared, but where they did begin, the Iron Wolves noted the bark had started to turn black, from the base of each trunk, creeping up. Each tree had developed symptoms to different degrees, each one at least half way up the main trunk, but some reaching the thickest lower branches. Here, not only was the bark a mottled, matt black and run through with fine red veins, the branches themselves had started to deform and twist, as if under the influence of a terrible disease. Many of the leaves, also, had turned matt black, interlaced with tiny red veins so fine they were like threads, or the spun web of a tiny spider.

"There's been a struggle." Dek nodded with his head towards the black maw of the doorway.

The whole door, in fact, had been torn free. Kiki drew her short sword and advanced with slow footsteps, ears pricking, eyes alert. To the left, deep in the trees, she saw where the huge, iron studded oak door had landed, flattening ferns. At the guard tower, she also saw the door had been torn free of hinges and bolts, which dangled against broken stone. She licked her lips.

"Something extremely powerful did this," and the hackles lifted on the back of her neck. Inside the tower, something shifted...

They came for her, a seething mass of tendrils like writhing snakes, and her right-hand sword came up fast in an outward arc, knocking half the tendrils aside and away from her face as, simultaneously, her left hand drew the blade on her right hip, and cut into yet more of the tendrils with sounds of chopping flesh. Some were hacked free and lay on the stone step of the guard tower, wriggling, like dying, severed worms.

It came for her, from the shadows: an elf rat, broad shouldered and hunched, with eyes like blood-red berries and snarling teeth like thorns in a twisted round maw. Both hands were held out, palms vertical, and from the core of each palm writhed the thick, snake-like tendrils. Kiki stumbled back and Dek ran in, long sword slashing down. He cut free several tendrils, but others slammed into his chest with pile-driver force, punching him back off his feet in rapid acceleration, face contorting in pain, sword clattering from his hand. Zastarte, also, darted in, rapier flickering with incredible speed, and chopping free yet more of the advancing tendrils. But more grew back, flowing from the creature, grasping for him. He ducked left, sword slashing right. A wriggling white worm hit the ground, but there was no blood.

"Wolves, to me!" yelled Kiki, backing away towards the road. Dek rolled to his feet, drawing twin knives, and he and Zastarte flanked Kiki. The elf rat stumbled towards them, leaving the sanctuary of the tower, giving them more room to fight. Kiki leapt in, both blades cutting and slashing, whilst Dek and Zastarte separated, coming in from different angles, dodging the elf rat's quests, cutting several free before Kiki managed to get in close enough to drive her sword down through the creature's clavicle. It gave a sudden high screech, left arm dropping to its side, the tendrils flopping suddenly to earth like an entwined rope made of thin snakes. Dek leapt in, plunging a long knife into the creature's neck, and Kiki's blade stabbed out, spearing through the creature's open mouth, snapping teeth before cutting through into the brain.

The elf rat hit the ground, and slowly the tendrils started to retract into its dead, motionless hands.

"What the fuck *are* they?" snapped Dek.

"They're like roots," said Zastarte, pushing the long slim tentacles with his boot. Within a half minute, they'd gone completely, leaving the hacked-open elf rat prostrate and, barely, human in its embrace of death.

Kiki glanced over at the tower, face grim. "'Thin roots which come from their hands, they can crawl inside your brains through ears and nose and mouth and rip your head apart with a simple tug'," she quoted, grimly. "Do you think that was one of them? Tree Stalkers, I mean?"

"I think, possibly," said Zastarte. "But Sameska seemed to think these Tree Stalkers were special elite hunters. This thing we killed, here, was a guard. I assume it was guarding something?"

"I reckon we caught it in the middle of something," agreed Dek, hefting his black sword.

"Let's go have a look then," said Kiki, and gave a cold smile, without humour.

She led the way to the tower entrance, and placed one foot tentatively over the step. The quests she had cut free were gone, shrivelled to an almost nothing of pale skin; like a shed snake-skin.

It was dark. It smelled bad. Metallic, like vinegar prickling at her nostrils. There were two rooms on the ground floor with nothing but basic furniture, several overturned chairs and three chests against one wall, all open, mostly empty except for some discarded weapons, axes and knives. In the corner, leaned three old spears. Kiki gave a silent gesture to ascend, and the other Iron Wolves nodded.

The stone steps led up a narrow channel in a tight spiral, a device used to make defending these stairwells beneficial to the defenders, and Kiki climbed with wary, carefully-placed footsteps. As her head breached the next floor, so the stench became incredibly over-powering, and she nearly gagged. A sound came to them, then, a low groaning, an ululation of constant sound, rising and falling, like breathing, and coming from many mouths... A short wall obscured Kiki's view. But then she came out into the wide open room and she stopped dead, staring. There were perhaps twenty people in the room, crouched naked and hunched into upright, near-foetal positions. There were a mixture of men and women, thin and fat, with different hair colourings, differing bruises and scabs on naked, scraped and battered flesh. But each one had a thick sprout of tendrils emerging from the tops of their skulls, then falling like tentacles of flesh to wind and curl and curve around the torsos and limbs of their victims, as if each person was in a prison of flesh-coloured, snake-thick strands, each winding and twisting on individual paths to create a cage purpose-built for that specific individual.

"What the fuck..." hissed Dek through clenched teeth.

In response to the sound, the tentacle coils slid greasily together, seemed to tighten around the people caught in these root-like traps. Kiki gestured for Dek to be silent, and they found themselves feeling suddenly sick. Whatever had happened to these poor people, their skulls had been invaded by some alien intrusion or device. As the tentacles, or quests, or whatever the fuck they were, tightened, so the sounds emanating from entrapped mouths increased in pitch, rising to a wail that made Kiki shudder to the very core of her being, hackles raised on the back of her neck and arms.

Kiki crept forward and knelt close – but not too close – to the nearest woman. Her sagging breasts were held unnaturally upright by a thick limb, which then curled tight across her belly and dropped between her legs, winding back up around her left thigh until it… Kiki turned and vomited through her fingers, a gagging acidic spray mimicking the stench in the air. Dek was beside her, cradling her, lifting her, and the Iron Wolves moved back to the steps, hurriedly down and out into the fresh air.

Kiki leaned against the stone. "One went inside her, up through her vagina, and another through her belly button."

"Like an elf rat umbilical cord?" said Zastarte.

"What?"

"A controlling device. Keeping them alive? Maybe controlling them?"

"Why don't they leap up and attack us then?" snarled Dek.

Zastarte shrugged. "Maybe they weren't… ready. I don't know. It's only a thought." He was pale, licking his lips nervously, left hand clenching and unclenching.

"Well, they're still alive," said Dek. "Suffering."

"What do you want to do?" Kiki's eyes were wide and she looked suddenly, incredibly vulnerable; like a child again.

"What you have to do when any decent creature is suffering. You end their misery."

"We haven't got time for this," said Kiki, weariness settling across her like ash from a crematorium chimney.

"You and Zastarte, go and check the city. I'll go get an axe," Dek growled.

Kiki met his gaze. It was hard as iron, his mouth a grim line.

"Maybe that's not the only way?"

"I'll try and remove one of the things first. If that doesn't work, then I'm not leaving our kind to suffer."

Kiki gave a nod and, with Zastarte, headed back to the road. Without a backward glance, Dek entered the dark doorway of the tower.

They were a hundred yards from the towering gates of Junglan when a shriek cut through the air, one of the most high, piercing sounds Kiki had ever heard in her life. It ended abruptly, and with a distant thud. Zastarte glanced back, but could see nothing; no sign of Dek, and no sign of any more elf rats.

"You OK, Kiki?"

"Yes."

"It was a savage sight, was it not?"

"Yes. One of the worst."

"Can you not... you know?"

"What?"

"Use the *Shamathe* thing? The earth magick, or whatever it is."

"It's a power born of rocks and trees and the mountains. And it's almost random, Zast. I don't control it. By the Seven Sisters, the bastard seems to control me!"

"Oh."

Their boots skidded a good distance before the gate, and they stopped, looking up at the vast, black edifice. Narrow archer shots could be seen near the top, and Kiki felt, again, incredibly vulnerable. It was not a feeling she enjoyed.

"They've taken it, have they not?" Zastarte's eyes looked just a little haunted.

"Yes."

"And if we go in, it'll be the same thing that happened back in Zanne?"

"I believe so."

Suddenly, Kiki cupped her hands around her mouth. " *Hello in there! Can anybody hear me? We're weary travellers looking for an inn for the night.*" Her words reverberated back to her from the vast gateway, metallic and strangely hollow. It made her feel less than human.

She glanced back, back up the road, to where Dek had emerged from the tower and placed the twin heads of the axe at his feet, both hands resting on the end of the shaft. The blades were covered in blood. Dek's face was ashen.

"We need to get moving," said Zastarte, voice gentle. "The city has fallen." Kiki gave a nod, felt herself crumbling, felt the whole of the fucking mess welling up inside her, forcing up from her belly through her throat and out through hot tears which coursed down her cheeks. Zastarte put his arm around her, hugged her, and they moved slowly back up the road. Dek and Zastarte locked gazes as they drew close. Dek's face was filled with a low-level rage, brows narrowed in a murderous look that sent a shiver down Zastarte's spine.

"You get it done?"

"Yes," said Dek.

"They're all dead?"

Dek looked away. "All of them," he said.

They climbed out of the valley on weary mounts, their morale low and ebbing further away. The rest of the day was spent heading east along sweeping dirt roads packed with snow, that finally climbed into high hills; the roads became increasingly winding, and the hills acted as a channel for driving winds, which made all three wrap in their blankets and lower heads against the wild shrieking, the violent buffeting.

The landscape had a wild, savage look, littered with massive rocks from an ancient ice-age, and sometimes even huge hunks of rusted iron. The trio stopped on several occasions, staring at massive blocks of rust, with ancient pipes and gear wheels, pulleys and levers. Some seemed to be mining devices, and the Iron Wolves could trace a long line of old cables down boulder-littered hillsides.

They camped in the lee of one such ancient behemoth, with its toothed wheels and cables thicker than a man's thigh, and which lay at a right-angle to a tall black wall of slate. Dek built a fire on which to cook some hot food, but also to try and cheer them up. The world seemed increasingly desolate, increasingly pointless.

They ate, and Zastarte produced a small flask of rum. It was bitter and strong, and Kiki drank deep before the tears left her and a rosy glow attended her cheeks. Dek had failed to comfort her during the long ride, and they'd eaten in silence; but now, he sat beside her, put his arms around her shoulders, and she snuggled her head to his chest.

"Do you remember that time in Drakerath? We were on leave for a week, not long after the War of Zakora had finished. We were still in high spirits, the Heroes of the Hour, and were pissed and honeyed up to our eyeballs in some leaf-peddling back-street cellar den run by the Red Thumbs."

Kiki glanced up. "We did that a lot, Dek. You thinking of any time specific?"

"Yeah." He frowned. "Some dandy bastard tried to pick you up. Twirled around in front of you, I actually think he was dancing, and I actually believe that *he* believed he looked rather grand."

"I remember that!" snapped Zastarte. "You broke his nose!"

"And he challenged you to a duel." Kiki grinned, and it felt good. "Yes. I do remember now."

"Out into the snow you two went, both drunk as lords, as high as an eagle's fart. You danced around for a while, missing each other with each sweep of your swords, until Dalgoran intervened and took away your weapons. Made you settle it with fists. But even then, you could hardly bloody hit one another!"

"You rolled around in the snow for a bit, then just lay there giggling, like children."

"Yes, yes, I remember it *very* well," said Dek, and hugged Kiki tighter. "Because it was the first night we made love under the influence of the honey-leaf."

"Ahh, the beautiful leaf," said Kiki, then saw the look in Zastarte's eye.

"Yes?" She tilted her head.

"We know you have some," said Zastarte, voice low and level. Non-judgemental.

"Saw you take it," agreed Dek.

There came an awkward silence. Kiki stared at Zastarte, then up at Dek, then down at the ground. She kicked her boot against the icy hardness, then leaned forward, and warmed her hands against the soft-crackling flames.

"Don't make me get rid of it," she said, her words little more than whispers on the wind. "It's one of the few things that keeps me going."

Again, Dek and Zastarte exchanged a glance over Kiki's head. Dek gave a sharp cough, and Kiki looked up. "Er," he said, then cleared his throat properly. "It wasn't that we wanted you to get rid of it, as such, Captain." He gave her a cheeky grin. "We wanted to fucking *share it*, girl. You're not the only one suffering through these harsh times."

Kiki met his gaze. Saw the grin, the skeletal baring of teeth, and yet *looked through* the grin and saw the pain hiding like a mask of silk strands beneath his real human flesh. She saw the glimmer of pain in his eyes. And she realised, *understood*, with sudden clarity – like being dropped naked into a pool of ice-melt – and a gasp, that gods, she wasn't the only bloody person in this damn miserable world who wanted, needed, a bit of chemical stimulation once in a while. And sometimes, sometimes ale and whiskey, they just weren't enough.

"It hit you hard, didn't it? Back at the tower."

"Let's say I've lived through better moments," rumbled Dek.

"So, come on, show us your stash," said Zastarte, holding out his hand, dark eyes glimmering with fire demons. "It was *coins*, right?"

Kiki nodded, and dug out her pouch, and coyly undid the string. "I'll share, but only on one condition."

"Name it," said Dek.

"I never have to clean another pan, spoon or plate for the rest of this mission."

"Sounds like a fair trade," agreed Dek, amiably.

"Now hold on," snapped Zastarte.

"What?"

"A man like me, well, he has his *fingernails* to think about."

Dek stared at him. Hard. "You *what*?"

"OK, OK," relinquished the dandy, with an almost feminine toss of his head. "I suppose I can clean *the odd spoon*."

Kiki handed both men a small coin of compressed, refined honey-leaf, and then took one herself and carefully replaced the pouch deep inside her clothing, in the secret pocket she'd stitched there herself. Close to her heart. Her *twin* hearts. The heart of the *Shamathe*…

"After you, gentlemen."

And slowly, all three placed a honey-leaf coin beneath their tongues, and their eyes grew bright, and they shared that intimate moment of the honey-leaf user, of knowing exactly – in an unpredictable way – of what was about to come. Because the beauty, or maybe the curse, of the *leaf* was that, each and every time, the drug manifested itself in different ways.

"You remember that time we were talking about?" said Dek, dreamily.

"In Drakerath? The first time we made love, after taking the leaf?"

"Yeah." He grinned. "Want to do it again?"

"I think that would be – magical." The fire, the stars, the moon, the world, all had taken on a glowing, surreal edge; and when she turned her head, every single point of light in the universe trailed sparks. Like she was a god.

Dek took her head gently in his huge hands, and kissed her. She tasted him, and he her, and their tongues played, and their lips moved languorously as the remains of the honey-leaf dissolved and flowed down their throats and into their veins and the world seemed soft as down…

A cough. Dek opened one eye.

"I have a proposition," said Zastarte, who was reclining against a rock, one leg kinked at the knee.

Dek broke the kiss with Kiki, and it took her a few moments to realise. Then her eyes drifted open and she turned, as if floating, and gradually focused on Zastarte.

"What do you mean?" she whispered, drifting out a smile.

"How about a threesome?" Zastarte gave a broad wink. "I am a skilled and generous lover." He fixed his dark eyes on Dek. "With women and with men."

Dek nearly choked. "Get fucked, you fucking queer!"

"That, I think, was the whole idea," smiled Zastarte, placing his fingertips together to create a steeple before him. "What do you say, Kiki? I am handsome, am I not? I have seen you watch my naked limbs in the forest, the times when I changed, the times I bathed in woodland pools. What say you?"

"I…"

"She fucking says no, is what she fucking says!" snapped Dek.

"Why don't you let her answer?"

"Why don't I snap your fucking neck?"

"Are you so afraid of the repressed sexuality every man carries within himself? Dek, my dear, dear love, there *is* no male, and there is no female; there is just fucking, and sensuous pleasure, and the constraints placed on us by a so-called civilised society. Let the honey-leaf free your mind, Dek. You'll soon realise my cock tastes as fine as any quim."

Dek went to surge to his feet, but Kiki clung onto him. "Wait," she said, "wait."

"As always, resorting to violence." Zastarte carried a

gentle mocking on his face. "The great pit fighter, more interested in defending a fake government imposed honour than actually using his *brain*, using his *body*, and pursuing that greatest of beautiful pursuits: physical ejaculation."

"I'll knock out all your teeth," hissed Dek.

"Yes?"

"We'll see how well you do with the ladies then." He gave a nasty smile. "And the men."

"Dek, calm down." Kiki slapped him, a sudden stinging blow, then rolled back, giggling. She turned on Zastarte. "The reason it has to be a *no*, Sweet Prince, is nothing to do with sexuality, or prudishness; but everything to do with mc being utterly, and totally, in love with Dek; and willing to bind myself to a concept of monogamy because of that all-consuming love. Now." She smiled sweetly. "Go to sleep, Zastarte. Or go and keep watch. Or pleasure yourself beneath your blankets. Me and Dek, we have some loving to catch up on."

And she fucked him. And It was amazing. The sensation, the flavours, the buzz running through her veins and through her brain. They writhed and moaned under their blankets, occasionally a leg or peeping breast highlighted by the orange glow of the flames. They no longer cared about the elf rats. They no longer cared about mud-orcs, or King Yoon or Orlana the Changer; the hunting Tree Stalkers or any of that fanciful fantastical horse shit. The sex was totally incredible: gentle and wild, subtle and brutal, vague and intense, the best sex Kiki had ever had. And even though Dek came, they carried on, and he came again as she clawed his back and bit his chest like a... she-wolf, and the honey-leaf tasted bitter in her mouth now and Suza was laughing a distant, sleazy laughter edged with the caw of crows plucking eyes on an ancient battlefield, and she thought of the Great Lie, and how if Dek knew about the Great Lie, how she had used the magick to change herself, how if Dek *knew* how she'd really looked at her moment of creation – well, how he wouldn't fuck her in a million years. Not even with Zastarte's dick. And she fell tumbling into an umbilical well of despondency and desolation; down the long dark slippery tube, and the fall lasted a million years, ending with a retarded birth.

They slept in late, dangerous with no sentry, but gone from the world and its realities with the lingering dregs of the honey-leaf. It did that to you. It fucked you over in *many* different ways. Dek made coffee in silence after they awoke, and they drank it strong and bitter, for they had run out of sugar – a crime Dek found hard to forgive. He blamed Narnok. "That old cut-up axeman bastard," he muttered, as he forced down the bitter brew, choking.

They packed and mounted up, and within an hour could see the Crystal Sea to the north. It had earned its name well, and glittered both with immense beauty, and yet sepulchrally. Despite the crystal clear waters leading to stunning beaches of polished rocks, the Crystal Sea was possibly the most treacherous stretch of water outside the Plague Ocean. The seemingly gentle waters, with their crystal qualities and gentle, shallow shores, were a dangerous siren to the uninitiated; for the sands of the sea bed sucked people down to their deaths, and powerful and random undercurrents meant once you were a few feet into the waters, you weren't ever getting out again.

"Some sailors call them the Death Waters," said Zastarte, conversationally. They had paused atop a high hill, where a track wound along the coastline. "Apparently, they have taken the lives of a thousand lovers, ten thousand exuberant children, a hundred thousand fishermen."

Dek threw him a sideways glance. "You're a fucking good man to enliven a party," he said, somewhat sourly. His head was thumping. So were his balls. His new partner was a demanding lover.

"I am merely imparting the rumours," said Zastarte.

"Get you hard, does it?"

"Not as much as watching you humping your bitch," smiled Zastarte.

Dek growled, but Kiki placed a hand on his arm. "Not here. Not now. We have bigger fish to fry." She glanced at Zastarte. "I hope you cleaned your blankets in the morning."

"With the skill of a practised voyeur," smiled the dandy, and kicked his horse into a canter.

They rode for another couple of hours, well past noon, until they spied the distant, vast canopy of Skell Forest stretching across distant hills like a green-black death-veil on a mourning widow.

"Look at that," said Dek, awed.

"Shit," said Kiki.

"Reminds me of The Drakka," said Zastarte, voice soft, manner wary. The Drakka was also known as the Suicide Forest; a place where people in their thousands chose to die. His eyes flickered to Kiki. "You OK with this, Captain?"

"Yes."

"Even after Dalgoran..." He left the sentence, and image, unfinished. He could not bring himself to say, "*killed himself*," although that was exactly what had happened.

Noble General Dalgoran. The man who created the Iron Wolves. The man who helped conquer Morkagoth the Sorcerer. And, after their subsequent disbanding and status as heroes of the War of Zakora, the man who brought them together again.

"Let's go," said Kiki, kicking her horse forward, hard.

Dek glanced at Zastarte. "Well done, horse cock."

Zastarte stared at him with cool malevolence. "Yes. You are correct. My cock is the size of a horse's. I gave you the option to experience it yesterday, but you were too cowardly to sample the experience."

"I warn you, Zast, you will push me too far."

"Then we'll see how it ends."

"I know how it'll fucking end."

"Big words from the Big Man. Just name the time. The tip of my blade will make you scream in ecstasy, and agony. And we both know I'm not talking about the steel in the sheath at my hip."

Dek growled a stream of curses, almost unrecognisable, and kicked his horse after Kiki. Zastarte sat his mount awhile, head lifted, smelling the cold air drifting up from this new and different forest. He could smell pine, and fire, and ice. He gave a sour grin.

Why do you taunt him so?

I do not know.

Yes. You do.

Maybe…

Yeah?

Maybe, sometimes, even I crave death.

There are easier ways to die.

Yes. I know. I have killed many.

And yet you would choose this?

Zastarte considered this internal monologue. Then he smiled, a warm and generous smile, and allowed a sudden warm breeze to ruffle his shirt, pleasuring his skin.

I believe your death should be as hard, and as painful, as possible. Only then will you achieve some form of salvation: a redemption. Only then, will you achieve some recognition in Heaven.

Dek will kill you hard.

That's what I'm hoping for, thought Zastarte, and kicked his horse into a canter after the others.

Skell Forest grew large and dark real fast. They stopped at the tree line, where the narrow road cut a swathe through the trees. Despite grey light spilling from the sky, inside, beneath that canopy, it was night dark and deeply claustrophobic.

"Don't like this one bit," said Dek, warily. "I remember the last fucking forest we had to travel through."

"There's no other way," said Zastarte.

"Who's asking you, cunt?"

Zastarte subsided, and Kiki placed her hand on Dek's. *Calm,* that gentle touch said. *Calm.*

"I'll go first. Dek, to the rear?"

"Why do I go in the fucking rear?" moaned Dek.

"Just *do it*," snapped Kiki, eyes wide, a sudden anger taking her face in contortion. Dek subsided, and allowed the others to fall into position. The clopping of hooves was immediately muffled as they headed under the canopy, and all three riders felt themselves duck involuntarily; as if the sky might fall down and crush them.

"It's as if the sky is pressing down," observed Zastarte.

"Maybe it is," said Kiki, voice barely above a whisper.

Thousand year-old pine trees towered all around, the lower limbs brown and dead, the higher limbs thick and covered in snow. Despite the gloom, their eyes soon adjusted and they found they could see just fine. What was more unnerving was the desolate silence that tumbled like a fresh fall of snow.

The horses moved in near silence on a carpet of dead pine needles. What modestly open sections of forest they came across were mud, now frozen solid by plummeting temperatures. And yet the close compact of pines kept the wind away, and after the harshness of the open, savage land, here it felt much, much warmer.

Within a few hours the sun eased from the sky, darkness rolling in much faster in the depths of Skell Forest.

They made camp, and for once finding fuel was not a struggle. They built a small fire, and Kiki cooked this time. Dek said his heart wasn't in it, but in reality, he was throwing Zastarte some evil looks and Kiki knew a foul mood had fallen on her lover. A dangerous mood. A killing mood.

Zastarte, however, seemed oblivious, and collected firewood and snow-melt for the pan. Within a half hour Kiki had made a fine stew, and they shared out the remains of their black bread. Rations were running low and now they'd run out of coffee and salt, as well as sugar. Dek cursed long and low and hard.

Still, Kiki fashioned a fine meal and Dek dragged some heavy logs around the fire to make a cosy circle. They reclined, with blankets around their shoulders and covering laps. With full bellies, weariness overcame them within minutes. As usual, Zastarte took the first watch. He was a man who needed little sleep. He said, all too often, in sleep he heard the screams of the women he'd murdered. Kiki suspected he did.

She came awake with a start. The fire was near-out. She blinked, feeling groggy, and then realised Zastarte had gone. She cut off the yawn that had taken over her mouth without permission, and eased herself upright enough to see further out from their small circle of created cosiness.

She moved her head with finger-breadth precision. And then saw him, edged in a sliver of silver moonlight. He had his narrow blade out. Was poised, totally motionless. Amazingly, he caught her movement and slowly, agonisingly, lifted his finger to his lips; then gestured with two fingers to the north.

Kiki gave a single nod, and pressed her boot into Dek's belly.

Dek gave a grunt, but Kiki leaned over and placed her hand over his mouth.

"What is it?" he mumbled.

She placed her lips against his ear. The words tickled Dek. "Zastarte has seen something," she mouthed, then silenced his dismissive snort with her finger. Slowly, moving with an infinity of care, Kiki rose from the ground and, keeping low, drew both her swords in smooth arcs. She crossed to Zastarte, but before she even reached him something leapt in a blur from the gloomy depths of the forest, smacking into him. They both disappeared in a flurry of limbs in the tangled undergrowth.

Kiki ran forward, boot on a log, flying through the air to land in a crouch. Zastarte rolled to his knees, found his sword, and glanced to Kiki. Blood was on his mouth. He looked severely pissed off.

"It's an elf rat," he spat. "It's been watching us."

Even as that last word came out, it leapt again from the darkness. It was tall, powerful, still distorted like the others, but elegant with it. It carried two swords of black iron, and Kiki found herself in a sudden, whirling swordfight. The sounds of clashing steel echoed through the trees. Dek leapt at the creature's back, but a reverse blade thrust checked him, and the second blade hammered for his head. He ducked, stepping back, as the Tree Stalker turned on him, focused on him with small black eyes like deep bore holes. A shiver melted through Dek. Kiki attacked, but the creature defended with ease, taking each blade against its own as Zastarte came at it around the other side. Suddenly, the creature doubled over and let out a high-pitched shriek, deafening them, and leapt over their heads. It landed next to a massive oak tree, stepped sideways… and melted into the wood.

Dek gasped.

Kiki ran at the tree, hacked at the back with her sword. Her blade bounced clear. The elf rat was gone.

"Did I just see what I think I saw?" said Dek, panting, licking his dry lips, rubbing at his eyes. "Or is it the dregs of the honey-leaf still burning in my veins?"

"I think we all saw the same thing," said Kiki. "It moved inside the tree."

"But that's impossible," growled Dek.

"It was testing us." Zastarte sat on a fallen log and rubbed at his jaw. He spat out more blood. "Either that, or it ran away; and with skill like that, I don't think any creature would be running."

"It caught us by surprise," said Kiki, eyes narrowed, contemplating what she'd witnessed.

Dek rolled his shoulders. "Yeah, and with some serious withdrawal! I'm shaking like a lost and smacked-down virgin in a sailor's drinking pit. Let it come at us when we're on top form!"

"That means no more honey-leaf," said Zastarte.

Kiki nodded, face pale. "No more honey-leaf," she agreed. "Let's get our shit together. This place isn't safe any longer."

They rode through the gloom, and the roadway widened allowing generous access. It had been several hours since the encounter with what Sameska had called a "Tree Stalker". Kiki racked her brains. What was it he'd said? *Then comes Aeoxir, a thief of shadows, covert in every word and action and deed. His intelligence is legendary. He plays life and death as if it is a board game; and he is always the winner. His special skill is that he can merge with the trees. Become completely invisible. Become a part of the woodland.*

So this was Aeoxir? And the bastards weren't just hunting the Iron Wolves; they'd found them.

Kiki remembered her dreams. And she felt suddenly very, very sick.

So, I always die, do I? Well, I'll fucking show them.

Suza laughed, a hollow mocking laugh from somewhere deep down a drug-tunnel full of honey-leaf smoke.

Dawn broke, icy grey tendrils fluttering through the high boughs of Skell Forest. It seemed to take an age to get light, and the three Iron Wolves cursed silently at this cold, grey world stinking of rotting pine needles, mud and ice.

Something moved on the road ahead; the flicker of a shadow.

Kiki reined in her mount.

From the trees stepped the Tree Stalker that had attacked them earlier. So. It had managed to get ahead of them.

It walked smoothly to the centre of the forest road, and drew both swords, twirling them with easy fluidity. It was tall, well over six feet, broad of shoulder, narrow of hip. The eyes were like black glass. And when it smiled, there were white needles for teeth.

"You are Aeoxir?"

"Yes." The words were low, and sibilant, but carried easily to the Iron Wolves. Then the creature gestured with one sword, smiling all the time with those unnerving teeth. "Get down from your horse, Kiki, Captain of the Iron Wolves."

"This is a challenge?"

"Yes." Aeoxir nodded. "Your friend, Zastarte, was correct. Earlier, that was simply a test. I could have killed all three of you in your sleep with some considerable ease. But... sometimes I am intrigued. We – us Tree Stalkers – are only ever sent out individually on a quest. And yet here, the five of us were sent after such a pathetic and weak little shambles. I am actually quite offended."

"I'll show you a pathetic, weak fucking shambles," snarled Dek, drawing his black long sword.

"You drink, and take the leaf, and rut by the fire, without thought of consequence. You are slaves to your base desires. You are a fucking disgrace to the name of soldiering, and the name of killing."

"Like that, is it? Right, you piece of elf rat shit..."

"No." Kiki's word hung in the air, then she kicked free of a stirrup and slid from her mount. She handed the reins to Zastarte. Glanced up at Dek. "It's all right. This is my fight."

"How do you work that one out?"

"Trust me."

"No, Keeks. We fight as a unit. That's the way it's always been."

"And yet this is a direct challenge; is that not so, Aeoxir?"

"It is."

"If I lose? Do the others go free?"

"Yes. I guarantee it. For without you at their core, the mission will fall apart."

"And if I win?"

Aeoxir seemed to consider this. Then his glassy, gleaming eyes fell on Kiki and she shivered to the bottom of her soul. "The others will come," he whispered.

Kiki moved forward, and faced Aeoxir on the pine-needle carpeted road. She dropped her pack, kicked it to one side, and drew on a pair of thin leather gloves. She drew both swords and felt her twin hearts increase in rapid acceleration. She felt power surge through her; and welcomed it, from the swaying trees all around...

"You are ready to begin?" said Aeoxir, politely.

"Let's do it," she said, and leapt forward with blinding speed.

WHITE LIONS

"So why do you take it, Kiki? The honey-leaf, I mean?"

The doctor sat in a high back leather chair in an airy office. Sunlight streamed through the windows, and outside cultured lawns drifted away to the fabulous white buildings of Drakerath University. Students walked by carrying armfuls of books, their faces animated in conversation and laughter. To the left there was a boating lake and beyond, sports fields where yet more students trained.

Kiki stared at the man. Professor Kaivertes, formerly Iron Wolves military and good friend of General Dalgoran – the man himself who had referred Kiki to the hallowed halls deep within the Ancient Quarter of Vagandrak's capital city.

"I don't know," she said, with a tight-lipped smile. "You tell me."

"It could be all manner of reasons." Professor Kaivertes fixed her with his own iron stare, and ran a hand through his bushy white hair.

"I agree."

"So which is it? Or do you not even know? Is it a topic that you have forcefully shut down inside yourself? Is it something repressed?"

384

Darkness. Lightning flickering on a hillside. Thunder, like the gods going to war.

"I do the honey-leaf because when my mind is flying, I fuck like an experienced whore."

"I watched my own wife murdered by brigands," said Professor Kaivertes, eyes shining. "They stabbed her in the throat, and attempted to rape her whilst her blood leaked out onto the forest lane."

Kiki sat, stunned for a moment.

"It takes more than a common, foul mouth to shock me."

"You stopped them?" she blurted out, almost forgetting where she was.

Kaivertes smiled kindly. "There were four of them. I executed them where they knelt, their hands up before them pleading, their eyes full of tears and fear. I chopped down, cutting off their fingers and hands. Then I left them howling in the mud whilst I tended to my dying wife. When she had finally passed beyond the Infinite, and we had exchanged our vows of love, I returned to my work with much vigour, I can assure you. It took those gutter motherfuckers two days to die. But then, that hardly matters, because it didn't bring back sweet Arolia, and I did not feel any sense of gratitude at having committed the deed. Everybody lost. Such it is with events and bad choices, sometimes. Such it is with the honey-leaf."

"Neat."

"So, will you talk to me?"

"I will try."

"Explain."

"I do the honey-leaf because I cannot stop."

"Why not?"

Kiki considered this. Then she closed her eyes, and she spoke slowly. "I have tried to stop. Many, many times, by Grak's Balls! I tried cutting it off. I tried other substances. I tried alcohol. I tried hard friends and locked rooms. But I think there is something wrong in my mind; something is badly wired. It does not work right. It does not connect. It does not respond. It does not listen."

"What started you using it?"

"The… *mana*. The *Shamathe*."

"It goes back that far?"

Kiki's eyes flickered open. "Did General Dalgoran tell you he took me in as a child?"

"No. I did not realise your relationship went back that far."

"It does. I was… *different*. But the power of the Equiem flowed strong in my veins."

"How different?"

"I could show you, but you'd vomit your lunch on the floor between those neatly polished brown shoes of yours."

"Try me. I had the stomach to feed my wife's murderers their own pulsing, excised kidneys."

Kiki gave a narrow smile. "As you wish," she said.

All those images flickered through her mind in a heartbeat and she remembered the Summoning and remembered the Rage and remembered the Heart and remembered the Earth and, finally, sought out the energy of the Equiem.

"You have been in my dreams," whispered Kiki.

"I know."

Aeoxir attacked, his sword a blistering trail of shining silver light.

Kiki parried, both swords clanging from Aeoxir's blades as she back-pedalled, boots skidding through dead pine needles on the forest road, and their swords exchanged blows in a dazzling array of double thrusts and blocks. Dek strained forward, like a dog on a leash, but Zastarte slapped him in the chest, shaking his head.

"No, she'll not thank you!"

"She'll not thank me if she ends up dead!"

"Er." Zastarte looked over Dek's shoulder. "I think we have other problems."

Kiki and Aeoxir fought backwards and forwards on the woodland road, a dazzling display of awesome skill, and with Kiki's confidence growing. Then she felt, more than saw, Dek and Zastarte step out behind her, with their backs to her, weapons drawn. She launched a dazzling attack which saw Aeoxir forced back, defending frantically with both blades, and she thought to herself: fucking chew on this you elf rat motherfucker, fucking Tree Stalkers is it, I'll give you a piece of Iron Wolf steel through your fucking heart – but managed a quick glance and her heart went cold.

On the road behind them, stood the other four Tree Stalkers. They were all tall, narrow of hip, broad of shoulder. They had black glass eyes and white needle teeth. Wreaths of smoke curled about their boots, and they carried swords and bows. They stood in a line, unmoving.

Kiki and Aeoxir circled one another warily, swords reaching out, touching occasionally with tiny *clings* of metal on metal. Their eyes were fixed, mouths grim lines, both having found somebody of fearsome match.

"You are faster than I imagined," said Aeoxir, voice a purr of falling pine needles.

"And you're a damn sight uglier in the flesh than in my fucking nightmares."

A smile. "You will all be ugly, Kiki, when the elf rat armies swarm across your lands and take what's rightfully ours."

"Show me."

Again, she launched, and their swords rang across the opening. She blanked out the idea that the other Tree Stalkers were waiting for her; that was a problem for another age, another lifetime; and maybe Dek and Zastarte would sort out that particular problem. Or maybe not.

Steel clashed, the four swords of the two combatants a shimmering blur as they moved backwards and forwards across the dead pine needles. Suddenly, Aeoxir launched at her, recklessly, and used both blades to slam Kiki's blades aside, and he front-kicked her in the chest making her stagger back; then he leapt in, one sword taking both her blades to the side in a circular sweep, whilst the other hacked for her neck…

Kiki spun low, dropping suddenly, her legs sweeping Aeoxir's from under him. Her right-hand blade hacked overhead, thudding into the ground where his head had been an instant earlier. He rolled smoothly to his feet, but Kiki launched another blistering attack, forcing him back. A thrust cut a long line across his cheek, and a low blow hacked a chunk from his knee a split-second later. Aeoxir, growling, suddenly drew back his arm and threw his sword like a spear. Kiki flexed left, and the blade whistled past her ear and clattered off between the boles of winter trees, lost in the darkness of the winter forest.

Kiki turned her head back, and stared at Aeoxir, and smiled.

He grabbed his remaining blade two-handed. "Come on bitch, come and die."

Without a word Kiki leapt forward, both blades shimmering in arcs of silver steel with blistering speed, displaying incredible agility and accuracy as the steel clashed and danced and sang a song of death across the forest road. Kiki drove Aeoxir back, and she felt triumph in her heart and quashed it savagely, for the fight was only done when the fight was done, and the killing only finished when the cunt was dead and headless on the road, corpse spewing a bloody fountain. She sensed panic in Aeoxir, felt him making tiny mistakes, slowing just a little as the worm drove deep into the flesh ripe apple of his confidence; and this pushed her on harder, her blades blurring as she threw every single ounce of skill and technique and experience into the battle that was, she realised, one of the hardest fights of her life. Suddenly, a savage horizontal cut took Aeoxir's blade from his hands and it skittered silently across the pine needles of the road. Kiki risked a glance at the other Tree Stalkers, thinking this was their moment to charge; but they stood motionless, like ghosts in the gloom and swirling mist. Immobile. A distant threat.

Is that what it's like with these Tree Stalkers? she wondered idly in the splinter of a second. They stand by and let their comrades die? Punishment for failure? A lack of team-work, a lack of camaraderie?

Suza sidled into her mind at this moment, with Aeoxir disabled, hands before him, face suddenly ashen, dark glass eyes gleaming with understanding as he backed away a millimetre at a time, and she gave a snort of derision.

You think you're special, bitch? You think the elf rats are somehow lower on the fucking nobility scale? What a load of horse shit. You Iron Wolves are a bunch of fucking scum lowlifes, you think you have honour because you cut up a few mud-orcs and put a spear through a sorcerer's eyeball? Well it soon changed, didn't it bitch? You all turned on one another. You couldn't wait to fill your hearts with hate. Look at Dek and Narnok. All that business with Dek shagging his wife and betraying his best fucking friend, betraying you, his lover and wife to be; and even you, bitch, cunt, you fucking turned on Dalgoran, the man who took you in as a deformed Shamathe child, who brought you up, who taught you the secrets of Equiem magick and how to channel it and how to ease away your pain, milk away your suffering, how to change your fucking shell into something that wouldn't get you burned at the stake as a witch or demon or devil. Because that's what you are, Kiki, a fucking devil.

Go to Hell. Burn in the Furnace. Suffer in the Chaos Halls.

I am already there, Kiki, my darling sister. Would you care to join me?

Kiki leapt forward, and her blade pressed against Aeoxir's throat, cold iron jerking up to lift his head so his eyes met hers.

"I thought your friends would help," she snarled, Suza's poison still ripe in her mind, her brain fluttering as she wondered what the fuck she should do. It wasn't their aim to destroy the bastard elf rats; the idea was to make them pure again. To *save* them in some twisted logic that harked back ten thousand years to the time when their decadent ancestors had persecuted a noble race. This fight, here and now… well, it wasn't *right*.

"We fight alone," said Aeoxir, smoothly, eyes fixed on hers.

"And you die alone?"

"Of course. Don't you?"

"We work together. As a team. As a unit. The Iron Wolves."

"Interesting."

Aeoxir's back was against a tree – and he simply *melted* into it. Kiki blinked, and in reflex stabbed forward her sword, the point of which embedded in solid wood. She whirled, fast, and saw the other Tree Stalkers still standing – immobile. Watching. Like sentinels. Dek cast a glance back at her, his own black sword out, his face grim as the Reaper.

Before Kiki could even react to Aeoxir's disappearance, a savage wind howled down the forest road, kicking up leaves and branches and pine needles. It screamed, and roared: a primeval thing, a raw elemental, like a wall of sheer force that slammed down, nearly bowling Dek and Zastarte over, and sending Kiki skidding across the ground still upright, her hair whipping around her head, her face filled with pain.

The wind dropped as suddenly as it came.

Kiki threw a glance to Dek, who shrugged.

Then it roared again, a solid wall of force that cannoned down the forest road, stirring up great piles of debris into a howling, spitting tunnel of branches, leaves and pine needles. Kiki started moving up the road with great, exaggerated steps, towards Dek and Zastarte who were watching the other four Tree Stalkers with suspicion and the threat of violence. Kiki found herself in the middle of the road, buffeted, her shouted words whipped away in an instant. She started to slide again, for the force was incredible, and Dek turned as if to move towards her, to offer help...

Overhead, two great oaks suddenly seemed to flex, leaning over the road towards Kiki who blinked, mouth dry, fear slamming into her mind as her hands raised above her to protect herself, and the great oaks loomed, branches stretching towards her with massive cracks and creaks and snaps. Thin roots slithered across the floor – pale white, anaemic, glistening with oil and sap – and began wrapping around her boots. She screamed, but the panicked noise was snapped away by the howling wind. Dek tried to run to her, but another tree bent, then slapped sideways, smacking into him, sending him flying into the darkness of the wintry undergrowth. All was chaos, all was bedlam, all was anarchy. Darkness fell like velvet dropped over the sun and moon and stars. Kiki found she could not move, through fear, because of the storm that screamed against her, and then roots whipped around her feet, and came snapping from the storm to fasten around her arms and body and throat. The ancient oaks flexed, and she was lifted screaming into the air, held apart like some religious icon, some virgin to be sacrificed, and panic slammed into her and down her and through her and she was completely at the mercy of the forest, of the trees, and of the creature that controlled them – Aeoxir, the elf rat, the High Lord of the Heartwood. Kiki felt herself stretched wide, and she knew with utmost certainty that this ancient woodland could wrench her apart in an instant and the irony ripped through her worse than any instant honey-leaf high; she'd thought she could beat the Tree Stalkers with good hard iron. How wrong she had been. How wrong.

And you deserve it, bitch, as you deserve every unpleasantness they throw at you…

Well that makes me feel better. The only consolation is that when I die, you die with me.

No! I live!

No, I understand you now, Suza, you piggy-back on my existence, on my survival; you are a fucking parasite of the worst order, you were a leech on your husband, working him into the ground until he died and you were free, and now you're a parasitical virus in my mind sending me over the edge for a whim, or for some petty personal revenge that you think you're entitled to. Well you're not, fucker. Because when I die, when I snuff out of existence, then you die with me.

No! impossible!

Look inside yourself. We are joined. We have always been joined by that same blood mother bitch who carried us; only I was a deformed fucking nightmare, and you were the pretty little blonde bitch. Mummy's little girl who got everything she ever wanted, and wanted for nothing, and I was jealous, and I despised you, I admit, but then we always get what we deserve, don't you think? And you got dead. The problem here, bitch, is that when I die – and you probably think I deserve that – then you *die with me. You're a malingering spirit because you're hooked on to me; in to me. But trust me when I say I'm going to Hell and beyond. I'm going to the Furnace. And you're coming with me.*

That is... impossible!

Think about it. But don't take too long, lest these oaks rip my arms and legs free...

And the pathway opened. It blazed like a bright golden trail before her, and Kiki felt the power, as if it resided in a vast golden lake beneath the surface of the planet, and all she had to do was reach down ever-so-gently and dip her finger into this well of massive energy. And she did.

She reached down. And the glowing gold opened before her. Eternal. A gathering of life and power and mana and purity. Pure energy. Pure life-force.

Kiki leaned forward a little.

Reached up, and brushed a few strands of hair from her face.

She reached into the power of the *Shamathe*. Left by the old gods. Left by the bad gods. Left by the *Equiem*.

It flowed inside her, like a new best friend, like a returned lover, like an infusion of purity.

And she welcomed it.

Dek wheezed in the darkness, feeling battered and beaten. He vomited into the woodland debris, and the world felt the wrong way round and the bad way up. Stars spun in his head and he realised that fucking tree had cracked two ribs. "That motherfucker," he snarled, and got to his knees, and clambered to his feet, dizzy and puking, and started staggering back towards the road, and the sound of Kiki screaming...

He accelerated and realised he'd lost his sword. In the glow he could see Zastarte stood, frozen, and to the right the other four Tree Stalkers, motionless, watching, smiling, aware that their *leader* Aeoxir could handle one little *Iron Wolf*...

"No!" he bellowed, words lost in the vastness of the forest and the howling storm as he saw the oaks shift, settle backwards, their roots and branches curled around Kiki, stretching her to the limit of human endurance and physical torture. He stumbled forward, hands clawing the soil, tripping over branches and fallen logs, his boots scrabbling in rotting leaves, his whole being stretching forward, yearning to be close to Kiki in this, her moment of death.

A noise boomed through the forest. It was so deep it was beyond human hearing, but came up through Dek's boots and belly and made him instantly vomit yet again. He hit the ground on his knees, and bright light washed over the scene as if the sun had exploded. He saw the four elf rat Tree Stalkers picked up and tossed away like dry stick kindling. The roots and branches holding Kiki in thrall whipped away as if cut by razors, snapping back and slapping other trees and the woodland floor. And yet Kiki still hung there, rotating softly and bathed in a golden glow. The booming sound, like the charging pulse of the ocean in the deepest caverns beneath the waves, rose up and up and up through the ground and trees and forest, and the oaks that had ensnared Kiki wavered, then bent backwards and their roots tore from the earth with terrible shrieks and then went spinning off through the woodland, knocking aside a hundred trees each. Dek ducked as one huge oak, easy three hundred years old, whirred above his head like cast-off driftwood, its bulk the largest moving thing Dek had ever seen in his life, its mass carving a wide path through the woodland that would last for a hundred years.

And then the storm died. And silence fell.

And Kiki hit the ground with a thud.

Dek floated for a while, and then consciousness drifted slowly back to him. He was lying on his side, curled in a tight ball, an embryo again. His ears were ringing, his mouth and throat burning with a dull throb, as if he'd been screaming until his lungs burst; but he did not remember. He breathed deep the scents of winter woodland, mud, damp undergrowth, mould and the aroma of decay. He forced open his eyes, which were filled with grit. The world swung into a lazy, blurred lack of focus. Dek rolled to his knees. He felt as if he'd been pounded with helves. He crawled forward, and soft, blurred light, a diffusion of reality, gradually moved into recognisable focus.

The dawn had come, spilling wintry light through the high treetops. The world was white and green, and the gods only knew what time it was; how long Dek had been enveloped in the bitter wings of unconsciousness.

He was lost. Disorientated. He crawled forward for a while, pausing to cough up balls of phlegm and spit them out. What he'd give for a long, straight glass of cool, fresh water.

He reached the edge of the road and, slowly, recognition tumbled into place like the levers inside a lock. And there was Kiki, lying on her back in the middle of the road. Around her was devastation. It looked like a world-killing hurricane had torn through the forest, destroying everything in its path, uprooting mammoth trees whole and flinging them around as if they were children's toys. Zastarte knelt over Kiki, and Dek watched for a moment, frowning, confused, for the scene did not look quite right. And then he realised Zastarte was talking to her, obviously trying to rouse her.

Dek forced himself to his feet, and Zastarte turned upon hearing his approach. He gave Dek a bleak smile.

"The horses have gone."

"How is she?"

"This little lady? She's fine. All her signs seem normal, she's just in a really deep, deep sleep."

"What the fuck did she do to them?"

"The Tree Stalkers? Way over there, and there, and there," Zastarte gestured, and grinned. "In a hundred pieces, I expect."

Dek nodded, and knelt by Kiki's side. He reached out and touched her cheek with uncharacteristic gentility. His bear's paws, with their scars and half-finished tattoos, looked strangely out of place against Kiki's pale skin.

Dek looked round at Zastarte. "Do you think you can track the horses?"

"I can try."

"And we'll need our weapons as well." Dek scratched his cheek, then shook Kiki gently. "Wake up, Keeks. Time to wake up."

She roused slowly, and was confused for long moments, staring at Dek without recognition. And then she sat up, and gazed around.

"Shit. Did I do this?"

"Yep. And destroyed the Tree Stalkers into the bargain, by the looks of things. I still think we should get moving, though. Who knows what other freaks of nature are on our trail?"

Kiki nodded, and Dek helped her to her feet. She groaned.

"What is it?"

"I hurt. I hurt *everywhere.*"

Dek took her face in both hands, and leaned forward to kiss her. "I thought you were going to die," he whispered.

"Takes more than the elf rats' finest to murder me," she croaked, and stumbled, Dek catching her before she hit the ground. She leaned against him, encircled by his massive pit fighter's arms, and grinned.

"You look like trampled horse shit."

"I feel like it. Let's find those horses."

Zastarte's tracking skill led them for two miles before they found their mounts, standing idle, their packs still intact,

cropping at winter ferns. With gentle coaxing the horses
were gathered and checked over; for, as Zastarte pointed
out, Kiki could have quite easily blasted every living thing
in the forest to the Furnace and back with her magick and
summoning. Dek snorted a laugh.

They rode for the rest of the day, but Kiki's exhaustion
forced them to halt early and build a temporary shelter
by the edges of Skell Forest. As they approached the
edges of the forest, so more snow was channelled into the
haven, blown by powerful surges of wind. Kiki suggested
an early night, and the others agreed. Skell Forest, for all
its brooding silence and the possibility it could contain
predators, was at least a place of shelter away from the
wild brutal elements that had overtaken Vagandrak.

Dek and Zastarte forced Kiki to rest as they cut
branches and ferns and constructed a lean-to, out of
the wind. Then Dek built a fire and cooked a thick soup
using wild mushrooms and onions he'd dug up with his
recently re-discovered sword, apologising to the blade for
this lack of honour. But when you were hungry, honour
had little place, and a sword made a damn fine spade, if
a little narrow.

Darkness fell, tumbling across the sky, and the three
Iron Wolves ate in silence, each lost in their own thoughts.
Zastarte seemed to have retreated into himself: no more
jokes or light-hearted banter, no talk of the women he'd
conquered or the fine wines he liked to sup. Now, his face
was lined with weariness and anxiety, his movements
tinged with lethargy. After eating, Dek said he'd take first
watch, despite his own weariness, and watched Kiki pass
into an immediate sleep reaching right down to oblivion.

Dek sat, watching the fire. A cool breeze whispered

through the trees, and beyond the orange flames the
shadows seemed darker than ink, and he shivered when
he cast his mind back over the last few months. What
wild times we live through, he thought sombrely. And
then he sank into thinking about his dear, departed mum.
He remembered the good times, he remembered the best
times, and found tears filling his eyes and running down
his cheeks. He hadn't contemplated her recent death;
indeed, had been so busy dealing with bastards with
swords trying to hack off his head, since the night he'd
burned down her house and cursed his brother, Ragorek,
and consigned the bastard known as Crowe to the flames;
well, he hadn't had much head space for contemplation.

Now, with only the fire as company, he remembered
the good times. His mum cooking at the stove, making
him sweet cakes and letting him run his fingers around
the bowl, licking their sweet stickiness. Playing with his
friends in the woods, swords made from hacked branches,
taking on the violent hordes of monsters from the Plague
Lands and beating them back, then running through long
ferns, jumping streams and getting home ready for thick
broth and Mum's homemade bread. Building a dam with
Ragorek using rocks and mud, then watching with patient
fascination as the water level built up to form a small
pond, then tying a rope above it to make a swing and
watching Ragorek swing across, slip and fall head first into
their newly created reservoir, all spluttering and cursing
to Dek's screams of laughter… and Mum's warm towels
by the hearth as she rubbed dry his hair and made soft
clucking noises. Lost days, distant days; love and warmth
long gone and dead and buried in the ashes of the fire and
distant memory.

Dek coughed, and rubbed the tears from his eyes, and felt an arm around his shoulders. He looked up into Kiki's eyes, saw the concern there, and forced a grin he did not feel.

"Are you okay, Dek?"

"Just thinking about my old mum," he said, his voice a little wavery.

"Come to bed."

"No, the Tree Stalkers might come back..."

Kiki closed her eyes for a moment, then shook her head, her eyes opening a fraction later. "There's nobody here in Skell, Dek. Trust me. There's no threat. We can sleep easy tonight, at least."

She led Dek into the shelter, and welcomed him under her blankets where they clung to one another like children, like young lovers, like newlyweds, like a couple waiting to die; and drifted off into a shared sleep and a welcoming oblivion of darkness.

Leaving the towering treetops of Skell Forest they rode east, hard and fast. Within a few hours they could see the distant city of Dunn, and beyond that, the towers of Kantarok, but they feared the worst and knew it was more important to push on, imperative they reached Zalazar beyond the White Lion Mountains. The land here was hilly, with some large climbs that forded them views of the White Lions – towering peaks, easily in the same league as the Mountains of Skarandos far to the southwest.

For the next two days Kiki, Dek and Zastarte rode the hills, and then foothills of the White Lion Mountains, which marched steadily towards them, mammoth, white-coated sentinels, tightly packed like teeth. More snow fell and the going was slow, but on the third morning after leaving the shelter of Skell Forest, they breached a rise that fell away, jagged vertical cliffs falling away to the sloping approaches of the first White Lion.

The land was snowy, but even the snow could not combat and cloak the huge rocks that littered this land. The Iron Wolves dismounted and tethered their mounts to a nearby stand of trees, and gazed down into the vast valley far below.

"You know the way through the mountains?" said Dek, and then his mouth fell open, for far below, and a little to the south, lay camped an army. Dek closed his mouth, and forced himself to remain very, very still.

"Elf rats," said Zastarte, finally.

"The army Sameska promised would march," said Kiki, her eyes shining. "On their way to deliver slaughter and mayhem to Yoon's armies, wherever they may be camped; on their way to bring blood and death to the men and women of Vagandrak."

"We're too late," hissed Dek.

"No, because we move faster than any damn army can. But it will be close, Dek. We know that now."

"How do we get through them? They're camped before the only fucking pass that runs through the White Lions, and that's being fucking generous, as we all know how treacherous that path is to walk."

"They are preparing to move," said Kiki, her eyes fixed on the encampment.

"How do you know that? Is this your magicking *Shamathe* powers at play again? I am mightily impressed."

"No." Kiki pointed. "Look. They're packing up their shit."

The three Iron Wolves lay on their bellies for an hour or so, watching the elf rats dismantling tents and packing bundles onto massive carts pulled by oxen, six beasts to a cart. Kiki estimated the army to number around six thousand warriors, with a third that number again in ancillary staff.

Eventually, they moved back to their horses and spent a while gathering wood, which they tied in bundles and to their horses' saddles; it was going to be a long trek across the mountains, and without fuel they would surely die of exposure.

Finally, when Kiki was happy they had enough fuel for the journey, they began looking for a way down into the valley, which took them several miles north, then onto a winding, man-made road of savage switchbacks cut into the rocky cliff-side itself. It was narrow and dangerous, especially in the snow and ice, and Kiki found vertigo a constant friend as she felt as if she teetered on the brink of some savage drop into an abyss. Hooves clattered and kicked in snow as they walked their horses down this descent, and they took their time, dropping carefully towards the distant valley floor.

Above them loomed the threatening shadows of the White Lion Mountains, and it was early afternoon, growing dark with stacked up storm clouds overhead, as they reached the valley floor and carefully picked their way towards the Kripzallandril Pass, simply known as *The Krip*, before which the departed elf rat army had been camped.

More snow began to fall, delicate little flakes that settled on their shoulders and hats and mounts. Dek glanced up, face a scowl, as they moved onwards and stopped in the deserted space the camp had occupied.

Zastarte went off to scout the locality, as Dek and Kiki turned to face the mouth of the pass. Here, it looked completely non-threatening. It was wide enough to take ten cavalry side by side and had only a gentle slope that had been trampled flat by the recent elf rat soldiers. However, both Dek and Kiki knew what lay ahead: the path, winding steeply up into the White Lion Mountains, narrowing to single file as it travelled up, up, up into the lofty peaks, treacherous for both men and horses alike, as howling icy winds blew hard enough to send an explorer careering off the path and into the void below. Dislodged rocks from above could crush a man's skull or, even worse, there were huge sections that were prone to avalanche. Not only was there a threat of being buried in such a horrific fall of ice and rock, but there was also the threat of reaching a section of previous fall and finding the path either gone, or buried. It was not a trek to make lightly, nor was it one for the faint-hearted.

"I remember training here," said Dek, gently, his voice oozing like smoke, his mind drifting back over the years. He glanced at Kiki. "You remember?"

"Not something you easily forget," smiled back Kiki, lips narrow.

"I'm not looking forward to this. We lost lots of good men. Back in the day."

Kiki nodded, and turned at the sound of Zastarte's approach. "They're heading southeast, following the range down towards Timanta. I would tentatively suggest they're using Zunder Fortress as a staging post; good defensive position, and you have the whole of eastern Vagandrak at your disposal."

"And what about the west?"

Zastarte shrugged. "They have more than one army."

"That's what worries me," brooded Kiki.

"You thinking what I'm thinking?" said Dek. "Maybe the whole of their forces haven't yet come meandering over the White Lions; maybe, and this is just a very sombre thought, just *maybe* we'll meet them high up on the peaks."

Kiki considered this. "We'll cross that particular cracking ice ravine when we come to it."

Despite the lateness of the hour, and with night falling fast, they began the trek up the wide snow road ahead of them, aware that time was of the essence, painfully aware that Vagandrak was *running out of* time. They moved with slow, measured steps, each lost in their own thoughts, each looking ahead at the mission to come – the stealing, or destruction, of the Elf Heart from under the very nose of the elf rat king, Daranganoth; unless he'd travelled south with his army – or armies. The whole mission stank like a ten day corpse and Kiki found familiar demons haunting her, found familiar doubts assailing her senses. The old *what ifs*. What if this didn't work? What if Sameska had been lying? What if they died in an avalanche? What if they were slaughtered the minute they stepped foot in Zalazar? Were Narnok and Trista still alive? Was there still a release from their *Iron Wolf* curse waiting for them back at Desekra Fortress, as General Dalgoran had promised? All swirled in a maelstrom of worry and doubt, with a constant underlying cackle from Suza, her dead bitch sister, waiting for her to drop down to the Chaos Halls beyond the Valleys of the Dead.

Dek found himself falling into a dark mood of desolation and doubt. As they trudged through ankle-deep snow, each footstep sapping just a little bit more strength, and with a biting wind chilling his face and finding tiny ways of intruding beyond his woollen clothing and oiled leather coat to make him curse and forever tug at the edges of his leaking clothing, so he glanced left at Kiki; glanced at that, some would say, *gaunt* face but a face that he found strong and beautiful. She was a proud woman, and he loved her dearly. But here and now, he felt like they were marching to their doom on an impossible task. Sometimes, Dek felt like he could take on the world. Here, in these godsforsaken lands, on this desolate mountain road heading for the poisoned lands of a hated, cast-out race, he felt a great weariness settle over his heart – like a gauntleted fist encompassing his dreams and goals and future. What future could they possibly have? They were going to die on this foolish fucking mission, and yet Kiki would not back down, would give her life to save her country despite her own deep problems, and that was why he loved her. That's why he'd follow her to the edges of the world and die for her on a distant battlefield, his blood mixing with the ice and frozen ground. *That's* why he loved her.

Zastarte, also, was moody and nostalgic. He thought about his childhood, joining the army, applying for and being accepted into the brotherhood of the Iron Wolves – Tarek's elite. He remembered being a hero: the cheering crowds, children thanking him in village squares for killing the sorcerer Morkagoth and bringing peace and security back to the lands of Vagandrak. And the women… oh, how they were thankful, throwing themselves at him, opening their legs willingly for this hero of Vagandrak, a *prince*, no less, with his dashing good looks and, even though he said so himself, a perfection of sartorial elegance. And yet. And *yet* somewhere along the line it had gone wrong. *Somewhere* his brain had become mis-wired; he'd always thought he'd end up married with bawling, boisterous kids ready to carry on the Zastarte name. Instead, he found himself in a torture cellar inflicting pain on innocent victims and watching them suffer, and burn.

He shivered, as a demon passed over his soul.

And now he realised he was in love with Trista. But, even if she'd lived after the events in Zanne, even if she'd survived the constant fighting without him by her side to watch out for her, would she ever return his love? How could she, knowing what he'd done in his dark and evil past? The atrocities he'd carried out in the name of... jealousy? Loathing? A base-level hatred of humanity? Because these things he had done, they were not born from love, or even desire or lust – no. They were products of a hatred that ran bone-deep, at the cellular level. They were genetic. Inherited, perhaps? Had his father carried the same warped desires?

Zastarte ground his teeth and marched on as darkness fell over the mountains and the world, and the biting wind brought him more pain.

"We're all going to die," he murmured, although his words were taken by the wind and snapped away to the snow-laden valleys far below their panoramic view, fading fast. He gave a twisted, sardonic smile. "And nobody is going to *give* a fuck."

They walked for half the night, deeper into The Krip, travelling inwards and upwards as if this were some insane military training exercise and a competition to see who had the greatest natural stamina. Dek finally called a halt, spying a cave down a narrow ice-edged cleft, and away from what had become a more severe and narrow path into the heart of the White Lion Mountains.

They just managed to squeeze the horses into the opening and tether them to nearby rocks. The place was a natural wind break and they unloaded wood from the horses, placing blankets across their backs, and Zastarte built a small fire at the mouth of the cave, where Dek brewed some hot tea and they all warmed savagely chilled fingers over the flames, sitting on their bedrolls to remove the seeping cold from the rocky ground.

The wind howled, a mournful series of ghost sounds, and Dek and Kiki huddled together, her head on his shoulder, staring at the dancing fire. Zastarte watched them from across the flames, his eyes hooded and dark, his cup in both hands warming his fingers, his mood brooding.

"You wish she was here, don't you?" said Kiki.

Zastarte gave a single nod.

"You've changed a lot since I found you in that torture cellar."

"Yes."

"Do you know why?"

Zastarte considered this. Eventually, just as Kiki thought he wouldn't answer and was going to prompt him again, he said, "I believe that I found myself. I found peace with myself. The inner demon was cast out."

"Inner demon?"

"Yes. A voice that spoke in my head. Prompted me to do bad things." Kiki's mouth went dry, and she thought about Suza.

"And you killed it?"

"I think, more, I exorcised it."

"Did your demon have a name?" said Kiki softly.

"Yes, but I will not speak it here, lest I conjure the bastard back from the Furnace." His head tilted to one side. "You know what I'm talking about, don't you?"

"Yes," said Kiki in a tiny voice. "I have a sister. Suza. She… died when I was much younger. It is her that haunts me, her that taunts me."

"No, no," said Zastarte, shaking his head. "I don't believe that; I don't believe your sister is inside your skull. This is something else. Something that came with our curse on that day Dalgoran and the other magickers created The Iron Wolves."

"You think so?"

"Yes. This Suza – she is a product of the curse. There will be a way you can kill her; or banish her from your mind. You just have to find the right trigger, the right pressure point, and she will be kicked screaming and wailing into the Pit."

"What was your trigger, Prince Zastarte?"

He leaned forward, and for a moment his eyes were visible by the light of the fire. They glistened with tears and he gave a woeful smile.

"I fell in love," he said.

They set off with the coming of dawn, and the track grew ever narrower, ever steeper. Many sections had had great steps hewn into the rock, staircases on which the horses struggled, their iron-shod hooves slipping and sliding. The snow had stopped, and the sky was the colour of the ocean, a dark thunderous grey, with rolling clouds like waves and a distant low-level narrow strip lit by the winter sun. It was bleak, and yet beautiful, and the more they climbed so the pastel panorama before them widened to reveal the land of Vagandrak in all its beauty; all its decadence. Distant castles dotted the horizon, and great swathes of forest were highlighted in stark patches of evergreen. Through drifts of cloud they could see Zunder the volcano, and noted trails of distant black oozing from its summit. The volcano had not erupted for nearly three hundred years, and most scholars believed the mammoth beast dormant. Here, though, now that the elf rats had invaded, and there were no scholars to witness, it appeared the mighty dragon would ignite once more.

They sat and ate a cold meal of dried pork strips and chunks of hard cheese, eating in silence, each lost in their thoughts. Their horses stamped and snorted steam, and Kiki moved to her mount, patting the gelding's neck and digging out a handful of oats. "Here you go, boy," she said, words gentle, and the horse ate, then turned, nuzzling her with quiet affectionate sounds. "We've been through a lot together, haven't we? And here I am leading you on a crazy mission to quite possibly a certain death. After all, we can't fight all the elf rats in Zalazar, can we? We can't possibly battle our way to the Mountains of the Moon through ten thousand enemies. We just haven't got the… the *strength*, any more. I'm tired, boy. Tired of this world."

They climbed for another hour, breaching the current peak only to see more, and higher, peaks unfolding ahead of them, like an undulating mass of mountain flanks, each one hiding a further, higher summit. "False summits", they'd called them during their training days. Designed by the gods to sap a soldier's morale; especially when humping a large, heavy pack up eternal, leg-breaking slopes.

Distantly, thunder rumbled.

They followed a trail well marked by the recent, passing elf rat army; and then onto another section of steep ascent. Dek was leading, and when he suddenly stopped up ahead, Kiki looked up from her morbid contemplation and halted her own mount.

"What is it?"

"There's been a rock fall. An avalanche of sorts. The fucking trail has gone."

Kiki and Zastarte hurried forward and stopped, dismay flooding them. The path had indeed gone; what now existed was a steep sideways slope of churned rock and gleaming ice and snow, cutting across right before them. It carried on, for as far as the eye could see, curving around the side of the mountain and out of sight.

"Horse shit," said Kiki, voice a monotone.

"There no other way around?" asked Zastarte.

"No. No other path. We'll have to risk it."

"We'll not get the horses across that," said Zastarte, frowning. "They'll slide to their deaths."

"You have to guide them," said Kiki, "but keep the reins loose in your hand. If you feel the creature begin to slip, let go, or it'll damn well drag you off the mountain."

Zastarte stared at her. "That seems a little harsh," he said, but forced a smile to hide his fear.

Kiki shrugged. "It's reality, my friend." She slapped him on the back. "Come on, it'll be all right. I'll look after you! After all, we're the Iron Wolves and we're on a mission of mercy to save Vagandrak! Chin up, be brave, you foppish dandy bastard."

Zastarte grinned, and gave an extravagant bow, extending his arm in a sweep. "After you then, good lady. Show me how it's done."

Dek went first, approaching the slope warily, his eyes scanning the lower flanks of the avalanche sweep, then looking up to see if it was likely more would come tumbling down on top of him. He looked back at Kiki. "You ever seen one of these bastards go?"

"A couple of times," she said, breathing deep. "But we have no other choice."

Dek nodded, and eased his way out onto the silent, gleaming slope. His mount, a solid chestnut gelding of south Vagandrak stock, was game for the traverse and, with only a little goading, stepped onto the sloping icefall and followed Dek, body tilting, rear haunches bunching as it fought to keep its weight moving forward.

Kiki gave a short prayer to the Seven Sisters, left a reasonable space, then followed Dek out, her own mount a little more skittish, but with kind words, and holding the reins loosely in her left hand, she started to make the crossing.

She glanced back. Zastarte was pale with fear. She gave him a smile, but he did not return it, instead, looking up at the sky where the clouds had darkened. Again, thunder rumbled in the distance and Kiki cursed.

"We have to cross now. *Now*, Zastarte. If that blizzard comes rushing in, we'll be truly fucked."

He gave a short nod, and stepped out onto the slope, his boots sliding a little. He gritted his teeth, felt his heart leap into his mouth, and cursed everybody from his mother to the gods to the demons of the Chaos Halls.

"Bastard, bastard, *bastard*," he muttered, and urged his mount forward with several clucks and clicks and "Come on, boy, come on," with gentle tugs on the reins. His horse stepped out onto the slope and gave a loud whinny of fear, ears laid back flat against its skull. Zastarte, leaning to the right to compensate for the steep, slippery slope angle, urged the beast on.

They started the traverse, and after a couple of minutes he looked up, sweat dripping from his forehead and off the tip of his nose. He saw the other side of the slope, where the path started once more. It looked like a thousand leagues away. He watched, as Dek made it safely, and he ground his teeth as the fear piled on and on and on, and he felt the beginnings of panic clamp his heart. His boot slipped, but he righted himself, and forced his mind into a state of calm.

Focus on each footstep.

Focus.

Just one at a time.

He glanced up. Kiki's mount stepped with a kicking of hind legs and a shower of stones and ice onto the pathway; and she led him forward, patting his mane and whispering words of encouragement into his twitching, laid-back ears.

Then she turned, almost in slow motion, to look back at Zastarte's progress…

At that moment, his horse slipped.

It screamed; the gelding screamed, and legs began scrabbling in a mad chaos of flailing limbs and a powerful shower of stones and ice. The horse slid down a section of the slope, hooves flailing, and Zastarte's arm was nearly wrenched clean from its socket. He was jerked, yanked after the sliding beast, his boots scrabbling, losing his footing on the scree and he hit the ground, and slid after the beast.

"Let go of the reins!" screamed Kiki, panicked, leaping forward onto the slope. "Let go!" But Zastarte could not let go, for in an unbidden, unconscious act, he'd wound the reins tight around his fist. He was connected to the horse by a tightened, thrumming umbilical – only this was a cord promising death, not life.

They slid further down the slope, the gelding losing its footing, hooves and legs flailing as it slammed onto its side. Zastarte slid after the creature head-first, his right hand trying desperately to free his sword so he could cut the reins; but his sword was trapped in its scabbard beneath him.

Rocks and ice tumbled around them. Again, thunder rumbled and the skies grew yet darker; more foreboding. Lightning split the sky in the distance, a brilliant flash that illuminated Zastarte's plight with an actinic crack.

"Zastarte!" yelled Kiki. Both her and Dek were on the slope now, beginning to edge down towards him as his mount, slowly, gradually, slid and ground to a halt. Zastarte carried on sliding, then bumped into the creature. It was snorting, chest rising and falling, and gave a feeble whinny, and Zastarte breathed deep, face ashen, looking up through lank rat-tails of sweat-streaked hair.

"Fuck," he breathed, then reached out slowly, and patted the gelding's muzzle. "Keep still, old boy. Keep real still."

Zastarte looked up the slope, to where Dek and Kiki, stick figures, had begun their own descent to help him.

"Get me some rope!" he shouted, and watched Dek turn back.

Zastarte peered left and right, but could see no edge to the slope. How far did it go? He could not see beyond the gelding's bulk, and he began to wriggle, trying to sit up. Pain lashed through him from his hand where the reins had dug in deep, cutting through flesh. Blood dripped from the leather leash, down his hand, trailing down his fingers and staining the ice.

Snow started to fall. Thunder growled like a caged bear. More lightning, closer this time. Cracks and booms echoed around the mountains. Zastarte managed to sit up, rocking himself into position, and gazed up at the snowflakes landing gently against his face. A strange serenity fell over him. A perfect, inner peace.

I am going to die, he realised. And he was not afraid.

"The rope isn't long enough!" boomed Dek, from the top of the slope.

"Kiki?" Zast's voice was perfectly calm. Kiki had halted her descent, and was staring up at the sky, then back up the slope, past the place where it had cut off their trail. There came a strange, rumbling, growling sound; only this time, it was not thunder.

"*Kiki*!"

"Yes?" Her head snapped around. She was too distant for him to see her face, but he knew in a moment of intuition that *she knew*. Understanding passed between them like a crackle of lightning.

"Tell Trista I love her," he said, the words slipping out.

Then, from further up the slope the rumbling turned suddenly into a roaring, grinding chaos and the gelding started to struggle violently, eyes widening. This set the horse sliding again, and Zastarte was yanked after the creature. From the upper slopes came a second wave of avalanche – a wall of snow and rocks, sliding, tumbling, racing down the slope. Dek leapt back from the edge and Kiki was sprinting, her boots sinking, as the wall loomed over her like a curl of violent, towering white surf.

Sliding further down the slope, Zastarte gazed up – and it looked as if the whole mountain had reared above him, a violent contrasting oil painting of chaos and panic and anarchy; a massive fist of rock and ice and snow and bent dead trees and crumbling blocks of granite... and it seemed to pause, this great terrible wall, and then came crashing down, enveloping him, slamming him and the screaming gelding spinning down the mountain and over the edge of jagged black cliffs, where they tumbled... spun silently, down into the deep black abyss below.

ENDTIMES

Mola stood in the snow-filled Gardens of the Winter Moon, rubbing his hands together, stamping his feet, blowing warm air into cupped hands, and wrapping his arms around his body. He was cold. No. He was *fucking freezing*. His breath streamed like dragon smoke. His teeth occasionally chattered, coming on in waves, then easing off again, for he was a wiry slim man, not a man with a lot of body fat.

His dogs paced around him, despite multiple warnings to "*Sit*!" and "*Lie*!" and "*Fucking lie down, bitch*!"

Mola looked around himself, wary. It had been over an hour since the others had scaled the walls and entered Zanne Keep, and he felt isolated, alone – despite the dogs. He felt more alone than he had in years and this puzzled him.

He checked his swords and knives.

Yeah. Right. Like simple steel would be much use against a horde of wandering elf rats intent on cracking his bones and sucking his blood and turning him into some tree-hugging motherfucker – because, and let's be honest here, Mola old chap, if the enemy decide to take you, really decide it, then you're fucked; no matter you have the best fighting dogs in Vagandrak at your heels. These elf rats are merciless bastards. Just like you. They'll chew you in a spit you out. You, and your hounds.

Mola blew into his hands, and rolled his wounded shoulder. Damn, that hurt. It just didn't feel right. Felt out of place. A little disjointed. A little… broken. And he knew with a sinking feeling that the injury would cause him shit for the rest of his life. Then smiled, a narrow affair on his brutal bleak face. That "life" might be a much shorter timeline than he realised.

Duchess whined, and looked up at him.

"Shh, girl." His hand touched her muzzle. The simple contact was enough to settle her. She gazed up at him. She was a pretty bitch; most beautiful. Her eyes shone with adoration. And that, *that* was why he loved dogs so much – much more than fucking *people*. A dog's love was unconditional. People always let you down. *People* always stabbed you in the fucking back when you least expected it. Best friends fucked you over. Brothers betrayed you. Cousins took your money or property. And where was it going? Did they love you? Nephews betrayed family by marrying into psychopathic, fucked up gene pools. And even lesser relations? The *greats?* Those who didn't even *know* you, much less care whether you lived or died? Why would they ever truly *give* a fuck? No. Just take a hefty slice of ill-gotten inheritance when you kicked the bucket, blood money of the worst order, and who gave a fuck where it came from, right? As long as they got their coin and pissed it away on pointlessness, the mercenary motherfucking pieces of shitty scumbags. Should be on a fucking noose hanging, neck bones grinding away as they loosened their bowels in their fancy pants trousers and pissed their way to the Chaos Halls.

Ha, he thought. I'm spending it all!

Or leaving it for the dogs.

Thrasher, the largest and most brutal of his beasts – fuck, he was almost as big as a pony, and Mola often wondered what beast, be it wolf or fucking bear, was in his lineage – stood and shook himself, and looked up at Mola, although not by a long way, and their eyes connected and Mola got that thrill that *fucking thrill* that he always got from the huge fighting dog. Would the bastard even *do* what Mola asked?

"Down, boy. Lie down."

By some miracle, the slab of muscle and savage rabid death lay down and put his head on his huge tufted paws. Mola breathed a little more calmly. It was always a close thing with Thrasher. Indeed. With all of them.

They were good boys and girls.

He loved them dearly.

But by their very nature, they lived close to the edge.

Close to the edge.

Just like him.

He grinned, a grin without humour, and wondered what he could do.

So.

Problem.

Zanne Fortress. Locked down to fuck, obviously. Or was it really so obvious? Were the elf rats really so... accurate? Or were they, like every other power-hungry bastard Mola had ever met during his miserable existence, *were they* filled with thoughts of their own supremacy and narcissism? Were they in love with their own fucking ideology and icons and pathetic fucking gods?

"Can't just stand here all night. Let's go and find out," muttered Mola. The dogs, *his* dogs, looked up at him; like loyal servants to their honourable Master. Mola saw the look. It filled him with pride. He loved his dogs. He *loved* his dogs.

He gazed around. The wild foliage of the Gardens of the Winter Moon seemed to gaze back; or at the very least, waver gently in the cold winter wind, sighing, and shifting, and casting long shadows.

"UP!"

The four dogs stood in an instant, were quivering, ready. They recognised the command in his voice. Maybe even the fear.

They padded along beneath the wall to Zanne Fortress. It reared high above, black and bleak, a towering vertical prison cell. Mola had his sword out, his eyes constantly scanning, but he knew the dogs were his early warning system, for their senses were far superior to his. Always had been.

Something's happened to the others. Inside. I can feel it. But the question is, if the Iron Wolves and the Red Thumbs and the Prison Boys weren't able to do anything – then what the hell can I do, on my own, like?

The gardens sighed in a cold gust. Snow flurries fluttered down, settling across Mola's shoulders, and his dark eyes flitted around the shadows, eyes narrowing. There was something there, he was sure of it. Something... watching him. He glanced to the dogs, but their senses hadn't picked anything up; which in Mola's books, usually meant there wasn't anything there at all except his paranoia. But still... the hackles rose on the back of his neck.

Damn, but you're spooked, old man.

He paused at a jutting corner of towering black stone, halted, glancing about. "To me, Dogs," he said, quietly, and they turned, stood by him, muzzles pointing outwards, eyes scanning, thick rolls of saliva pooling to the frozen ground. Thrasher panted, fangs like razors glinting in the moonlight as gentle snowflakes settled on his raggedy black coat. Mola reached out, patted the dog, and for an instant thought Thrasher would take off his hand. Instead, the great beast licked him, and Mola chuckled.

"*Good boy.*"

They moved across silent, frozen ground and stopped before the great gates of Zanne Keep. Mola had been here before, during happier times; the gates were twenty feet high and two feet thick. Solid oak banded with iron and studded with bronze. Impressive. Huge. Solid. Mola prodded the gates with his boot, then poked them with his sword, half hoping they would swing wide; maybe some miracle would occur and Narnok's scarred and ugly face would peer out and grin at him... but that didn't happen. There came a solid little *thunk*. The gates were as immovable as the Mountains of Skarandos.

Duchess gave a tiny, tiny growl. Her round black nose quivered. Mola turned from the gates, and glanced down, then looked up. The gardens with trees and ferns and exotic bushes containing spiked leaves were a solid, inky mass. Snowflakes settled through the air with casual gentility. There was an ornate iron trellis, an archway, matt black and almost hidden in the gloom. Mola blinked, and there was a figure stood beneath its arch.

Mola brought his sword around.

"Horse shit," he muttered.

It was an elf rat. And a tall one at that.

"Dogs," he said, and Duchess looked at him. He pointed. "Kill."

Duchess, Duke, Sarge and Thrasher leapt forward, muscles powering them into attack in a seething mass of fur and snarling jaws, slamming them towards the elf rat. Mola observed. It was tall, seven feet at least, and had narrow bony limbs in skin that reminded Mola of bark. It carried no weapons in hands with long fingers like claws. With a shudder, he realised it was watching him.

It made no move as the dogs charged, and Mola started forward, following them up with his sword in case of other surprises. He was in no doubt his dogs would tear this creature apart, but there might be others. Hundreds of others…

Duchess was quickest, and as the bitch leapt, snarling, jaws glinting, the elf rat's hand suddenly lifted, fingers together, palm to the ground. Duchess hit the frozen grass limp and unconscious, and in the blink of an eye, the other dogs followed. They landed, Thrasher rolling, and lay unmoving.

"NO!" screamed Mola, and charged forward, his sword in one fist.

"They are sleeping," said the elf rat, his voice a gentle hiss like the wind caressing oak leaves in a dreamy forest on a summer afternoon. Mola felt *something* hit him, like a wave of pressure that forced a need to sleep into his system. He faltered, his aggression and hate leaking away, and his sword lowered, his charge slowing.

He stopped, and knelt by Duchess. She was breathing deeply.

Mola's head came up. "Who are you?" he slurred, feeling drugged, sleepy.

"I am Sameska," said the elf rat, dark eyes gleaming. "Your Iron Wolf friends, Kiki and Dek and Zastarte, are on a mission into elf rat lands to find the Elf Heart and destroy it, freeing my people; *purifying* my people from an ancient curse. And yet, they walk into a terrible trap – for here, Bazaroth aea Quazaquiel holds a spell over the Elf Heart; ancient Equiem magick. When they get close, they will be torn apart by primal elemental forces. If the Tree Stalkers don't kill them first."

"My friends, they have gone in there," Mola gestured to the Keep, "seeking this sorcerer, Bazaroth. They will kill him."

"They have already failed," said Sameska, stepping forward from under the iron archway. He knelt by Duchess, and stroked her fur. "They are imprisoned in Zanne Dungeons, even as we speak."

"Then I will go to their rescue," said Mola, despite feeling only a need for his bed.

"I will help you," said Sameska, his voice hypnotic. He fixed his dark eyes on Mola. He grinned, and his teeth were like splinters of thorn. "We will find Bazaroth together, both you and your dogs, and I will help you kill him." Sameska stroked Duchess. "Or else the Iron Wolves will surely die."

Narnok groaned. Fuck me, that was one hefty session on the whiskey! I hope I didn't do anything I shouldn't. I hope my bastard axe didn't get me into any more trouble. Actually. I fucking wish I hadn't even been born.

Narnok's head pounded. His mouth tasted like a sewer. His knuckles throbbed, and he groaned again inside; that was *never* a good sign. What local strutting farmer had he taken apart this time?

Then he opened his eyes, and the world spun around and into focus and reality came crashing in, along with his memories, and his fear. He was in a black stone dungeon. The walls were damp and festering with thick mounds of mould. His arms were chained above his head, and he sagged against his chains, his wrists burning and cramped. He spat on the floor before him, and a cool breeze drifted across his hot, fevered features. He looked to his left, where Trista was watching him from her own chains, a sardonic smile caressing her face.

"I think we fucked up," she said.

"What were those tentacle things coming out of Randaman's face?" blurted Narnok, and shuddered. Then he manoeuvred his chained hands and started poking at his own mouth. "They've not done it to me, have they, Trist? You can't see anything sprouted out of my face, can you?"

"Only your unkempt nostril hair," said Trista, wearily.

They hung there for a while, in silence, contemplating their fate.

"We've been in worse shit than this," said Narnok, eventually.

"Yes. Possibly."

"We'll sort something out."

"Again, possibly."

Narnok moaned and wriggled. "Your stitches are holding up well," he said, maybe a little too brightly.

Trista gave him a stern look. "Well, it's always good to know one's handiwork is appreciated; especially when one is about to die."

"Don't be like that, Trista."

"What? Pragmatic?"

Narnok suddenly realised others were chained up with them; hard to see in the gloom, further down the stone wall filled with chains and manacles at a variety of handy heights. There was Veila, unconscious, head hung low, arms above and behind her in an inverted "V". And squinting, Narnok could just make out Dag Da. Beyond that he could see Cunt and Meatboy, and other figures whom he assumed to be the prison boys.

"I wonder how many of us survived?" he muttered.

"That's academic," said Trista.

"How do you reckon that?"

"Because we'll all soon be dead."

There came a distant scraping of iron. The sound of heavy tumblers in a lock. Boots on stone.

Three figures could be seen, shadows at first bearing lanterns before them which illuminated faces in pale circles of glowing orange; demons drifting through the dark.

Narnok grunted when he saw Randaman and Faltor Gan. They stopped, one lantern swinging gently, and surveyed Narnok with narrow smiles.

"What do you cunts want?" he growled.

"Brave words from a man who's chained up," said Randaman.

Narnok shrugged. "I'm impressed you can speak, Red Thumb dregshit, last time I saw you, *you* had all this tentacle shit spewing from your mouth like you was something dredged out of the sea, dead – and better off there, if I don't say so myself."

Randaman's face shifted into a scowl. "*You don't know of what you speak!*" he snarled.

Narnok stared back, his single eye bright and focused, his scarred face hard and brutal. "I know I'd rather be dead that have octopus legs for a face. And as for him," he gestured to Faltor Gan, with a nudge of his head, "what's the matter, sea creature maggots got your tongue?"

"We are operating at a higher level than you could ever imagine," said Faltor Gan, and gave a brittle smile. He lifted the lantern a little higher, as if better to regard Narnok. "The elf rats are now All Powerful across Vagandrak, Narnok of the Axe. You are dumber than a dead donkey if you can't see the power shift in this land; we *volunteered* ourselves to the Great Sorcerer, Bazaroth – and as a reward, he gave us the *gift* that you witnessed in the Hall of Zanne Keep. We are truly *honoured* to be taken in by the elf rats; to be trusted, to be treated as equals; to be given the power of the *quests*."

"You've got fucking tentacles in your mouth, boy!" roared Narnok, with booming laughter. "That's not evolution, it's a child's evil fucking nightmare!"

Randaman drew a short, curved blade, and moved close, his eyes narrowing. "You are about to witness the greatest power shift Vagandrak has ever seen, you ugly old fuck; and *we* will be there at the forefront, serving the king, working with the armies, bringing the elf rats to total domination over human scum like Yoon, whose ancestors betrayed them all those centuries ago! But then, you'll be able to see *fuck all* if I cut out your remaining eye, eh lad?"

He was close now, *closer*, and Narnok had reined back on his chains when they first entered the dungeon with their lanterns. Now, he surged forward and delivered a massive smashing headbutt that crushed Randaman's nose into a broken flat pancake and sent him spinning around, arms outstretched, screeching, his dagger clattering to the stone floor as he finally sat down and pressed his hands to his nose. They met blood and sharp shards of bone and cartilage and he screamed at the touch, then looked up, eyes bright with hate, and he searched the ground for his dagger and crawled to his feet.

"I'm going to gut you now," he said in a terribly calm voice.

"Enough!" snapped Faltor Gan, stepping in front of Randaman and gesturing for him to get rid of the knife. "Stop being a horse dick. You know why we're here. You know what we have to do."

Narnok, splattered with Randaman's blood, grinned. "What you going to do, use those facial tentacles to arse-fuck us to death?"

"On the contrary." Faltor Gan smiled, and gestured down the line. Now, by the light of the lantern Narnok could see the others awakening, groggy, faces filled with confusion and fear. Veila was muttering, her eyes wild. Dag Da was silent and stony-faced. He could see Bones, Meatboy, Darkdog and Cunt, who was scowling enough for all of them, his great thunderous brows touching in the middle.

"What are you going to do?" whispered Trista.

"We are going to make you one of us," said Faltor Gan, and a fist-thick core of tentacles erupted from his mouth like organic vomit, like a tube of snakes. And behind him, grinning, Randaman did the same.

Narnok held his courage in place, strong and hard and true; managed to hold on well; right up to the point where the thrashing, oiled tentacles touched his face, like a caress from a warped snake lover, and then ran down his scarred jawline, touched delicately to his lips, forced them apart like a powerful, forked lover's tongue. And he could taste them, taste their wriggling, bitter tang, like rotting bark, like ancient mushrooms, like rotting meat long dead in the forest.

It was only as they pushed inside his mouth, that Narnok began to scream.

The mugginess of sleep was leaving Mola, and Sameska led him to the massive gate of Zanne Keep. Duchess and the other dogs were awake now. They'd whined a little, then crossed to Sameska and – to Mola's utter, total amazement – licked his bony fingers as if he were their master.

"Charming," he muttered, just a little put out.

They stood there, the tall spindly elf rat, the short, narrow-faced ex-Iron Wolf, and four dogs of renowned fighting heritage. The snow was falling more heavily, now, and Sameska turned his face to the heavens, eyes closed. He seemed to be tasting the air. Suddenly, quests emerged from his right hand and sank into the soil, moving deep, pushing aside soil and leaves and snow. Sameska sank to one knee and lowered his head. He seemed to stay like that for a long time.

Mola hopped from one foot to the other, glancing occasionally at his dogs. They seemed... *odd*. They were behaving in a very strange fashion. They kept glancing towards him as if they only half knew him; and that made him very nervous.

"Duchess. Here, girl. Good girl."

She stared at him hard, then reluctantly, padded to his side.

This is turning into a long and evil fucking night, he thought sourly.

Finally, Sameska roused and stood. The quests retracted into his hands like slippery sliding worms into a vat of jelly. Mola stared, and felt his stomach turn over with a mighty churning, as a shudder wracked through his body.

"We don't have much time," said the elf rat, voice husky.

"You know where Kiki and Dek are?"

"Yes. They are in Zalazar. We must find Bazaroth, or they will face certain destruction."

Mola stared hard at Sameska. "You do realise I don't exactly have much love for these people," he said, after a few moments. "You do realise I only love my dogs. Right?"

"Of course," said Sameska. "However. If you do not wish you – and your dogs – and your entire *people* to be enslaved by the twisted, poisoned elf rats under Daranganoth and his pet sorcerer, Bazaroth, then we must act. Do you have no loyalty for your country?"

Mola considered this. "Not much, I reckon," he said. "But I hear what you're saying. Let's do it. Er. What exactly are we going to do? This door is looking pretty fucking thick and impenetrable to me, my new spindly, bark-faced elf rat friend."

Sameska gave him a smile, and extended his hand. Quests surged out and entered the oak portal – all twenty feet of it. They extended through the wood, making cracking sounds, spreading out like a pale spider's web just beneath the surface, racing through the grain and then, suddenly, there came an almighty titanic *crack* like thunder, like mountains breaking up, like the end of the world. The giant gates guarding Zanne Portal broke into thousands of pieces, jagged chunks of timber like so many axe-hacked logs. Wood dust billowed out, and for a moment Mola felt as if he stood in the midst of a sawmill during a violent storm. And then it blasted past him, filling his eyes with grit and making him sneeze with its warm, invasive passage.

"Follow me," said Sameska, and strode forward.

Still clutching his sword, Mola followed and, in silence, his dogs came after him.

It was like a dream, a blurring of reality, a honey-leaf drugsmoke vision. Mola followed the elf rat, loping through endless corridors of opulence, through carpeted halls, through great vast libraries lined floor to ceiling with ancient tomes and wood panelling; they moved through chapels of religious calm, through great rooms with intricate tapestries of ancient battles and rich oil paintings of long forgotten monarchs. And all the while, Mola's dogs panted after him, and he panted after Sameska, and he wondered what the fuck he was doing and maybe, *just maybe*, he should turn around and do the right thing – run away from this place, head alone for the mountains and seek out a simple life of solitude in a crude log cabin.

But it never works out like that, Mola.

If you run away, the past always comes to haunt you. To hunt you down.

If you flee, the fucking elf rats will find you in the end.

They always do.

It always comes back to get you.

They stopped. Sameska turned and looked at Mola. They were in an ancient series of passages, hewn from some kind of rock chamber. The walls were rough. Mola suddenly realised they were underground; probably underneath Zanne Keep itself.

"Yes?" he found himself saying, and kicked himself mentally. He sounded like a dog panting and begging to its bloody master.

"Through this door is Bazaroth aea Quazaquiel. The elf rat sorcerer. Servant of the elf rat king, Daranganoth. Are you ready to face your nemesis, Mola of the Dogs?"

"Well, actually, I've just been thinking about that..."

"We must act now!"

"Er. I meant to say, Sameska, I'm not your average hero-type material, you know? I mean, I have my fighting dogs and everything, but to be brutally honest with you, all that war and hero stuff was a long time ago." He waved his sword. "I haven't used this thing properly in years. You could say I'm a bit rusty."

Sameska stared at him. "You are one of the Iron Wolves of legend," he whispered. "You *will* overcome."

And with a quick movement, he blasted the oak door from its hinges. Duchess and the others began snarling in vicious hate and surged forward, then stopped just within the interior. It was an incredibly ancient chapel, rough hewn walls carved from the rock itself beneath Zanne Keep. There was a throne, but this was not like the pompous, glossy, glitzy Yoon throne that squatted up in the main hall of Zanne Keep like some actor's prop on a stage. No. This was a basic chair hewn from the living rock of the chamber itself. It was inlaid with strange bones, their shapes unrecognisable to Mola's eyes in his swift appraisal of the scene before him.

But what he *did* see was the sorcerer, Bazaroth, seated on the rock chair with his face displaying... ecstasy?

Mola stepped forward, sword out, his dogs growling at his knees and midriff. Saliva drooled from fangs ready to kill. Muscles were bunched. Mola's dogs were poised, ready to attack. Ready to kill.

"Welcome," said Bazaroth.

There were others in the chamber, which was lit by soft candles in alcoves which circled the room. In fact, it seemed more than just a chapel. It felt like some deep religious altar. It felt, to Mola in those fleeting seconds, like some portal to a different time, a different world, a different religion.

The Equiem, whispered something in his mind, in a cracked voice of breaking tomb lids.

The Old Gods.

The Bad Gods.

The Seeds of Chaos.

The Takers in the Dark.

"I think we need a talk, mate," snapped Mola, puffing out his chest and reverting to his brisk military stance. It was all he knew. All he could do. He felt Sameska come in behind him, drifting like a ghost. He eyed the figures in heavy brown robes and frowned. There were some shapes there he recognised. Some... *faces* that in the candlelight looked a little bit like...

"*No*," mouthed Mola, eyes widening.

Narnok smiled, throwing back the hood of his brown robe. A fist of tentacles thrust from his mouth, and it appeared he was screaming in silence as they wriggled and squirmed before his face, hissing like a writhing pit of snakes.

And they were all there. Trista. Veila. Randaman. Faltor Gan. Meatboy. Darkdog. Even Cunt turned, his shaved and tattooed head glowing under the soft light of the candles and, as his mouth opened, so tentacles squirmed free and wriggled in front of his face like so many oiled eels in a tube...

Bazaroth lowered his head. His eyes were old. More ancient than the mountains.

Narnok drew out his double-headed axe, and his eyes were dark and evil as the parasitic snakes in his mouth and throat and chest squirmed and fought and stretched out towards new fresh meat...

"Kill them," said Bazaroth, and his servants charged.

CHILDHOOD'S END

Kiki and Dek travelled in silence for the rest of the day, each lost in philosophical contemplation of their friend, now gone and dead, their mission to *save* Vagandrak yet further compromised. Even as a trio it had been going to be a tough assignment; but with Prince Zastarte dead down some dark mountain crevasse, and just the two of them to now carry the torch, their increased vulnerability weighed heavy on sombre minds.

The storm had continued for a while, thunder rumbling through the mountains, ancient gods battling with sword and shield. The path wound on to higher and higher peaks, the wind biting like a fighting dog, snow flurries further making progress and comfort more difficult.

They halted at one point, huddling in a shallow cave whilst Dek made a hot thin soup with their meagre rations. They ate in silence and warmed hands over the fire. Kiki found herself lost, deep in thought; she remembered the early days with Zastarte, his well-groomed beauty, his witty lines, the fights, the wine, the drugs, the sex...

"I'll miss the dandy bastard," said Dek, eventually. "Although I hated his perfume. He stank like a rancid prostitute."

"I can't believe he's gone."

"But to be fair, you hadn't seen him for a couple of decades."

"Yes."

"And he had taken to torturing young women. Don't forget that."

"Yes. I know."

"So, to all intents and purposes, he was a stranger to you."

Kiki stared hard at Dek. "Are you intentionally trying to fuck me off?"

"No! No, not at all. I just…"

"You just what? Wanted to desecrate the memory of a man who fought with us, died for us, and his corpse isn't even fucking cold yet?"

"It'll be cold in that ice, I can promise you that." He saw Kiki's face. "However, I can see what you mean," he mumbled, and ladled more soup into his maw, averting his eyes and trying to absorb some of the meagre heat from the fire.

Kiki said nothing. And they repacked in silence.

Another night travelling through freezing darkness. Another bleak morning catching a few hours beneath too-thin blankets and wondering if the ice demons would take them in the night.

Never had Kiki needed the honey-leaf more. And she took what little she had, and kept her addiction at a stable level, and did not tell Dek. After all, would he understand? Could he ever understand?

Dek was torn and exhausted and done. He hadn't meant for it to sound like he didn't give a fuck about Zastarte. Zastarte had saved Dek's life on thirteen separate occasions, and he'd had a certain fondness for the bisexual, sartorially challenged, murderous and murdering motherfucker. But at the end of the day, they weren't in this thing as a game. The odds were serious shit – stacked against them. They were Iron Wolves. They'd fought through a million battles. They knew the fucking risks and Zast knew the fucking risks. And his luck had run out. On a long enough mission, all their luck ran out.

The stars were twinkling diamonds.

The horses were unhappy, snorting and stamping.

The path was a weaving, winding, nightmare.

Days seemed to blend into one another, and time no longer meant anything, no longer mattered; and Vagandrak no longer mattered, and the elf rats no longer mattered. They were battling the White Lion Mountains. And the White Lion Mountains were a savage, merciless mistress – willing to snuff out life in an instant. No regrets. No emotion. That's the way it was. Life and death. But shit, mostly death.

They sat in a cave Dek had carved out of a snow wall with a hand axe. They were slowly freezing to death. They had burned the last of the wood bundles they'd brought on their mounts, and food was running low. The next stage was to kill one of the horses, eat as much as they could, bundle up the rest of the best cuts and travel on. Dek seemed nonplussed at the thought of slaughtering one of the geldings; Kiki, however, couldn't even bear the thought.

A blizzard had driven them to shelter, and the hours blended into one another. Kiki and Dek shared the last of the honey-leaf, entwining under their blankets. They had no idea how long they'd been travelling. No idea how long it was since Zastarte was swept over the mountain and claimed by the Ice Demons. Disorientation ruled them.

They ran out of food, and Kiki said she would not, absolutely *would not* kill the horses.

So they embraced one another, and got high, and waited to die.

The sun rose, painting a strip of violet across the horizon. Kiki opened her ice-encrusted eyes, and drank in the view beyond their tiny cave entrance, and breathed. The blizzard had subsided. And the view that opened up before her was one of an awesome, vast world – beyond the White Lion Mountains.

"Dek," she croaked. "Dek!"

She looked down, and his face was deathly white. At first she thought he was dead and panic slammed her in the chest like a sledgehammer. She shook him, and slapped his face, and he murmured and gradually came awake. Sombrely, they realised how close to death they were. Skipping along the edge of a razor.

And then they looked out beyond the mountains.

Zalazar stretched away beyond, endless rolling plains, and lakes, and forests.

Zalazar. The elf rat lands.

In silence, they descended sweeping paths down this, the final border mountain to Zalazar. With each hundred feet of descent the wind dropped, and the temperature started to rise. There was no greenery of any kind, but the warmer breeze was a welcome break from the relentless buffeting of snow and ice. Gradually, the snow started to disappear and there were more glimpses of black rock breaking up the endless white; huge jagged boulders dotted the mountainside, and maybe half way down Kiki and Dek sat on two large rocks and surveyed the elf rat lands.

Rolling hills spread away, green and patched with rocks, patched with snow. The winter was less harsh here. To the north and southeast were great swathes of... forest. But instead of the evergreen they'd expected, these forests were entirely black. Black tree trunks, black leaves, black pine needles. Branches were crooked, disjointed, like arthritic limbs. The soil was soaked with something like fish oil.

Distantly, more mountains lined the horizon.

"It never ends," said Kiki, sighing.

"The Mountains of the Moon," said Dek, quietly. "We've seen them before."

"I remember."

They scanned the landscape. It had been a long time. Twenty-five years, or more. A different world. A different lifetime.

"There they are," said Kiki, with reverence.

"The White Towers."

"Yes."

And they both stared at the distant towers that rose from the centre of a matt black forest sprawl. Twin needles of glistening white, as if the towers were created from ice. They shot up from the forest, impossibly high for structures made by man. But then, they were not made by man. They had been built by the Elves, over a thousand years previous.

"This is an impossible mission," said Dek, his chin on his fist, despondency his mistress.

"Perhaps."

"Look at it. The pride of the elf rats. The seat of their power. They're in the process of taking Vagandrak apart – with absolute fucking ease. Yoon's armies are in disarray; ignore that. Yoon's armies are non-existent. Disbanded. Demoralised. Those who weren't killed by Orlana's mud-orcs have probably run off home to wives who deserve them. Those who stayed… well. There can't be that many Yoon didn't send home."

Kiki looked at him. "I love you, Dek. You know that."

"I know it, sweetie," he rumbled, with a broken-toothed smile.

"As long as you know. In case we don't make it."

Dek chuckled.

"What is it?"

"If we go down there, Kikellya Mandasayard, there's no going home."

"And yet you'll still come with me? Knowing we ride to certain death?"

"Of course." He frowned. "What the fuck else have I got to do?"

She laughed, then, a genuine peal of laughter that brought a ragged wide smile to Dek's face, and they got up, and brushed themselves down, and checked their weapons, and headed down the mountain with two battered, wild-eyed horses looking very much the worse for wear – and maybe unconsciously aware they'd escaped the cooking pot by the skin of their equine teeth.

It was early afternoon when they reached the valley floor and rode into the first forest of black trees. It was silent. There were no birds, no leaves, no sound at all. It was perfectly still. Still as a church. Still as a thousand year tomb.

The horses' hooves clopped on a road of frozen mud. The trees were large, angular, unreal. They were like no other trees Kiki had ever seen. Their branches were angular, as if beaten from old iron swords. And yet they were living. *Must* be living, after a sort.

"The elf rats are bonded to their Heart Trees," said Dek, eventually, when the eerie silence had become too much.

Kiki nodded. "Yes."

"We should burn the forests."

"No. That's not the way."

"Sounds like the right thing to me." He tilted his head.

"Trust me, Dek. This is not about murder. This is about salvation."

They rode for hours through the endless trees of black. Occasionally, they came upon a clearing and saw the distant spikes of the White Towers, the twin glittering spires of bright white, white, as if they were glowing, as if they were the exact antithesis to these twisted, stunted, warped and blackened trees. As if the White Towers themselves had sucked all the life out of the land: all the colour, all the energy, all the spirit.

The White Towers.

Or... what lay within them.

Eventually, Dek and Kiki rode out onto a green hillside. They climbed slowly, weary, tired to the bones. As they reached the summit, they stopped.

Below them, sat a motionless army of elf rats.

Kiki hissed.

"Fuck me," said Dek, eyes wide, teeth forming an unholy grin. "Are they waiting for us?"

There must have been ten thousand soldiers. Winter sunlight glinted from their black armour. Violet fire shone from the points of ten thousand spears. They turned, in gradients, as one single unit.

Kiki shrugged, and stared down at the warriors who looked up, dark eyes under matt black helms fixing on her. There was no doubt about it. They were there, between the two remaining Iron Wolves, and their goal: the White Towers.

Dek's horse pawed the frozen grass.

"What do we do?"

"We ride down."

"They'll fucking cut us to pieces!"

"Then they cut us to pieces."

The soldiers spread away like an ocean. Armour glinted. The sun shifted and extra rays of light glittered across the warriors ranged before them.

"There's two of us," said Dek.

"Yeah," said Kiki.

"We're Iron Wolves."

"Damn. Fucking. Right."

"I reckon we can take a couple of hundred," he growled. "What do you reckon?"

Kiki scowled. "I reckon we're going to find out. Because I turn back for no man, woman or fucking toxic elf rat."

She kicked her horse into a canter, and rode down the hillside, hooves crunching snow and icy grass. Dek followed, unsheathing one of his swords in a smooth, fluid movement. If he was going to die, it was going to be with a blade in his hand. A man could ask for no more. And his mam would damn well expect it.

They cantered down towards the elf rat army, and Kiki reined in a hundred paces from them. Their black and silver uniforms were immaculate. Their spears were held in perfect stillness. They stood, eyes turned to Kiki and Dek without emotion. They made no move, no sound, no gesture.

"I think it's time to die," said Kiki, and kicked her horse forward.

"I'm with you, girl," growled Dek, and followed, his heart racing.

They approached the army, and smoothly it split apart, soldiers marching aside and stamping to attention. They created a road through their ranks, and stood, eyes staring straight ahead, now ignoring Kiki and Dek.

Kiki halted at the opening of this elf rat road. She gave a wicked grin. "You're joking, right?"

Nobody answered.

" *You! Elf rat! Fucking answer me!*"

Nothing. No indication the Iron Wolves even existed.

Kiki kicked her horse at the nearest soldier, reining in at the last moment with a savage tug, the gelding twisting its head. The elf rat did not move. Did not flinch. She drew her short sword, and held it to his throat.

Nothing. No reaction. No attack.

Kiki looked back at Dek. "I expect," she said, "that we're expected."

"I expect we're going to be tortured," muttered Dek.

"I truly don't think that's the case."

"What is it then? Idle curiosity?"

"Aren't *you* curious, Dek? Come on. Ride beside me. Let's end this adventure together."

Dek kicked his horse forward, and together they cantered through the ranks of thousands and thousands of elf rat warriors. Perfectly armed and armoured soldiers. Crimson painted their helms and breast plates and spears and swords. They could have killed Dek and Kiki in a minute. In an instant. But they did not.

The hill dropped, and Kiki and Dek rode side by side through the elf rat ranks, until they reached the end of the army and entered another woodland road. Kiki rode with her shoulder blades itching, expecting some shaft at any moment to punch between them, skewering her lungs.

But it did not come.

"I cannot believe that," said Dek, shaking his head.

"I know."

"I thought we would die."

"Me, also."

"What now?"

Kiki turned to him. "We ride to the White Towers," she said.

The snow came; a wild blizzard blasted across Zalazar. And in the midst of the blizzard, emerging from a forest of twisted black trees towering high above them, the great limbs like the crooked arms of dead and cooked burn victims, Kiki and Dek came across a second army. There were less soldiers this time, maybe four or five thousand. Once more they stood in silent ranks, blocking the way to the White Towers. These had swords drawn, and were stood perfectly motionless, as the snow whipped and blasted around them. Their black armour was crusted with ice and snowflakes. They were taller than men, but still twisted, poisoned by the very land and trees that had spawned them; they wore black helms and black eyes gleamed like glass behind visor slits.

Kiki rode towards the front ranks, and they parted, the entire army splitting down the middle to create a road between their ranks. Kiki rode in a straight line, looking neither left nor right, and Dek followed, hand on his sword hilt, marvelling – and dreading – this turn of events. Because something was quite obviously wrong. There was a game being played, and Dek hated not knowing the bloody rules.

The thousands of black-armoured elf rats made no move, until Kiki and Dek had passed through the entire army. And then, with a many-replicated clink of armour and stamp of boots, the ranks closed to form an impenetrable wall of swords and shields and armour.

Dek glanced back, face grim, but Kiki did not.

"I guess we're not going home in a hurry," he said, voice bitter.

"I don't think we ever were."

"Well I fucking was," snapped Dek. "There's still an ocean of whiskey to drink; a million hog roasts to consume; and I'd hoped, one day, we might have children…"

"Children?" Kiki halted her horse, and turned, and stared at her lover. "Oh, Dek…"

"It's all right. Don't get soppy now, you hard-hearted bitch." He smiled to take the sting out of his words. "Just a dream I had, that's all."

"Why did you never have children before?" Snow settled on her hair and shoulders. To Dek, Kiki looked like a queen.

"Because it was never with you," he replied, voice husky.

They rode on. Towards the White Towers.

Light was failing as they emerged from another forest. Zalazar was practically one huge forest, from the White Lion Mountains all the way to the Mountains of the

Moon – which loomed above them now. Maybe because every elf rat had to be linked to a tree? A Heart Tree?

They stood their geldings, stamping and snorting, and gazed up at the White Towers ahead of them.

"I expected another army," said Dek, breath steaming like demon-smoke.

"Me, also."

"Are we going in?"

"I think that's the plan."

Kiki led the way down a narrow path, which led into a valley. The White Towers dominated a central position, and shot up into the heavens with smooth, slick sides like polished marble. There were no doors or windows in the entire twin structures, just solid walls of gently glowing white; gleaming, as their polished surfaces reflected the winter sun. Above, maybe a thousand feet in the sky, the twin White Towers curved inwards, ending in perfect points.

Kiki slowed her approach, and Dek mimicked her pace. Finally, she stopped, and kicked herself from the saddle. Her eyes searched for doorways, an entrance of some kind. But there was none. She put her right hand on her right sword hilt, and walked forward with Dek close behind. But there came a sound, from the edge of the trees, and they emerged like four dark wraiths, gliding through the snow, each one bearing two drawn swords. It was the Tree Stalkers.

"Shit," snarled Dek, drawing his own weapon. "I thought they were dead!"

"They have tracked us over the mountains," said Kiki, and drew both her own swords.

"Shall we run?" hissed Dek. "I don't think we can take all four!"

"I agree," said Kiki, bitterly, standing her ground.

They moved closer, each nearly seven feet tall, their limbs twisted just a little, their black glass eyes fixed with fanaticism and hate on the two Iron Wolves. There was Villiboch, his bow slung over his shoulder, his swords black and matt and razor sharp. There was Sileath, the female, her face long and pointed – a little like a rat's. There was Ffaefel, taller and more elegant than the others, and finally Ugrak, hulking, broad shouldered, a power-house of a creature.

The Tree Stalkers halted ten feet away.

"You have one missing," smiled Kiki, her eyes glinting.

"You killed Aeoxir in Skell Forest," said Villiboch, stepping forward. "Now, however, you have come far enough."

A distant howl echoed through the forest, as if punctuating Villiboch's statement. It was long and mournful. Nobody moved.

"Do that thing," muttered Dek from the corner of his mouth.

"What thing?"

"That thing with the earthquakes and the storms and shit," he muttered. "Go on. Throw some fucking trees at them."

"We are in their world now," said Kiki, eyes locked on Villiboch's. "That power is denied me."

"Horse shit. So we have to rely on good old Vagandrak steel?"

"It would appear so," growled Kiki.

Then, from the edge of the trees they came, padding on silent paws through the snow and iced grass. They were wolves, a pack of large wolves moving fast, four feet tall at the shoulder, their fur the thick grey of heavy winter coats. There were thirty or forty of the beasts, and the Tree Stalkers saw Kiki and Dek look past them...

Villiboch spun and swiftly strung his bow. Three shafts hissed through the air, taking down three of the great beasts, which rolled, blood staining the snow in great, pissing arcs – but the wolves increased their pace, charging across the clearing with growls and snarls to leap, and they were on the Tree Stalkers in an instant, growling and tearing, jaws snapping and breaking and the fight was incredibly brutal. Three wolves dragged a screaming Ugrak to the ground and chewed through his throat. Sileath's head was snapped clean off with one giant bite. Within seconds, the Tree Stalkers were reduced to so much strewn and bloody meat and severed limbs.

During this fast, savage battle, Dek had backed away, face pale, and readied himself for attack. But Kiki was cool, her eyes watching the wolves. Then she turned to Dek. "It's all right," she said, voice low, and husky, and filled with an incredible well of emotion. "They are... not our enemies."

"Bollocks!"

"Sheath your sword, soldier," she said. Her eyes were fixed on his. "Do it, if you want to live."

Dek sheathed his weapon at the third attempt.

Kiki, ignoring the wolves with their bloody muzzles and narrowed eyes, turned her attention back to the White Towers – and walked swiftly towards the gleaming white walls. As she walked, she closed her eyes and felt the magick of the land. Felt the *polluted* magick. This place was poisoned beyond repair; toxic, beyond cleansing;

dark, beyond the possibility of light. And yet these two towers stood like beacons. And inside, she knew, was the Elf Heart – a device created by the ancient kings and magickers of Vagandrak in order to twist their enemies, the elves, imprisoning them here; and in the process, polluting and twisting an entire nation.

Kiki searched outwards, and downwards, and felt the incredible power charged in the land; in the rocks and twisted trees, in every blade of grass, in every tiny worm that crawled and struggled through the soil.

Her eyes flickered open, and she stopped a foot away from the wall. She reached out, but did not touch the surface.

"This place has been waiting for me," she said.

"Yeah, but how do we get in?" said Dek uneasily, one eye still on the bloody, panting wolves which made no attempt to attack. It's a bloody miracle, he thought. A bloody bastard miracle!

Kiki closed her eyes again, and tentatively felt her way forward with her spirit force – there came some kind of sudden *crack* and Kiki was picked up and accelerated backwards across the clearing, hitting the snow hard and rolling over maybe twenty times, like a broken rag doll. Dek stood for a moment, mouth open in shock at what he'd just seen, then ran to her, dropping to his knees and cradling her head. Her eyes opened, and blood trickled from her mouth.

"Get away from me!" she hissed. "Bazaroth... he is inside me... usurping my powers... sucking out the Equiem magick..."

"What can I do?" cried Dek, feeling helpless, like a young child again.

"Nothing…" murmured Kiki, and she began to change; like some terrible vision, her hair started to crawl back into her skull, retreating and changing to a jet black, like a clump of thick wires, until only a central clump remained. Her skin paled, bleaching yellow, and became gently ridged as if she had scales. Her nose twisted, and her teeth cracked and narrowed to little points. And then there came more snapping sounds, and Kiki's skin shrivelled around her hands, her fingers closing, fusing together to form solid spikes. Within her boots, her feet did the same, and the useless items were kicked away as she began to thrash and scream and Dek stared down at this horrible creature below him, his Kiki changed into some incredible monster. There was a hiss as his sword cleared his scabbard and confusion slammed like a meteor through his brain. Was this Kiki? *Really* Kiki? Where had his love gone? Emotions raged through him, burning him and turning his mind inside out. What can I do? *What can I fucking do?*

There came a feral growl, and the wolves moved towards Dek and this shivering, horrible creature vulnerable on the floor.

"*Kiki*!" screamed Dek, looking around frantically as the wolves loped towards him with blood-slick muzzles. He knew he was fucked. There was no way one man could fight three wolves, never mind this pack of monsters. And they had shown how terribly efficient in the art of death they really were. The massacre of the Tree Stalkers had proved that.

"*Kiki*!" he bellowed again, and then the creature on the floor sat up, and its head rotated, and it looked at Dek with iron-dark eyes. Slowly, it spoke.

"I'm sorry, Dek. Sorry you had to see me this way."

Dek froze, and the wolves formed a circle around the two. They were panting, lolling pink tongues hanging out and dripping Tree Stalker blood, their eyes fixed not on Dek, but on this creature on the ground before them. Dek felt one of the wolves nudge him in the back of the legs, and he closed his eyes for a moment, breathing deeply, and summoning a strength of will to *not attack*. To make a single strike was to die. He knew this instinctively.

"Kiki?" he said again, softly this time, disbelief raging through him.

The creature stood, painfully, swaying as if learning to balance, and Dek's eyes travelled down, fixing on the points where human fingers had once been. "Kiki, what did that bastard sorcerer *do* to you?"

"He took away the powers of the *Shamathe*," said Kiki, her voice the same and yet curiously different. As if heard from a long distance away; through decades of twisted years. "He took me back in time. He turned me back to Lorna. Into the shape in which I was born. When I became powerful, I changed my physical shell, Dek. I changed myself to look like the beautiful people around me. Or so I thought. For not all beauty is in the face, is it?" She smiled, and it looked wrong on her twisted, yellow-scaled face.

"You were *born* like this?" sighed Dek.

"Yes. I'm sorry. I wanted to tell you, so, so many times. I wanted to show you. To test your love."

"Why did you not?"

"Because I was afraid," said Kiki, tears running down her mottled cheeks. "Afraid you would leave me if you knew what I really was, under the skin. The real me. The monster hidden inside the beautiful shell."

Dek clamped shut his teeth, and narrowed his eyes, and asked himself the question: would I have left? And to his very great shame, he did not know the true answer.

Suddenly, the wolf pack growled as one, a low rumbling of threat like thunder, and one stepped forward towards Kiki, a heavy, ponderous approach as its lips drew back into a terrible snarl. The wolf was a touch larger than the others, and had a black slash of fur across its muzzle. Its great fangs opened before Kiki's face, eyes fixed on her.

"No!" screamed Dek, and, with sword lifting fast, he leapt to the attack.

Mola braced himself, face dropping into a hardened place of combat. The world seemed to slow. He remembered Dalgoran standing over him with a vial of bright green liquid. And the drops leaking down into his mouth. They had tasted… sweet. But that had been the last of it. The last of the pleasure. The rest had been a world of pain. A world of shit.

And now he was here.

His dogs growled.

But he growled deeper…

Eain doam shalsoar. The Art of the Shapeshifter. It reared inside him unbidden. It roared through his veins like the most powerful drug. His skin darkened, hairs like iron bristles easing across his skin as Narnok and Trista and Faltor Gan and the others turned and lurched towards him; towards his Dogs.

"Take them," he slurred, words hardly human as his own muzzle emerged, pushing slowly outwards from his face with subtle crunches of rearranging bone and muscle. The images were bright in his mind; brighter than a furnace.

"You *are special, Mola*," said Dalgoran.

"*I am?*"

"*You are the only one who can do it alone…*"

Duchess, Duke, Sarge and Thrasher launched at the gathered enemies in the rough cut stone chamber. A vicious fight ensued. Narnok issued a great, strangled roar and the tentacles thrashed from his opened maw. His axe screamed through the air but Mola's dogs were too fast. Fangs snapped and tore. Duchess and Thrasher, especially, were in their element: eyes bright, hearts wild.

Mola's fangs emerged from his engorged muzzle, and it hurt. Hurt like no other pain in the fucking world. But then. But then…

"Go on," urged Sameska.

And Mola charged through the throng, his great, heavily-muscled body smashing enemies out of the way, his goal single – and simple. Bazaroth saw him coming, and directed more of his followers, more of his puppets, towards the charging… wolf. But Duchess and Thrasher were there, tearing free limbs, chewing out throats, working as a unit to clear a path for Mola as he charged on all fours, a huge and terrifying *werewolf*, and leapt…

There came a mighty cracking, snapping sound. Mola rode Bazaroth's corpse to the ground, and spat out the head, which bounced across the stone chamber. Blood poured from the elf rat, thick black blood, which smelled old and sour and rancid. Smoke rose from the foul-smelling ichor. Bazaroth's ancient claws clenched and unclenched in a rapid death spasm.

Mola lifted his muzzle to a sky above deep stone walls and frozen soil, a sky filled with fire and clouds and evil. And the moon. A full moon.

Mola howled.

"No!" screamed Kiki, as some unseen wolf hit Dek in the back, slamming him to the ground. He lay perfectly still, stunned, waiting for the great fangs to close over his head and rip it free. His face was scrunched up, waiting for the pain, waiting to feel fangs puncture his skull, bringing instant death.

But it did not come.

After a few moments, the weight lifted from him. He lay still, and he could just see his sword a couple of feet away. Instead, he rolled over and sat up. He looked across at Kiki and she forced a smile.

"Bazaroth's spell has been broken," she said, simply. And gestured with a splintered arm towards the White Towers. They were shimmering, and a single portal had appeared at the base. "I must go inside. I will find the Elf Heart. I will destroy it. I will free these creatures from a thousand year spell."

"No," said Dek, a terrible fear invading his heart. For he knew; he *knew* she would not return. She wasn't explaining her actions. She was saying goodbye.

Climbing to his feet, he moved towards Kiki, and took her in his arms. "No," he repeated. "Stay with me. You owe the elf rats *nothing.*"

"I will destroy it," she said, gently, and her eyes met his. And in there he saw the *old Kiki,* or at least, the woman he knew and loved. He hugged her tightly to him. "You know I will not return."

"No," he wept.

"I must. We owe these elves their freedom. It is the right thing to do."

Gently, she disengaged from Dek, and reaching up, struggling with the points of her arms, she removed a key on a chain from around her neck. She looped it over his. "In a chest beneath Drakerath Fortress, Dalgoran stored the means for lifting the curse of the Iron Wolves. This key will open it. You can all be free, Dek. All of you."

"But not you?"

"My path was chosen from the day I was born," said Kiki, words like smoke. Her eyes shone. "I was bestowed with the power of the *Shamathe* for a reason – with the power of the Equiem. I was born to right a terrible wrong. And that is what I must do."

Leaning heavily on the wolf with the striped muzzle, she started towards the White Towers. The other wolves loped after them, forming a protective circle. Kiki reached the doorway leading inside; leading to the Elf Heart.

She turned, and looked back at Dek. He raised his hand, and held it there, as white light blossomed around Kiki, his woman, his lover, his love. She stepped inside. The glow brightened, then died. And she was gone.

Dek slowly lowered his hand, and the wolves turned as one and stared at him. He blinked, and realised the portal had vanished, also. Again, the White Towers were impenetrable.

"What are you lot fucking staring at?" he snarled, reaching down and picking up his sword, and gripping it tightly. "You want some of this?" He waved the blade.

The wolves turned, and loped off through the snow. Dek watched them leave, waiting until they'd vanished into the trees. Then he walked to the walls of the White Towers and reaching out, touched the smooth, cool surface. It felt like glass. He banged his fist against it. It felt depressingly solid.

"Shit."

What now?

What to do?

Where to go?

Dek turned, and realised the horses had bolted; either at the appearance of the Tree Stalkers, or maybe the pack of wolves; or maybe both.

"Sons of bitches," he growled, and started back towards the trees. When he reached the edge of the black, twisted forest, he stopped and looked back at the White Towers. The place where his love had sacrificed herself for a race of creatures they found it hard to comprehend. He had a strange feeling he would one day return.

Dek straightened his back, sheathed his sword, and snapped a smart salute. "Farewell, Captain Kikellya Mandasayard of the Iron Wolves. You were an honourable woman and a brilliant soldier. Wait for me in the Hall of Heroes, won't you? I'll see you there… one day."

He smiled. Wiped away a tear.

Then Dek turned, stepped down the path, and was swallowed by the black, twisted forest.

EPILOGUE

There was no flash of lightning, no great storm, no fireball, no violent wash of bright holy light. There were no singing angels, nor cheering crowds. No great mob uprising. No massive slaughter of invading elf rats. No battle of massive armies. No great conquest by a handsome king in shining armour. There was simply a *pulse*. It began in the White Towers, and spread slowly through Zalazar, across the mountains, and on to Vagandrak – and beyond. It travelled through the mountains and the forests, through the plants and the insects and the earth. It radiated outwards, and it purified the land of the man-made toxins which had poisoned the world. It broke the ancient spell of the magickers of old. It removed the curse which had plagued the elf rats.

And it brought with it some kind of peace.

Across Vagandrak, people slowly came out of hiding. Gates were opened, doors and windows thrown wide. Thousands awoke from deep dark sleeps, and put their hands to their mouths, for they'd suffered a million nightmares of growing squirming roots from their very own throats and tongues and lips. For many, these nightmares would last until the day they died. The dead were taken beyond the many city walls, and burned in huge funeral pyres, along with any remaining elf rats who were captured. People chopped down twisted black trees, which had grown through the streets. Black smoke filled the skies over Vagandrak for many months.

Sameska left Zanne, and crossed the mountains, and took up his rightful rule after it was discovered that his brother, Daranganoth, King of Zalazar, was murdered by the evil sorcerer, Bazaroth aea Quazaquiel. He led two armies, both numbering ten thousand, who came across the White Lion Mountains and met the remains of Bazaroth's dark and treacherous elf rats, the ones tainted with evil deeds of murder and control and human puppetry. The battle was decided on one wintry morning, on the Kantarok Plains north of the Rokroth Marshes. Sameska's elf rat forces, bedecked in black steel helms and armour, carrying black swords and black shields, and even in this short time showing a reduced toxicity: a straightening of backs, a clearing of eyes, a fluidity of movement. In eerie silence, except for the thudding of charging boots, the two armies clashed. The battle lasted three hours, and ended with the surrender of two thousand of Bazaroth's elf rats.

Sameska had them executed the following morning, and buried in a massive pit. He returned with his armies to the lands of Zalazar as, on the horizon, Yoon sat with his own battalions and watched, a snarl on his face.

A month after Bazaroth aea Quazaquiel's killing, the first leaves of green sprouted on a tree deep in a forest in the centre of Zalazar. Within a week, and despite the winter chill, green could be seen on every branch and tree throughout the once poisoned land. Within another month, and with the coming of spring, Zalazar was unrecognisable. Plants and bushes and hedgerows dotted the lands, and the tens of thousands of trees, many of which were Heart Trees to the population of surviving elves, blossomed. Life and colour flooded the once toxic land between the Mountains of the Moon and the White Lion Mountains.

The elves of Vagandrak were free.

The elves of Vagandrak were noble once more.

Narnok of the Axe sat in The Fighting Cocks in Drakerath, across from Dek, Trista and Mola. Narnok drank a half flagon of beer, then reached up and touched his mouth tentatively, as if exploring swollen lips with his stubby, powerful fingers.

"Will you *stop* fucking doing that," snapped Dek, draining his own tankard.

"Ha! You weren't the one who had fucking tentacles growing out of his fucking face, were you? Have some respect for a man's private nightmares, will you?"

"Guys, can you two be quiet?" snapped Trista, patting her freshly washed and oiled blonde curls into place, and smoothing down the creases in her rather fetching red dress. "Some of us are busy searching for a handsome young man for the night."

"No, it's him," said Dek, scowling and pointing directly in Narnok's face. "Tell him to stop, Trista. He keeps fucking with his face!"

"I'll fuck with *your* face in a minute," growled the large warrior.

"Oh, here we go," growled Dek, slamming down his tankard. "I suppose you'll start moaning about the fact I shagged your wife now, won't you?"

"Well you did!" roared Narnok.

"Yeah, and we've been through this a hundred times, man. I apologised. You broke my nose. That's the end of it."

"I *don't* like your tone, laddie!" snarled Narnok.

"Oh yeah? You want to take this out on the cobbles again do you, Big Man?"

"Any fucking time!" roared Narnok.

"I'm taking bets!" yelled Weasel, pulling out a well-worn stub of a pencil and a small, tatty notebook.

Trista whipped out two slender daggers, and held one under each man's chin against bobbing Adam's apples. Dek and Narnok were still as statues, locked in place by razor-sharp steel. And, amazingly, they fell into sudden silence like heavy stones dropped down a well.

"Gentlemen." Trista smiled, and removed the daggers, sheathing them neatly in hidden places within the folds of the red dress. "Calm your anger. For it is finally time for us all to get properly drunk."

Eighteen months had passed.

King Sameska of Zalazar sat in his study at the Palace of Heartwood, deep within the Mountains of the Moon. He was tall, and elegant, his skin smooth like polished oak, his eyes wide and a deep, dark green, and very kind. He was studying a vellum scroll as two great doors at the end of the chamber opened, and an elf strode forward wearing woodsman's garb, and carrying a longbow of yew across his back.

"Well met, Zardona," nodded King Sameska. "You seek refreshment after your long journey from foreign lands?"

Zardona waved his hand to the side. He looked deeply tired, deeply troubled. "After I have imparted the information I discovered, Sire."

"Go ahead," said Sameska, drawing up a high-backed chair of hardwood, skilfully carved and inset with valuable gems.

"Unfortunately, your deepest fears were correct, Sire."

"Yoon still builds his armies?"

"Yes, Sire. I am sorry to report."

Sameska rubbed his chin, then glanced up. Zardona had a pained look on his face. A deep fear glittering in his azure eyes.

"There is something more?"

"I overheard a conversation. In a tavern in Vagan, their War Capital. It is said Yoon has somehow summoned Orlana the Changer, otherwise known as the Horse Lady. And with this, his new Demon Queen, he intends to bring his armies north." Zardona swallowed, averting his gaze from Sameska. "Across the White Lion Mountains. To Zalazar."

"That is… not good."

"There is more. Yoon has reformed the elite units of old; the Iron Wolves, they are called. It is said they recruit and train new Wolves even now, after giving these special warriors some kind of deep magick; some evil that hides in their bones."

Sameska stood, and with hands clasped behind him, walked towards the high windows at the far end of the study. He gazed out at the beauty of his restored land. At Zalazar, the land of the elves.

And he remembered the Old Hate that had destroyed his race a thousand years ago; and it burned him.

"Come then, King Yoon. This time, your reception will be very different," King Sameska said.

ACKNOWLEDGMENTS

Thanks, as ever, must go to my wife Sonia, and my boys, Joseph and Oliver, for making me laugh so much, so hard and so long. Our *Singstar Nights* are the Stuff of Legend. Greetings and thanks to my old comrade, Ian Graham; never a scruffier, beard-touting, tweed-wearing man will you ever meet; but also never a stauncher comrade. He is indeed a man to walk the mountains with, and I recommend you check out his fantasy debut, *Monument*.

Thanks must also go to all the people who worked with me on our little film, *Impurity*; it was tremendous fun, and I love you all (although Brad still needs a haircut!).

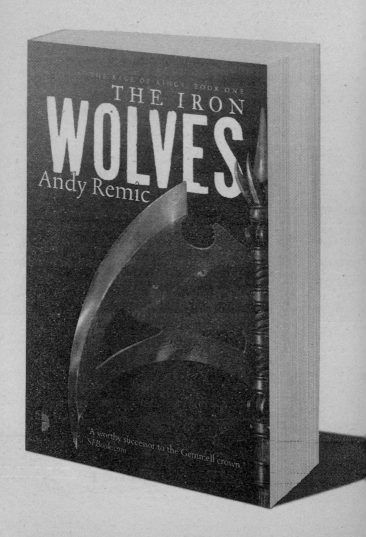

THE RAGE OF KINGS: BOOK ONE

THE IRON WOLVES

Andy Remic

"A worthy successor to the Gemmell crown."
SFBook.com

**It's Supernatural meets Men in Black
in a darkly humorous urban fantasy
from the author of Nekropolis.**

PEACEMAKER

MARIANNE DE PIERRES

"TWO LINE AUTHOR SHOUT ABOUT THE FANTASTIC PEACEMAKER WILL GO HERE."
AUTHOR NAME